You Can't
Break Me

Sue Langford

To all of you who need to be reminded that nobody in the world can ever break you.

"And one day she discovered that she was fierce, and strong, and full of fire, and that not even she could hold herself back because her passion burned brighter than her fears." — Mark Anthony.

Chapter 1

"There is no way in hell I am letting a guy like that ruin everything. Not happening. No how, no way. No guy is tearing down what I've spent years building up. I'm nominated for a dang award and the press isn't gonna stop asking now. The man takes his damn clothes off for a living," Piper said as the weight of the problem seemed to feel heavier and heavier. "Piper, we can't make him leave you alone. We tried a cease and desist. He hasn't backed off. It's like someone's paying him to come after you. Whoever you ticked off isn't about to back off that easily," Char said. "Then find out who," Piper replied.

* * * *

"Piper, tell me you're coming out tonight. Please," Caroline said. "I have to keep a low dang profile if we go out, we're not going anywhere there's a ton of people," Piper said. "Girl, it's a girl night. She finally broke it off with Kelvin. She wants a I'm finally single night. One won't kill you," Caroline joked. "If there's no security and it's a huge club, there's no second thought on it. I won't be able to," Piper said. "You've been working on music all day. One night out," Caroline said. "Fine, but it better be somewhere tiny with a lot of security," Piper said. "Done. She already has the place picked out," Caroline said as she joked. "You realize that if she goes somewhere shady," Piper said. "I know. You'll leave," Caroline joked.

Piper Adams had finally got a break and a record deal from one of the biggest labels she could get. She was almost 5 foot 9 and had that long blonde hair and blue eyes. Only thing she was missing was the size 2 figure and the golden tan. The closest she ever got was sort of red. She lived for her spray tans and girl night with the friends who'd been there since she was just a songwriter in Nashville. Luckily, Piper had stayed in Savannah surrounded by her friends. She had the ammo she needed for the music and the friends to remind her who she was. She was determined not to blow the only chance she had. Nobody was standing in her way.

Caroline French had been the center of attention most of her life. She was the picturesque beach girl. From the long bleach blonde hair to the long tan legs, she looked like sex on a stick to most of the guys in town. She was a model by day and a party girl by night. She had any guy she wanted, including the 5 or 6 guys she'd stolen away from Piper. She was almost 5 foot 7, almost 5 foot 10 in her stiletto heels that she always wore. Her motto, the shorter the skirt, the higher the heels. Needless to say, she was trouble with a capital T.

"So, where'd you decide on goin," Piper asked. "Dinner then we're going out to a bar so we're away from the crazies," Caroline said. "Funny," Piper replied. She went upstairs and slid into her leather pants and her sexy red top. She did her hair, her makeup and even painted her nails before they headed out. "Looking good there Piper," Caroline said from her bedroom as she slid on the sexiest skirt she had. "You couldn't just put jeans on," Piper asked. "Girl, I am wearing the skirt. I'm just as single as she is," Caroline teased. "Y'all are just gonna play every dang guy in the room," Piper said. "That was the plan," Caroline teased. She put on her perfume and Piper put on some of her magnolia perfume. They headed off and Caroline headed straight over to the Grey. "This is where y'all wanted to go," Piper asked. Caroline nodded. "It's either here or we went to Lady and Sons. Honestly, you know this place rocks," Caroline joked. They got a table, sat down and ordered and Piper pulled out her notebook. "You have your nose in that all night and I'm throwin it into the dang river," Caroline said. Piper shook her head. "Whatever," she said.

Dinner showed at the table not long later and Eve showed a little while later. "Hey ladies," Eve said as she gave them each a hug. "I got a table booked for us at the bar. All ready and yes miss thang there's extra security," Eve joked. "Good," Piper said. Something about how Eve said it set Piper off. Something wasn't right. She was up to something, and 90% of the time, she was up to no dang good at all. "You telling me where we're goin," Piper asked. "It's the ultimate girls night," Caroline said. "Talk," Piper said. "We're heading over in 20 minutes," Caroline said. "Alright. Fine," Piper replied. "This mean we got a table," Caroline asked. "In the back, but yeah," Eve said. "Thank you," Piper said. "Not a problem," Eve said. They finished up dinner and left to go over to wherever it was that Eve had booked the table.

They headed off to the bar and the minute Piper saw the front door, she opted to head home. "Girl, it's girl night. Just come," Caroline said. "Not happening. I'll be at home," Piper said. She got back in the uber and headed back to the house. Not a word was said all the way home. She got to the house, went into her bedroom and we determined to stay as far away from them as possible. Why on earth Caroline would even think of taking her to a strip club, she'd never know. Kinsey sat down in her room and did her best to get work done on music. Avoiding all of the insanity was what she needed. Privacy and no drama for the tabloids was the best bet. When her agent called, Piper was even happier that she hadn't indulged in the insanity.

Not long later, her phone buzzed. "Yep," Piper said. "This is Colt Jensen. From the gym. Just calling to book your training session," Colt said. "I need to get going on it. Probably 3 days a week at least," Piper said. "Not a problem. Are you okay with early morning," he asked. Piper took a deep breath. "Sure. I'm always up early anyway," she said. "Alright. We'll see you at 7," Colt said. "Alright," Piper said. She hung up with him and went and set her alarm for the next morning. She sat down to try and relax. Maybe a half hour later, Caroline called. "Hey," Piper said. "What are you doin," Caroline asked. "Getting work done so I can pay the bills. Y'all having fun," Piper asked. "I met a hot guy for you. Like super hot. He said he wanted to meet you," Caroline said. "I'll pass," Piper said. "He works on Broughton. Come on," Caroline said. "I'll talk to you tomorrow," Piper said. "Fine, but you're coming next time. We're going to the better than sex bar," Caroline said. "One-track mind always," Piper said. "Understatement. You need to get out more," Caroline teased. "I'm starting with a trainer tomorrow. Honestly, right now, that's all I can deal with," Piper said. "Girl, at some point you need to come socialize," Caroline said. "I will. I'm just not going to somewhere seedy," Piper said.

The next morning, Piper woke up and headed over to the gym. "You must be Piper," a man said as he walked towards her. "Colt," Piper asked. "Yes ma'am. You ready to get goin," he asked. Piper nodded, knowing that she really wasn't. He got her going on a machine or two, opting to try and sweet talk her. "So, what do you do," he asked. "Musician," Piper said. "Oh really? Anything that I've heard," he asked. "Just got the record deal. I've played a few places around," Piper said. "Then all the more reason to look that much hotter right," he asked. Piper nodded. "Whatever you say," Piper said. They finished the workout almost an hour and a half later. "Now the best part," he teased. "Which would be," Piper asked as she guzzled down water. "That would be food," he teased. He grabbed her a protein shake and a breakfast sandwich and sat down with her. "You did pretty dang good for not comin to a gym for a while," he said. "Never said I didn't work out. I just don't come to the gym," Piper said. "Well, you are definitely a lot stronger than you think," he said. "I'll take that as a compliment," Piper said. "It is. I still can't figure how you're single," he said. "You can quit tryin to hit on me," Piper said. "I wasn't trying. I was succeeding," he teased. "Whatever you say," Piper replied.

She finished her breakfast and headed off. The minute she got home, Caroline called her again. "And how did your workout go," Caroline asked. "You driving into work," Piper asked. "Of course. How was it," Caroline asked. "Not bad. The trainer is kind of hot, but the ego. Dang. Nothin like a completely over inflated ego to completely make a hot guy a total turnoff," Piper joked. "You going back tomorrow," Caroline asked. "Every day," Piper replied. "You realize you look just fine the way you are right," Caroline said. "Just fine isn't enough anymore. If I'm gonna be on stage in front of a ton of people, I can't just be happy with just fine," Piper said. "Girl," Caroline said. "I know, but I have to. If only just to look better in whatever craziness I get for wardrobe for press and stage stuff. There's way too much to get ready for. If I ever got to Carrie Underwood or Jason Aldean level, I have to be in shape. Nobody will accept me," Piper said. "Whatever you say," Caroline joked. "Go do some work or something," Piper said. "I will. We're going out tomorrow night. That includes you," Caroline said. "As long as we aren't going to the shady bar that you went to last night," Piper said. "We'll talk. I'll do my best but she seriously needs a girl night," Caroline said. "I know," Piper said.

Piper spent most of the afternoon working on song after song. When it got closer to dinner, she headed off to Tybee for dinner. She grabbed take out at Bubba Gumbo's and headed off to the beach. She sat down on the warm sand with her beach towel, slid her shoes off and had her dinner as she looked out at the sunset. Just as she took one last bite of the amazing dinner, her phone buzzed. "Yep," Piper said. "So, I have a favor to ask," Caroline said. "Which is what," Piper asked. "Eve can't find a place to stay that's even available.

You know that there's no room at my place. Would you be okay with Eve hanging at your house until she finds a place," Caroline asked. "Tell her to call me," Piper said. "Why do I hear waves," Caroline asked. "Out at Tybee. Just relaxing a bit before I head home," Piper said. "You went to Bubba's didn't you," Caroline asked. "Talk to you in a while," Piper said. "Fine. I'll meet you at your place in an hour or something," Caroline said. They hung up and Piper shook her head.

Piper looked back out to the water, watching the waves go in and out. There was something overtly calming about it. No matter how bad things got on land, the waves still went in and out. The water still held every ounce of beauty, but somehow, it turned that fire that she had into calm waters. It washed the anger away like it was putting out a flame. She shook her head and got up to head back. Just as she did, she heard someone running down the beach. She walked back towards where she'd parked and bumped clear into Colt. "Long time no see," Colt said. "What are you doin out here in the dark," Piper asked. "Watched the sunset. Too dang pretty not to," he said. Piper shook her head. "We could go grab a drink or something," Colt said. "And I'd be doing that why," Piper asked. "You determined to give me a hard time or what," he asked. "I just don't date. Haven't in a while," Piper said. "A drink wouldn't kill you. Think of it as a test date," he asked. "Fine, but only one drink," Piper replied.

She shook her head and messaged Caroline that she was going for a drink with a friend. When she didn't get a reply back, she figured that Caroline was probably giggling away. They got to a bar near the beach and sat out on the outdoor patio, watching the water. "What are you doing out here anyway," he asked. "Sorta wanted to get away from the noise for a while. Clears my head out here," Piper said. "That's why I go for a run out here. I don't even need the music," Colt said. "So, do you just workout at the gym and train people or is there something else," Piper asked. "Now that's a date question if I ever heard one. I model too," he said. "Like I couldn't guess that," Piper teased. "Girl, you're dang beautiful. I just don't get why you are still single," Colt said. "Because I made a decision that until I meet the right person, I'm staying single," Piper said. "And how do you know if they're right unless you give them a chance," he asked. "Colt, I get it. I do. I get you want to get some attention. I'm just not the girl," Piper said. "Just want a chance. That's all," he said. "Let's just leave it at trainer and gym time," Piper said. "You realize that you have to let people in right," he asked. "Colt, I appreciate it, but you're not my therapist or my father," Piper said. "Still shut off," he said. Piper shook her head, got up from her seat and went to pay for her drink. "I think I can handle one drink," Colt said. "Thanks," Piper said. She headed off, went down to her truck and left.

She got back to her place, locked up the truck in the garage and went to head inside when her phone rang. One look at the call display and she ignored the call. She texted Eve that she was home and went to head upstairs when Eve called her. "Hey," Piper said. "Where'd you disappear to," Eve asked. "Just went to the beach to try and relax a bit," Piper said. "You alright if I come stay for a little bit," Eve asked. "Definitely. There's a ton of room," Piper replied. "You sure," Eve asked. "There are one or two house rules, but nothing insane," Piper said. "Sounds a lot more relaxing than my place with him," Eve said. "See you in a little bit then. Just buzz when you get to the gate," Piper said. "I will," Eve said as they hung up.

Piper went and got changed and grabbed her guitar, bringing it downstairs to the TV room. She got her notebook and started working away on lyrics and trying to get the song out of her head that had been stuck there for days. She worked on it for what felt like hours. When Eve finally showed, she was at the door complete with what looked like a lifetime of clothes. "What did you do? Empty the walk-in closet into bags," Piper asked. "Something like that. I walked in on him with someone else already. I took my stuff and pawned half his stupid jewelry so I had money for a new place," Eve said. "You realize he's gonna lose it," Piper said. "He knows. I told him while she was screwing him in our bed," Eve said. "Dang," Piper said. "That's why there's no dang problem with what Caroline and I did last night. Not one dang thing," Eve said. Piper shook her head, joking around and did her very best to keep Eve positive.

They hung out for a while then Piper went and turned in for the night. Not 10 minutes after she laid down in the bed, her phone buzzed. She took one look and shook her head. "Yep," Piper said. "Tomorrow we're doing 7am. You alright with that," Colt asked. "Fine. Just remember that we're leaving this at trainer and workout person," Piper said. "For now," Colt said. Piper shook her head. "Goodnight," Piper said as she hung up. She shook her head, knowing that there was a lot more to that call than just him wanting her to come in early. There was something that she was determined to fight off at all costs. Sure it would come in handy having him around, but she wasn't about to let him in. Not when she finally had the record deal. Not when she finally had a chance to live that dream of being as big as Patsy Cline.

Piper got up the next morning and got changed and headed to the gym. She intentionally went in a t-shirt and her workout pants. "Lookin great," Colt said. "Like I said, trainer client," Piper said. "Not a problem. I'm not gonna say you don't look smokin hot right now," he said. "Harassment," Piper said as she walked over and started her circuit training. He shook his head and helped her. The more she did, the more she got that look from Colt. "Stop watching my backside," Piper said. "Can't help it," he said. Piper shook her head. She finished her workout and grabbed a protein shake. She shook her head and walked out, calling the gym for a new trainer. "Unfortunately, he's the only one with time. Is there an issue," Colt's boss asked. "It's fine. He's just on my last nerve," Piper said. "I'll chat with him about keeping things professional," his boss said. "Thank you," Piper said. "You're most welcome," he said.

Piper got home, had breakfast and did her yoga. "What are you doin," Eve asked as she yawned her way into the kitchen. "Breakfast before every muscle I have seizes up," Piper said. "Coffee," Caroline asked. "Mug is on the counter for you," Piper replied. "So, what's up with the gym? Hot guys," Eve asked. "Did you ever think that maybe you might be better off staying single a while until you meet the right guy," Piper asked. "If you stop tryin, you'll never find him," Eve replied. "Oh really," Piper asked. "I mean there was one guy that was kinda fine at the bar, but I don't think I could even think about dating a guy like that," Eve said. "And what kind would that be? The one who charges by the hour," Piper teased. "Funny….by the dance," Eve said. "Girl, you deserve better than that. Everyone does. You deserve a guy who'd bend over backwards to keep your attention instead of doing whatever those guys do in those bars. Before you even get the idea, I'm never stepping foot in one," Piper said. "You do realize that at some point you have to try dating again," Eve said. "If it's not you, it's Caroline. Seriously. I can handle things. When I'm ready to date I will," Piper said. "Girl, you need to get out of the dang house and have a real date," Eve said. "Then we go to a normal bar or something and meet normal people," Piper said. "Fine," Eve replied. "You're killin me," Piper said. "That was my plan," Eve joked. "Tomorrow is Saturday. We can go out, but I'm going to church on Sunday so we are not staying out until 3," Piper said. "Done," Eve replied.

Piper kicked herself knowing what she'd just agreed to do. She almost wished she'd just got more friends along the way. Piper went upstairs and got changed for the day and when she came downstairs, Eve was on the phone. "We're going tonight," Eve said. "I sorta have plans," Piper said. "Girl, if sitting around here and working on music is the plan, you can do that tomorrow night," Eve said. "And where are we going," Piper asked. "The Grey," Eve said. "And," Piper asked. "Couple other bars. It'll be fun," Eve replied. "Fine," Piper said kicking herself all the way into the office. She checked her emails and within a matter of minutes, she got a call from her manager.

"Hey Char," Piper said. "So, we have three interviews set up for this upcoming week. One in Atlanta, one in New York and one in LA. All three include performances. Are y'all prepared," Char asked. "Just going to head into rehearsal today with them. We almost have something together for when the time came. It's just a matter of getting the set list together," Piper said. "I have the rehearsal space reserved for the rest of the day. All yours until 7," Char replied. "I'll let the band know. Do you know what song they want us to do," Piper asked. "Revenge," Char said. "Of course," Piper joked. "That's the first release. You know it's zooming straight to number one," Char teased. "Alright then. We'll work on that and Breaking point so we have two ready," Piper said. "Work on Follow me Home as well. That's gonna be the third release. Might as well get prepared," Char joked. "Will do. Are you coming down," Piper asked. "Yes. I'll bring the wardrobe for next week as well," Char said. "Alright," Piper replied.

She got off the phone and called the band, giving them the details then grabbed her guitar, purse, phone and water. "Where you headed," Eve asked as she came downstairs to head off to work. "Going to rehearsal. I'm not gonna be ready until after 8," Piper said. "Not a problem," Eve joked. "If y'all want, come down and hang at the rehearsal when you're done work," Piper said. Eve nodded. They both headed out and locked up then headed off for the day.

When Piper got to rehearsal, she was about to flip her phone off when she got a text from Colt:

Looks like I'm coming with you for the interviews. Call you in a little bit – C

Piper shook her head. "Seriously," Piper said. "Problem," Char asked as she walked in. "I didn't really need the trainer coming on location," Piper said. "If you're gonna do the fitness thing then you need the trainer with you, even if you're travelling," Char said. "I am completely capable of doing the workout alone. Honestly, we don't click at all. I'm not comfortable with him being my trainer period," Piper said. "When you're on that stage, it's a lot more work than you think. You need to be in the best shape possible. You know that. It means you have to do the workouts and you'll have to have the trainer with you," Char said. "Then I want a different trainer. Anyone else. Preferably a female trainer," Piper said. "While we're tracking someone down, you're working with him," Char said. "Fine," Piper said. "What's shakin superstar," her guitarist Kurt asked. "Nothing. Y'all know that we have to do those performances next week. We have to get them down just right so it looks easy," Piper said. "Not a problem," Jack her drummer said. "And," Keith, her other guitarist, asked. "And we have to make it perfect since it's probably gonna be replayed on YouTube a million times. Perfect," Char said. "Done boss lady," Keith teased. Harley came in a little while later. "And," Harley asked. "Your three faves," Piper said. "Done," Harley replied.

They worked away all afternoon on the staging, the songs, the steps and everything in between. When they stopped for lunch, Char came in with something for everyone and handed

Piper a chicken Caesar and She Crab soup. "So, everyone else gets real food and I get this," Piper joked. Char shook her head and headed off, knowing they had everything under control. "I still don't get why you need a trainer. You look amazing," Harley said. "Not a size 5," Piper replied. "You still look great the way you are," Keith said. "Just means beating her at her own game. Kick some butt at the gym," Kurt said. "Gotcha," Piper joked. "You realize your phone is buzzing right," Harley asked. Piper took one look at it and saw Colt's name. She pressed ignore and a text came through:

Tomorrow at 7. We're doing a run in the park then to the gym. Meet you at Forsyth Fountain at 7. Don't be late. PS see you later – C

Piper put her phone in her bag. "He can't be that bad if he's a trainer," Harley said. "Self-absorbed, yes. Over inflated ego, hell yes. Pushy and figures he runs the world, definitely," Piper said. "You still have to deal with his stupid butt for a week or two. Make the most of it," Harley teased. "I'll pass. You can have him," Piper teased. "I may take you up on that if my hubby says it's alright," Harley teased. They joked around and finished up dinner. As soon as they were going through their last run through, Eve and Caroline showed to watch. They fixed the mistakes and got three songs done perfectly. Piper looked over and saw Eve and Caroline cheering. "So, we managed to entertain these two. The world is next," Piper said. "Tomorrow," they asked. Piper nodded. "Meaning what," Eve asked. "Meaning I'm not staying out late since we're rehearsing tomorrow," Piper said. "You're havin a ladies night. Go," Harley said. "You're comin. You realize that," Caroline said. "Then it's a real ladies night," Harley joked. Piper thanked everyone and got freshened up and changed, Harley got changed and they headed off for the one night that she almost dreaded.

When they showed, everyone was turning around and looking at Piper and Harley. "Great," Piper joked. Caroline smirked. "It's dinner," Eve teased. They hung out, had a drink or two and when they were just about done, the waitress came over with a drink for Piper. She shook her head. "From the gentleman at the bar," the waitress said. Piper looked and swore she saw Colt. She handed it to Harley and when they were all finished, they headed off. They got to the next bar, and it felt like someone was right behind them. They got a private table in the back and Piper was determined not to touch a drop of alcohol. She went as far as getting a jack and coke hold the jack. Nobody noticed anything. It wasn't until she felt someone walking towards them that she realized what was going on.

"May I speak with you a moment," she heard as she got goosebumps. She turned around and Eve's jaw dropped. Piper turned to face Colt, knowing that none of the ladies were going to hold her back. "And what do you want," Piper asked as Caroline nudged her leg. He put his hand out and Piper shook her head. She got up and walked over to the bar with him. "And what do you want," Piper asked. "To make up for acting like an idiot," he said. "Colt, leave it at professional," Piper said. "I can't," he said. "Then learn," Piper said. She went to walk away and he grabbed her hand and pulled her back to him. "What," Piper asked. "Let me buy you a drink at least," he said. "Answer was no at The Grey, and it's no now," Piper said. He handed her a soda. Piper shook her head. "Come on," Colt said. "I'm not drinking. Period. Leave it be," Piper replied. She walked off and went back to her table. "And who the heck was that," Harley asked. "The trainer," Piper said. Eve nudged Caroline. "Damn," Harley said. "Don't even," Piper replied.

They hung out with Colt still watching them. When Piper went to head out, Harley pulled her back. "One drink," Harley said. "I'll see y'all. Eve, I'll see you at the house," Piper said. She went to head out and Colt was right behind her. "Is there a reason you're following me," Piper asked. "Because I don't take no for an answer," he replied. Piper walked over to the rehearsal hall, got in her truck and went to head back to the house. "Piper," Colt said. "What," she asked. He grabbed her hand, pulled her to him and kissed her. It was hot and almost like he was intentionally trying to make her knees go weak. She pushed him away and got in the truck, leaving and heading straight home. She locked the truck up and headed into the house, making sure that the truck was safe in the garage. She locked the door behind her and saw a text from Colt come through:

Please. Just give me a chance. – C

Piper washed up, got changed and slid into bed, ignoring the text and deleting it completely. She was about to fall asleep when her phone rang. "Yep," Piper said. "What's up with the hottie," Eve asked. "The annoying trainer. It's fine. I'm home," Piper said. "He left when you did," Eve said. "I know. Where are y'all headed now," Piper asked. "Couple other places then I'm crashing at Caroline's on the sofa," Eve said. "Alright. I'm getting some rest," Piper said as she hung up. She was just falling asleep when her phone rang again. "Yep," Piper said. "You home safe," Harley asked. "Yes. You home," Piper asked. "Yep. He's out so I can actually get sleep tonight," Harley joked. "Sweet dreams," Piper said. "Back at ya," Harley said. They hung up and finally, Piper rolled over and got some sleep.

The next morning, after her run, she headed to the gym and got a workout in, trying her best to avoid Colt altogether. She saw the manager and he came in to check on her. "Miss Piper," the manager said. "Am I allowed to complain and request someone else," Piper asked. "We're working on it.

We have a few female trainers. May be an option, but for the time being until there's availability...." "I get it, but honestly, I think I'd rather just do it on my own," Piper said determined to try and keep what'd happened the night before out of the situation. "Is there someone other than him that I can work with today," Piper asked. "Yes ma'am," the manager said. The female trainer came over and Piper spent over an hour trying to talk the trainer into working with her. "I can see if I can fit you in but it'd be early morning," the trainer said. "Perfectly fine. I just don't want to work with that other trainer," Piper said. "Not a problem," she said as she held back a laugh. Piper got her info and sent it to her manager telling her that she was coming instead of Colt.

Piper headed off and got breakfast then headed back to the house to get showered and changed for rehearsal. When she walked in, her manager was there with the wardrobe they had set up for the interviews. "Mornin," Piper said. "Morning. So, I got your message about the trainer. He already signed on to do it," Char said. "I don't want him on the plane or a bus or anything else. I got another trainer," Piper replied. "You gonna tell me what happened," Char asked. "He followed me out and kissed me. That's what. This is supposed to be professional," she said. "Piper," she said. "That's what I'm doing. I don't care if he doesn't like it," Piper said. "Was it that bad," Char asked. "If he's on that bus or whatever, I'm not. End of discussion," Piper said. "Alright then," Char said. "I don't want to be snarky or rude about it, but he's pushing that line and I don't like it," Piper said. "Alright. I mean, if it's that bad then I'll handle it," Char said. "Thank you," Piper said. "For what," Harley asked as she walked in with oversized sunglasses and a giant-sized coffee.

"I have the wardrobe for the performances. I just need you to try it on and make sure it's alright," Char said. Piper grabbed her pieces and went and tried them on. When she tried each one on, somehow it looked better, felt better and she had that much more confidence. When she came out to show Char, her jaw dropped. "Now that's what I was hoping for," Char said. Piper was in leather pants and a sexy top that showed just enough. It showed off what she wanted to show. "One question. Am I wearing heels or my boots," Piper asked. "We're thinking heels since it will look better on TV. For when you sit down for the interview, you can switch to a heel boot or leave on the heels," Char said. "Alright, and what are we doing for the other performances," Piper asked. "Just changing up the color of the top or the pant. I'll have everything in a bag for you by tomorrow night," Char said. Harley came out with her outfit then the guys one after another. They looked good. For the first time, almost professional. They got down to rehearsing and maybe an hour later, Piper's phone was ringing. Char silenced it and put in in Piper's purse and watched the rest of the rehearsal. "Sounds amazing. Now, you know that you're leaving tomorrow at 6 right? We'll send drivers to pick you up and I'll meet you in LA since that's the first one," Char said.

"That means no party night to shake off the nerves," Harley said. Piper almost laughed. "That means sound check is 5am. I'll wake you up at 4 at the hotel. Early night," Char said. "Alright then," Piper said. They headed out after rehearsal and Harley pulled Piper to the side. "What's up," Harley asked. "Who was the guy really," Harley asked. "The trainer. I got a new trainer so it's not really an issue," Piper said. "He's hot. I'm married and I still think he's hot," Harley said. "And I officially pass. I don't need that in my life," Piper said. "You need something that makes you happy. I don't care if it's a house or a new truck or what. You need something that makes you feel good," Harley said. "I have that with the music," Piper replied. "Girl, you have every power song in the world on there but not one that's a sappy love song," Harley said. "You think that's what's missing," Piper asked. "I know," Harley said. "If I said anyone other than him," Piper teased. "Done," Harley joked. They laughed, hopped in the vehicles and headed off and Piper headed straight home. When she got there, Eve was hungover on the sofa. "You realize it's almost 3 in the afternoon," Piper joked. "Stop screaming," Eve joked.

"So, what did you want to do tonight?" "Well, since I'm leaving tomorrow for LA, I'm getting a decent night of sleep without guy problems," Piper said. "You blew him off? Seriously," Eve asked. "I'm taking a hard pass," Piper replied. "The guy is hot. Really hot. Cover of a romance novel hot," Eve said. "Not mine," Piper replied. "Alright then. Do we get to come see those performances," Eve asked as she guzzled her Gatorade. "You can PVR them for me and watch them," Piper said. "Girl, seriously? You're going to LA and New York and we're not invited," Eve said. "It's work," Piper replied. "What's close," Eve asked. "Atlanta before we come back. It's early morning," Piper said. "Then we'll meet you in ATL and make a weekend out of it," Eve said. "If that's what you want to do, all the more power to you. Just make sure you bring soup with you," Piper said. "Girl, you and that Pink House soup," Eve joked.

Piper went and got packed up. She got her toiletries together and her chargers. "You could just do that tomorrow you know," Eve said as she sat down on the edge of Piper's bed. "I'm getting it done so I can go to church and come home to relax before we leave," Piper said. "You sure you don't want company," Eve asked. "You have work. Just promise me that nobody comes into this house. No dates, no nothing," Piper said. "I get it. Privacy. Security. The whole nobody knows where thing," Eve said. "Can you agree," Piper asked. "Fine. If I meet someone I go to their house," Eve said. "Also, just make sure that the alarm is on and all the doors are locked

when you leave for the day," Piper said. "Alright boss lady,"
Eve joked.

Piper went and got some work done on the music and social
media then checked through her emails. When Harley said
she was in world war three with her husband, Piper took
things into her own hands. "Come crash here tonight. We're
leaving tomorrow anyway. Just bring your stuff. It'll be an
inside girl night," Piper said. "You sure that's alright," Harley
said. "I'll get some extra wine," Piper said. "I'll grab a case on
the way over," Harley said. "Thank you. I'll order dinner for all
of us," Piper said. "Ladies night," Eve teased. "I'll see you in a
little bit," Harley said as they hung up and Piper got cleaning
up. "Girl, this place is cleaner than a dang hospital. Chill," Eve
said. She finished getting everything together, got the bag put
into the closet to take with her the next day then messaged
Harley to bring church clothes.

Within maybe a half hour, Harley was at the door complete
with a case of wine. "Girl, I thought you were kidding," Piper
said. "Nope. We're bringing it on the tour," she joked.
"Whatever you say," Piper said. "And what movie are we
watching tonight," Eve asked. "Pick a movie," Piper said. She
opened the wine and got a glass for each of them. They sat
down and went through a bunch of movies, opting for Magic
Mike. "Of course that's what you chose," Piper said. The
ladies watched it while Piper was working on lyrics again.
When her phone rang, one look and Piper ignored the call.
"Who is it," Harley asked. Piper shook her head. An hour
later, her phone rang. Harley grabbed it. One look said it all.
"Go," Harley said.

Chapter 2

"What do you want Colt," Piper said. "I heard you were working with Tessa today," he said. "And she's my new trainer," Piper said. "Then that means we can go out," he said. "Leave it be. I'm not doing it," Piper said. "You're that scared of one freaking date," he asked. "Don't even think that you can instigate a dang fight. I'm not your type and you aren't mine either," Piper said. "I guess we'll see what happens then right," he asked. "You really need to see someone about that obsessive thing you have going on," Piper said. She hung up and went back to watching the movie. Within maybe 15 minutes, another message came in:

I'm not giving up.

Piper shook her head. "What," Harley asked. Piper showed her the text. "Are you serious? He's stalking you now? I mean seriously," Harley said. Piper nodded. She filled Piper's glass and they went back to watching Channing Tatum get semi naked. When the movie was finished, Piper showed Harley to her room and Eve opted to watch part two. "You alright," Harley asked. "Honestly, the guy is ticking me off. I mean who the heck does he think he is," Piper asked. "Something about it has me feeling like something else is up. Somethin big. Like someone plotting somethin," Harley said. "You have a point," Piper said. "You don't think those girls are starting a problem you can't fix do you," Harley asked. "I wouldn't exactly put it past them, but that's insane to even think it," Piper said. "Did you ever think that maybe they're seriously doing somethin to cause this," Harley asked. "They wouldn't be dumb enough to piss me off. They'll be gone," Piper said. "Tomorrow, we figure it out. We have time on that stupid flight," Harley joked. "True," Piper replied. "If they're planning all of this, we have to do something," Piper said. Harley nodded, gave her a hug and went to get ready for bed.

Piper went into her room and relaxed a little. When she heard the TV go off, Piper went downstairs. "Hey," Eve said. "I need to ask you something and I want the honest truth," Piper said. "Which is what," Eve asked as she put the glasses in the dishwasher. "Have you met that Colt guy before," Piper asked. "The trainer guy," Eve asked. Piper nodded. "I mean we've seen him out at the bars and stuff, but personally, no," Eve said. "You sure," Piper asked. Eve nodded. "Girl, I wouldn't do that to you," Eve replied. "And if I find out that either one of you are lying," Piper said. "Alright. Honestly, he looks like a guy we saw, but that's not him," Eve said. "You sure," Piper asked. Eve nodded. "Girl, the man is smokin hot. I still don't get why you don't just take a chance," Eve said. "What is up with you and pushing me into dating someone? Of all dang people, you really want that," Piper asked. "I want you with someone who isn't a dang pushover. Besides the fact that he's hot, you deserve happy in your personal life. Give yourself a dang break," Eve said. "I'm not going near that. Period. Do not pass go, don't collect the money. Not happening," Piper said. "Why," Eve asked. "He's self-centered and in love with his own dang reflection. I'm the only one that ever told him no," Piper said.

The next morning, Piper woke up and went to the gym with the new trainer then came straight home and they all headed off to church. "We couldn't have just slept in," Harley asked. "Meaning," Piper asked. "Hangover and church don't really mix," Eve said. "I need all the help I can get this week," Piper said. When church was finished, they all headed back to the house. Piper made something for a big lunch and Harley got a few things she'd forgotten at home. When the car showed at 3 to pick them up, Harley pulled in and put her truck in the garage beside Piper's and locked it up. Piper locked the garage up with the security system and came out to the car, hopping in while the driver loaded the bags. Harley hopped in with her and they said goodbye to Eve.

Within an hour, they were all at the airport and getting settled on the plane. "Tell me you aren't getting nervous," Harley asked. "Beyond. The fact that we're performing a song in front of a live crowd and we're gonna be on national TV is about enough to make me need an oversized drink," Piper said. "Girl, you'll be fine," Harley said. "Maybe once we're done the first one I'll be fine," Piper said. "Girl, it'll be old hat by the end of the week. You'll be fine. You know you will," Harley said. "Will what," the rest of the guys asked. "Nothing. Boss lady has nerves," Harley joked. "Then we say a prayer before we leave. Deal," they joked. "Alright. We might want to wait until tomorrow before we go on though," Harley replied. "Done," the guys said. The hair and makeup team headed onto the plane alone with Char and a few other people. They took off and Piper did her best to keep her mind off everything. They even tried singing through the songs to get her mind off of the nervousness. "And when is the trainer guy coming," one of the guys asked. "He's not," Piper said. "The trainer is meeting us there. She is taking a separate flight out since she has clients until 6," Char said. "We could wait for her," Piper said. "She's flying out at 6:45. It's fine," Char said.

They took off and headed straight to LA. The longer they were on the plane, the more nervous Piper got about the performance. "You realize that by the time we're done, all of this is gonna be easy," Kurt said. "Whatever you say. I'm still nervous performing even when it's at a bar. I always have been," Piper said. "Then why would you go and do all of this," Keith joked. "Would you quit pickin at her already," Harley said. They joked around and when they finally landed, they headed over to do sound check. "We need sleep," Piper said. "Girl, you'll be fine. I promise you," Char said. They did a quick run through of one of the songs, got the sound check done and headed off to the hotel. Piper walked into the suite and saw the flowers waiting that were from Colt. "I mean seriously," Piper said. An hour later, as she was finally soaking in the tub and relaxing before bed, Colt called.

"What can I do for you," Piper asked. "Come downstairs for a drink," he said. "Colt, I'm going to bed. I have to be there at 5am tomorrow," Piper said. "Then I'll come up to your suite," he said. "Good night," Piper said. "You don't want to date your trainer, fine. You aren't. She's your trainer now," Colt said. "I'm not having this conversation. Good night," Piper said as she hung up. She slid out of the tub, dried off and got changed for bed, opting for a little yoga before bed. Just as she slid into the comfortable oversized bed, her phone rang again. "Yep," Piper said. "One drink," he said. "Colt, enough," Piper said as she hung up.

The next morning, Piper woke up at 4:30, got up and did a quick workout with her new trainer and got showered and changed. They headed to the studio and did a quick sound check again then went straight into hair and makeup and got ready. Just as she was taking a deep breath before heading out, there was a knock at the door. "Come in," Piper said. "Hey. You ready sunshine," Harley asked. "As I'll ever be," Piper replied. They walked out together and said a quick prayer in the hall hoping that all of it didn't blow up in her face. They headed on, Piper looked at the band and nodded. They started the first song and the crowd started going crazy. "And a special welcome to the one, the only, Piper Adams," the host said. Piper started the song and then the next. When they finished the second song, the host came out to interview them.

"Well Miss Piper, you are just outstanding. Isn't she," the host asked as the crowd cheered. Piper spotted Colt in the crowd.

"Well thank you to all of y'all," Piper said. The fact that her stomach was flip-flopping and she was nervous as all get out was besides the point. "I have to ask, where have you been hiding? These songs are just amazing," the interviewer said. "To be honest with you, I've been writing music for years. It took a pretty amazing band to get me where I am. I don't know where I'd be without them," Piper said. "And we heard that you have a big announcement. What's the big news," the host asked. "Well, since I know y'all love these new songs, as of Friday this week, the new CD is out! It's called Shotgun," Piper said. "And we all know this one is hitting number one the minute it's out. It's a fantastic CD," the host said. "Luckily I had a few of the best songwriters to work with. They're all right here," Piper said. "Well, those two songs were amazing. Any special guy inspire them," the host asked. "Being single is the only inspiration I need," Piper joked. "Alright everyone. You heard it. She's single. So, what do you have next," the host asked. "Well, if y'all want it, we have one more song for you," Piper said. "Alright. Give it up for Piper Adams," the host said as she headed off and Piper and the band started the final song.

When they finished, they thanked everyone, signed a few autographs and headed off. Colt walked straight towards the security and demanded to go backstage to talk to Piper. When security wouldn't let him, he texted her over and over. Ignoring him was the highlight of her morning. They signed a CD or two for the hosts of the show and left to head to the hotel. Within maybe an hour, they were checking out and headed to a radio station or two for interviews before they left to head to the next interview. She was asked over and over again if she had a boyfriend and it about drove her nuts. When they finally got on the plane to leave, Piper had officially had enough. "What's wrong," Harley asked. "If I get asked one more dang time if I have a boyfriend, I'm gonna scream," Piper said. "They ask because you're a new person on the show. It means when you do, they're gonna be all over you. We had 15 more interview requests since you left the show this morning," Char said. "Why is everyone so dang concerned about my dang social life? They need something else to talk to me about," Piper said. "Then we get you nominated for the music awards," Char said.

They arrived at the next stop and finally had a day to relax. "Three radio interviews and then you go to do the morning show performance. Same three songs," Char said. "Then we're rehearsing in the suite," Piper said. "We have a floor. Not an issue," Char said. "Alright. What time do we have to be at the interview," Piper asked. "8. Performance starts at 9:30," Char replied. "Then we can relax a bit and try to get over the stupid time difference," Piper joked. They were cracking jokes and relaxing over lunch when they arrived. "We going shopping a while," Harley teased. Piper shook her head. "Honestly, a hot bath and a massage is all I need. That and a decent night of sleep," Piper said. "Totally agree with you," Harley said. "Massage therapist is coming up now. Just be prepared for tomorrow," Char said.

They got massages and just as Piper was lying down on the bed to try and relax a while, Colt called. "What are you doing? Stalking me now," Piper asked. "Trying to convince you that we belong together," he said. "My god. First off, I barely know you. Second, I don't want to, and third, leave me alone Colt. I'm not going out with you," Piper said. "I'm getting on a plane. We can go out tomorrow," he said. "Answer is still no. Get over it already," Piper said as she hung up. She shook her head, let Char know what was going on and shook her head. Not long later, Harley came over. "I brought wine," Harley joked.

"Honestly, I don't get why he's practically stalking me. I mean, what the heck did I do to deserve this," Piper asked. "You ignored his stupid butt. I mean, the guy is good looking and everyone would stop asking about your private life if you did date him. It's up to you," Harley said. "I'm not dating a guy who'd rather date the one he sees in the dang mirror. Normal works. 9-5 life normal is what I want. He just doesn't fit," Piper said. "Then have fun. Leave it at fun. You don't have to marry the guy," Harley said. "Really? Who me? Fun? I'm not that person Harley. I never have been," Piper said. "You can date the guy without making it into more. If you fit, then you fit. It's not like he isn't begging for it," Harley joked. "I'm not putting myself through that. He's not worth the time," Piper said. They ordered dinner not long later, had dinner in their robes then turned in for the night, attempting more sleep.

By the time they'd finished the interviews and performances in New York, Harley was beyond tired. They got back to the hotel and chilled while Piper did her best to try and work on new music. When her phone went off at 7pm, she shook her head. "Hello," Piper said. "Come downstairs for a drink," Colt said. "You're turning into a stalker. I mean seriously," Piper said. "Then tell them to let me upstairs," he said. "No," Piper said. "Please," he asked. Piper shook her head. "Fine, but you're not staying," she said. If it meant telling him face to face to get him to leave, she'd do whatever she had to. When there was a knock at the door maybe 20 minutes later, she was almost getting butterflies. She opened the door and there was Colt, complete with a bottle of wine. "What would you like," Piper asked. "You inviting me in," he asked. "Nope," Piper replied. He shook his head and came in completely ignoring what she'd said.

"I'm not drinking. You realize that right," Piper said. "And why's that," he asked. "Because I have 24 hours to relax before I have to do another performance then head to Atlanta. That's why," Piper said. "Which means an actual night to relax. Just have a glass," he said. "Answer is still no," Piper said. She got herself a glass of sweet tea, handed a glass of wine to Colt and went and sat down in the chair intentionally. "You're seriously planning on givin me that dang hard of a time aren't you," he asked. "You stalked me across two states. I'd say yes," Piper replied. "I just want a chance. You got a new trainer. Now you don't have that as a dang excuse to say no," he said. "I still have an excuse. I'm not gonna date you. I don't want to," Piper replied. "Then let me have one dang date," he said. "This is all you're getting," she replied. "Tell me one dang good reason why," Colt asked. "I don't have to. Answer is no and it's staying no," Piper said. "Why," he asked. "Because I am not doing this. I have a job where I'm in the dang public eye. I don't want you in it," Piper said. He shook his head. "What?" He got up, grabbed her hand and pulled her to him on the sofa. "Let go of my hand," Piper said. He managed to get her two inches from him.

"You don't ever take no for a dang answer do you," Piper asked. "Not if I don't have to," he said. "You're not my type Colt. You aren't. You never will be," Piper said. "Says who," he asked. "I've lived as far away from the city as I could most of my dang life," Piper said. "And I've always lived beside the beach," he said. "Colt," she said. "I get it. We're opposites. Doesn't mean that we can't work," he said. "It means no," Piper replied. "Just convinced that you deserve better or that I do," he asked. "That I'm better off staying single," Piper replied. He shook his head. "You deserve to be happy. To have someone with you who actually wants you," he said. "And who would that be," Piper asked. "Me," he said. "Right. For now, until you get someone skinnier or whatever," Piper said. He shook his head, pulled her to him and kissed her, devouring her lips. Piper pushed him away, got up and knocked on Harley's connecting door. One look and Harley knew. Piper was about to either kick Colt or have him banned. "I think you need to leave," Harley said. "We're talking," he said. "We're done," Piper replied. He shook his head. "I asked for one dang drink," he said. "And there's the door," Piper replied. He shook his head and as she walked him to the door, he kissed her again. "Out." She pushed him out the door and locked it behind him.

"He even smelled good," Harley said. "I know, but I honestly don't want to go near him. There's something that he's not tellin me," Piper replied. "Like what," Harley asked. "Eve and Caroline keep pushing me to go out with him. I mean, the two of them were at a dang strip club. From that dang day on, the two of them were pushing. How do I know that they don't have that planned," Piper asked. "I thought those two were your friends," Harley asked. "They are, but that doesn't mean that they aren't totally plotting somethin," Piper said. Harley shook her head. "Girl, only you would have friends that try this stuff," Harley joked. "I don't want him around if all he's doing is causing trouble," Piper said. "You can't just be a guy and have fun with it," Harley teased. "Because I'm not. I have to watch my back to make sure the press doesn't get wind of anything. Dating a trainer isn't me," Piper said. "Girl, it doesn't matter what he does. All that matters is that he's in it for the right reasons. If he does work at that stupid bar then you'll know. One way or another you will," Harley replied. "I'm not running the chance," Piper said. "You telling me that if you had a chance, you wouldn't go near him with a ten-foot pole," Harley asked. "Like I said, I don't date guys like that," Piper replied.

The next morning, Piper got up early, did a workout with the trainer then came back up to the suite and went for a run on the treadmill. When Harley got up, she came in with coffee, handed a mug to Piper and got breakfast ordered. When it showed, Piper hopped off the treadmill and they ate. "So, we have a couple interviews then we head to Atlanta," Harley asked. "Yep," Piper said as she inhaled her breakfast. "Damn," Harley said. "That mean you're gonna give the guy a chance or no, because he's been pestering security all morning to get you to talk to him," Harley said. "Doesn't change that the answer is no. I don't need a stalker, I don't need a crazy fan and I don't want any of that," Piper said. "And if y'all were both in a room together, you telling me that if he wasn't just a trainer you wouldn't go out with him," Harley asked. "I just can't," Piper said. Harley smirked, gave her a hug then went and got ready to head off for the day. Piper went to get in the shower and heard a knock at the door. She shook her head.

She slid her hoodie on and answered. "Yep," Piper said. "That gentleman that was up here last night is riding my last nerve. He is pestering," her security said. "We're leaving this afternoon anyway. When we head out let him up," Piper said. "Alright then. That mean y'all are packing up," he asked. Piper nodded. "We're out of here within the hour," Piper replied. "Alright. I'll be back to help y'all with your bags," her security said. Piper nodded and went back to have her shower and get ready. When she stepped out, her phone was buzzing with texts from Colt. Piper called Char. "What's up," Char asked. "I need to change the phone number," Piper said. "For your cell phone," Char asked. "Colt has now texted 5 times since 6am. This is getting out of hand," Piper said. "I'll get it changed while we're on the way to Atlanta," Char said. "Thank you," Piper said. "No problem," Char replied. They hung up, Piper finished getting packed up and they all headed out. Just as they were going through the lobby," Colt grabbed her hand and pulled her to him. "What do you want Colt. I have a plane…." He kissed her again, devouring her lips. He walked back out with her to the waiting car. "Let go of my dang hand," Piper said. "No," Colt said. Security blocked him from getting into the car. They broke his grasp on Piper and she got in the car and left with everyone else to head to the airport.

"What in the hell was that," Kurt asked. "That's called thank god I have a different trainer," Piper said. "I don't know what's up with him. You'd think he would snap out of this stupidness," Piper's new trainer Jess said. "Like I said, he's nuts," Piper replied. They got two more quick interviews in and headed to the airport. When they landed in Atlanta, they were taken straight to their hotel. They got their suites and Piper called Eve and Caroline. "And how goes everything on tour," Eve asked. "If either one of you is behind all of this stupid crap with Colt then say it now. If it's a dang game, say it," Piper said. "We met him and thought you two would hit it off. That's it. Girl, we just wanted you happy," Eve said. "And," Piper asked. "He said he was going to talk to you. That's it," Eve said. "He's followed me to every dang stop. He's going overboard. I'm changing my number," Piper said. "Girl, you don't need to take it that far. It's not like he's a psycho," Eve said. "He's getting to that point. I'm done playing stupid games Eve. I don't want him near me," Piper replied. "You're telling me that you aren't even curious," Eve asked. "No," Piper replied. "Fine. I'll tell him to back off," Eve replied. "He's going way past overboard," Piper said. "Maybe you'll meet someone else," Eve said. "Agreed. We're in Atlanta if y'all are heading down," Piper said. "We're on the way in a couple minutes," Eve said.

Char came in to talk to Piper. "What's up," Piper asked. "So, we're doing another performance tonight. You alright with that," Char asked. "If the rest of the band is," Piper replied. "They're on board. I have the clothes for the performance," Char said. "Then I'm on board," Piper said. "Alright. I got your friends passes for the performance," Char said. "I appreciate that. They'll love it," Piper replied. "Which means three interviews, three performances and we're leaving in an hour for the round of radio interviews. Two then an afternoon performance then one after dinner and one at one of the big bars in town. You ready for the spotlight," Char asked. Piper nodded. She went and got changed, did her makeup and hair and just as she was about to step out of the suite, Haley knocked. "Ready," Harley asked. Piper nodded.

They headed off and went to the radio interviews, the late afternoon performance then to dinner before they went on for another show then left for the last one of the day. When she walked in and saw Eve and Caroline in the audience, she almost laughed. She got up and blew the performance out of the water. On top of it, and according to Eve and Caroline, Piper looked amazing. She finished up and everyone was tripping over themselves to try and get an autograph. Eve saw what was going on. Whatever Colt was doing wasn't enough to get her attention. He either needed to step up his game or he was gonna be replaced. What Piper didn't see was that Colt was right behind them. Like they were a group package.

As soon as they were finished, Piper sent a drink over to Caroline and Eve with a note that she was heading back to the hotel. She left with Harley intentionally. "You realize they were here to see you," Harley said. "I'm just freaking exhausted. Honestly, bed and bath is all I can handle right now," Piper replied. "You should tell them at least," Harley said. "I did. I sent Eve a note," Piper replied. They got in the car and went back to the hotel. Harley walked in to a bottle of wine in the bedroom and a hot bath. It was all she wanted and needed. She relaxed and within maybe an hour, she was out cold in bed.

The next morning, Piper got up and did her workout with the trainer and went upstairs to get showered and packed up to head home. Just as she was about to zip up the suitcase, security called. "Yep," Piper said. "Two ladies are here to see you. Miss Eve and Miss Caroline," her security guy said. "As long as it's just the two of them," Piper said. "There is a man here with them," he said. "Just Eve and Caroline. He's not allowed up here," Piper said. "Yes miss Piper," the security guy said. Eve and Caroline came up and Piper zipped up her bag. She slid it off the bed and put it by the door. When they knocked, Piper opened the door to see Eve and Caroline both beyond hungover. "Well hello there party people," Piper teased. "You started it with those drinks last night," Eve said. "Y'all didn't have to follow them up with a dozen more," Piper said as she handed them each a bottle of water. "You were amazing last night by the way," Caroline said.

"Well thank you," Piper said. "Y'all rocked that," Eve said. "That's what all the hard work was for," Piper joked. "By the way, Colt is a little annoyed that he's not allowed up here," Eve said. "He's not gonna be," Piper replied. "Girl, come on," Caroline said. "And since when were all of y'all friends," Piper asked. "He saw us together at that bar once already," Eve said. "And now I know where all of his insanity is coming from," Piper replied. "Girl, come on," Caroline said. "No. I'm in control of my own life. Period. I don't need y'all setting me up and I don't need anyone telling me who to date," Piper said. "I want you to have someone. If it's not him, fine. I just don't want you to be alone," Caroline said. "I can handle my own social life. Trust me," Piper said. "You know that he does want you around right," Eve asked. "I appreciate it, but honestly, I'm good. If I want a set-up, I'll tell you," Piper teased.

Piper got her bags and got the band and they headed down to the waiting SUV. "You flying back," Eve asked. Piper nodded. "Did y'all fly in," Piper asked. "Drove up. We decided to go shopping," Caroline joked. "Have fun. I have to go back to do the press stuff in Savannah and a bunch of radio interviews when I get to the house," Piper teased. "We'll see you tomorrow then. We can go out or something," Eve said. Piper nodded, gave them a hug and thanked them for coming and headed off before Colt broke through the security to get to Piper. Just as the door closed on the SUV, Colt got up to the SUV. "Piper," he said as he knocked on the window.

The SUV pulled out and he shook his head and tried texting her. When it didn't go through, he about snapped. Piper got to the airport and Harley had her hand tight in hers. "You sure you're alright," Harley asked. "I told them they were out of line," Piper said. "You need to figure out what you're gonna do with him," Harley said. "I know. Honestly, I don't think he's gonna give me a break on anything. They're up to something," Piper said. "Then decide what you want. You can't be the single girl forever. Even that chick from Sex and the City got married," Harley teased. "Girl, are you sayin that you actually sat and watched Sex and the City? You laughed at me for watching it," Piper joked.

They landed back in Savannah not long later. Piper hopped off the plane, thanked the band and headed back to the house with Harley. "So, now what," Harley asked. "Now, I get to sleep in my own bed and go for a walk or whatever here. What are you doing tonight," Piper asked. "Taking you out for a night out," Harley teased. "Serious," Piper asked. "You need a night out with that guy not involved. Maybe meet someone else," Harley said. Piper almost started to laugh. "If that's what you wanna do," Piper said. "I also kinda want another night off from life," Harley joked. "Done. I'll get us a reservation at the Olde Pink House and we can go from there," Piper said. "Sounds like a plan," Harley said. Piper went and made the reservation and Harley called her husband and let him know she'd be home the next day.

They relaxed and got mani/pedi's at the spa in town then went for a walk and went shopping for a while. They headed back to the house and Harley's phone went off. "Hubby," Harley said as she answered. She talked to him on the way back and just as they got back to The house, Piper's phone buzzed with a text:

Can we talk?

Piper shook her head and checked to see if her number was changed. When she realized it wasn't, she shook her head and sent a reply:

Not on your life. I'm done. Stop messaging me. Nothing is gonna change.

They walked in the door and got changed. They left and headed out to dinner, while Piper completely ignored her phone. They had a long relaxing dinner then headed out the door and went off to their ongoing ladies night. Bar to bar, drink to drink, they had fun and got rid of all of the insanity of the week. When they went to head home, Piper saw Colt. "Home or talk," Harley asked. "Home," Piper said. "Piper, two minutes," Colt said. "I'm not your property and I don't want anything to do with you. You don't get that," Piper asked. "I want two minutes. I ran all over the dang country. Please," Colt said. "You're ridiculous," Piper said. He grabbed her hand and pulled her to him. Harley intentionally stayed close by. "We need to talk," Colt said. "No we don't. We have nothing to talk about. I don't even know you and honestly, after all of this crap, I really don't want to," Piper said. He shook his head. "What," Piper asked. He kissed her and Piper pushed so hard he fell backwards. She walked off with Harley, went to the waiting uber and went back to the house.

"What is up with that," Harley said. "Not you know why I want to whoop his butt to the moon," Piper said. "He is persistent. Almost as much as my husband was before we got married. Girl, my husband didn't stop until he put a ring on my finger. He's not the kind to stop either," Harley said. "I'm not playing with him. Not when everything I do is in the spotlight now. I'm not doing this with him. I don't need a guy like that anywhere near me. He's never gonna be my type," Piper said. "Give him a chance. One chance," Harley said. "Answer is still no. I'm not doing it," Piper said. "Then be prepared. Guys like that don't take no for an answer and my hubby was no different. He never took no for a dang answer. That's what got me three miscarriages," Harley said jokingly. "Girl, you love him even if y'all were in the middle of world war three y'all would still be alright," Piper said. "Then you need to go looking for the guy that you want to have world war three stuff with," Harley said. "Right now, we need water and a bed. We can drop you at home," Piper said. "Nope," Harley replied as the alcohol kicked in and she started slurring.

They got back to Piper's and she helped Harley inside and up to the guestroom, got her in bed in her pajamas and got her water. Piper locked up and turned the alarm on then grabbed a Gatorade and went upstairs. By the time she reached the top step, Harley was guzzling down the water. She grabbed a G2 and handed it to Harley. "How are you not drunk," Harley asked. "Took my time," Piper joked. "Goodnight girl." Piper went down to her bedroom and slid into bed, guzzling her water. Just as she was about to close her eyes, her phone buzzed with what felt like the millionth text:

Gate of Wormsloe. Five minutes. Please. – C

Piper shook her head. She knew that it wasn't that far of a walk, but she didn't want to even give him a chance. Not when she was drinking and not when she was so against ever going out with him. She shook her head and maybe 2 minutes later, he called her. "What," Piper asked. "Please," he asked. "No. I was drinking. I'm not getting behind the wheel of a car," Piper said. "Then I'll come over there," Colt said. "Answer is no. End of discussion. Just stop. I don't want to date you. What don't you get," Piper asked. "I'll send a car to get you. Please," he asked. "Colt, enough. I'm done. This conversation is over," Piper said as she hung up. The more he pushed, the more pissed she got.

The next morning, Piper woke up to 5 missed calls from Colt. She deleted the calls and went into the gym for a workout. Just as she was leaving, she saw Colt. He handed her a smoothie and walked her outside. "What," Piper asked. "We need to talk. Enough with the avoiding me thing," Colt said. "We have nothing to talk about. I'm not going out with you. Take the no and accept it already. Just leave me alone," Piper said. She shook her head and got back in her truck with the smoothie and headed home. She got in the door and Harley was just waking up. "You're seriously back already," Harley asked. Piper nodded. "Breakfast," Piper asked as she drank the last of her smoothie. "Definitely," Harley replied.

Piper made breakfast and had her turkey bacon and fresh juice. "So, what did psycho guy want," Harley asked. "He decided to keep pestering and see if I'd go out with him. The answer is still no whether he accepts it or not," Piper said. "The man is not gonna accept that no," Harley said. "Then I find someone who I actually want to be with," Piper said. "That means more girl nights. I think I'm up for that," Harley joked. "Good. Honestly, after going out with Eve and Caroline, I think I may just be hanging with you instead," Piper said. "They went to that stupid strip club place right," Harley asked. Piper nodded. "Eve had just broken it off with her boyfriend. That's what she needed. I just removed myself from it. Char would lose it if I was spotted in there," Piper said. Harley shook her head. "Then hubby and I will introduce you to a few guys we know are good people," Harley said. "I'm in on that one," Piper said.

They both got showered and changed and after a quick hug, Harley headed home and Piper cleaned up the house before Eve got back. Maybe 20 minutes later, her phone went off. "Yep," Piper said. "So, I have some news," Eve said. "Which would be," Piper asked. "I got word back about a place. It's exactly what I wanted. Is that alright," Eve asked. "You know you're welcome here whenever, but yeah. That's amazing. You'll have to tell me all the details," Piper replied. "I will. We are on our way back to the house now," Eve said. "Alright girl. I'll see you soon," Piper said as she hung up. She finished cleaning up, went and got groceries and came back to just relax for a while. She opened the wine and poured herself a drink then sat down on the sofa and tried to chill. When she heard a car door closing, Piper got up and saw Eve in the driveway with Caroline.

"And how was the trip," Piper asked. "We had a blast. Honestly, if we can, we are so going to a Falcons game. That stadium is amazing," Eve said. "I'm glad y'all had fun," Piper said. "You should've come with us," Caroline joked. "I had so much to get done it was insane," Piper said. "So, what's the plan for the rest of the week," Caroline asked. "Getting work done, writing and probably a million radio interviews. What's up with y'all," Piper asked. "We're doing a girls night. We need one. We're going to Mrs. Wilkes then we are having a night on the dang town. We're finding you a boyfriend if it kills me," Caroline teased. "I appreciate the gesture, but honestly, I'm good. When and if I ever meet the right person then it'll click. I don't need any help," Piper said. "Girl, you are always cooped up in the house or working. You need someone. Just admit it," Caroline said. "I need air, food, water. What do you want me to say? I don't need a guy to make me happy. I don't need to have someone in bed with me every night," Piper said. "Then stop closing yourself off. Colt's actually..." "Seriously? Colt is a psycho. I'll pass," Piper said. "Girl, he's trying to get your attention," Caroline said. "And he can quit any dang time now," Piper replied.

Caroline finally headed out a little while later and Eve got packed. Piper finished working on some lyrics that she had stuck in her head then went and put something on for dinner. When Eve caught a whiff, she walked downstairs following the amazing smell. "What are you cookin," Eve asked. "Stuffed lobster and little steaks," Piper said. "Damn. That is one thing I'm gonna miss," Eve said. "When are you goin," Piper asked. "Tomorrow. I lucked out on the place. The people that wanted to rent it had to back out," Eve said. "You know that you are always welcome over here," Piper said. Eve nodded and gave Piper a hug. "Still think that set up thing would be alright. I think Caroline just likes Colt for some odd reason," Eve said. "Blind," Piper joked. She threw a salad together and they sat down and had a relaxing dinner.

As soon as they were finished, Harley texted that operation find a man was a go. It was starting that night. "You have another night of fun in you," Piper asked. Eve smirked. "Definitely. Should I call Caroline," Eve asked. "If she can accept that it's not gonna be Colt," Piper replied. "I can't promise a dang thing, but whatever we do we'll have fun," Eve said. Piper nodded and gave her a hug. "Tuesday," Piper asked. Eve nodded. "I'm gonna get some work done. Do you need any help packing up," Piper asked. "I'm good. I'm getting a mover to help instead," Eve joked. "And what's his name," Piper teased. "Jeremy. Caroline's brother," Eve said. "Alright. You do know that if anything happens, you can always come back here right," Piper asked. "Oh I know. I was sorta hoping a guy would be keeping you occupied though," Eve teased. "You and Eve are seriously pushing way too dang hard," Piper said. "Girl, all I'm sayin is that I want you happy.

You deserve a great guy. You always have," Eve said. "And when one is created, I'm sure he'll become a psycho when he meets me," Piper joked. "Funny," Eve said.

Eve got a few things packed up and put into the trunk of her car then turned in to pack up the little things and a few important fragile items. Piper, on the other hand, went and tried working on music until her phone started going off for the millionth time. One look at the call display and she shook her head. "What do you want now," Piper asked. "Come for a drink with me," Colt said. "What part of leave me alone don't you get," Piper asked. "The part where all I ask is for one stupid date and you ignore me," he said. "I said no. Accept it," Piper said. "Please," Colt said. "I said no. End of discussion. Colt, I'm not your client at the gym anymore. You have no dang reason to call me. Enough," Piper said. She hung up, got the phone number changed and sent the information to Char, the band and Harley. She told Eve and Caroline that she'd changed the number and emailed her folks so they had all the updated information.

Piper finally managed to relax and finish a few songs she'd been working on. When she got the information down, she sent it to the band and they opted to go in and work on the music in the rehearsal studio. She went to go to sleep and there was a buzz at the gate. "Yes," Piper said. "It's Caroline," she said. "You alone," Piper asked. "Of course," Caroline said. Piper buzzed her in, made sure the gate was locked up behind her and went downstairs. "What are you doin here so late," Piper asked. "Got into a fight with the boyfriend," Caroline said. "Good thing I have 3 bedrooms," Piper said. "You sure," Caroline asked. "Eve's leaving tomorrow and moving into her place. More than welcome as long as you don't try giving Colt any info. Deal," Piper asked. Caroline nodded. "I get it. Honestly, I just want you happy. That's all," Caroline said. Piper got her set up in the other guest bedroom and locked up, turned the alarm on and made sure the house was all safe. She turned the lights off and went upstairs to go back to bed.

Chapter 3

The next morning, Piper got up and went for her workout with her trainer and just as she was about to head out, Colt saw her. "Can we talk for a minute," Colt asked. "Didn't understand the meaning of no," Piper asked. "Two minutes," he said. "No," Piper said as she tried to push past him. He grabbed her hand and pulled her to the side. "Let go," Piper said. He walked her into an office and closed the door. "Colt, enough. I'm going home," Piper said. "All I wanted was a chance to talk to you," he said. "Answer is no," Piper replied. "Am I that bad," he asked. "You want the truth? Pushing until I do what you want is stupid. That's not how to get someone to go out with you. Second, I said I wasn't interested. I'm still not. Leave it alone Colt. I'm done," Piper said. She got up and went to head out. "Piper," he said. "Leave me be," Piper replied. She walked out the door, got into her truck and headed back to the house.

She walked in and saw Eve and Caroline packing up. "How goes the packing," Piper asked. "Never realize how much stuff I had with me," Eve said. "You know that if there's anything you forgot, you can always come over," Piper said. "I appreciate it," Eve said as she gave Piper a hug. Piper went and got breakfast on and got the ladies a mug of coffee while she inhaled her breakfast. The ladies took a break and had their breakfast then Piper helped Eve get her things packed up into the moving van. "What happened to the movers," Piper asked. "They're packing my furniture up from the storage locker. My mom is helping out," Eve said. "Is there anything else you're gonna need," Piper asked. "Nothin. Honestly, I think I may be eating takeout for a couple days, but everything's all good," Eve said. Piper sat down and put an order in for grocery delivery then got Eve's new address and put the order through. When Eve finally headed out before lunch, Piper got showered and changed and went and helped Eve get settled at the new place. When the order showed not long later, Eve accepted it and looked at Piper. "Did you do this," Eve asked. "Who wants take out," Piper joked. "Girl, you are too much," Eve said as she gave Piper a hug.

Piper finished up and headed back to the house, getting some quiet time alone while she could to work on her music. When Harley called, Piper almost laughed. "What can I do for you," Piper asked. "So, it got that bad that you had to go changing the number," Harley asked. "Understatement," Piper said. "You up for a jam session on those new lyrics," Harley said. "Definitely. See you soon," Piper said. They hung up and Piper relaxed. Within a half hour, Harley was at the house complete with her guitar. "You ready," Piper asked. "You mean considering that those lyrics are about to out that idiot," Harley joked. "There's more than one. I just think we need to put those lyrics out," Piper said. "You never did come up with a title," Harley said. "Never give up," Piper asked. "That could work. It does kinda go along with the lyric," Harley said. "Good. The question is, do you think it would even make it on the charts," Piper asked. "Girl, any woman who was screwed over by a guy would be all freaking over it," Harley replied. "We'll run it past Char and the label then. See what they think," Piper said.

They finished working on the song then started on a few others that Piper had been trying to work on. They finished up a few and got everything down the way they wanted then recorded the song the way they wanted it. They played it back and it was amazing. Harley grabbed Piper's cell and forwarded it to the rest of the band and to Char. When she got nothing but positive replies, Harley smirked. "I told ya," Harley said. "Alright. Fine, but we have to have more than a song or two to do a cd. We both know that," Piper said. "You finished the first one. Char said something about a way to

41

record on the tour bus when we travel. It's gonna be fun when we actually get to go and do more than just the odd tv performance," Harley said. "If and when," Piper said. "You never know. It could happen," Harley joked. "So, what you up to tonight other than buggin me," Piper teased. "Hanging with my friend," Harley joked. "Ladies night," Piper asked. "At home, yeah," Harley teased. "Done. We can get takeout Chinese and just hang here," Piper said. "After what the hubby pulled, I think this is a pretty good idea," Harley said. "And what did he do now," Piper asked as she put the dinner order in on her phone. "He doesn't think that I'm taking care of him enough," Harley said. "Then what on earth are you doin here? Go have a date night," Piper said. "I tried that. He said he didn't want to," Harley said. "Girl, you need to do somethin. I know how much he loves you," Piper said. "Girl, he does, he just forgot how to show it," Harley said. "Then we do a performance and you put those sappy songs in that you love," Piper said. "Done," Harley said.

"Do we even have any performances," Harley asked. "I can ask Char, but we can come up with something. There's always something," Piper said. "We can do something in Forsyth. They already have the bandshell," Harley said. Piper nodded. She sent the info to Char and within a matter of minutes she got one heck of a reply. "Well, Char's on board. She actually suggested doing it for a benefit. What do you think," Piper asked. "I think I'm already on board," Harley said. "Done," Piper said. She sent the idea off to the rest of the band and they were all on board. "Well, it's all you girl. What day are we planning it for," Piper asked. "We can say it's for breast cancer research and make it on our anniversary," Harley said. "Perfect. We can have it set up for a picnic dinner or something. What do you think," Piper asked. Harley nodded. "You can come up with a million dang ideas, but you're still on your own. Something isn't right about that," Harley said.

42

"Girl, don't worry about my love life. Whatever's meant to happen will when it's the right time," Piper said. "Whatever you say girl," Harley said. They hung out and relaxed, had their Chinese food and tried to just laugh all their troubles away. They played around with lyrics, watched a movie or two and just hung out. When Caroline came back, Harley headed home and everything was cleared away like nobody was even there. Just as she came up the steps, her phone buzzed with a call from Colt.

"What's up," Caroline asked. "She changed her number. Help me out," Colt asked. "Maybe stop pushing so hard," Caroline said. "I can't stop thinkin about her. Since the day you told me about her, I couldn't get her off my mind," Colt said. "You need to calm down. She's gonna snap if she knows that it was because of me," Caroline said. "Just get her to talk to me," Colt asked. Little did Caroline know, Piper heard the entire conversation. "What was because of you," Piper asked. She handed the phone to Piper, knowing that she was about to snap. "What can I do..." "Piper," Colt said. "When are you gonna take a dang hint," Piper asked. "Just come out with me. One date," Colt said. "So now you're going through Caroline to get attention? Give me a damn break," Piper said. "We can have one night. One. We can have dinner or something. Walk at Forsyth. Please," Colt said. "I already said no," Piper said. "I'm not gonna give up. I just want a chance," Colt said. "Answer is still no," Piper said. "If it doesn't work then I'll back off and leave you alone," Colt said. "Just..." "Please," he begged. "One date. Period. End of discussion," Piper said. "Alright. Tomorrow night," Colt said. "Seriously," Piper said. "Please. I'll come pick you up at the house or something," Colt said. "No," Piper said. "Then we meet nearby," he said. "I'll meet you at the restaurant," Piper said. "We're going to the Pink House," Colt said. "You do realize you need a reservation right," Piper said. "I know a guy. I'll meet you there at 5 tomorrow," he said. "Fine, but if this backfires, you leave me alone," Piper said. "Alright," Colt said.

Piper hung up with him and handed the phone to Caroline. "And," Piper said. "I met him when Eve and I were out. I thought you two would make a good couple. When he said y'all didn't work, he just called and said that he wanted to go out with you and he couldn't stop thinking about you. I know he's a good person," Caroline said. "Answer is still no. After tomorrow night, he'll see it the same way I do. It's not gonna work," Piper said. "And," Caroline asked. "And nothing. He'll figure it out. It's not gonna work," Piper said. "Alright. Whatever you say," Caroline said. Piper shook her head. "I appreciate that you want to help with finding the right guy for me, but honestly, I'm all good," Piper said. "I want you to have a good guy," Caroline said. "Then maybe you need to check your eyesight. He's the complete opposite of it," Piper said.

Piper walked into the master bedroom and laid down on the bed. "What the hell did I do now," Piper thought to herself. She went and slid into a long hot bath and leaned back, trying to relax. When she slid out and drained the tub, Char called. "What's up," Piper asked. "Choice of charity for it," Char asked. "Either kids hospital, breast cancer or cancer research. Something everyone can get behind," Piper said. "What about something like musicians on call or St. Jude," Char asked. "I'll poll the band and see what they think," Piper said. "They said yes as long as you'll help do promo for it and it goes to charity. They just want to do something like canned goods instead of tickets and buying t-shirts with the proceeds going to charity. What do you think," she asked. "I think it's a lot to do in a month. We have to do a set list and wardrobe and everything else. All of it is insane," Piper said. "We have it handled. We have the shirts that have the cover photo on them, then we can do ones with you and the band by Forsyth

Fountain or something and go from there. Something quick and easy. What do you think," Char asked. "Done," Piper replied. "Alright. I'll get going on it and let me know when the band decides. What else do you need me to do," Char asked. "Maybe doing food from local restaurants or something," Piper suggested. "Works for me," Char said. "Alright then. We're a go. Now comes the insanity," Piper joked. "By the way, did you check your email? We got a request and I need your input," Char said. "I'll check it out. I'll give you a shout tomorrow," Piper said. "Alright girl. Get some rest. You're gonna need it," Char said as they hung up.

The next morning, Piper was up early. Ideas were running in her mind all night. When she got back from the gym, Caroline was just getting up. "Hey," Caroline said. "Mornin," Piper replied. "Your phone was blowing up all mornin by the way. What's the big news," Caroline asked. "Not sure yet. I didn't even check my email, but we are doing somethin else kinda cool. We're doing a live show at Forsyth," Piper said. "When," Caroline asked. "Before you say anything to your little friend, I'm intentionally keeping this quiet until we have everything in place. It's not for public knowledge," Piper said. "Sounds like a big somethin," Caroline said. "It will be," Piper said. "As long as you promise I can come when it does happen," Caroline said. Piper nodded.

Caroline headed into work and Piper got in touch with the band and had a group conversation. "Is everyone on board," Piper asked. "100%," they all agreed. "Y'all know that means rehearsing right," Piper joked. "Char said she had big news. Did you find out what it was," Keith asked. "Hold on," Piper said as she went into her email. When she saw what the big news was, she almost dropped the phone. "What's up," Harley asked. "Well, there's other news. Seems like we have one heck of a huge request that's gonna mean being away a lot," Piper said. "Meaning," Harley asked. "Meaning we were asked to be opener," Piper said. "For who," Keith asked. "One opener one lead act. Us then Jason Wright," Piper said. "What," Harley asked. "I guess this means that the CD is bound to hit the top ten…and we have a heck of a lot of work to get done," Piper said. "We're rehearsing today if that's what we're doing. We have to get new wardrobe and everything," Harley said. "I guess that means we need to meet up today if you have the time," Piper joked. "We'll meet you at the rehearsal space," they all decided.

Piper messaged Char about what time they were heading to the rehearsal space. When she replied that she'd booked it so they could all go through wardrobe and set lists. Piper went and got showered and changed to head over and messaged the band. Just as she did, Caroline forwarded a text she'd got from Colt:

We're going to dinner in Hilton Head. I'll meet you down on river street near the dock near the Marriott. Hope you're alright with it. – C

Piper shook her head. Leaving town with him wasn't in the cards and wasn't exactly an option. She shook her head, messaged Caroline and told her to let him know she would. She knew deep down that she was gonna regret it. She headed over to the rehearsal space and the minute they walked in, the band was there waiting. "So," Kurt asked. "So, I talked to Char. Emailed her actually. It's kinda what we all wanted. A big tour, opening act but that also means a ton of wardrobe and rehearsing and lighting and everything else. That other event, we sorta have to choose the charity it's going to go for. Harley, we're doing this for other reasons so you get first option," Piper said. "I chose breast cancer research. Up to y'all," Harley said. "Breast cancer is a good plan for me," Kurt said. Everyone else agreed. "Good. Now that's done," Piper teased. "So, what do we want to do for the set list," the guys asked. "Well, that's the thing. If we're doing the tour, it means doing a few videos for the songs we're gonna have in the set list. What do you think," Piper asked. "I'm good. Whenever you want me," Harley said.

They all agreed and maybe a minute or two later, Char came in with wardrobe for all of them. "Alright. So, now we have to start goin through all of this. We're picking out ideas for wardrobe. If it's not perfect, it's fine. We'll work with the idea. Sound alright," Char asked. They all agreed and Piper waited until the end. She went through the wardrobe for all of it and they managed to get an idea of what they wanted to do for all of it. By the end, everyone else's wardrobe was done and she was starting on hers. Sparkle and everything else came out from that dressing room. "And," Piper asked. "The sparkles work and the denim thing is good. You know you're gonna want to switch things up along the way," Harley said. "Tweak, not switch," Piper joked. "So, does this mean we can actually get back to rehearsing," Harley asked. "Definitely. We have to get everything good for whatever the heck our set list is gonna be for opening. We're working on the second CD anyway so we can use a couple of those as we go through," Piper said. "What did y'all decide on for the set list," Char asked.

The rest of the afternoon, they had the set list set and were doing rehearsal until they all needed a break. "We'll meet back over here tomorrow," Piper asked. Everyone agreed and Harley smirked. "What," Piper asked. "Have fun tonight," Harley teased. "Funny. Honestly, I would rather go to bed early," Piper said. They all headed out and went off to wherever and Harley followed Piper back to the house. They headed inside and Harley helped Piper get ready. "You know I can do this solo right," Piper teased. "Girl, I need time off from my man like you need a date. Just show me what you're gonna wear," Harley said. Piper showed her and Harley almost smirked. "You're joking right," Harley asked. "That's what I'm wearin," Piper replied. "Girl, you two are goin to dinner. White jeans? Seriously," Harley asked. "I'm not wearing a dress. Not around him," Piper said. "Dressy pants," Harley asked. Piper handed her white leather leggings. "Damn. Alright then. What top," Harley joked. "Silver or baby blue," Piper said. "Silver," Harley said. "Bringing a sweater. Not about to freeze," Piper said. "Alright then. You have everything you need except shoes," Harley said. "Wedge sandals," Piper replied. "Do you need my help with anything else or do you want me to go grab a bottle of wine," Harley teased. "I'm not drinkin around him," Piper said.

Harley got a glass of wine and got Piper a glass of ice water. Piper did her hair and her makeup and then opted to paint her nails. "You look amazing," Harley said. "Thank you. Now I have just enough time to cancel and have a girl night with you," Piper said. "You're goin. What's the worst that could happen," Harley said. "Fall off the boat, get attacked, killed, food poisoning and get arrested," Piper teased. "You need to chill. If you want me to, I'll drag hubby there so you have backup," Harley said. "He's not gonna stop until I go, but if it were up to me you'd be there," Piper said. "You have to chill. When you want to come back, if he is being an idiot, call me and I'll come get you myself," Harley said. Piper gave her a hug and when Harley finished her wine, they left and headed off.

Piper gave herself a pep talk the entire way there. She charged her phone, put her backup in her purse and talked to Harley one last time. "You got this. When you get back, message me," Harley said. "I will. Cross your fingers," Piper said. They hung up and Piper locked up her truck and headed down to the dock. She saw a big boat and just as she turned to walk away, she saw Colt pop up from the boat. "Good timing. I was just getting everything organized. Come on aboard," Colt said. He held out his hand. She slid her sandals off and hopped aboard. "Well, this is cute," Piper said. "Figured it was a lot faster to get up there by boat. We can drive if you want to," Colt said. "It's fine. I'm just not drinking," Piper said. "Totally get it. I grabbed us a couple sodas," Colt replied.

They sat down and he handed her a cold can of ginger ale. "Glass," Colt asked. She shook her head. "Thank you though. Where are we goin," Piper asked. "Restaurant on the water in Hilton head. Cute place that I've gone to for years," he said. "Alright," Piper replied. "Do you want to go now," he asked. "Probably a good idea. I do have to go in to rehearsal tomorrow," Piper said. "Before we go," he said. "What," Piper asked. "I'm sorry for acting a fool before this. Honestly, I overstepped a hell of a lot. I went too far," Colt said. "Understatement. Let's just go," Piper said. "You really don't want me near you do you," he asked. "Colt, I said I'd go. Beyond that, I don't even know. We just don't click," Piper said. "Then we'll just go," he said. "Colt, it's honestly nothing personally against you. I just don't know if I want a relationship at all. I have a tour coming up. I don't even know if I have time for a private life," Piper teased. "If you hadn't banned me from the tour, I could just come hang with you," he said. "Following me and demanding to talk to me at every stop wasn't the smartest idea," she said.

"I'll admit that I acted like an idiot. Tell me what I have to do to make it up to you," Colt said. "One night without any pressure," Piper said. "Done," he replied. He gave her a hug and then started the boat up. They headed off and made their way to the restaurant. Part way, she got up and stood beside him and he pulled her to him. When they finally arrived, she sat back down until they tied to the dock. He helped her out of the boat and they headed over to the restaurant. He slid his hand in hers. She shook her head and smirked. "What," Colt asked. "Nothin," Piper said. They got their table and were seated. "Cute little place," Piper said. "Was hoping you'd like it," Colt joked. One look at the menu and it's like he could read her mind. "So, what do you feel like," he asked. "No idea," Piper said.

They finally got their drinks and ordered dinner then there was an awkward silence. She almost wanted to just cut and leave, but she knew she couldn't. "So, I know that Caroline told you that we met," Colt said. "Where is the question," Piper said. "I was out with some buddies that night and Caroline thought we would hit it off," Colt said. "Just seems odd that she'd be out with Eve and think that we could hit it off," Piper said. "She asked me about work and stuff and I told her how I was a big country music fan. She told me about you and I pestered her to introduce me," Colt said. "Well, you got your wish," Piper teased. He had that look. One that said that one way or another, she'd want him and he wouldn't stop until she did. That look that said he was already hooked. That look like he was imagining her without a stitch of clothing on. "Quit looking at me like I'm dessert," Piper said. "You look good tonight. What do you want me to do," he teased. Piper finished her dinner while he continued to attempt to taunt her and tease. "You realize that you aren't getting anywhere right," Piper said. "All I wanted was dinner," he teased. Piper shook her head.

She knew his type a long way off. The muscles, the killer blue eyes, the short blonde hair, the smile that was always meant to pull a woman in. All of it was a façade. She'd known guys like him and they were up to no good at all. He was almost six foot three and was showing that off. Every inch of him. The tattoos, the earring. He wasn't her type, but he was determined to act like he was. Like someone had put him up to it. "One thing I don't get," Piper said. "Which is what," he asked as he ordered dessert for them to share. "Why me,"

Piper asked. "You're the one that came in to the gym. First I heard about you, you were coming in for training at the gym," Colt said. "Colt," Piper said. "Eve told me about a friend she wanted to set me up with. Trust me. If I'd known she was talking about you, I would've jumped at the chance immediately," he teased. "I don't even know if I can trust you," Piper said. "You can. Just give me the chance to prove it," he said. "Colt, you're still assuming there would ever be another date," Piper said. "If I said that I want there to be one," he asked. "I said only one and I meant it," Piper said. "Tell me why," Colt asked. "Because you aren't my type Colt. You never will be," Piper said. Dessert showed and it was one of her favorites. How the heck did he know? "And what makes you think that," Colt asked.

She knew it was a game to him. It always was with guys like that. "You aren't. Second, I'm always rehearsing or performing. I have a ton of stuff coming up and I don't have time for a guy in my life other than the guys in the band," Piper said. "Then I'll come as your trainer," Colt said. Piper shook her head. "We should go," Piper said. "One date," he said. "And as of now, it's over," Piper replied. He got the bill and Piper headed down to the boat and messaged Harley that she wanted out of there immediately. She went and sat down outside and just as she was about to call Harley to come get her, Colt came down behind her. "You ready to head back," Colt asked. "I'm gonna get a ride back," Piper said. "I'm not trying to intentionally come after you or attack or something. I said I'd get you back there safe and I meant it," Colt said. "I'll pass," Piper said. "Then at least come sit with me until your ride gets here. I get you're mad Piper, but can't you just open up a little? I get that you've probably been hurt a million times over, but I'm not those guys. I just wanted a dang chance," Colt said. "I'm gonna say this and I know it's gonna sound blunt," Piper said. "Just say it," Colt said. "You followed me to 5 different cities. That's almost stalker level," Piper said. "What do you want me to say," Colt asked. "Going that far is a little insane. It tells me that you're practically a stalker. Saying no and walking away isn't something you can even accept. You're gonna have to," Piper said. He shook his head.

"I'm not a bad guy," Colt said. "That's your opinion. I'm going home alone. Period. No second date," Piper said as she felt her phone buzz, no doubt with a message from Harley. She looked and saw a message that she wasn't far from there and was on her way. "Piper," he said. "What," she replied. "Tell me you aren't serious. I was trying to get you to talk to me. One minute we're good, the next you're avoiding me and telling security to block me from coming near you. I wanted to know what the heck happened," he said. "Colt," Piper said. He shook his head. "What," she asked. "Before you go blowing me off for the rest of your life," he said. "What," Piper asked again. He kissed her. That kiss was so hot, it lit a flame in her. He got up and went to walk her down to the boat. "I'm just gonna go," Piper said. "What's wrong," he asked. "Colt, honestly, it's not gonna work," Piper said as she got up. He kissed her again, pulling her to him. That arm of steel wrapped around her and held her so tight it was almost like she had no way of walking away. "Just come down to the boat," Colt asked. Her phone buzzed again that Harley was in the parking lot. "I'm going," Piper said. "Come with me," he said. "Good night," Piper replied. She broke away from him and walked up to the restaurant and out to the parking lot, hopping in Harley's truck.

"What's up with that," Harley asked. "Just go," Piper replied. They pulled out just as Colt made his way out the front door. "You have to get your truck," Harley said. "I thought you said you were nearby? I figured you'd be here with hubby," Piper said. "I drove up and went and grabbed dinner. I figured I was close just in case," Harley said. "Is it really that bad," Piper asked. "He had to work. Two passing ships and all that," Harley replied. "I'm kinda glad you were here," Piper said. "What went wrong," Harley asked. "He's not for me Harley. He's not ever gonna be my type," Piper said. She shook her head and they finally made their way back towards Savannah. "Details," Harley said. "I called him on the stalker attitude and he made an excuse for it. I'm just glad that's finally over," Piper said. "Girl, we are seriously hunting down a guy for you," Harley said. "As long as that isn't it, I'm good," Piper said.

They got back to the dock and Harley went to get in the truck and saw Colt walking up towards the parking lot. "You really hate me that much," he asked. "Colt, we don't click. The spark isn't there," Piper said. "And the reason why you're running off and taking off is what," Colt asked. "I'm not your girlfriend Colt. It was one stupid date that we shouldn't have gone on in the first place," Piper said. "Then we're finishing the date," Colt said. "Says who," Piper said. He kissed her. "We were supposed to go over to the Grey," Colt said. "I'm going home," Piper replied. "Tell me why you're so determined to get rid of me," he asked. "I'm not playing this game with you Colt. I'm going home. Date is over," Piper said. She went to open the door of the truck and he closed it, pinning her against the side of the truck. "What," Piper asked. He kissed her again and with one swoop, she pushed him away from her making him lose his balance. She got in the truck and left to head home.

One minute in the door and she was almost paranoid about locking the doors. She shook her head and went upstairs and let Harley know she was home. Within a matter of minutes, her phone rang. "Hey," Piper said. "Hey yourself," Harley teased. "So, did he try calling?" "Not yet anyway," Piper replied. "You pissed," Harley asked. "Nope. He tried kissing me again when I picked up the truck, but I'm even more convinced now that there's no point," Piper said. "Then we're on for tomorrow night. I'm finding you a good guy if it kills me," Harley teased. "Like there was ever a doubt," Piper teased. "I'm thinking that I need to talk to the hubs about all of this avoiding each other thing," Harley said. "I agree with you," Piper said. "He's just pulling in. I'll call you back," Harley said. "Tomorrow. Talk to him," Piper replied. They hung up and Piper went and got changed for bed. A half hour later, she was just about to turn the light off when her cell buzzed. It was a text from Caroline:

So, how did the date go?

Piper didn't even bother answering. She just curled up under the covers and went to sleep.

The next morning, Piper went down to the gym for her workout and bumped right into Colt. "Excuse me," Piper said walking around him. He grabbed her hand and pulled her into his office and closed the door. "Colt, I have an appointment," Piper said. He kissed her. "You walked off on me," he said. "Intentionally," Piper said as she went to walk out. He closed the door and locked it. "Colt, enough," Piper said. "What's wrong with us going out and having fun together," he asked. "You want something from me that I'm not giving you. That's what," Piper said. "You know that last night was good right," he said. Piper unlocked the door and stepped out, walking into the gym and getting to work with her trainer. By the time she was done, she was about ready to kick Colt's butt to the moon. "We need to talk," Colt said as he walked back towards the office. He grabbed her hand and she shook her head and brushed him off. Whatever it was that was driving her nuts, he was making everything worse. She walked out the door and walked straight to her truck. She hopped in and took off before he did something else.

Piper got to the house and got showered and washed up and had a quick breakfast. Just as she was about to head off to rehearsal, Caroline was calling her phone. "What's up," Piper asked as she hopped in the truck and put Caroline on Bluetooth. "So, how did the date go," Caroline asked. "Not gonna be happening again," Piper replied. "Was it seriously that bad," Caroline asked. "Yeah it was. End of discussion. I'm done playing games with him," Piper said. "What's goin on," Caroline asked. "Like I said, that's never ever happening again," Piper said. "He was trying to get in touch with you," Caroline said. "Answer is no if I'm thinking what you are. I don't want him having my dang number," Piper said. "Can I forward the call then," Caroline asked. "I said no Caroline. I get that you're trying to help, but it's only gonna make things worse," Piper replied. "That bad," Caroline asked. "Definitely worse," Piper replied. "What am I supposed to tell him," Caroline asked. "That I'm not interested and I never will be," Piper said. "Damn. You're being a little harsh there lady," Caroline replied. "That's being nice," Piper said. "Alright. We can talk about it tonight. We're doin a girl's night," Caroline said. "Busy," Piper replied. "Dinner," Caroline replied. "And if he shows, I'm out," Piper replied.

She finally got the details for dinner and headed into rehearsal, opting to work on music until everyone else showed. When Harley snuck in so she could hear the music, she leaned back and heard the lyrics that Piper was singing. It was painfully obvious that it was a song of revenge. Harley knew it after she heard that first phrase. "You can come over here if you want," Piper said when she finished the song and wrote down what she wanted in it. "Didn't want to interrupt," Harley joked. "Funny," Piper said. "It's really good. I get where the inspiration came from," Harley teased. "Honestly, all of it drove me insane. I had to do somethin," Piper teased. "About what," Keith asked as he came in.

"Came up with another song, but I'm not sure if it's CD worthy," Piper said. "It's good. Run it by Char and see what she thinks when it's finished," Keith said. "Well thanks," Piper joked. "So, what time is everyone supposed to be here," Keith asked. "Soon," Piper said. Kurt came in a few minutes later then the drummer came in. "Ready," Kurt asked. Piper nodded and they got up and got going on rehearsal.

By the time they were finished for the day, it was almost 5pm. "I'm taking y'all to dinner," Piper said. "And where are we goin," Keith asked. "Name the place," Piper joked. "We can go to that little restaurant out of the city. What do you think," Keith asked. "I'll follow you up there," Piper said. "I'm riding with you," Harley said. Piper nodded. They got organized, locked up and headed to the truck. "What happened to your truck," Piper asked. "In the shop," Harley said. Piper looked at her. "The truth," Piper asked. "I told him to take it. Honestly, things are just getting worse. He's starting to resent me doing all of this music stuff," Harley said. "Maybe that performance would help," Piper said. "I think that it may just be a lost cause altogether," Harley replied as they hopped in the truck. "We do the performance and whatever happens beyond that, we stick together even if it means you staying at my place," Piper replied. "You sure," Harley asked. "If you love him, just remember to hold on with both hands. The single life isn't all that exciting," Piper said. "Girl, trust me when I tell you that I am not lookin forward to that either. I just don't think either of us are happy. That's all," Harley said. "Then you work on it. He couldn't possibly be worse than Colt," Piper said.

Harley almost laughed. "Girl, he drove me insane when we met. He was determined to marry me and I was determined to keep him at arm's length. Eventually it just clicked, but now it's like the spark went out," Harley replied. "It's sorta up to both of you to figure out if you want to leave it out or re-spark it," Piper said. "What are you talkin about," Harley said. "The performance in the park is next week. We don't start the tour for another couple weeks. You can bring him if that's what you want. He can fly in for the big shows. I'm sure I can get Char to do something to help. We can come home during the week and be touring on the weekends. If you want him in your life, say the word," Piper said. "Alright," Harley said. They stopped at the restaurant and Piper gave her a hug. "We'll figure it out," Piper said. "I know. Thank you," Harley said. Piper nodded.

As soon as dinner was done, Piper got Harley home and headed home herself when she saw a truck coming up behind her. "What in the hell," Piper thought to herself. When she finally caught a glimpse of the driver, she pulled over onto the gravel as it flew in the air. She stopped, shaking her head, and hopped out, seeing Colt get out of his truck. "What in the dang world do you want," Piper asked. "You," Colt said. "So, you're stalking me now," Piper asked. "You won't let me call. What do you want me to do," Colt asked. "Leave me alone like I asked," Piper replied. "I don't get why you hate me so dang much," he said. "You push one more time and I swear I will kick you so dang hard you'll pass out," Piper said. "All I want is a chance," Colt said. "Just leave me be Colt. We agreed," Piper said. "And I didn't get fair treatment. You walked out half-way through," Colt said. "If you don't stop, I'm gonna push this even more. You're gonna end up unemployed," Piper said. "I want to finish the date," Colt said. "It is finished. If you don't stop, I'm calling the sheriff," Piper replied. "Then you won't get mad when I do this," he said as he grabbed her and pulled her into his arms, kissing her. She hit him so hard that he fell to the ground. "I meant no," Piper said. She walked back to her truck and left, seeing him still on the ground.

When she got home, she headed inside and locked up, opting to get ready for bed. Just as she stepped into her bedroom, her phone buzzed. It was the front gate. Harley was there. Piper shook her head, buzzed her in and went downstairs. She opened up the front door and Harley was coming up the steps. "What happened," Piper asked. "He snapped. Honestly, I think going on tour is a much better idea then I thought," Harley said. "Your room is all clean," Piper said. Harley gave her a hug. "What you up to," Harley asked. "You mean other than winding Colt," Piper asked. "Dang," Harley said. "He tailed me from your place. He's driving me insane. I'm almost at restraining order level," Piper said. "If we're on the road, he won't be able to start a problem," Harley said. "You mean if he doesn't tail us all over the continent," Piper replied. "Then we add more security. It'll be fine. Either that or we find you a hot single guy to date that can kick his butt," Harley teased. "He doesn't exist," Piper replied.

Piper poured a glass of wine for each of them and they went and sat on the back patio of the house, watching the stars. "We're doin girl night tomorrow. You good with that," Harley asked. "I guess. Honestly, part of me thinks that we should just go somewhere completely different. Somewhere I don't usually go where there are actual normal people instead of guys like Colt," Piper said. "I have the perfect place. Its mostly white collar guys instead of the norm. We can go before dinner," Harley said. "Done," Piper said. "We can go and hang a while then head home early so my hubby doesn't start world war three again," Harley said. "Sounds like a plan," Piper said. They finished their wine and Harley helped her figure out what to wear the next night. "Girl, why don't I just get an outfit out of that giant pile of clothes the stylist picked out? So much freaking easier," Piper said. "We'll figure somethin out. Pick a couple ideas out and see how it goes," Harley joked.

Piper got a few ideas together and showed Harley. After glass 3 of wine, they managed to figure out two options for ladies night. "I'll figure something out at home. I swear, I am gonna have it out with him. At some point, he either has to accept the music stuff or leave. I can't keep doing this," Harley said. "Just take some time to think about it. We can hang tomorrow night after whatever that bar entails and you can stay here. After that, you can head home with a clear head and figure out how to get him to Forsyth," Piper said. "Is it bad that I almost think it's pointless," Harley asked. "You have to make that decision lady. The single life isn't exactly great. That I will warn you of," Piper teased. Harley gave her a hug. "You're like family now. You know that right," Harley said. "You always have been," Piper said. "I'm gonna need that if things backfire completely," Harley said. Piper nodded. "You will always have a space here if you need to stay," Piper replied. Harley nodded. "I'm going to get into bed and try sleeping today's insanity off. I'll see you in the mornin," Harley said. Piper nodded, cleaned up and got the house locked up. She headed upstairs to bed and as she was closing the door, Char messaged.

Piper called her. "So, what's up," Piper asked. "Well, the sound check is day after tomorrow. Are y'all prepared for it," Char asked. "Completely," Piper replied. "Alright. Sound check is gonna be at noon. We can't do anything about it," Char said. "Alright," Piper said. "And we have the set list organized. We're doing the performance and announcing the tour the same day. When the event is on the last song, we're doing a video call for Jason Wright since he's doing a fan party. It's gonna be announced on the big screen at his performance and at yours then it hits Instagram and all the social media and press. It also means there's gonna be more interviews," Char said. "Fine with me," Piper said. "Alright. Second, the trainer can't come out with us if we're travelling.

You alright with that," Char asked. "Doesn't mean I'm gonna stop working out," Piper said. "You sure you don't want me getting that other trainer out with you," Char asked. "Answer is a hard no. I don't even want him near me," Piper replied. "Alright. I'll see what I can do. If not, we just work with what we can. You sure you're ready for the tour and the performance," Char asked. "Yep," Piper said.

Chapter 4

The next day, after rehearsing all day, Harley and Piper
headed off for the so-called ladies night. They walked into the
bar and it was like every head turned when they walked in.
She grabbed a table with Harley, ordered a drink and they sat
back and just relaxed. Within a half hour, they had 5 free
drinks. They still hadn't managed to meet a decent guy yet.
"Is it bad that I'm thinking we need to leave," Piper asked.
"Not when that is here," Harley said noticing a guy who was
handsome and was totally Piper's type. The short sandy
brown hair, the green eyes, the beach baby tan and the
muscles that showed how much he took care of himself.
"And," Harley asked. "Alright fine, but if he's a stripper or
something, I'm out," Piper replied.

When he saw Piper, he shook his head. He took a deep
breath and walked over. "Hey," he said. "Hey yourself," Piper
replied. "So, did y'all want a drink," he asked. He was just as
nervous as Piper was. "Sure," Harley said. The waitress
brought over wine for the table and put it on his tab. "So,
what's your name," Harley asked. "Jamie Hastings," he said.
"Jamie, I'm Harley and this is the most amazing woman in the
world, my bestie Piper Adams," Harley said. "Nice to meet
y'all," he said as he sat down beside Piper. "And what do y'all
do," Jamie asked. "I write music and I perform," Piper said.
"And I'm her kick butt lead guitarist," Harley said as she
fidgeted with her wedding ring. "Dang. Would I have heard
anything," Jamie asked. "Not sure. The CD just came out,"
Piper said. "Wow. CD," Jamie asked. "You heard about that
impromptu concert at Forsyth this week right," Harley asked.
He nodded. "That's our show," Piper replied. "Then I
definitely have to come," he said. "You're more than
welcome," Harley said.

"How exactly are you two both single and nobody had the guts to come over here," Jamie asked. "Must be intimidating or something," Piper said. "May I," Jamie asked. Piper moved over in the booth and he slid closer to her, doing his best to hit on her subtly. "So, what do you do," Harley asked. "I work in a music label downtown. I sort of help in the studio with the production stuff," Jamie said. "What label," Harley asked. "Dirt Road Records," Jamie said. Piper smirked. That was the studio that she'd be working on the second CD in. She almost laughed. "What," Jamie asked. "Nothin. My boss said that's where we were recording the next CD," Piper joked. He shook his head. "That means you're kinda stuck with me then," Jamie joked. "I guess that means we'll probably be bumping into each other," Piper said. "Does that mean I can ask you out," Jamie asked. Harley smirked and got up to grab a drink. "That means that you have that option," Piper teased. He grabbed his card from his pocket and wrote his personal cell number on the back. "So, what are you up to this weekend," Jamie asked. "Performance at Forsyth Park. Other than that, probably doing rehearsal," Piper said. "Then maybe dinner or something," Jamie asked. Piper nodded. "Sounds good," Piper replied. He kissed her cheek. "Now that we have that out of the way," he teased as he snuggled in a little closer. Piper felt her phone buzz. "This is gonna seem so rude, but I have to check this," Piper said. "Go ahead," Jamie said as he kissed her shoulder. She saw a text and 3 emails:

Come outside asap. We're leaving.

"Crap," Piper said. "What's up," Jamie asked. "I have to go. Something happened to Harley," Piper said. "At least let me walk you to your truck," Jamie said. Piper nodded. They headed outside and Harley was losing her marbles in world war three with her husband on the phone. Harley hopped in and Jamie walked around to Piper's side. "Call me tomorrow," he asked. Piper nodded. "As soon as we finish sound check," Piper replied. He kissed her. It was a two-second, I want to do more but you'd kick my butt kinda kiss. "Tomorrow," he asked. Piper nodded. He gave her a hug, kissed her again and got her door for her. She hopped in and started the truck and they headed out. When Harley finally managed to contain the fight that wouldn't end, Piper got them back to the house and they headed inside.

"What happened," Piper asked. "He decided I was cheating by being your dang wing woman. Honestly, this performance thing is the last dang straw. I might as well start moving my stuff out," Harley said. "If that's what happens, then you know you have somewhere to stay," Piper said. "Girl, I appreciate it. I really do. I just think that my ass of a husband is about to get what's coming to him. He's gonna regret ever pissing me off," Harley said. Piper shook her head. "Perfect," Piper teased. "So what's up with that Jamie guy," Harley said determined to get her mind off her own problems.

"He's handsome and even if it's just his best behavior, he is kinda nice. Honestly, I don't know what to make of him yet," Piper said. "Music material," Harley joked. "Happy song maybe," Piper said. "Works for me. Did you want to work on it," Harley teased trying to come up with an idea and a reason to hang out. "We can. Not tonight, but we have time. We're gonna be on tour soon enough," Piper said. "Can't come soon enough. I do know that after tonight, I have a feeling that Jamie isn't gonna be too happy about you goin," Harley said. "He works at the label that we're recording the next CD at. He works in those studios. We'll be perfectly fine. I was planning on dinner with him this weekend maybe," Piper said. "Nice," Harley said. "We'll see if it was best behavior or the real deal," Piper said. They locked up and got changed out of the party clothes and curled up downstairs with a glass of wine and played around with lyrics. By the time they were two more glasses into the wine, Piper texted Jamie to say hey. Within minutes, her phone was ringing.

"Hello," Piper said. "Hey yourself beautiful," Jamie said. "Just thought I should message you and say hi so you knew that I was for real," Piper teased. "Well, if it's of any benefit, I got a ticket to that show at Forsyth. I'm determined to see you," Jamie said. "Well, I know that show isn't gonna be an early night. Maybe we can meet up on Saturday," Piper said. "How about this. I come down to the show and we go and have a glass of wine on the beach after," Jamie teased. "I guess I could," Piper said. "I'm heading to church early Sunday anyway," he said. "Probably the same one," Piper teased. "Wouldn't be surprised. I'll meet you at the park," he teased. "I can meet you at the house after. What do you think," Piper asked. "Send me the address and I'll be there," he said. "Alright. I'll see you Saturday," Piper said. "Goodnight beautiful," Jamie said. "Night handsome," Piper replied. They hung up and Harley had a grin ear to ear. "Told ya so," Harley joked. Piper shook her head and they went back to working on the music before bed.

Within a matter of days, they were doing sound check and getting ready for the performance that would make or break Harley's marriage. Her husband had barely heard a word about the performance except that she was rehearsing for a tour. When the day came, Piper helped her figure out what to wear and had set up that perfect picnic dinner. Piper got hair and makeup done and the rest of the band got ready, had a quick dinner while Harley was having a picnic dinner with her husband, then warmed up backstage.

"What is all of this about," Harley's husband asked. "I wanted us to do something romantic on our anniversary," Harley said. "Last ditch effort," her husband asked. "Stop. Just try to enjoy having some quiet time alone. That's all that I'm doing,"

Harley said. "This isn't working. We both know that. There's really no point in fighting a war that neither of us want to fight," her husband said. "Meaning what," Harley said. "Meaning just call it what it is. It's done. You're happier out with Piper," her hubby said. "You don't love me anymore," Harley asked. "There's no point," her husband said. "Are you hanging out for the performance," Harley asked. "Why? It's not like y'all are singing anything new," he said. "Just stay and listen for once. We're singing one that I wrote," Harley asked. "Fine," he replied. Harley kissed him, even though there was no emotion behind it, and went backstage. She got changed, warmed up and fought off tears.

"What's wrong," Piper asked. "I'm moving in," Harley said. Piper shook her head and gave Harley a hug. They said a quick prayer and headed onstage a few minutes later. The first song had everyone running towards the stage. By the second song, the park was getting crazy busy. By the song that all of it was put together for, and Harley didn't see her husband. He was gone. Even the blanket and picnic basket were gone, according to security. They did Harley's song and as soon as they were done, they finished up the set list and did the big end. "Now, I know that y'all are so excited with all the new tunes you just heard. Here's the big thing..." Just as Piper said it, her phone rang. "Y'all wouldn't mind if we took this call would you? It's a FaceTime y'all," Piper said. The band all had smiles ear to ear. "Hello," Piper said. "Miss Piper. Long time no talk," Jason Wright said. The crowd went insane and the press started snapping away with photo after photo.

"And how are you," Piper asked. "Well, that's sorta what I wanted to talk to you about. I'm in need of an opener for my new Heartbreak Ride tour. Do you know of any huge new bands that could come hang out on the tour with me," Jason said. "Well, I mean, we're not busy, but I could suggest Destiny or Love Heroes," Piper said. "Well, I was gonna ask if y'all might be interested," Jason said as the press and the fans went crazy. "Well, let me check with the fans. Would y'all come see me on tour with this guy," Piper asked. The crowd roared. "I guess this means that we're saying yes," Piper said. "Alright then y'all. I'll see y'all on tour," Jason said. The crowd went crazy. "I guess that means one more song before we take off on tour with Jason Wright y'all," Piper said. The crowd roared and started chanting their names. Piper looked at Harley. "This one is for you," Piper said quietly. They all agreed and sang the one song that Harley had just finished that Char hadn't even heard yet. When they finished it, the crowd was going insane and then Piper let everyone know. "So, I have one other thing y'all. Who still hasn't got their CD," Piper joked. They all went crazy. She looked over and Char nodded that the CD's were at the merch table. "Well, brand new merchandise and the CD are all available right back here. The first 50 people over there get the CD's autographed by all of us and a photo. Who wants one," Piper joked. They all took off running. "Can't wait to see y'all on the road," Piper said as they headed off stage and over to do the meet and greets.

They didn't even finish up with the meet and greet until almost 11:30. When they managed to head out, Piper got Harley home and headed back to the house to see Eve and Caroline waiting. "And what are y'all doin here," Piper asked as she headed upstairs to get changed to go out with Jamie. "Wondering where you disappeared to," Eve said. "Meet and greet after the performance and I'm goin out," Piper said. "It's 11. Normally you're goin to bed early," Caroline said. "Y'all can chill. I have plans," Piper said. "Meaning what," Eve asked. Just as the words passed her lips, her phone buzzed. She took one look, sent the address to Jamie and finished getting changed. "Where are you goin," Caroline asked. "Out with a friend. I have a feeling that Harley's coming back over here tonight." "Where are you goin," Eve asked. "I have a date," Piper said. She finished freshening up and re-doing her makeup then headed downstairs. Caroline and Eve finally left and Piper heard a truck coming down the street.

Just as Eve and Caroline left, she got a message from Jamie that he was at the gate. Piper buzzed him in and when he came down to the front door, his jaw almost hit the floor of his truck. "Hey handsome," Piper said as he hopped out. "Hey yourself superstar. You were amazing tonight," Jamie said. "Well thank you," Piper said as he gave her a hug. "You ready," he asked. Piper nodded, making sure the house was locked. He got her door for her and they headed off. "So, where are we goin," Piper asked. "Two options. We can go down to the beach or we can go over to my place and hang out. Porch swing and all," he teased. "Beach," Piper joked. "I totally called that. We can grab coffee and go," he said. Piper nodded. He slid his hand in hers and kissed her hand. "You really were amazing tonight," he said. "Maybe next time you can hang side stage instead," Piper said. "This mean that we're havin another date," he teased. "We'll see," Piper joked. He kissed her hand again, they stopped and got iced lattes and they headed to Tybee. "I have a happy medium to that decision," he joked. "The swings on the beach," Piper asked. Jamie nodded.

He smirked and they left the Starbucks and headed down to the swing. "How messed up is it that you can read my mind and we barely know each other," Jamie asked. "That's kinda my spot at the beach. Always has been," Piper said. "And that's not just because Channing Tatum had a scene on that swing in Magic Mike," he said. "The XXL one for your info," Piper teased. "Oh I know. My sister watched it like a million times. She's obsessed. Better topic. What are you up to tomorrow," Jamie asked. "Church then dinner with the girls. Nothin else really planned. Why," Piper asked. "Then we're goin out tomorrow night. You and me," he teased. "And where did you want to go," Piper asked. "Come over to my place. We can hang out and just relax and watch a movie or hang and talk on the patio or somethin," he said. "You think tonight's going that good," Piper joked. "I think that we need more time," he said. "Oh really," Piper asked. He nodded. He parked the truck, paid for parking and got her door for her. They headed down to the beach hand in hand and walked straight to the swing.

They sat down and he slid her sandals off. "What are you doin," Piper asked. He slid her legs over his lap. "Well thank you," Piper said. "You worked your dang tail off tonight. You deserve some happy tonight," he said. "Well thank you," Piper said. He pulled her to him and she leaned her head on his shoulder. "Thank you for this." "For coffee and an old porch swing in the sand," he asked. Piper nodded. He looked at her. "What," she asked. "How the heck are you single," he asked. "Picky and busy," Piper said. "And now," he asked. "Kinda met someone," Piper teased. "Do I know him," he teased. "He bought me coffee," Piper said. "So I do know him," Jamie said. She got a silly little grin. "So far, I think things might be going okay," Piper teased. "That's good," he joked. "And why's that," Piper asked. "Because I met a woman I kinda like," he teased. "Nice," Piper said. "And I kinda asked her out for tomorrow night," he joked. "Hope she's sayin yes," Piper replied. "Are you," he asked. "You mean since you got me the perfect drink for tonight," Piper teased. "Since I want to see you in daylight," he teased. "Done," Piper teased. "Good," he teased. "What," Piper asked. He looked in her eyes.

"What's with the look," Piper asked. "Nothin," he said as his hand slid to the side of her face. He leaned in and kissed her. That kiss had her almost trembling in his arms and him pulling her that much tighter to him. That kiss got hotter until they

opted to get up before things went way too far. They finished
their drinks and opted to walk down the pier. When they got
to the end, they threw out their coffee cups and he leaned
her against the railing. "Yes," she said. He leaned in and
kissed her again, devouring her lips. "You are so dang hot," he
said. "What am I gonna do with you," she said. "Tomorrow
night," he teased. "Alright," Piper said. He kissed her again,
leaning into her arms. "I should probably get back so I don't
sleep through church," Piper said. "Well, we could or we just
walk," he teased. "We can walk back towards the truck,"
Piper said. He kissed her. "Alright. As long as we're still going
out tomorrow night," Jamie said. Piper nodded. "Without a
doubt," Piper said. He gave her a huge hug and when he felt
her hug him back, he was almost breathing easier. His panic
faded and he realized he actually was starting to fall for her.
He kissed her and then opted to walk back to the truck with
her before he whisked her off.

He got her door for her, hopped in and they headed back
towards her place. "Thank you for this tonight," Piper said. He
linked their fingers and kissed her hand. "Thank you for
saying yes," he teased. "So, what's the big plan for tomorrow
night," Piper asked. "Dinner and a movie and we just hang
out and relax. Nothing huge. Time for you to just chill and
relax. What do you think," Jamie asked. "You sure I can't
bring anything," Piper asked. "Just you," he replied. "You
sending me an address," Piper asked. He nodded.
"Definitely," he replied. He kissed her hand again and they
pulled into her driveway. "Do you want to come in," Piper
asked. "Thought you'd never ask," he teased.

They headed into the house and the minute the door closed
behind them, he pulled her to him and devoured her lips. He
walked her backwards into the kitchen and had her leaned
against the counter within a matter of minutes. "Jamie,"
Piper said. "Can't help it," he teased as he kissed her

shoulder. "What am I gonna do with you," Piper asked. He kissed her again. "I should go before I end up romancing you right into the bedroom," he said. "Sounds like a plan," Piper said as he kissed her neck again. "You are one heck of a bad influence." He kissed her, devouring her lips again. "That was my plan," he teased. "Jamie," Piper said. He kissed her and she walked him to the door. "Call me when you get home," Piper asked. "Alright beautiful girlfriend," he teased. Piper kissed him and he finally headed off.

Piper locked up and went upstairs. She checked her phone and saw 3 missed calls from Eve. She texted her back that she was home and went upstairs and went to get ready for bed. Just as she was getting changed, her phone rang. "Yep," Piper said. "Just wanted to tell you that I was home," Jamie said. "Do you live down the street or something," Piper asked. "Sorta," he teased. "Meaning what," Piper asked. "Meaning more like a house or two. Maybe a 2-minute drive," Jamie said. "Seriously," Piper asked. "Meaning if you miss me you can always walk over," he teased. "Or run by in the morning," Piper said. "Tease. So, I'll walk over and meet you tomorrow," he teased. "Sounds like a plan," Piper replied. "Get some rest or you're gonna be sleeping through church." "Alright sexy. See you tomorrow," Jamie said. "Sweet dreams," Piper said. "Back at ya beautiful," he replied. They got off the phone and Piper finally got some sleep while she could.

The next morning, Piper got up and got changed for the gym. She headed out the door, walked into the gym and was face to face with Colt. "Piper," Colt said. She shook her head and tried walking past him but he blocked her. "We need to talk," Colt said. "About what? I have an appointment and I'm not gonna be late because of you," Piper said as she pushed him out of the way and walked into the ladies locker room to put her things in the locker. When she came out, Colt grabbed her hand and walked her into his office. He closed the door and Piper shook her head. "What," Piper asked. "Who's the guy," he asked. "Meaning what," Piper asked. "Don't go playing stupid," Colt said. Piper shook her head and walked out of the office. She went in and met up with the trainer, intentionally avoiding eye contact at all costs. As soon as she finished, she got her breakfast and headed back to the house. She came in, locked back up and sat down, trying to get some down time. Just as she sat down, her phone buzzed.

"Yep," Piper said. "What time are you heading to church," Caroline asked. "As soon as I get showered and dressed," Piper replied. "Alright. I'll meet you over there," Caroline replied. "Alright," Piper said. She got up and got showered and ready to go. Just as she stepped out the door, she started wondering what Jamie was really up to. She hopped in the truck and headed to church to see the most familiar truck right behind her. For once, it wasn't Colt. She was almost doing a double-take. When she parked, the truck parked right beside hers. She slid out and saw Jamie. "What are you doin," Piper joked. "Guess this means we can carpool," he joked. Piper shook her head and he kissed her cheek, giving her a hug. He slid his hand in hers and they headed into church side by side, hand in hand. He even went one step further. He sat beside her.

Caroline shook her head. She elbowed Piper and sat down beside her. "Caroline, this is Jamie. Jamie, this is one of my friends Caroline," Piper said. "Nice to meet you," Jamie said. The service started and Jamie barely let go of her hand. As soon as they were finished, Jamie headed right out the door with Piper. Nothing stopped him. They got out the door and he got her to his truck. "What are you up to," Piper asked. He kissed her. "I've been wanting to do that since we got there. Had to go wearing the sexy dress," he whispered. "Far from it," Piper said. He kissed her cheek and gave her a huge hug. "And what are we doing this afternoon." "I have to get some work in before next week. We can still go hang tonight," Piper said. "Excuse me," she heard come from behind her. Piper turned around and saw Colt two inches from her. "And what do you want," Piper asked. "We need to talk," Colt said. "I have nothing to say. I told you then and I'll say it now. Leave me out of your little plan," Piper said. "So, you'd rather go out with a nobody," Colt said. She shook her head and looked at Jamie. He gave her a look saying silently, "Do you want me to handle this idiot." Piper shook her head and turned to face Colt. "I'd rather go out with someone who doesn't need to have an over-inflated ego and push people around when they'd rather be alone then date you. Got me," Piper asked. She turned around and walked back to her truck.

Jamie hopped in his truck and when Piper pulled off, he followed, leaving Colt in the dust. That's how Piper wanted it. Scene or not, Colt wasn't getting what he wanted. She was over the stupid stuff he'd been pulling. Jamie might not have been a millionaire or a super huge country star, but he was a good guy. For once, she thought maybe she'd found a good one.

They got back to Piper's and Jamie pulled in behind her. "What the heck was that," Jamie asked. "Guy I had one date with that thinks he owns me," Piper replied. "And," Jamie asked. "He thinks it's alright to push people around. Caroline probably set the dang thing up," Piper replied. He slid his hand in hers and pulled her into his arms. "And," he asked. "I made my decision and he wasn't even part of the equation," Piper said. "This mean that I get to take you out tonight," he asked. "Let me get changed out of church clothes and we can go do whatever," Piper said. He kissed her and leaned her against the side of the truck. "What," Piper asked. He kissed her again and she headed inside to get changed. He followed and went into the kitchen. She came downstairs maybe 20 minutes later in jean shorts and a tank and he leaned against the counter. "Pretty sexy there woman," Jamie said. "Figured if we were going out…" "Good point. If I said we were just relaxing and hanging out," he teased. "Then I'm good," Piper said. He shook his head, kissed her and walked her out to his truck. She locked up behind her and they headed over to his place.

They walked in and Piper saw flowers on the counter. "What's this," Piper asked. "For you," he replied. "Well thank you," Piper replied. He kissed her and picked her up, sitting her on the kitchen counter. "Jamie," Piper said. He kissed her, devouring her lips and wrapped her legs around him. "And," Piper asked as he nibbled at her lower lip and kissed his way down her neck. "Movie or we sit outside," he said as his hands worked their way down her back to her back pockets. "I think maybe the sitting thing would be a better idea," Piper said. "I just don't get how you're single," Jamie said. "I appreciate the compliment, but," Piper said. He kissed her again before she said another word. He picked her up and walked into the TV room, leaning her onto the oversized sofa. "Jamie," she said. "What," he asked as he kissed her ear. "While all of this is really nice, I think maybe we should get up," Piper said. He kissed her again and when he let her up for air, she pushed her way up. "What," Jamie asked. "Vertical," Piper said. "Your fault that you taunted me," he teased. Piper shook her head, went into the kitchen and grabbed her purse. He didn't even move from the sofa. She shook her head and walked out the front door and back down to her place. What was with the guys around that city? She wasn't a dang toy.

She locked back up and made dinner, opting to eat alone. She had her wine and sat outside, enjoying her meal. When her phone buzzed with a text from Colt, Piper shook her head:

Caroline gave me the number. I just wanted to know who that guy was.

Piper shook her head and blocked his number. Within a matter of 10 minutes, she heard the gate buzz. She took a deep breath, took a gulp of wine and answered. "Yep," Piper said. "I'm sorry," Jamie said. "It's fine. Just getting changed to head out," Piper said. "You mean since you're hanging out in the back having dinner," Jamie asked. "Go home," Piper replied. "Come over," he said. "Not tonight," Piper replied. She leaned back, finished her wine and her phone buzzed with a phone call. "Yes," Piper said. "I messed up. I get it. Just come hang and watch a movie," Jamie replied. "Not tonight," Piper said. "Because I messed up," he asked. "Because I'm not there because you're in the dang mood," Piper replied. "Piper," he said as she heard him go into his house. "I'm not playin a game Jamie. You said you wanted to date me, but 3 seconds into a date, you're trying to get me onto the sofa," Piper said. "Just come," he asked. "Not gonna happen tonight. I'm goin to relax," Piper said. "It's 3 in the dang afternoon. Come on," Jamie said. Piper shook her head. "I'm going for a hike around Wormsloe before they close up for the night. Other than that, I'm stayin home," Piper said. "Then get your hiking boots on and we'll go," he replied. "Fine," Piper said.

She slid her runners on and cleaned the dishes up. She went to pull out to go to Wormsloe and saw Jamie walking down the street. "What are you doin," Piper asked. "Going," he teased. He hopped in the truck with her and they headed over. "I'm sorry about earlier," he said. "Jamie, I'm not saying it's bad. I'm just saying that you're going way too far too fast," Piper said. "What do you expect me to do," he asked. "Act like a gentleman like you did at the beginning. Just stop rushing," Piper replied. He nodded and kissed her hand. They pulled in, parked and paid then started the walk. He went with her and they walked it side by side. When they were done and they got back to the truck, he shook his head and handed her a bottle of water. "In all the dang time I've lived here, I never did that walk," he said. "It was kinda pretty," Piper said. He kissed her. "So, now that you're done the walk," he asked. "Heading home and getting work done," Piper said. "Walk on the beach," he asked. Piper shook her head. "Not tonight," she said. He kissed her and leaned her up against the side of her truck. "You sure I can't talk you into it," he asked. "Jamie," Piper said. He had her almost pinned. "We can watch a movie at your place," he said. "And…" He kissed her again. "Fine, but we're watching it," Piper said. He nodded.

They left to head back to the house and he slid his hand back in hers. "Jamie," Piper said. "What," he asked holding on a little tighter. "Just remember that slow was the plan alright," Piper asked. He nodded. "Oh I know. Doesn't mean that I like waiting, but I can handle that if it means you and me together at the end," Jamie said. "Thinkin long term and it hasn't even been two dates," Piper teased. She stopped at the light and he kissed her. "What," Piper asked. "Too dang cute," he teased. "Nice. Cute like a puppy," Piper teased. He shook his head and kissed her neck. They got back to her place and headed inside. "So what's up with that guy who was pestering you," he asked. "As in the annoying guy who was at church," Piper asked. Jamie nodded. "Like I said, a Caroline setup. He constantly pesters me at the gym and beyond that, he begs me to date him. I said no a million times. There's just something about him," Piper said. "Which would be," he asked. "Which means that he's pushy as all get out and he doesn't deserve the attention he gets. Knowing them, he's a stripper or something," Piper replied. He kissed her again, they got a drink and went and chilled on the sofa. Piper turned a movie on and he snuggled her into his arms. "What,"

Piper asked as she felt him hold her a little closer. "Nothin,"
he replied. Piper shook her head and they finished the movie.

As soon as it was finished, he pressed stop on the movie and
turned her to face him. "What," Piper asked. He kissed her.
"Promise me that this stupid guy isn't gonna be a problem,"
Jamie asked. "He isn't and never will be. Obnoxious yes. In
the way no," Piper replied. He kissed her again. His hands slid
to her backside and into her back pockets. "So, I had an idea,"
Jamie said. "Which is," Piper asked. "Would you be pissed if I
said I kinda wanted to see if we could really date," he asked.
"Meaning," Piper asked. "Be my girl," he said. "Can we talk
about it whenever next time is," Piper asked. Jamie kissed
her. "I just wanted to put the feelings out there," he replied.
"Jamie," Piper said. "What," he asked. "It doesn't mean no. It
means we figure it out as we go and take our time," Piper
replied. "As long as you don't take off," he teased. "I have no
idea when that tour is even starting," Piper said. "Are you
gonna at least let me come see you," Jamie asked.
"Whenever you want to," Piper replied. He kissed her. "And if
you change your mind," he said. "For now, I'm not. We just
need to take our time alright? No more tryin to jump into my
pants," Piper teased. "You sure," Jamie teased as he pulled
her tighter to him, pulling her legs around him. "I'm sure,"
Piper said. He kissed her again, devouring her lips until he had
to find some restraint. "Dang tempting," Jamie replied. "For
what," Piper teased. "You don't stop teasing you're gonna be
under blankets on this sofa," he teased. Piper shook her
head. "Then we should probably get up since you have work
tomorrow and I have to get into rehearsal early," Piper said.
He kissed her again.

"Or we could just stay right here and keep doing this," Jamie
replied. "What am I gonna do with you," Piper asked as he
flipped her to her back and leaned into her arms. "Then pick
another movie," Piper replied. He kissed her, leaning into her

so she could feel every muscle against her torso. "Or we just…" "Pick a movie," Piper teased. He picked one, pressed play and kissed her again, leaning in for another kiss. When she heard the theme song, she shook her head. "Jamie," Piper said. "You said pick," he teased. "You seriously picked the Notebook," Piper asked. He devoured her lips. "Right mood," Jamie joked. "You realize we're watching it right," Piper asked. He kissed her neck and snuggled into her. He pressed stop and turned the TV right off. "Instead of a movie," he teased. Piper shook her head and he kissed her neck again. "Jamie," Piper said. "Yes beautiful girlfriend of mine," he said. "We really should get up," she said. "Five more minutes," he teased. He kissed her again and they ended up making out like two horny teenagers on the sofa. Finally, she managed to get up. "You sure," Jamie asked. "I'll see you in the morning," Piper said. "You mean since I don't have to be at work until tomorrow afternoon," Jamie asked.

"Since when," Piper asked. "Since I don't have to be there until 11ish. We were there until just after 6," Jamie said. "When," Piper asked. "Saturday. Went in on my day off on top of it so they gave me Monday morning off," he teased. "Then I guess that means you're coming to rehearsal with me," Piper said. "Then if you want, I could just stay," he teased. "Then it's kinda pointless since you live 2 doors down," Piper said. He kissed her. "I'll go to the gym with you," he said. "Jamie," Piper said. "I'm only suggesting it because that guy is getting on your last nerve. That's it. I don't want him ruining your good mood," Jamie replied. "Fine, but I have a trainer," Piper replied. "I've seen you at the gym lady. I get it," he said. "Meaning," Piper said. "Meaning I was there this morning," he replied. "What," Piper asked. "You left before I could come over," he said. Piper shook her head.

"Fine. I'm leaving at 6," Piper said. "Perfect. That's what time I usually head over myself," Jamie said. Piper shook her head. "Then you should get some sleep," Piper said as he slid his arms around her. He devoured her lips again. "Jamie," Piper said. "Just kissing my woman good night," he replied. She walked him to the door, one last kiss goodbye and he finally headed off. Piper locked up, turned the alarm on, cleaned up and went upstairs to bed. Piper got changed, cleaned up and went to slide into bed when her phone buzzed. "Yes," Piper said answering her phone. "Thought I'd say goodnight," Jamie replied. "You were just here," Piper teased. "See you in the morning," he replied. "See you then," Piper said. They hung up and Piper slid into bed and flipped off the light. Little did she know that someone was watching from the street.

Piper was up the next morning, got her water and was about to head out the door when she heard her phone. "Yep," Piper asked. "We're going into rehearsal at 8. You good," Harley asked. "Yep," Piper said. "And how is the hottie," Harley teased. "Comin with me to the gym. I take that as a good sign," Piper teased. "You know you're spilling at rehearsal," Harley said. "He's coming with me," Piper replied. "Dang. Alright then. We can wait until he heads out," Harley joked. "See you in a bit," Piper said. They hung up and Piper headed out. As she was about to hop into her truck, Jamie pulled in. "I'll drive," Jamie said. Piper smirked and hopped in his truck. They headed over. As soon as they showed up, he slid his hand in hers and they headed in together.

Within minutes, Colt came out of his office and saw Piper with Jamie. "Piper," Colt said. She ignored him and they kept walking. They got into the gym and started warmup side by side, intentionally avoiding Colt. "Miss Piper," her trainer Jess said. "Jess, Jamie. Jamie, my trainer Jess," Piper said. "Oh we've met," Jamie said. "Meaning," Piper asked. "Probably know him better than you do," Jess said. "Anything I need to know," Piper asked. "Jess is my sister," Jamie said. She shook her head. "Of course," Piper replied. They did their workouts and when they finished up, Colt started walking towards Piper again. Jess stopped him to give Piper and Jamie time to leave. They hopped into the truck and went to her place. "Nice of you to tell me," Piper teased. "Honestly, I didn't think she was workin today. I mean, the fact that you are her secret client that she told me about almost makes me laugh," Jamie said. "You are seriously ridiculous," Piper said. "Kinda glad she is. It means that if you're on tour, she's coming. It also means I can come visit both of y'all," Jamie teased. "Oh. So that's why," Piper joked. He slid his hand in hers and kissed it. "You think that's a bad thing," Jamie asked. "I think that you're treading on going a little too far," Piper said.

"You saying that you don't want me coming," he asked. Piper shook her head. "It means we'll see," Piper replied. "Alright then. When is the tour starting anyway," he asked. "Honestly, probably a week or two. We have a ton of work to do still," Piper said. "Then I'll make us dinner tonight," he said. "Oh really," Piper asked. He kissed her at the light. "Really," he said. He drove her up towards the front door. "And what time are we going to the rehearsal," Jamie asked. "We? I'm going over once I get showered and changed and eat," Piper replied. "And I'll follow you over," Jamie said. Piper smirked. "If that's what you want," Piper said. He hopped out and got her door for her. "Jamie," Piper said. He kissed her. "I'll see you in a half hour," he asked. "Around there," Piper said. "Alright. I'll see you in a half hour then beautiful," Jamie said. He kissed her again and she shook her head and went inside.

She had a long hot shower, a huge breakfast then went and got changed for rehearsal. Just as she was cleaning up and grabbing her drink, Jamie showed up. "Hey beautiful," he said as he came through the gate. Piper unlocked the door and grabbed something for a snack for rehearsal. "You ready to go," he asked. Piper nodded. "You can follow me over," Piper said. He looked at her. "What," Piper asked. "I'm drivin," he teased. "I'm bringing my truck," Piper said. He shook his head. "Whatever you say sexy," he replied. She locked up and hopped in her truck and he followed her the entire way over. When they arrived, nobody else was there yet. Piper headed in, put her bags down and got a water. "I always wondered what this would look like," Jamie said. Piper shook her head. "Not exactly exciting," Piper replied. Jamie slid his hand in hers. "What," Piper asked. "Come here for a second," he asked as he pulled her towards him and into his arms.

Chapter 5

"What are you up to," Piper asked. Jamie leaned in and kissed her, devouring her lips. Coming up for air wasn't even a thought at that moment. He nibbled at her top lip with a kiss so strong, her knees were almost crumbling. "Still think I should be your assistant on tour," he teased. "What am I gonna do with you," Piper asked. Jamie leaned in and gave her a hug. "Maybe you should hang around and figure it out," he teased. "Maybe I might after the tour," Piper said. He kissed her again. They sat down and he continued to try and convince her into being with him. Just as he had finally got close enough, he heard the door. "Hey Harley," Piper said. "What are you up to girl," Harley asked. "Hangin out. You remember Jamie," Piper said. "Nice seeing you again," Harley teased. "So, what are we working on?" "We have to do a rehearsal and come up with the proper set list for the shows. I have the timing figured out but we have to do staging and everything else," Piper said. "And," Harley joked. "This mean I get to see the dry run," Jamie joked. Piper shook her head. "If you want to," Piper replied. He kissed her and Piper got up and got warmed up. Within a matter of minutes, the rest of the band showed. Piper introduced them to Jamie and they got going. "Here's the ideas for the set list. Let me know what you think," Piper said as they all went through it. "Dang girl. You sure about this," Kurt asked. "That's just enough time for that plus a little extra talk time and joking around with the fans," Piper said.

They played through the set list as they would at a concert and Jamie was in complete and utter awe. "Damn," Jamie said. "Anything you think we're missing," Harley asked. "Other than wardrobe and lights, not a dang thing. That was insane good," Jamie said. "And that's not just because you have a thing for the leading lady here," Harley joked. Jamie started to blush and his phone went off two minutes later. He went into the hall and Harley shook her head. "I mean dang," Harley said. "What," Piper asked. "The man is fine, but what's up with the leaving the room thing," Harley asked. "Why don't you ask him," Piper said. She went and got a drink and went for the bathroom. Harley was two steps behind her.

"What the hell," Harley asked. "Don't. I barely even know him. I don't get to complain when I don't know him," Piper replied. Harley looked at her. "Then stop lookin like someone just kicked your cat," Harley asked. "I'm not assuming that it's bad alright," Piper said. "Just keep your eyes open," Harley said. They came out a few minutes later and Jamie was sitting down with the guys. "And what are all y'all chatting about," Harley asked as Piper took a gulp of her water on the stage. "We were talking about the tour stops you know about," Jamie said. He looked over at Piper and she was checking over her emails then walked over to her and sat down beside her. "You alright," he asked. "I'm fine," Piper replied. "Then why do you look mad," he asked. "I'm fine Jamie," Piper replied. "My sister said she had just signed on to come on the tour and asked if you were gonna let me come," he said. She shook it off. "We'll see," Piper said. "What's wrong," he asked. "Nothing," Piper replied. He shook his head. "Do you want me to go," he asked. "Jamie, it's fine. Hang out as long as you want to," Piper replied. She got up and hopped back on the stage going through the other songs they can put in place of others in case she started getting sick of them.

Jamie went and sat down with Harley. "What's goin on," he asked. "Just let her breathe," Harley replied. He shook his head and got up to talk to Piper. "Piper," he said. "Yep," Piper said. He walked over, grabbed her hand and walked into the hallway. "What," Piper asked. He kissed her, devouring her lips. "Tell me what the heck is wrong," he said. "It's fine," Piper said. "It obviously isn't if you're all upset," Jamie said. She shook her head and he pulled her to him. "Just say it,"

Jamie asked. "I can't," Piper said. He shook his head and kissed her again. "You think it was something else," he asked. "Jamie, leave it alone," she said. "It was my sister. She was joking that she was about to set us up before she saw me with you at the gym," he said. "Alright," Piper replied. "I wasn't talking to someone else if that's what you were thinking. Trust me. I know what I have in front of me," he said. "I have to go in," Piper replied. He kissed her again. "Alright," he said. She nodded. "For now," Piper replied. He shook his head.

He walked her back inside and took a seat while Piper hopped back up on stage to go through a few of the alternate songs that she'd picked. They rehearsed them and when they were done, Piper looked over and Jamie was still there. "Alright. I think we actually have it down. We didn't even need lyric sheets," Piper teased. "Which means we can all head home early so I can surprise the wife," Kurt asked. "Go ahead. I'm just gonna write out a few ideas for backdrops and lighting," Piper said. Harley walked over to her. "He's not movin Piper. Just go and talk to him," Harley said. "Already did thanks," Piper replied. "By the way, the husband served me," Harley replied. "When," Piper asked. "When I went to go get the last of my stuff. Looks like I'm gonna need that room full-time. He even put the house up for sale," Harley replied. "That says a whole heck of a lot," Piper said. "He planned all of this. Honestly, that event at the park was pretty amazing, but I don't think it made a difference at all. My lawyer said he supposedly talked to the lawyers weeks ago," Harley said. "You know that room is all yours. You have a key right," Piper asked. Harley nodded. "Then whenever you want to start bringing stuff let me know," Piper said.

When Piper took a quick glance over to Jamie he was walking out the door with the phone on his ear for what felt like the second time. "Stop. The guy likes you or he wouldn't have been here," Harley said. "Whatever," Piper said. They stepped off the stage and Piper grabbed her purse and Harley grabbed her things and headed out, leaving Piper and Jamie alone in the rehearsal space.

Just as Piper was about to walk out and past Jamie in the hall, he grabbed her hand and pulled her to him. "Alright. It's not a problem. It's cancelled for the day. Just start feelin better," Jamie said. He finished his conversation, hung up and kissed her. "You heading home," he asked. Piper nodded. "Well, luckily I have the rest of the day off. The band I was supposed to be recording aren't feeling up to studio stuff. There's a cold goin on with them. Just means I get to hang with you," Jamie said. "And I'm going home to play around with a few ideas Harley and I came up with for music," Piper replied. "Or we go to the park and you can work on it under the live oaks. I can get us lunch," he said. "Jamie," Piper said. "What," he asked. "I'm not..." He kissed her again and pulled her to him, wrapping both arms around her. "I just want to hang with you a while. What's wrong with that," Jamie asked. "I have to get real work done on this," Piper said. He shook his head. "What's the real issue," he asked. "Nothing," Piper said. "Then we'll go to the house, get your writing stuff and have a picnic. I have to work on email stuff and you work on the music stuff," Jamie replied. "Fine, but we're getting healthy stuff. If I have to be on a stage, I need to try to get healthier," Piper said. "Just because you aren't a dang size 2 doesn't mean that you aren't sexy," he said. "Tell my manager that," Piper teased.

They left and he followed Piper back to the house. She dropped her truck off, got her notebook and they headed off to get a picnic lunch together. When they finally found the perfect spot, he laid out a huge beach blanket. "Think we have enough space," he asked. "I guess," Piper said. He kissed her and they sat down and tried to relax a bit. He handed her a glass of chilled wine and then sat down, leaning her into his arms. "Yes," Piper asked. "Dang sexy girlfriend I have," he joked. "Since when," Piper asked. "Since you quit worrying I was talking to another girl," he teased. "Just looks bad when you leave the room," Piper said. "It was a work thing. I didn't want to interrupt," Jamie replied. "As long as I don't get lied to," Piper replied. He kissed her cheek and snuggled her to him. "I'm not like those other idiots. Walking away isn't an option," Jamie said. "It is," Piper said. "If it makes you feel any better, to me it isn't," Jamie said. They relaxed together and they both got work done. They just spent the rest of the afternoon relaxing, watching the Spanish moss sway in the wind. They watched the tourists wander through the park and intentionally just leaned back and relaxed. Nobody bothered them and not one person even realized who she was.

By the time they got up, their stomachs were almost demanding dinner. "I'll get something and we can hang at my place. I promise to be a gentleman," Jamie said. "Just don't make me regret this," Piper said. "Only thing you're gonna regret is not letting me cook," he teased. "Then we stop at the butcher and get dinner," Piper replied. He kissed her. "I like the way you think," he teased. They did just that. Once they had everything, they went back to his place. Piper headed down to her place to get freshened up and got changed. Just as she was about to head back out, Harley pulled in. "Hey girl," Harley said. "Hey yourself. I guess this means that you're movin in," Piper said. "Yup," Harley said. She headed upstairs and put the first of her bags upstairs. "Do you want help," Piper asked. "You go hang with the hot guy next door. I'll be fine," Harley said. "I'm like 2 doors down if you need anything alright," Piper asked. Harley nodded. "I will," Harley said as she gave Piper a hug. Piper headed back over to Jamie's and saw a car in the driveway. She shook her head and knocked at the front door. When there was no answer, she texted him. Again, there was no reply. She shook her head and walked back to the house, closing the gate behind her.

Piper walked into the house and saw Harley in tears on the steps upstairs. "You alright," Piper asked. "What are you doin here? I thought you were hanging with the hottie neighbor," Harley said as she brushed her tears away. "He had other ideas," Piper said. "Then we're doin dinner and a ton of alcohol," Harley said. "Sounds good to me," Piper said. Harley gave her a hug. "Who would've even thought that this would be happening? It feels like he just proposed and now we're over and he's throwing the house away," Harley said. "Just means you can find a better house that makes you happy. You get to do whatever you want with it," Piper said. "That was my dream house. We picked every inch of it out together," Harley said. "You'll find something that you get to do totally the way you want. It'll work out," Piper said. "I guess," Harley said. "Just give yourself a little time," Piper said. Harley nodded and Piper got shots of Jack. She handed two to Harley and as she was about to drink hers, her phone buzzed. She looked and saw Jamie's name on the call display. She ignored the call and did the shots.

Within 5 minutes, her phone went off again and Piper turned it off. "Talk," Harley said. "It's perfectly fine," Piper said. "And that's why you turned it off," Harley asked. "Don't worry about me. It's all fine," Piper said. "You know that he's gonna come over here," Harley said. "And it has nothin to do with me. I'm hanging with you," Piper said. Harley gave her a hug. Piper went and got a snack together and they sat down. Piper put a movie on and they curled up on the sofa and started off their girl night. 10 minutes later, the gate buzzed. Piper looked and ignored it. "You can invite him in," Harley said.

"I'll pass," Piper replied. He called 2 minutes later. "Just answer it already," Harley said.

"What would you like," Piper asked. "You coming over," he asked. "Depends. You wanna tell me who was in the driveway," Piper asked. "My sister. She was giving me the schedule for being away with y'all. Just come over already," Jamie said. "I'm hanging with Harley," Piper said. "Stubborn is one thing. We had a good day, Just come over," he said. Harley grabbed the phone and buzzed him in. "We're havin a girl night," Piper said. "Then talk to him and we can get on with it," Harley said. She gave Harley a hug and headed upstairs to unpack. Jamie knocked at the door and Piper shook her head, walking to the door. "What," Piper asked as she opened the door. He grabbed her hand, pulling her to him, and kissed her. "What do you want," Piper asked. "We had a good day. Just come. Pease," he said. "What do you want me to say," Piper asked. "That you're coming," he said. Piper shook her head. He kissed her again. "The barbecue is warming up," he said. "Then you should go eat," Piper said. "Harley," Jamie said. "Yep," Harley said. "Come over for dinner," he asked. "Cook and I'll be there," Harley said. "Then let's go," Jamie said. He grabbed Piper's hand. Harley grabbed her purse and Piper's and their phones and keys and headed off with them.

Piper got to the house with him and they went outside. Jamie put the steak on and got Harley and Piper a drink, intentionally double-shotting Piper's drink. She looked over and saw him coming outside. He handed a glass to Piper and one to Harley and went back to working on the steak. Harley shook her head and went inside. She poured the drink in a bigger glass and added soda. When she came back outside, she sat down and sipped on her drink. Jamie took one look and realized what she'd done. He sat down on the chaise behind Piper and she got up and went and sat in the chair. He shook his head. Harley noticed that look and shook her head. "What," Jamie asked. "Nothin," Piper said. He got up, walked over and grabbed her hand, walking her into the house.

"Just say it," Jamie said. "Say what," Piper asked. "What's wrong," he asked. "You mean you double dosing my drink or the fact that you're full of crap," Piper asked. He shook his head. "And what do you think I'm lying about now? First it's flipping out that I left the room. Then it's not answering the phone when you call. What," he asked. "That how you want it? Fine. I'm going home. Don't call," Piper said as she went to walk out the front door. He caught up to her, grabbed her hand and pulled her to him. He kissed her, walking her into the office and closing the door. He sat her on the desk and pulled her legs around him. "Stop worrying that I'm gonna do something completely stupid. I'm not the cheater type," he said. Before she could even say a word, he kissed her again, leaning into her and pulling her legs tight around him. "I want...you," he said between kisses. She couldn't even back away. He was holding her tight to him. "You get that right," he asked as he kissed down her neck. "Stop," Piper replied. "What," he asked. She shook her head. "You don't get it do you," Piper asked. "I'm not lying to you and I'm not about to mess my dang chance up. Stop assuming I will," he replied. Piper shook her head and he kissed her again. That kiss got hotter.

He was about to go as far as pulling his shirt off when Piper stopped him. "You're gonna burn the steak," Piper said. He kissed her, devouring her lips. "Enough with the fight alright," he asked. Piper shook her head and he kissed her again, walking her back outside. He checked the steak and Piper took her drink inside and got a sweet tea. When he came inside, he saw her. "What you doin," Jamie asked. "Getting a sweet tea," Piper said. He pulled her to him. "That determined to avoid havin fun," he asked. "Just keeping a

clear head. That's all," Piper said. He shook his head. "Fine,"
he said. He walked her back outside and sat down. They all
tried to talk a while and when Harley's phone went off, she
took one look. "I have to take this," Harley said as she went
inside. "She alright," Jamie asked. "You mean since she got
served divorce papers? I highly doubt it," Piper said. He kissed
her neck. "Stay tonight," he asked. Piper shook her head.
"That would be a no," Piper replied. He nibbled at her neck,
then her shoulder. "Jamie," Piper said. "Please," he asked.
She went to get up and he pulled her back. "Turn around," he
asked. She shook her head. "Piper," he said as she got
goosebumps. She got up and he pulled her back to him,
wrapping her legs around him. "What," Piper asked. He kissed
her and his hands slid deep into her back pockets, pulling her
tight to him.

"Quit," Piper said. He devoured her lips again and Piper tried
getting up. "Where are you goin," he asked. "Getting up,"
Piper replied. "Nope," he said. She got up and sat down in the
chair. He shook his head and checked the steak. When he
realized it was done, he put it on the platter, sliced it and he
took the platter to the patio table. He got the salad and came
and sat down at the table with Piper when Harley came out.
"You alright," Jamie asked. Harley nodded. "Just glad that
alcohol was invented," Harley said. They dug into dinner and
Harley tried as hard as she could to drink the feelings away.

As soon as they were done, Jamie texted a buddy to come
over to keep Harley occupied. His buddy Jake showed a little
while later and they finished dinner and went inside to watch
a movie. Jamie pulled Piper aside before they went in.
"What," Piper asked once Jake and Harley were busy talking
on the sofa. "What," Piper asked. He walked her out of
Harley's eye shot and leaned her up against the wall. "What,"
Piper asked. He kissed her, devouring her lips and picked her
up, wrapping her legs around him. He walked over to the

chaise and leaned her onto it, leaning into her arms. "Jamie," Piper said. "What," he asked as he went to peel his shirt off. "They're inside. We're going in," Piper said. "Pool yes. Movie with them, no," he replied. He devoured her lips again, linking their fingers and almost pinning her to the chaise as he kissed down her neck. "Let go of the hands," Piper said. "Tell me what's so dang wrong with just being together," Jamie asked. "Because I'm not sleeping with you," Piper said. He kissed her again, taking her breath away. "You that scared of a real relationship," he asked. "Up," Piper said. "Answer me first," he replied. She shook her head, pushed her way up and walked into the house, grabbing her phone, keys and purse and walked out the front door.

Within a matter of minutes, Harley got up and went after her. "I got this," Jamie said. "Maybe y'all just need time alone," Harley said. "Something isn't right," Jamie said. He walked out the door and went after her. "Piper," he said. "Leave me alone," Piper said. "Talk," he said. "You think I'm seriously afraid? Not jumping into freaking bed with you like you want is the only reason why you're pissed," Piper said. "I just want to be with you. What's wrong with that," he asked. Piper shook her head, went in the house and he stopped the door from slamming in his face and went in behind her while Harley came in and went upstairs to her room.

"What," Piper asked. "You seriously that freaked about all of this," he asked. "Jamie, leave it alone. Go home," Piper said. He tried to pull her to him and she fought him off. "I'm that damn determined not to make another stupid mistake. That's what. The whole relationship fear stuff is BS. If you don't know that then there's no dang point in you being here," Piper said. He shook his head. "Just go with the dang flow," he said. "Go," Piper said. He shook his head. "You can't push me out," he said. "Leave," Piper said. He kissed her, pulling her back to him. "What do you want from me," Jamie asked.

"To be a dang gentleman for one. Slow the heck down and quit trying to get me into bed," Piper replied. "I just want to be with you. There's nothing wrong with that," he said. She broke away from him. "Just leave it alone," Piper said. He grabbed her hand, pulling her to him again. "Enough." "Piper, stop flipping out. Just be. Just enjoy being together," he said. Piper shook her head. "Slow the heck down," Piper said. "Then be with me. Date. Hang out. Stop putting on the breaks every 10 seconds," he said. Piper shook her head. She pushed him away and walked to the door. "What," he asked. "Go," Piper said. He shook his head. "This is what you want," Jamie asked. "You need a dang cold shower," Piper said. Jamie grabbed her hand and walked her outside.

"What," Piper asked. "You think I seriously want to keep having fights about this," he asked. "Jamie, just…" He kissed her again as he cradled her face in his hands. "I get you don't want me pushing, but it's like every single time we're alone and enjoying ourselves, you stop me. I don't get it," Jamie said. "I'm not jumping into bed with you," she said. "Then just relax. Whatever happens, happens," He said. Piper shook her head. "Quit. Leave it as it is," Piper said. He kissed her again. "Stop fighting then," he replied. "What do you want from me," Piper asked. "I want you to be my girl instead of keeping me at arm's length," he said. "Then quit trying to get me in bed 3 seconds after I arrive," she said. "Then quit showin up all sexy and smelling good," he teased. "You're just so…." He kissed her again, walked her back down to his place and in the door. "What are you up to," Piper asked. "Enjoying our date night instead of fighting," he said. Piper grabbed her phone and let Harley know she was at Jamie's and they sat down to watch the movie he'd picked out.

"And what exactly are we watching," Piper asked. "Longest Ride since I know you want to watch it. I'm not saying you aren't gonna be distracting the heck out of me," he said. He got up and got them each a drink, putting a double shot in each and getting a big huge glass for each of them. "Jamie," Piper said. "I can walk you home. You're fine," he said. He took a gulp of his, putting it on the table. "What concoction is this now," Piper asked. "Jack and Coke," he replied. Piper shook her head. He turned the movie on and curled her into his arms, leaning her against his chest. His arms slid around her and he pressed play on the movie. He nibbled at her neck before the opening credits even started. "Jamie," Piper said. He kissed the edge of her ear and his hand rested on hers. "Movie," Piper said. He slid the strap of her shirt off her shoulder and kissed her shoulder. She grabbed the remote and paused the movie. She turned to face him and he pulled her to him, devouring her lips. "Am I allowed to kiss my woman," he asked. "Depends. Who is she," Piper teased. He shook his head and pulled her legs around him. "So, is that a yes," he asked. "As long as you don't assume it's gonna be more," Piper said. "How about we just see where things go," Jamie said. "How about we just watch the movie," Piper asked. He kissed her. "If I said I wanted more than that and you're too dang tempting," he asked. "Then I'd say you need some ice," Piper said. He kissed her.

He kissed her again and that turned into making out on the oversized sofa. He leaned her onto the sofa and peeled his shirt off. "Jamie," Piper said. He went to undo her jeans and she shook her head and stopped him. "Quit," Piper said. "At least throw me a bone," he teased. "We just had this..." he kissed her and peeled her shirt off. "Jamie..." He devoured her lips. "What," he asked. "You aren't getting your way," she said. He kissed her again. "Slow works," he said. "This is as far as you're getting," Piper replied. "I can handle this," he said. He devoured her lips and forgot all about the movie. When the TV turned itself off, he picked her up and walked upstairs to the master bedroom, leaning her onto the massive bed.

"Jamie, stop," Piper said. "Just more room to relax," he said. "Not falling for it," Piper said. He kissed her again and she shook her head and got up. "What," he asked. "Maybe you didn't hear me," Piper said. She walked downstairs, slid her tank back on and grabbed her stuff and went home. She walked in, closed the gate and locked up. "Hey," Harley said from the sofa.

"What you still doin up," Piper asked. "Stupid freaking lawyers. I got the papers and went through them. He wants everything. I told him what I definitely wanted. Now it's just negotiating to get it," Harley said. "Girl, let the lawyers stress. We're rehearsing, finishing up with styling and doing lighting and the backdrop ideas. We're good. A couple weeks left and we're out," Piper said. "Why do you look pissed again," Harley asked. Piper shook her head. "Doesn't matter," Piper said. "Another double shot," Harley asked. Piper nodded. "I'm going to bed before he starts more drama," Piper said. "You know you're tellin me in the morning," Harley said. Piper shook her head and went upstairs to bed.

The next morning, Piper got up and went to the gym. As soon as she got there, Jamie was talking to his sister and doing a quick workout. Piper went and started stretching out when Colt came over. "Want some help," he asked. "Seriously, that's the last dang thing I need. Go away," Piper said. He sat down on the bench beside her. "Colt, seriously, screw off. I've had more than enough from you," Piper said. He went to kiss her, and she pushed him so hard he fell backwards. Piper went and started her workout in complete silence. Jamie came over a couple minutes later and Piper went over to start her workout with his sister. Not a word was said between her and Jamie. When she finished her workout, Piper went to leave and saw Jamie waiting by her truck.

"What would you like," Piper asked. "You," he said. Piper got in the truck and shook her head. "You took off," he said. "And," Piper asked. "You seriously that mad," he asked. "You didn't listen to a dang word I said did you," Piper asked. "At some point you have to stop and just let things go the way they're meant to," Jamie said. "Just like every other dang guy in the world. Wouldn't want to be original," Piper said as she got in her truck and left. She got back to the house, got changed, had breakfast and headed off to the rehearsal studio. When she arrived, Char was there going through work emails.

"Well hello there," Piper said as she gave her a hug. "So, what's on the list for today," Piper asked. "Backgrounds and staging so we have it organized. Here's what I came up with so far," Char said as she showed it to her on her iPad. "It looks amazing," Piper said. "Means having a tour where you're a big name. The crowd is gonna be singing back every lyric. The CD special edition with those new songs is coming this week. What do you think," Char asked. "Since we did all the interview stuff already you mean," Piper asked. "And there's more this week. It's radio interviews and a couple TV interviews. They're all local though and the label is letting you use the private jet for them," she said. "Works for me. I'm good leavin town for a bit," Piper said.

"The trainer is on board for it. She's coming with us," Char said. "And you're coming," Piper asked. Char nodded. "What's goin on? I can see it in your face," Char replied. "Nothing. I'm good. Just frustrated. It's personal stuff," Piper said. "What's what," Harley said as she came in. "The stage ideas are all put together. Are y'all on board for the interview stuff next week," Char asked. "I can leave now if you want," Piper teased. "By the way, someone popped over when I was leaving," Harley said as she handed Piper the flowers that Jamie had dropped off for her. Piper shook her head. "You can keep them," Piper joked. Harley handed her the card and put the flowers on the table. Two minutes later, her phone buzzed. One look and she shook her head. "Excuse me for a minute," Piper said. She went into the hall and answered.

"What on earth do you want," Piper asked. "I get it I screwed up last night," Jamie said. "Maybe you just need to take out the ear plugs," Piper said. "One night and we just let whatever happen," Jamie said. "Wrong number," Piper said. "Piper," he said. "I'm going," Piper said as she hung up. She went back in and wardrobe came in with the racks of clothes for the interviews and the tour. They went through them and got everything packed and organized to head out. Just as she stepped into the parking lot, she saw Jamie. "Seriously? You're stalking me now," Piper asked. "I actually have a meeting," Jamie said. Piper shook her head, got in her truck and left before Jamie had a chance to say anything. She left with Harley right behind her. When they got back to the house, her phone went off. Just as they were hopping out, Harley took one look. "This is seriously driving me nuts," Piper said. "Then answer," Harley said.

"Yep," Piper said. "I'm going into the studio. I'll meet you at 7 so we can talk. Deal," Jamie asked. "Nope," Piper replied. "I'll be waiting," Jamie said. "After all of that, you're seriously starting this," Piper asked. "I messed up. Gimme a chance to make it up to you," he asked. "I have to go," Piper said. "Seven," he said. "Fine," Piper replied. They hung up and Harley shook her head. "Go figure," Piper said. "Girl, give him a chance and quit pickin a fight," Harley said. "Every dang time we're alone, he's trying to get me into bed. I don't see that being the smart idea on his part," Piper said. "Girl, things happen. If you're comfortable then do whatever works. You don't have to keep pushing him away," Harley said. "I just don't want to go there with someone and take off for a tour. He's gonna mess around and we all know it. "He hasn't looked away once. The guy wants to come and be there while we're touring. What's wrong with that," Harley asked. "The fact that I don't want him starting all of this stuff right before I leave. That's what. Why can't he just be a decent guy," Piper asked. "Because he only has so much will power," Harley teased. "Funny," Piper said. "Just go and see what happens. If you want to go further then go. He's not exactly biting at the bit for you to leave," Harley said. "Still doesn't mean that anything is happening. I'm not gonna do it Harley," Piper said. "Then stand your ground and tell him you aren't going to until you're dang good and ready," Harley said. Piper nodded.

Just as Piper was finishing getting organized to make dinner, her phone buzzed. "Yep," Piper said. "Finished up early. I'm getting the steaks on now. You ready," Jamie asked. "Just about to put dinner on for me and Harley," Piper said. "Then I'll bring the steaks there and we can do a big dinner," he said. "Jamie," Piper said. "Not taking no for an answer. Even got your Kale Caesar that you like," he said. Piper shook her head. "Fine, but we're talking and nothing else," Piper said. "And after dinner we can come hang here," he said. "Fine," Piper said. "No walking off," he asked. "As long as you're a dang gentleman," Piper replied. "In other words control myself," he said. "Exactly," Piper replied. "I'll do my best," he said. "And we're having an actual conversation that you're gonna hear," Piper asked. "Just open the dang gate," Harley said. "Thank you," Jamie teased.

Piper opened the gate and within maybe 15 minutes, he was on his way over. Piper shook her head when she heard Jamie coming up the drive. "If he starts, he's out," Piper said. Harley shook her head. "Whatever you say girl," Harley said as she opened the door for Jamie. "Hey neighbor," Harley said. "Hey yourself," Jamie said. He came in, headed outside and put the steaks onto the grill. Piper shook her head. He walked in, grabbed her hand and kissed her. He walked her outside and sat down with her. "What," Piper asked. "Tell me what's wrong with just being together," he asked. "You seriously think that after three dang dates that I'm just gonna do what you want and let you have your dang way," Piper asked. "What's wrong with just being together," he asked. "Not happening," Piper replied. "What's wrong with it. Give me one dang reason," Jamie asked. "Because sleeping with you isn't on my list of priorities," Piper said. "And," he asked. "And I'm not sleeping with you. Not now. I get that's what you want, but if you're expecting me to just give in, you're totally barking up the wrong tree," Piper said. "And if I say that I'm not walking away," he asked. "Whatever you wanna do," Piper said. "I just wanna be with you. I don't care if that means in bed or not," he said. "Fine," Piper said.

They finished making dinner and Harley came outside with the salad. "So, what's the plan for tonight," Harley asked. "Do-over from last night," Jamie said. Piper shook her head. She went inside, got a refill of her drink and was about to head upstairs when Harley spotted her. "Girl, what are you doin," Harley asked. "I'm not playing with him. He wants to act like an idiot then I'm not even gonna bother," Piper said. "Go and talk to him. You know dang well that you like him. Just give him a chance," Harley said. "No," Piper replied. She shook her head. "He's here for you not me," Harley replied. "Fine, but if he starts again, I'm kickin his butt," Piper said. "Want a target," Jamie said as he came in to top off his drink.

"Funny," Piper replied. "Maybe we need to talk," Jamie said. "Maybe we just need to leave it alone," Piper said. Jamie shook his head, walking outside with Piper, and Harley went to grab dessert. "Maybe you need to quit pushing everyone away. You can work and do the tour and have a guy in your life. You know that right," he asked. "I know. Fact is that I don't know if you're that person and I'm not gonna drag someone into that spotlight unless I know they are," Piper said. He shook his head. "What's wrong with us," Jamie asked. "You want something that I don't. You want it when you want it despite anything that I'm saying," Piper replied. "I get that you don't want to go that far yet, but come on," Jamie said. "Go home. Do me a favor and just leave," Piper said. He shook his head. "I'm not leavin until you hear me out," Jamie said. "I already did," Piper said. "I just want to date you. I don't care what else I have to do to make you understand that," Jamie said. "And I don't…" He shook his head and got up, kissing her. "Stop making all of this so dang difficult. All I want is you. What the heck is wrong with that," Jamie asked. "Then don't push," Piper said.

"Tell me what I have to do," Jamie asked. Piper shook her head, almost pushing him away. He finally stopped her. "Tell me," he said. "Because I'm not sleeping with someone that I know isn't gonna be here the next day," Piper replied. He shook his head. "I already proved I would be. Name once that I actually left and didn't come back," Jamie said. "Leave it alone," she said. "Who messed you up so dang bad," Jamie asked. "Doesn't matter," Piper said. "I'm a good guy Piper. I'm not the walk away type. Just let your dang guard down," he asked. "I can't," Piper said. He kissed her and pulled her into his arms. "You know you're gonna end up tellin me right," he teased. "Just leave it be," Piper replied. "Come watch the movie. We can just hang out period," he said. "Jamie," Piper said. He kissed her again and hugged her, trying to convince her that things would be alright.

When Harley came back outside, she saw them sitting side by side. "What's the dessert," Jamie asked. "Cobbler," Harley said. "She bakes when she's upset," Piper said. "Frustration," Harley replied. "Well, it looks amazing," Jamie said. Two bites in and he was in love with the cherry cobbler. They all finished and Jamie was full of compliments for Harley. "You are one amazing chef there miss Harley," Jamie said. "Well thank you," she replied. "Does this mean I gave you enough time to make up?" "Tried," Jamie said. "As long as nobody starts getting ahead of themselves," Piper said. "I get the hint," Jamie said. "Then yes," Piper said. "Good, because I have a hot bath with my name on it," Harley said. "You sure," Piper asked. Harley nodded. "I'm good. Y'all have fun," Harley said hinting at Piper. "You comin," Jamie asked as he got up. Piper nodded.

She grabbed her purse, keys and phone and headed over to Jamie's with him. "You that worried," he asked. "I just don't have the energy for another fight tonight," Piper said. "There won't be one. We're watching a movie. I have a million of them," Jamie said. "I bet," Piper teased. They headed inside and he opted for something else. "Want a glass of wine," he asked. "I'm good with ice water," Piper replied. "Whatever you say," Jamie said noticing the look on her face. He handed her a glass and walked her outside to the back patio. "What," Piper asked. "Tell me why you're so stressed out about the whole idea of dating," he asked. "Jamie, all I'm saying is that jumping into a relationship where sex gets involved is a mistake right now," Piper said. "And you're worried about us sleeping together why," he asked. "Because I've already been through it. I got dumped when things got too hard," Piper said. "I worked this dang hard to get you to even go out with me. You really think I'm gonna walk out," he asked. "I think that the minute I leave to do the tour, everything goes up in smoke," Piper replied. "Except the fact that I'll still be around. My sister is coming to be your trainer," he teased. "And," Piper asked. "Alright. I get it," he said. "Jamie, it's not like you're a bad guy. I just don't want to start something and have it blow up in my face again," Piper said.

"You know that at some point you have to stop and just take a chance," he said. "I'm just not ready to yet," Piper said. He kissed her. "I get it," he replied. "I just want to enjoy the relaxation and fun for a while," Piper said. He kissed her again and walked her to the chaise, intentionally curling up with her. "What are you up to," Piper asked. "Making up for getting you all mad," he replied. Piper shook her head and he pulled her into his arms. "I wasn't mad," Piper said. He kissed her neck. "You were peeved," he replied. "Annoyed," Piper said. He kissed and nibbled at her earlobe. "That mean we can make up," he teased. "As long as you don't get all carried away," Piper replied. "Meaning," he teased as he held her a little closer. "Meaning we can either hang and watch the movie or go for a walk or something," Piper replied. He kissed her neck. "Movie works," he said. They got up and headed inside, curling up on the sofa. He kissed and nibbled at her neck through most of the movie and the minute the credits rolled, he slid into her arms. "And what would you like handsome," Piper asked. He kissed her, devouring her lips. "Hey," Piper said as he came up for air.

"Hey yourself sexy woman of mine," he said. "Since when," Piper asked. He kissed her. "Since the minute you said you'd come over here," Jamie teased. Piper shook her head. "And," Piper asked. He kissed her again. "When you decide you're ready then tell me," he said. "I will. I just need to figure all of this out. I don't want to drag someone else through it," Piper said. "I just want to be there to cheer you on. That's all," Jamie said. "And what about work? You can't just take off," Piper said. "I can when they want me helping you with the new music. The tour bus that you're going on has a small recording area in it," Jamie said. Piper shook her head. "Nice excuse," Piper replied. "Means that when you're not working, you get recording in," he said. Piper shook her head. "Nice plan," Piper teased. "Which means that I have a reason to be out there. Even if I only use my sister as reason, I can come out wherever you are," Jamie said. "Just slow down and take it easy. I don't even know when we're leaving," Piper said. He kissed her. "Whenever it is, just tell me," he replied. Piper nodded. He kissed her, snuggling her tight to him. "Now about that whole idea of you not wanting to be my girl," he teased. "What about it. "You accepting the offer or do I have to spend the rest of the night convincing you," Jamie teased. "Fine, but I'm allowed to say you can't come," Piper said. "As long as you don't disappear on me," he replied.

Chapter 6

Just as they were starting to relax, Piper's phone buzzed. "Don't even think about it," Jamie teased. "I have to," Piper replied. He shook his head and nibbled at her neck as she answered the phone. "Hello," Piper said. "It's Char. I thought I'd let you know, all of the travel is organized. We're leaving a week from Friday," Char said. "So dang soon," Piper replied. "I have VIP passes for Jamie and backstage access for them. I take it they're travelling with us," Char asked. "At least partial," Piper replied as the kisses trailed down to her shoulder. "Alright. The announcement for dates went out today. They're already sold out in most of the places which means we may have extra dates added," Char said. "As long as on breaks I can be back home to relax," Piper said. "Alright. Already set up for whenever we can get back," Char said. "Perfect. What else do you need me to do," Piper asked. "Performance on Friday night in New York," Char said. "Alright," Piper replied. They hung up and Jamie looked at her. "What," she asked. "And this means," he asked. "Want to come to New York," Piper asked.

He kissed her and buried himself in her arms. "Tell me when and I'll be there," Jamie said. He kissed her again and pulled her legs around him. "You may want to check with work there loverboy," Piper said. "I will in the mornin. Tonight, we get to relax," Jamie said as he leaned in and kissed and nibbled at her neck again. "Taunting," Piper joked. He kissed her. "This mean that you're gonna stop pushing me aside," he asked. Piper shook her head. "You have to wait," Piper replied. "And where exactly would I be sleeping when I come visit," he asked. "You seriously have a one-track mind," Piper said. He kissed her and peeled his shirt off. "You get me hot and freaking bothered. Your fault," he said. She shook her head and he nibbled down the front of her neck. "What are you up to," Piper asked. He kissed her. "Trying to tell you that I'm a good guy," he replied. "We'll see," Piper teased. He kissed her again and snuggled against her. "You sure you don't want to stay," he asked. "Not tonight," Piper said. He kissed her again. "You never did answer me. Where would I be staying," he teased. "I have absolutely no idea," Piper replied. "Then I have 2 weeks to talk you into more," Jamie said. She kissed him and just as their lips touched, her phone went off. "Don't you dare," he said. "If it's…" He devoured her lips until he felt her toes curling. They kept going until her phone went off again. He picked her up and walked upstairs. "Jamie," Piper said. "Nothing else. Just a better view," he teased. "You better," Piper teased as he kissed her again and leaned her onto the bed in the master bedroom. "And where's this better view," Piper teased.

Jamie shook his head, got up and grabbed her hand and walked her outside to the upper balcony. When she looked, it's as if the sky cleared and the stars were shining brighter. "Like I said, much better view, he said as he leaned into her and wrapped his arms around her from behind. "What are you up to," Piper asked as she turned to face him. He devoured her lips and walked her back into the bedroom. "What," Piper asked. "Still think that you can't trust me," he asked. "Jamie," Piper said. He kissed her again and they fell onto the bed together. "Stay," he asked. Before Piper could even reply, he leaned in for another kiss. She got a warm feeling head to toe and he pulled her legs around him. "I have to go," Piper said. He shook his head. "Not allowed," he replied. "I have to," Piper said. He kissed her again, trailing the kisses down her neck to her shoulder. "I have to," Piper said. "Then we're doing something tomorrow night," he replied. "I'm doing rehearsals. After that show in New York, we leave to head out on the road. We're probably doing promo along the way," Piper replied. "Then you have company like it or not," he replied. Piper shook her head and he devoured her lips. "Fine, but just remember this is work," Piper said. He nodded.

Piper got home and Harley was sitting on the sofa almost laughing when the door opened. "Hey," Harley said. "Hey yourself," Piper said. "I heard that we're going to New York," Harley said. "You're totally gonna ask if that includes Jamie and his sister," Piper said. "I know it does. My question, can he bring a good single friend to a show for me," Harley teased. Piper shook her head. "Funny," Piper replied. "And what happened with you two," Harley asked. "Nothin. We just hung out and talked," Piper said. "Girl, quit holding out. Does that mean that y'all are all good or still picking a dang fight," Harley asked. "We're good. We talked things out," Piper said. "And," Harley asked. "And nothing," Piper replied. Harley looked at her. "What," Piper asked. "Girl, just tell me what happened," Harley said. "Maybe going to sleep and talking about it in the morning," Piper asked.

Piper locked up, turned the alarm on and went to head upstairs to bed with Harley right behind her. "What," Piper asked. "Spill it," Harley said as she sat on the edge of Piper's bed. "We talked. Nothing else to it," Piper replied as she went and changed into her pajamas. "So is he on the bus with us or getting his own transportation," Harley said jokingly. "For now, on the bus when he can come out. Period. Nothing else," Piper replied. "At least you let up on the poor guy," Harley said. "I'm giving him a chance. One. If he screws it up, it's done," Piper said. "He actually agreed to that," Harley asked. Piper nodded. "That was the agreement. It doesn't mean he's not gonna keep trying to talk his way into my bed," Piper said. "Go figure," Harley replied. "Meaning I'm going to bed. Period," Piper said. "And when are we heading to New York," Harley asked. "Next week. Friday. As soon as that's done, we head off to the first stop on the tour," Piper replied. "Am I allowed to say that I'm glad we're going," Harley asked.

"I almost wish I could just come back here every night," Piper replied. "We'll be fine. We can put pictures up in the bus of all the cool places you love here," Harley said. "Still. I finally have the house I want and now we're just disappearing," Piper replied.

"Girl, it'll be fine. Don't worry about it," Harley replied. "Just over-thinking as per usual. I'm exhausted. I'm goin to bed," Piper replied. "Alright girl. See you in the mornin," Harley said. Harley headed out and went to her bedroom and got ready for bed. Piper on the other hand, got a phone call that she wasn't expecting in any way. "Yep," Piper said. "It's Colt," he said. "And how in the heck did you get my dang number," Piper asked. "I grabbed Caroline's phone for a minute. I wanted to talk to you," he said. "Colt, leave me alone. Don't you even get it? I don't want to date you. I don't want anything. I just want you to leave me alone," Piper said. "You think that it's that easy to walk away," he asked. "If you cause a dang problem, I swear you are gonna be jobless," Piper said. "Making threats is a big mistake there lady," Colt said. "Goodbye," Piper said as she hung up. She messaged Char and let her know that Colt was an issue and what he'd threatened and within minutes, her phone rang. "I'll talk to the police in the morning and we'll make sure he's not gonna be near you. Do you want to talk to the gym about him," Char asked. "I think it's a good idea. I know he's not used to no. Who knows what he can pull after this," Piper said. "I'll get info on the manager for the gym. It'll be all handled," Char said. "Thank you," Piper replied. They hung up and Piper finally went and tried to get some sleep.

The next morning, Piper went to head into the gym and saw Jamie. "Hey beautiful," Jamie said as he came up behind her. Piper turned around and he picked her up, kissing her. "Hey," Piper said when he let her up for air. "What are you doin here so dang early," Jamie asked. "Have to handle something before I go for my workout," Piper said. "You alright," he asked. Piper nodded. He opened the door and they headed in. Piper went to talk to Colt's boss and Jamie went to talk to his sister.

"Miss Piper," Colt's boss said. "I need to speak with you about Colt," Piper said. "I did see the restraining order from the police. What happened," his boss asked. "He tried getting me to date him and when I turned him down he practically tailed me all over the press circuit. He was practically stalking level. He's gone too far. He's even come after me here," Piper said. "I'm so sorry about all of this," his boss said. "I appreciate it. Honestly, any help with the whole avoiding him would help," Piper replied. "And if we just switched his shift so he was late instead of early," his boss asked. "I just don't want to have to see him here," Piper said. "Completely understandable. I'll take care of this for you," his boss said. Piper nodded, thanked him and went into the gym to warm up before her workout with Jamie and his sister.

"You alright," Jamie asked as he sat up from his crunches. Piper nodded and he kissed her. They got going and Piper started her workout. "Y'all are making me nauseous already," his sister joked. "She's happy. Leave my girl alone," Jamie said. "Well that's new," his sister joked. Piper shook her head and kept going on her workout. When they finished, his sister stopped her. "Question. Do you need me next weekend for New York," his sister asked. "Not really. I mean this guy here is determined to come so we can sorta do the workout," Piper said. "You sure," she asked. "I got this. I promise," Jamie teased. "Alright. I have to finish up and get my clients going with the other trainer then I can come meet you guys for the rest of the away stuff," his sister said. "Not a problem," Piper said. "Alright then. You two go make everyone else nauseous while I get back to work," his sister joked. Jamie hugged her and he headed out hand in hand with Piper.

"So, what was the whole meeting thing about," Jamie asked as he handed her a smoothie. "When we get outside," Piper said. Jamie walked her outside and over to her truck. "Spill it," he said. "House," Piper said. "Then I'm following you to your place," Jamie said. Piper nodded. They left and went back to her place, then headed inside. Piper made the omelets while Jamie made the rest of the breakfast. "Just say it," Jamie said. "That Colt guy is an ass," Piper said. "Always has been. What's the problem," Jamie asked. "He won't back off and leave me alone and he started calling from Caroline's cell since I blocked his. It's insane," Piper said. "And what did you do," Jamie asked. "His boss knows plus there's a restraining order now," Piper said. "Dang," Jamie said. She nodded. "It's too much. Honestly, dealing with his stupid butt is driving me nuts," Piper said. "Did you tell him we were together," Jamie asked. "I told him to back off. So far, that's all that I've done. I'm not adding to the stress," Piper replied. "And," he asked. "And nothing. My manager has it handled," Piper said. "You sure," he asked. "Jamie, I promise that it's fine. If he starts a dang rumor, you know why," Piper replied. He nodded. "Just promise me that if he starts another problem, that you tell me alright," he asked. Piper kissed him. "I will," Piper replied. He kissed her and they sat down to breakfast.

Just as they did, Harley came downstairs. "Mornin," Harley said as she poured herself an oversized mug of coffee. "Morning," Jamie said. "So, what do y'all have planned for today while I'm cooped up in a studio," Jamie asked. "Rehearsal, staging, lighting and going through the background setup. Nothing exciting," Piper said. "Do y'all need help with getting stuff together for on the road," Jamie asked. Piper shook her head. "We have a ton of time," Piper said. "Remember what I said alright," Jamie asked. Piper nodded. "It'll be fine," Piper said. "Whatever you say. We're doing something after I finish today if you're good with that," Jamie asked. Piper smirked. "Alright," Piper said. He kissed her and left to get ready for work. Harley looked over at Piper while she picked at her breakfast. "Glad to see that y'all are finally trying," Harley said. "For now," Piper teased. Piper cleaned up and put the dishes into the washer then went up to get ready for the day.

By the time they were finished rehearsal, everyone was exhausted. Harley went back to the house with Piper and as they pulled in, Piper saw flowers at the gate. "I don't even wanna know," Piper said. Harley got out, took one look at the card and slid it into her pocket, pulling the truck in. Piper closed the gate and they went inside. Harley handed Piper the phone the minute they were through the door. She locked up and turned the security alarm on and Piper looked at her. "How the heck does he know where I live," Piper asked. "You need to call Caroline and Eve and call the police," Harley said. Piper grabbed her cell and called the police. She gave them the information and the officers decided to come to Piper's. As soon as they were off the phone, she called Caroline.

"What's up superstar," Caroline asked. "You wanna tell me why Colt had your cell," Piper asked. "What," Caroline asked. "Last night. He grabbed your cell. He has my phone number," Piper said. "How the heck did he do that," Caroline asked. "Wherever y'all were, he got your phone long enough to call," Piper replied. "Crap. I'm sorry girl. If I'd known," Caroline said. "Where were y'all last night," Piper asked. "A bar downtown. I'll let Eve know too to avoid him," Caroline said. "I have a restraining order against him now. If you do see him, keep your phone close," Piper said. "Thanks for letting me know," Caroline replied. "I have to call Eve. Just please be careful around him," Piper said. "I will," Caroline said. Piper hung up with her and went through the same conversation with Eve. "Where were y'all anyway," Piper asked. "The bar where he works," Eve said. "And what bar is that," Piper asked. "The one you refused to walk into," Eve replied. "What," Piper asked. "Caroline said she needed a girl night," Eve said. "And this is the guy you seriously think that I'd want in my life? What kind of crazy is in your heads," Piper asked. "Piper," Eve said. "I have to go. The police are here," Piper said. She hung up, shaking her head and Harley let the police officer in.

"Miss Piper," the officer said. "Thank you," Piper said. "We have the flowers and now the card. We have taken him into police custody. He's not going to be starting anything else for the next while. Did you want to press charges," the officer asked. "Yes. 100% yes," Piper said. "We need to get some other information from you," the officer said as he sat down with Piper to go through everything. By the time the officer was leaving, Jamie came straight down the driveway. He hopped out of his truck and went to the front door. "What the heck happened," Jamie asked. "He left flowers at the gate," Piper said. "How the heck did he find out where you lived," Jamie asked. "Good dang question. I talked to my friend Caroline and Eve and they never said a word. He's nuts," Piper said. "If he's getting this close, and starting this much, I want you somewhere safe," Jamie said. "I'm not leaving this house other than for the tour and everything," Piper said. "Then you need more security. I mean, even when you're on tour your house has to be safe. Please," Jamie said. Piper nodded. "Alright," Piper said. "Meaning," Jamie asked. "Meaning the security situation is expected. Char knows and there's going to be extra security here," Piper said. "Piper," he said. She shook her head. "It'll be fine," Piper said. He gave her a hug. "You sure," Jamie asked. Piper nodded.

They hung out a while and after a quick kiss, Jamie headed home with a promise that Piper would be coming over within an hour. "Dang. You're really giving him a chance. That's totally not normal for you," Harley teased. "So far, he's being a good guy," Piper said. "Like you're expecting a train wreck," Harley joked. "Sorta," Piper said. She went upstairs, showered, got changed and got ready to head to Jamie's. A few minutes later, her phone buzzed:

Putting the shrimp on. You comin for dinner or what?

Piper shook her head and went downstairs to see Harley on the phone. "I'm heading over. If you need me call me," Piper whispered. Harley nodded and Piper grabbed her purse, keys and cell and went over to see Jamie. She walked in and heard him making dinner. "What are you up to," Piper asked. "Shrimp and Pasta. Figured you might like it," Jamie said. He leaned in and kissed her. "That I probably will," Piper said. He poured her a glass of wine and handed it to her then went back to finishing making dinner. "Pick a movie," he said. "What no walk," Piper asked. "5 of them on the table in the tv room," he said. Piper shook her head and walked into the tv room. She saw the movies, the blanket, the pillows and the movies he'd picked out. When she saw all three Fifty Shades movies, Sliver and Basic Instinct, she almost laughed. "Nice selection," Piper said. She came back into the kitchen and saw him plating the food.

"So, which did you choose," he teased. "Sitting outside and watching the sunset instead," Piper said. "Whatever you want," he said as he leaned in and kissed her. "And what did you make there handsome," Piper asked. "Spaghetti with fresh tomatoes and shrimp," Jamie said. Piper smirked. "What," he asked. "Nothin," Piper replied. They sat down and had dinner. It was quiet and even by candlelight, but Piper kept wondering one simple thing – was he thinking that he was gonna get some? Did he think that he had to save her from everything? Something about it had her more than turned off, but there was nothing she could do about it. They finished dinner and she helped him clean up. "Why are you so quiet," Jamie asked. "Just thinking," Piper said. "About what," he asked. "Nothin. Just this stupid crap that keeps happening," Piper said. "Why do I get the feeling that you want to kick my butt right now then," Jamie asked. "Did you think I was really gonna give in," Piper asked. "Meaning what," he asked. "I get the hint," Piper said. "Baby," Jamie said. She shook her head. "Nothing else," Piper said. "It was so we're comfortable," he said. "Right," Piper said. She finished her glass of wine and he looked at her. "Just hang out. Stay and just talk or whatever you want. Please," Jamie asked.

"If you're under the assumption that…" Jamie kissed her. Before another word was said, and before she stormed out the door, he kissed her. He pulled her tight into his arms and devoured her lips. "Those were the only ones we hadn't watched that I had. I wasn't assuming anything," Jamie said. "Then you definitely need some Netflix in your life," Piper replied. He shook his head and hugged her. "Whatever you want to do. I can open another bottle of wine and we can sit," he said. Piper nodded and he grabbed another bottle from the fridge, opened it and filled their glasses then walked her outside to the side by side chairs.

"You sure you're alright," Jamie asked. "I'm fine. It'll be handled," Piper said. "Babe," Jamie said. "I'm perfectly fine," Piper said. "And if I think you're safer with a lot more security at the house," Jamie asked. "Char said it's handled," Piper replied. "Still worried about you," Jamie said. "I'll be fine. It's a tour," Piper said. "And when you're back," Jamie asked. "I may just keep the extra security on. It's that or I move," Piper teased. "Not funny," he said. "The house will be safe. I promise," Piper said. "Only thing I worry about is you," Jamie said. "You'll be there and when I'm back, I'm safe," Piper said.

He kissed her. "Come here a minute," Jamie asked. Piper shook her head. She got up and he grabbed her hand and pulled her into his lap. "And what do you want," Piper asked. He kissed her, devouring her lips. "I'll give you a hint," he teased. "Funny," Piper said. He kissed her again. "No movie, just sofa," he asked. Piper shook her head. "You're behaving," Piper said. "That is behaving. Trust me," Jamie teased. "Nope," Piper said. He shook his head and kissed her again. "What," she teased. "Just think. Yesterday you were all mad," Jamie teased. "Still stickin to that slow down thing," Piper said. "Or we just enjoy it and take our time," Jamie said. "You're horrible. One-track mind every minute of every dang day," Piper said. "When it comes to you," Jamie replied.

"Jamie," Piper said. "How long," he asked. "Meaning what," Piper asked. "You know what I'm asking," he said. "I'm not having this conversation," Piper said as she went to get up. He pulled her back to him. "Answer," he said. "No," Piper replied. She got up and got her drink, finishing the glass. "Piper," Jamie said as he came up behind her and wrapped his arm around her waist. "What," she asked. "You just refuse to talk about it or what," he asked. Piper shook her head and walked inside into the kitchen. "Talk," Jamie said as he put his glass down and turned her towards him. "I'm not having that conversation Jamie. Period," Piper said. "It's you and me and nobody else. Just say it," he said. "I'm not having that conversation," Piper said. "How long," he asked. "6 years," Piper replied. "What," Jamie asked. "Happy now," Piper asked. She went to walk off and he pulled her to him. "Where are you going," Jamie asked. "Back to..." He stopped her and kissed her. "Stay," he said. Piper shook her head. She tried to step away and couldn't. He pulled her back to him and devoured her lips. "Jamie," Piper said as they came up for air. "What," Piper asked. He grabbed her hand and walked her into the TV room.

"Jamie," Piper said. He sat down and pulled her into his lap. "What," he asked as he nibbled at her neck. "Stop," Piper said. "Why," he asked. "Because we're not doing this," Piper said. He kissed her. "We're not doing anything," Jamie said. "Just stop," Piper said. "What are you so petrified about," Jamie asked. "I'm not. I'm saying that I'm not doin anything until I decide," Piper said. He kissed her again and wrapped her legs around him. "We're not doing anything," Jamie said. "I know what you're up to," Piper said. "The air conditioning gets cold. That's all," Jamie said. Piper shook her head. "Nice," Piper said. He pulled her to him, devoured her lips and leaned her onto the sofa. "Don't start," Piper said. "You're the one that showed up all sexy," he teased. "Just quit," Piper said. He leaned in and kissed her again. "What in the world are you so dang scared of," Jamie asked. "I'm not doing it so don't even start," Piper said. "Tell me what you want," Jamie asked. "Drink," Piper said trying to come up with the only thing she could to get room to breathe.

He kissed her, got up and went and got them each a drink, coming back over to her and putting it down on the table. He leaned into her arms, leaning her onto the sofa. "Jamie," Piper said. "What," he asked as he nibbled at her neck and his hand slid up her shirt. "Jamie," Piper said as he slid her shirt over her head. "Yes, sexy girlfriend of mine," Jamie asked. "You are getting ahead of yourself," Piper said. He kissed her and peeled his shirt off. "Before I get ahead of myself," he said as he got up and locked the front door and the patio door. He walked back in and leaned into Piper's arms. "Hey," he said as he slid his arms around her. "What are you up to," Piper asked. "Seducing my woman," Jamie said. He kissed her and nibbled his way back down her neck. "And the sexy lingerie too," Jamie said. "Jamie," Piper said. "What," he asked as his lips met hers and their eyes locked. "What do you want from me," Piper asked. "Just you. That's all," Jamie said. "And," Piper asked. "I just want you in my life. I don't care how much, and I don't care if it means I miss you more than I can even imagine. I just want you," Jamie said. Piper looked at him. She felt his warm arms wrapped around her. She felt the softness of his lips against her neck. Fact was, she wanted him just as much. Her only worry was what would happen if things backfired completely and she lost him because of the tour. It was a nagging thought in her head. With one more kiss, that fear just fizzled away like a raindrop disappearing in the summer heat.

"What's goin on in that sexy head of yours," Jamie asked. "Just thinking. I just don't want to jump 20 feet ahead. That's all," Piper said as he curled up with her. "Then tell me why you're so worried," Jamie said. "You want the truth," Piper asked. He nodded. "Just say it," Jamie said. "I don't want to regret all of this," Piper said. "There's nothing to regret. I'm not going anywhere," Jamie said. "I just don't think that we should," Piper said. He kissed her again. "Then we just take our time," Jamie said. "I need to..." He kissed her, devouring her lips and holding her tight to him. "Just stay tonight," Jamie asked. "I have to be up for rehearsal tomorrow," Piper said. "Please," Jamie asked. She noticed his watch and saw it was almost 11. Saying she was tired wasn't an option. Telling him that she didn't want to be with him until she was sure that he wasn't after her for the fame of it wasn't an option either. He kissed her again and she got lost in that moment.

He curled her into his arms and didn't even think to let go. They kept going and the only thing that managed to break that kiss was her phone going off. She broke away from him and grabbed her cell phone. "Yep," Piper said as Jamie was kissing down her neck. "I'm sending a car to pick you and Harley up in the morning. We have an interview in Nashville and one in Charlotte in the next 24 hours. Acoustic performance. That alright," Char asked. "Yep. Did we happen to find out who was gonna look after the house before I go," Piper asked as he kissed down her chest. "All organized. Higher level security like you wanted," Char said. "Thank you," Piper said. "They'll be there at 10 tomorrow. Interview is Wednesday at 7am," Char replied. "Alright. Thanks," Piper said. They hung up as Jamie was about to undo the lace bra. "I have to go," Piper said. "Not allowed," he teased. "Jamie," Piper said. "Where are you goin," he asked. "I have to pack and get things together to go do interviews," Piper said. "Am I allowed to say that I hate that phone," he asked. She kissed him and he still wasn't letting her up. "Come and get me in the morning," he asked. "As long as I'm home and ready to go before 9," Piper replied. "Then we're going to the gym early so we have time," Jamie said. "For what," Piper asked as she saw the Cheshire grin come across his face. "You'll see," he teased.

Piper slid her shirt on as he put his on. "What are you up to," Piper asked. "Let's just leave it at if you ask me what's going on in this head of mine, you'd never make it out the door," Jamie teased. Piper kissed him. "Tomorrow," Piper said. "At least let me look after the house while you're away. I know you aren't gonna let me come to wherever you're goin," Jamie said. "I'm gone 48 hours. I'll be home before you even notice that I'm gone," Piper said. Jamie leaned her up against the back of the door and kissed her. "I'm gonna notice the minute you leave tomorrow," Jamie said. Piper kissed him. "You sure," Piper asked. "Just don't be surprised if I bump into Colt and whoop his butt for getting you all mad," Jamie said. Piper shook her head. "You're ridiculous," Piper said. "Nobody hurts you and gets away with it," Jamie said. "I'll call you when I get there," Piper said. He kissed her and nodded. "Just let me take care of the house," Jamie asked. "Alright. I'll give you the key tomorrow," Piper replied. He nodded and wrapped his arms around her like it was the last time he'd ever see her. Piper kissed him and he walked her back to her place. "Promise that you'll call me tomorrow," he asked. "As soon as I get there. We're going to the gym tomorrow anyway," Piper said. He kissed her. "And," Jamie asked. "And what," Piper asked. "You're back before you go do the first shows right," Jamie asked almost desperate for an answer. "I'm not leaving without saying anything. I promise you," Piper said. He nodded, gave her another hug and kissed her.

Piper headed inside and Jamie left and went home. "What's up," Harley asked. "We're going to Nashville tomorrow. We have to get packed," Piper said. "Dang," Harley replied. "Performance too," Piper said. She sent the rest of the band a text to let them know the plan and that they had to meet at her place by 9am. Everyone agreed and Piper locked up and went to start packing. "And what happened with you and loverboy," Harley asked. "Nothing. We just hung out and talked and stuff," Piper said. "Girl, just say it," Harley said. "Nothing happened. He's worried about the house being safe when we're gone. He's worried about me walking off," Piper said. "Why are you so freaked out about being with the guy," Harley asked. "Because I don't know that the minute I leave he's gonna be with someone else," Piper said. "You don't know that he's in love with you? I mean seriously," Harley said. "I'm not going something until I'm good and ready," Piper said. "Do you like him," Harley asked. "Don't you have packing to do," Piper asked. "Answer," Harley replied. "Yeah I do, but I'm still not sure," Piper replied. "If it were me, I'd seriously be all over that," Harley said. "And when that time comes it comes," Piper replied. "Alright girl. I'll leave you so you can get packed," Harley said as she left and went into her bedroom to get an overnight bag together.

The next morning, Piper was about to step out the door to go to the gym and saw Jamie pull up to the gate. "Hey handsome," Piper said. "You ready," he asked. Piper nodded and they left for the gym. They got there and out of the corner of her eye, Piper saw Colt. "Go," Jamie said. "Don't you start a dang fight over him," Piper said. He kissed her and signaled to his sister then went straight over to Colt. "We need to talk," Jamie said. Colt walked him into the office and closed the door. "What's the problem," Colt asked. "Either you stay away from my girlfriend or I'm throwing your butt in a jail cell," Jamie said. "Excuse me," Colt said. "You heard me. Leave her alone. Don't call her, don't text her and stay away from her friends. Leave my woman alone," Jamie said. "I was sleeping with her last night. More like stay away from my woman," Colt said. "Excuse me." Jamie said. "Why do you think she won't sleep with you," Colt said. Jamie about snapped. He threw a punch and knocked Colt to the floor.

When Jamie finally made his way into the gym, he looked like he was about to completely explode. Like an atomic bomb that was about to demolish the world, Piper could almost see the smoke shooting out his ears. He walked off and went and worked out with the boxing equipment. His sister left Piper to do her treadmill to warm up and walked over to where he was. "What happened," she asked. "Leave it alone. When I calm down," Jamie said. She walked back over to Piper and shook her head. "What's going on," Piper asked. "I don't know. I'll get you home if he is still blowing off steam," she said. "Thank you," Piper said. They finished up the workout and just as Piper was about to leave, she looked and saw Colt with a black eye. She left with Jamie's sister and went back to the house. She got breakfast, showered and changed and was ready to go when the band showed. Harley looked at her. "Where's Jamie," Harley asked. "No idea. I just want to leave," Piper said. A minute or two later, the bus came to pick them up. They all headed out the door, Harley and Piper made sure the house was locked up and they got on the bus and left. Piper didn't even bother to call Jamie.

The bus left and Harley wouldn't even look at his house. "You alright," Harley asked when she got to the master bedroom. Piper shook her head and leaned back to work on lyrics for a while. When they arrived in Nashville, Piper hopped off and went up to the suite that she was sharing with Harley. "You alright," Harley asked. "He went off to mouth off at Colt and the next thing I know he's avoiding me. Honestly, if that's what's going on then I'm glad I didn't sleep with him," Piper said. "Girl, you need to figure all of this out," Harley said. A few minutes later, Char was knocking at the door.

"Yep," Piper said as she answered. "The security is all settled at the house. They aren't going inside, but there's two at the back and two at the front gate and front door. Just wanted to make sure you knew. Wardrobe is coming this afternoon with the clothes for the next day or two of interviews. I have a rehearsal space set up for y'all. If you're okay with it, you could go down now," Char said. Piper nodded. "I'll let everyone know," Piper said. "I'll get everyone together. We'll meet at the elevator in 20," Char said. Piper nodded. "You need to call Jamie," Harley said as she grabbed her phone and got her things together. "I'm not gonna even bother," Piper said. "You need to talk to him at least," Harley said. Piper shook her head, got her things and walked down the hall to the elevator.

When they got back from rehearsal, Piper opted to have a long hot bath. Harley ordered dinner and grabbed a bottle of wine that she'd intentionally brought. "Glass," Harley asked. "Bottle," Piper replied. Harley handed her the glass and went to get changed to hang out for the night. Maybe 2 minutes later, Piper's phone buzzed. Harley looked and saw Jamie's name on the screen. She knocked on the bathroom door. "It's Jamie," Harley said. "Ignore the call. Just leave it be," Piper said. Harley shook her head. "Fine, but if he calls again, you're answering," Harley said doing as Piper asked. Dinner showed and Piper hopped out of the tub, wrapping herself up in her pajamas. She came and sat down to her seafood dinner and as soon as they were done, she finished the second glass of wine. "What's really goin on," Harley asked. "I have no freaking idea. Honestly, if throwing punches is his solution then I don't want that in my life Harley. Not even a little," Piper said. "What do you wanna do? You know his sister is gonna be on the tour," Harley said. "Doesn't change anything. She can come. He just won't," Piper said. "You need to figure this out. You need to handle it," Harley said. "Not tonight I don't," Piper said.

The next morning, Piper got up and did her workout. She came back to the room not long later and they got showered, ate and got ready to head to rehearsal. They got down to the performance place and got sound check done and went straight into hair and makeup. "Did you talk to him," Harley asked. Piper shook her head. They finished getting ready and after a quick prayer, they went and got ready. As soon as the interviewer mentioned them, they started their performance. It blew everyone's minds. The bonus being that the first 10 people that had shown to come into the event had won tickets to the concert. They did a third song and when they finished, they got a few autographs done and headed back to the hotel to pack up and head to Charlotte.

When they finished the second performance, Piper almost dreaded going home the next day. "Girl, you know he's gonna lose it if you don't talk to him," Harley said. "How many days until we leave," Piper asked. "Less than 5. We have to do that performance in New York first," Harley said. "And if I said that I wanted to just not go back and go to New York now," Piper asked. "You're avoiding the inevitable. Just do whatever," Harley said. Piper shook her head. "If that's how he's gonna act," Piper said. Harley gave her a hug. "Let whatever's gonna happen just happen," Harley said. Piper nodded. They stayed the second night in Charlotte then headed home.

When they got back, security stayed at the house. The cars faded away leaving only Piper's and Harley's. They went inside and she got settled. Within maybe 15 minutes, her phone rang. She looked and saw Jamie's number on the screen. She ignored the call and went and put something together for dinner instead. Maybe 10 minutes later, the security guard was knocking at the door. "Miss Piper, there's a gentleman here to see you," the guard said. "Who," Piper asked. "He said his name is Jamie," the guard said. Piper nodded.

"You didn't even call me to tell me that you were there safe," Jamie said. "Go home," Piper replied. "You gonna tell me why you didn't call," Jamie asked. "Leave," Piper replied. "Talk," Jamie said. "You seriously think throwing a punch at someone is gonna fix all of this," Piper asked. "Did you sleep with him," Jamie asked. Piper shook her head, went to the door and asked security to remove him. "Yes or no," Jamie said as they walked him out the door. Piper shook her head, finished making dinner and when Harley came into the kitchen, Piper was two glasses of wine in. "What happened now," Harley asked. "Colt told him that we slept together," Piper said. "What," Harley asked. "Honestly, I just want to be away from here," Piper said. Harley gave her a hug. "You need to talk to the cops," Harley said. Piper nodded. She called the officer that had taken her statement and asked him to come to the house to discuss the Colt problem. Within maybe 10 minutes, the police officer was at her front door.

"Miss Piper," the officer said. "He's now started spreading rumors. This is a major problem," Piper said. "I can completely understand that. The manager of the gym said that he's been let go as of today. He's banned from the premises. I gather something happened this morning," the officer said. "A few days ago before I left to head out of town. He put his hands on a neighbor of mine at the gym. I want him silenced. If he starts another problem and puts it into the press, there's going to be a huge problem," Piper said. "We can't stop him from starting a rumor, but we can prevent him from being within 1000 feet as the restraining order says," the officer said. "He's gone too far," Piper said. "It's up to you to charge him with stalking or harassment," the officer said. "Then we charge him. He's even going after my friends," Piper said. "Then we'll take the statement and take it to the chief," the officer said. Within a half hour, the statement was made and the officer headed out.

"You seriously went through all of that without saying a dang word," Harley said. "That's the detailed version," Piper said. "My god lady. How the heck does this happen," Harley asked. "Good dang question. Like I said, being with someone who's so dang willing to believe what Colt said isn't exactly a smart idea," Piper said. "He was in shock. Give the guy a chance. He lost his marbles. He wouldn't have thrown a punch at Colt if he hadn't," Harley said. "He has to figure out how to handle it better then. I just can't deal with him," Piper said. A little while later, her phone stared to ring again. "I'm not answering if it's him," Piper said. Harley looked and saw Jamie's name on the call display. She walked into the kitchen and answered. "Piper," Jamie said. "It's Harley. She's livid. Beyond pissed. She just made another police statement. Whatever you did that got her all mad is just brewing and getting worse," Harley said. "Can you just let me in," Jamie asked. "Not unless she's alright with it," Harley said. "Please," Jamie asked. "I'll talk to her, but she's gonna end up saying no," Harley said. "Just please talk to her," Jamie said. "I will," Harley said as they hung up.

Chapter 7

"And what does Jamie want," Piper asked. "You need to talk to him. Even if it's just on the dang phone," Harley said. "No. He threw a dang punch in public. This is insane," Piper said. "Girl, you still need to talk to him. Whatever the heck happened, just hear him," Harley said. "Not tonight I'm not," Piper said. She walked upstairs, grabbed her cell and went and soaked the anger away in the huge master tub. An hour and a bit later, her phone buzzed with a text from Jamie:

I never should've even mentioned it. It set me off and I lost control. I don't want to lose you. Please just talk to me. – Jamie.

Piper shook her head. When she saw the dots come back up like he was sending another message, she turned her phone on silent and put it on the floor. When it buzzed again, she shook her head. She leaned into the water, submerging herself, trying to drown the anger away. When she came back up, she shook her head and drained the water out. She dried off, put her phone on the charger and within minutes it was buzzing again. When she ignored it, it buzzed again with a call. Finally, she just answered. "What do you want," Piper asked. "I messed up," Jamie said. "A lot more than messed up," Piper said. "Piper, please," Jamie said. "You threw a punch in a gym. What did you expect me to do," Piper asked. "I made a mistake. A huge mistake. I should've kept my cool, but after what he said I couldn't even think," Jamie said. "I know. I just wanted you to try and think. What would make you think that I would ever go anywhere near him," Piper asked. "You need to talk to me instead of walkin away," Jamie said. "And you need to stop being an idiot when it comes to him. I'm not playing this game Jamie. If you can't deal with it then walk," Piper said. "I'm not going anywhere. Piper, please," Jamie said. "As long as we don't have to have this conversation again," Piper said. "Next time, I'll just tell him where to go," Jamie said. "Good," Piper said.

"This mean that we can get together tomorrow," Jamie asked. "We'll see," Piper said. "Can we do the gym in the morning," Jamie asked. "Honestly, I don't even know if it's a good idea," Piper said. "Please," he asked. "We'll see in the morning," Piper replied. "Piper, honest to god, I'm sorry that I let it go that far," Jamie said. "I know. I just need time to cool off," Piper said. "Tomorrow we can talk," Jamie asked. "Maybe," Piper said. "Get some rest tonight then. If you want to come with me, I'll meet you tomorrow at the end of the driveway," Jamie said. "Okay," Piper said. They hung up and Piper set her morning alarm.

The next morning, Jamie and Piper headed to the gym and there was no sign of Colt anywhere. They got through the workout and when they were just about to leave, he came up with an idea. "I have an idea," Jamie said. "Another one," Piper asked. "We have breakfast at my place. What do you think," Jamie asked. "Don't you have work or something," Piper asked. "We still need breakfast," Jamie said. "You're ridiculous," Piper said. "So are you coming or what," Jamie asked. "I have to go home and get things organized before I leave," Piper said. "Then we're eating at your place," Jamie said. "Jamie," Piper said. "I finally got you talking to me again. I am not about to let you vanish into the sunset," Jamie said. "Fine," Piper replied. He kissed her and they hopped into the truck to head back to her place. When they got there, two cop cars were guarding the front gate. "What's going on," Piper asked. "A package was delivered with your name and nothing else. We have it secured now. You can go in," the officer said. "You're not staying here," Jamie said. "I'm fine. The police have it handled," Piper said. He shook his head. They got out of the car and Jamie walked her into the house. "This is completely insane," Jamie said.

Piper went into the kitchen and made breakfast. Just as she did, Harley headed downstairs. "Piper, this is nuts," Jamie said. "I'm gone in a couple days. I'm not exactly worried," Piper said. "And if your house gets torched? This is dangerous. What if something happened," Jamie asked. "I won't be here. The cops have things handled," Piper said. "You telling me that you aren't even worried," Jamie asked. "I'm worried, but they got it. It's fine," Piper said. "What in the world are y'all talking about," Harley asked. "A package got delivered to the dang house and the cops took possession. Whatever it was, it was bad," Jamie said. "This is insane. You know that right," Harley asked. "I know. They got it before anything happened," Piper replied. "And if they didn't, something could've happened to you and Harley. Piper, this isn't right," Jamie said. Maybe 10 minutes later, there was a knock at the door.

"Yep," Piper said as she came to the door. "Miss Piper, the package was from the gentleman that you have the order against. We have taken it to the court so they have what they need to charge him," the officer said. "Am I allowed to ask what it was," Piper asked. "If I even mentioned it, I would be in trouble. It was something suggestive. We do have a photo of the note," the officer said as he showed it to Piper:

If that's who you're gonna be with, you're gonna need these. When you want a real man let me know.

Piper shook her head. "What," Jamie asked. "Just ignore it," Piper said. "Do you want us to do anything else," the officer asked. "Just keep him away from me and my friends. Period. Nothing else," Piper said. "We'll let you know if anything else happens," the officer said. Piper nodded and the officer headed out. They finished making breakfast and sat down to eat. "You gonna tell me what the stupid note said," Harley asked. Piper shook her head. Jamie finished his coffee and looked at Piper. "I'm going to get ready for rehearsal. Y'all talk," Harley said as she cleaned off her dishes.

Jamie looked at Piper. "Tell me," he said. "It's just a bunch of BS. He's a complete fool if he thinks that he'd get anywhere doing that stuff," Piper said. "Answer me," he asked. "It was adult toys and a note saying that if I was with you I'd need them," Piper said. "You happy now?" Jamie shook his head and went to do dishes. Piper knew that was his way to cope with it and that he really wanted to haul out and kick Colt's butt. "Piper, I'm tryin dang hard to keep my cool right now. I really am. If that's the drama he's gonna start then you need to kick his butt with those cops. He's gone too dang far," Jamie said. "Exactly why I'm glad that I'm not gonna be here and I'm gonna be on the tour," Piper said. "Speaking of that, my boss said that I could go be on the road with y'all from Thursday to Sunday during the week. I think you'd be back here when you could right," Jamie asked. "That's sorta the plan if I can do it," Piper replied.

"Then we're good. I can go with you," Jamie said. "You don't have to be there the entire time," Piper said. "I know. I just want to be able to be there," Jamie said. "Just remember that sometimes I may not be able to get back," Piper said. "I get it. As long as you're safe and the house is safe when y'all are back, you'll be fine," Jamie said. "I just want to be in your life. That's all," Jamie said. "I know. Just try to remember that all of this is work for me," Piper said. Jamie shook his head. "Still don't trust me," he asked. Piper shook her head. "Stop giving the girl a hard time," Harley said. "Nothin to do with it," Jamie said. "Whenever you can, you come out. Leave it at that," Harley said as she got another mug of coffee in her travel mug. "I have to get ready," Piper said. "I'll call you when I'm back," Jamie said. Piper nodded. She walked him out, kissed him goodbye and went upstairs to shower and change to head to rehearsal.

They got back from rehearsal late that afternoon and Piper was beyond exhausted. "When do we leave on Friday," Harley asked. "Can't be early enough," Piper said. "Girl, he's worried. If I'd known that package was here, I would've lost my marbles," Harley said. "Harley, none of this has to do with the stupid package. It has to do with him trying to stake his claim," Piper said. "Girl, would you think for two seconds? He wants you in his life and he's willing to go wherever he has to so he can make that happen. You deserve a good person who wants that. Why can't you see that," Harley asked. "Because every time I give someone a chance, it blows up in my face. What happens if Colt goes that much further Harley? What happens when he goes 250 points overboard? Is he just gonna assume that I did what Colt accuses me of," Piper asked. "He is in love with you. I can see it Piper. I know that look. It's the same dang look my husband gave me when we first met. When things were good and we were happy. That's the same dang look. I'm not letting you walk away from that," Harley said.

They had dinner and instead of wine or water, Harley was on her second glass of whiskey by the end of dinner. "I get that you're upset. Honestly, I do. I get what you want me to do. I just need to take time with this. When I'm ready it'll happen, whatever that is," Piper said. "Just give him a chance. That's all. Not every relationship backfires like mine," Harley said. "I know. Right now I have to concentrate on the tour stuff until it gets going," Piper said. "Jason has a dang family. He's gonna be coming back too. It's not that big of a deal," Harley said. "I get it. I just don't wanna go too far and get in over my dang head," Piper said. "Jump in. Quit testing the dang water," Harley joked. "I'll try, but I need to feel it out Harley. That's just how I am and you know it," Piper said. "I know. No matter how much I try to drag you out of that, I know," Harley joked.

Around 9, Piper's phone went off. "Yep," she said. "I know it's insanely late. I just got back. Did you want to come over for a bit," Jamie asked. "For a little while," Piper said. "See you in a couple then," Jamie said. They hung up and Harley looked at her. "Remember what I said. He's a good guy," Harley said. Piper nodded. "Thank you for that," Piper said. Harley nodded and Piper got freshened up and headed off. When she got to Jamie's, he was in the midst of an overly loud call. From what Piper heard, he was fighting with a woman. She knocked and he opened the door, grabbing her hand and bringing her into the house then locking the door behind her. "I'm not having this fight again. It's done. Over. Finished. Stop calling my dang phone," Jamie said. He hung up and kissed Piper. "And who was that," Piper asked. "An old girlfriend who decided to try to start world war three. She showed up at my work and tried to start a dang fight," Jamie said.

"Okay," Piper said. "What," he asked. "Nothing," Piper replied. He could tell by the look on her face that she wasn't impressed. He poured each of them a drink and Piper went and sat outside on the oversized chaise. "What's wrong," Jamie asked. "Just trying to make sense of things," Piper said. "What kind of things," Jamie asked as he sat down beside her. "I know that you don't get it and that Harley doesn't, but we barely know each other Jamie. A week or two isn't enough. I have to go do the tour stuff and it's like we're skipping over the whole dating thing," Piper said. "We can't date if you aren't here," Jamie said. "Then we date when I'm on the road. I'm not jumping into bed with you because there's no other way. I'm not," Piper replied. "I wasn't saying that we were gonna just jump in," Jamie replied. "I'm willing to try the dating stuff, but I just can't do things how you want to Jamie. You being out there every weekend is too much," Piper said. "Piper," Jamie said. "Every other weekend or something. I just can't do things any other way," Piper replied. "That's why you came over here? To tell me that all of this is too much? Seriously," Jamie asked. "I just don't want to rush things. If things were meant to happen, they'll happen either way. We just need to slow down a little," Piper said.

"As long as I'm not losing you from my life completely, I'll do it. Whatever you want me to," Jamie said. "I just need time. It's nothing against you," Piper said. He kissed her and wrapped his arm around her, snuggling her closer. "You alright," Jamie asked. "I am. Honestly, I just thought things over today while we were at rehearsal. I talked to Harley and she said a whole other bunch of stuff," Piper said. "She's on my side," he teased. "Something like that," Piper replied. He kissed her forehead. "I just want to be with you even if it means missing you something crazy," Jamie said. "I have to go to New York on Friday. You don't have to come. You have work," Piper said. "I can be there whenever you want. I'll come down the first weekend. We'll go from there," Jamie said. "Okay," Piper said. "Means we are still goin to the gym right," Jamie asked. Piper nodded. "Means we can still hang out and do breakfast and stuff," Piper said. "You know this is all I wanted all day," Jamie said. "What," Piper asked. "You and me. Didn't matter what, I just wanted you and me time," Jamie replied. "I know. I don't know what the future is gonna hold," Piper said. "As long as I can be around, that's all I want," Jamie said. "You will be," Piper said.

That changed things so much he didn't even say it. He didn't want to say a thing. Risking what that one sentence meant to him wasn't an option. He kissed her neck. "What," Piper asked. "Come here for a sec," he teased as he got up. He held his hand out and surprisingly, she took his hand. He walked her inside, they finished their wine and he leaned her against the counter. "What would you like," Piper asked. He kissed her and devoured her lips, leaning up against her. "What you want," Piper asked. He kissed her. "I'm not trying to push, but every inch of me wants you right now," Jamie said. "You think," Piper asked. He kissed her again. "I could so totally not behave right now," Jamie said. "Oh really," Piper asked. "I could totally peel those jeans off right now," he whispered as goose bumps appeared and she got a shiver down her back. "You are trouble with a capital T," Piper said. "And," he asked. "And nothing. Before you go way too far, I'm going," Piper said. He kissed her again, picked her up and sat her on the counter. "Jamie," Piper said. He pulled her legs around him.

He devoured her lips and she peeled his shirt off. "You know that if you start I'm finishing," Jamie said as she got a silly grin. "Oh I know," Piper said. "Before you change your mind," he teased. "What," Piper asked. He slid her into his arms and walked upstairs, leaning her onto the bed. The moonlight was the only thing that was lighting up the room. It gave the entire thing a glow that was almost movie like. He leaned into her arms and kissed her. She could smell the cologne that she loved and the fading scent of the body wash that he loved. It was like the bedroom was covered in April fresh scents mixed with the salty air. When the kiss broke, he peeled her shirt off. He leaned in and kissed her again, devouring her lips and getting lost in the kiss. For the first time in forever, he started hesitating to go further. The only way he was, was if Piper made the first move. Her hands slid to his back and he kissed her even more. "It's up to you," Jamie said. He leaned in and devoured her lips. "What am I gonna do with you," Piper asked. "I have a hint," he joked. Piper kissed him. "Jamie," Piper said. "What," he asked. "You gonna get mad if I say not yet," Piper asked. "Nope," he teased. Jamie devoured her lips again and slid her sandals off.

They barely managed to come up for air between kisses. It wasn't until his phone went off that they even realized what they were doing. "Not answering it," Jamie said as he kissed her again. "I should go," Piper said. "You could stay," he said as he kissed down her neck and held her tight to him. "And if I stay, something else is gonna be going on," Piper said. He kissed her shoulder. "Just stay tonight," Jamie said. "And if I did, neither of us would be sleeping would we," Piper asked. "Probably not," Jamie said as he went for the button of her jeans. "I need to go," Piper said. "Please," he asked. Piper kissed him and managed to get up, sliding her shirt on. "Damn," he said. "I'll see you in the morning," Jamie said. Piper nodded, leaned over and kissed him and slid her sandals back on. "I'll walk you back," Jamie said. Piper shook her head. "I'm fine," Piper replied. He got up, kissed her and slid his flip flops on with a hoodie. "Jamie," Piper said. He kissed her, walked her downstairs and walked her home. No matter how bad he wanted her to stay, he knew that pushing wasn't gonna do any good for anyone.

He walked Piper the few steps back to her house and kissed her at the door. "What," Piper asked seeing the look on his face as he pulled her to him. "Stay tomorrow night," he asked. Piper shook her head. "I don't know," Piper said. "Think about it. Stay tomorrow night. Please," Jamie said. "Jamie," Piper said. "I don't care if you sleep in the bed and I'm on the floor," Jamie said. "Can I think about it," Piper asked. He nodded and kissed her. "See you in the morning beautiful," Jamie said. Piper nodded and kissed him. "See you in the mornin," Piper said. He kissed her again and headed off as Piper headed inside.

"What you doin back so early," Harley teased as she finished putting the dishes away. "I was tired," Piper said. "And," Harley asked. "And nothing. We talked. Everything is good," Piper said. "You decide what you wanted to do about him," Harley asked. "I made a decision," Piper replied. "And that was," Harley asked. "We're giving it a real try. We're just taking our time," Piper said. "So y'all are alright," Harley teased. Piper nodded. Piper locked up, turned the alarm on and went upstairs. She slid into her pajamas, got ready for bed and within a matter of minutes her phone was ringing.

"Yep," Piper said. "Hey. It's Caroline. I wanted to call and see how you were," she said. "I'm good. Just heading to bed. What's up," Piper asked. "You around tomorrow," Caroline asked. "Rehearsal then getting ready for Friday and the tour," Piper replied. "Oh. I was gonna see if you wanted to have a girl night or drinks or something," Caroline said. "Honestly, I'm tryin to get as much rest as I can before we head out. I can't really be up that late," Piper said. "We can do dinner or something," Caroline said. "I'm gonna be honest with you," Piper said. "After the whole Colt thing, I'm kinda hesitant about hanging out with you. I mean, we were gonna have a ladies night and y'all went to a strip bar. That's not my thing and it never will be. Even if it's a bachelorette I wouldn't," Piper said. "We can go to the Pink House or something," Caroline said. "Maybe a barbecue here or something," Piper replied. "Can we do it before you leave," Caroline asked. "As long as you don't invite Colt," Piper said. "I mean, we're friends, but I wouldn't invite him there knowing how you feel," Caroline said. "Tomorrow y'all can come by, but I'm gonna have to make it an early night," Harley replied. "Alright. I'll come over around 4," Caroline replied. "And yes Eve can come," Piper teased. "We'll see you tomorrow," Caroline replied. "Yes," Piper replied.

The next morning, Piper was getting ready for the gym when Jamie texted:

Outside when you're ready gorgeous

Piper smirked, grabbed her phone and keys and headed off, locking up behind her. "Hey sexy," Jamie said. "Hey yourself handsome," Piper said. He held her hand the entire way to the gym. When they arrive, Piper saw Colt's truck. "We have a problem," Piper said. "I saw it," Jamie said. "I'm not goin in there if he's there," Piper said. "I'll take you in myself. Just don't let go of my hand," Jamie said. Piper nodded. He got her door, locked up the truck and walked in with her hand in hand. The manager saw them, nodded and they went into the gym. There was no trace of Colt, luckily, so they weren't thrown off. They worked out with Jamie's sister then headed out without a problem at all. When they went to leave, Colt's truck was gone. "Lucky," Jamie said. Piper nodded. "So, I should be home by 8. I'll come over and get you," Jamie said. "The girls are comin for a little bit, so don't be surprised when you see a bunch of girls," Piper said. "Guess that means I have to be extra charming," Jamie joked. "Something like that," Piper said. "So, about what I said last night," he teased. "About what," Piper asked. "Staying tonight. There's only two more days until you're gone on the tour," Jamie said. "It's not like it's a deadline," Piper replied. "It is for being able to romance you," Jamie joked. "I swear, you are just a sweetheart sometimes," Piper said. "One of the last nights we're really alone," Jamie said. "I get it," Piper said. "And," he asked as he linked their fingers while he drove them back to the house. "I'll think about it," Piper replied doing her best to put him off.

They got back and he dropped his stuff at his place. They walked over to Piper's and saw Harley making breakfast. "Good timing or what," Jamie teased. "Couldn't sleep, so I figured I'd make breakfast," Harley said. They sat down together and Harley said the words that Jamie was dreading. "Char called by the way. We leave at 6 tomorrow morning," Harley said. "I can get out of going the studio," Jamie said. "And the bus is picking us up at 5:30 at the house," Harley said. "I'll be out early. My boss knows," Jamie teased. "If you don't, it's not that big of a deal," Piper said. Jamie gave her one of those looks. "They dropped the clothes and stuff off for us and it's put into the cases so we have it. We just have to pack up everything else," Harley said. "Almost half-finished anyway. I'll be ready to go tomorrow," Piper said. "You getting nervous yet," Jamie asked. "Not even a little," Piper replied. "Maybe you aren't, but I am," Harley said. "This coming from the girl who couldn't wait to leave town," Piper joked. "Just nervous about the whole performing in front of tons of people," Harley said. "We've done it before. You were great last time," Piper said. "It's a heck of a lot more people," Harley said. "Piper is right though. You'll be great," Jamie said. "I dang well hope so," Piper replied. "So does this mean that y'all are off today," Jamie asked. Harley nodded. "I'm gonna check on a few things and make sure what we need for the bus is there," Piper said. "In other words, two boxes of her wine," Harley teased. "It's a necessity," Piper joked.

They cleaned up while Harley went and got changed. "You sure you'll have everything," Jamie teased. "Yup," Piper replied. "Tease," Jamie joked. "You are so getting it later." Piper shook her head and he kissed her shoulder. "I didn't do a darn thing," Piper said as she dried off the dishes and put them away. "So, what time are they coming," Jamie asked. "4. At least that's the plan. If you want to come over then come," Piper said. "Done," Jamie said. "Then I'm all yours until you have to go to work," Piper said. He kissed her devouring her lips. "I'm gonna call you out on that tonight," Jamie whispered as she got goosebumps. "I know you will," Piper said. He kissed her neck and his phone buzzed. "You have work," Piper said. "That's probably who it is," Jamie said. He grabbed his phone and took one look. "Crap," Jamie said. "What," Piper replied. "I have to go. They're comin in early," Jamie said. "I'll see you tonight," Piper said. He kissed her and headed home to get ready to go to work.

Piper locked up and got ready for the day. She packed, did laundry, cleaned and put something out for the ladies night.

She got what she needed for the bus and packed it into a grocery bag. "Anything we're missing," Harley asked. "Nope," Piper teased. "We have extra toiletry stuff right," Harley asked. "Of course. We have everything including that tea and extra Starbucks," Piper said. "Thank goodness for that," Harley joked. "We have everything," Piper said. "And one thing you did forget about that I'm packing for you," Harley said. "I don't even wanna know," Piper said. "Girl, I'm making sure that the tour goes the way you want it to," Harley replied. "You can cool your jets if it's what I think" Piper teased. "Girl, you do what you want to when you want to. Just be sure it's what you want," Harley said. Piper nodded. "How are you doing with the divorce stuff by the way," Piper asked. "It's final in a week or two. He asked to speed it up. Quickest divorce ever," Harley said. "You alright with it," Piper asked. She shook her head. "Not exactly," Harley replied. "Then we have a girl night," Piper said. "To keep my mind off it," Harley asked. Piper nodded. "That's the plan," Piper said. "Done. Even if I'm hung over tomorrow, I'm in," Harley replied.

They hung out the rest of the day, opting for manicures and pedicures to start the tour off right then they headed back to the house. Piper got dinner together and Caroline called. "We're on the way girl," Caroline said. "See you in a couple," Piper replied. She got the dinner going and opened the wine. When everyone started to arrive, Piper almost laughed. "Come on in ladies," Piper said. Caroline and Eve came in. Harley came downstairs and Piper got drinks. "So, what's the plan for tonight," Harley asked. "Well, since Piper said that we had to have an early night, barbecue," Caroline said. "We're drinking. That's all I know," Harley said as she got a bottle of Jack and poured herself a glass. Piper shook her head and went and put the steaks on. "So what are you makin," Eve asked. "Steaks, got the kale salad inside and grilled veggies," Piper said. "Girl, you are outdoing yourself," Eve said. "Last big night before we head out. I even got shrimp to grill if y'all want it," Piper said. "Dang," Caroline said. Piper got the food together while they all talked. Instead of a glass of wine, Piper had sweet tea intentionally.

"So, how goes the boyfriend stuff," Eve asked. "Good. I met a good guy," Piper said. She walked over and checked the steaks. "And what does he do," Caroline teased. "Y'all can ask him yourself. He's comin by," Piper said. "Colt said to say hi," Eve said. "He can rot in a hole where he belongs," Piper said. "He's a good guy you know," Caroline said. "You mean since he's a sleaze and a bully? There's a reason for the restraining order," Piper said. "Where did you meet him anyway," Harley asked. "A bar that we were at. It was that same night that we were goin out after dinner," Eve said. "You met him at a dang strip bar," Piper asked. "It was a bar next door," Caroline said giving Eve a look. "You're full of it," Piper said. She walked into the house and heard her phone buzz. She looked and saw a text from Jamie that he got out early. Piper texted him back and said to come asap before she kicked butt. She shook her head and poured herself a drink. When she heard the phone buzz that he was at the gate, Piper messaged Harley that she needed to cool off a minute. She went out front and Jamie walked over to her and wrapped his arms around her. "What happened," Jamie asked. "He's a stripper. The man is certifiably insane," Piper said. Jamie kissed her. "We play nice until they leave," Jamie said. Piper nodded.

They headed inside hand in hand and Jamie put her drink back in the bottle. "You don't need it. Trust me," Jamie said. He poured her a glass of wine and handed it to her, walking outside to check on the steaks. "You must be Jamie," Eve said. "Nice to meet y'all," Jamie said. "Eve and Caroline, this is Jamie," Piper said. "So, when did y'all meet," Caroline asked. "Couple weeks ago. It was ladies night at a bar near my work," Jamie said. "Harley and I had a girl night," Piper said. "I guess we weren't invited," Caroline asked. "We were just hanging out because I had got divorce papers," Harley said. "That's not good," Eve said. "Was a long week. We decided we needed a night out so we went," Harley said. "And I'm lucky as all get out that they did," Jamie said as his arm slid around Piper. "So, what happened with Colt," Caroline asked. "Let's just leave that topic alone," Jamie said coming to Piper's defense. "Why," Caroline asked. "You're seriously causing a dang problem," Piper asked. "I just don't get why you're so determined to ruin him," Caroline said. "I'm not playin this game. If this is what you're gonna do then walk your butt out the door," Piper said. "You got him thrown in jail," Caroline said. Harley shook her head knowing exactly what was about to happen. Piper shook her head and Jamie's hand held Piper's that much tighter. "Caroline, come inside for a minute," Piper said. Jamie kissed Piper and she went inside to talk to Caroline alone.

"What," Caroline asked. "I'm gonna say this nicely and I'm only saying it once. Colt is never coming near me again and if he does, he's thrown into a cell in the basement of the dang jail. He pushed me around, tried to force me into things and started leaving threatening packages at my door. I don't care where you met his pathetic butt, but he's not coming anywhere near me again period. End of discussion. You bring his butt up again, you're leaving and you're done as my friend. Got me," Piper asked. "He just wants to be with you," Caroline said. "It's not happening. Period. Do you get that? You want him to have a girlfriend so dang bad then you date him. I'm done," Piper said. "You could've called and told him that," Caroline said. Piper went outside, got Caroline's purse, came in, handed it to her and walked her out the door and out to the street then closed the gate. She came back inside and grabbed her cell, blocking Caroline's number.

"You alright," Eve asked. Piper nodded. "Where's Caroline," Harley asked. "Don't really give a crap," Piper said. "Damn," Eve said. "Like I said, anyone mentions that idiot again in this house and they're gone," Piper said. "She kinda hit it off with him. They were sorta hanging out if you get my drift and when he saw a picture of you with Caroline, he said he wanted to meet you," Eve said. "I have a permanent order against him. I want nothing to do with him or Caroline after hearing that," Piper said. "Steaks are done. Who's ready to eat," Jamie asked. They all got something to eat and had a nice quiet dinner. Jamie wanted Piper so much it was killing him to sit there. "So, what are your intentions towards my friend," Eve asked. "Not letting her out of my dang sight. Kinda like being able to hang out because we live so close," Jamie said. "He lives two doors down," Harley said. "Dang. Well that's luck," Eve teased. "Something like that," Jamie said. "I don't think I've seen Piper smile that much in what feels like forever," Eve said. "Definitely inspires some of that music," Harley teased. "Funny," Piper said. "I guess y'all are all pumped about the tour though. Isn't that kind of the best thing that could happen music stuff wise," Eve asked. "Something like that," Harley said as Jamie's arm slid around Piper's shoulders.

Jamie kissed Piper's shoulder and got up to refill their wine glasses. "Did you want a refill," Jamie asked. "Thank you," Eve said. Harley went inside with him and left Eve and Piper to talk. "If I'd known that he was that crazy, I never would've even let her think about introducing y'all," Eve said. "What's done is done Eve. He's not coming near me again. Never. He got fired from the gym. He left a dang package by the front gate. Jamie snapped when he found out. He's worried about the house," Piper said. "I can look after it while you're away. Anything you need me to do," Eve said. "I appreciate that, but I think we figured it out," Piper said. "I'm so sorry," Eve said.

Harley came outside with Jamie. He had wine, Harley had the heavy drinks. "So, when do y'all leave," Eve asked. "Tomorrow mornin," Piper replied. "That is gonna be one early mornin," Jamie said. "You're going with them," Eve asked. "For a while," Jamie said. Piper smirked. "As long as y'all are happy. Do I get to come visit too," Eve asked. "Sure," Harley replied. "It's definitely gonna be an adventure," Piper said. Jamie kissed her. "So, what else do y'all have planned. Are you gonna be back for the holidays," Eve asked. "We'll be back. I think the dates finish up beginning of December for a break for the holidays," Piper said.

They sat around and talked for a while longer, Piper got dessert together and they finished that a matter of minutes later. When they finished up the drinks, Eve opted to head out. "I'm gonna go check on you know who. Let me know when you're home or when you're close," Eve asked. Piper nodded. "I definitely will. Once the you know who stuff calms down with Caroline, maybe I'll talk to her," Piper said. "I'll get her to chill out," Eve said. Piper nodded. "Whatever you say," Piper teased. She gave Eve a hug, Harley gave Eve a hug and she left to head home. "I swear I thought you were gonna throw Caroline to the wolves," Harley said. "I almost threw her in the garbage disposal," Piper said. "I'm kinda glad you didn't," Jamie said. Piper shook her head and kissed him. "I'm going to have my long soak in the tub for the last time," Harley teased. "Have fun," Piper said. Harley gave her a hug, turned the dishwasher on and headed upstairs. "Get your bag," Jamie whispered. "Two minutes," she said. "I'm countin," Jamie replied.

Piper knocked on Harley's door. "What are you getting all worried about," Harley teased as she opened the door. "You know what," Piper said. "Go. I'll be right here. I'll make sure you're up in time to get on the bus," Harley said. "And if I come home instead," Piper said. "Whatever you want girl,"

Harley said. "My stuff is in the office. If I get back late…" "Girl, go. Whatever happens, everything's fine. I'll even make sure you have breakfast before we go," Harley replied. Piper gave her a hug. "Go," Harley said.

Piper headed downstairs and saw Jamie, grabbed her overnight bag, her keys and phone and headed to Jamie's with him. "You okay," Jamie asked. Piper nodded. "Just wanted to make sure she had a couple things that she said to remind her about. What's with the big ole cat that ate the canary grin," Piper asked. "Just happy that you're here," Jamie said. "I'm sorry about Caroline being a psycho," Piper said. "Babe, she's your friend. He got to her and started world war three intentionally," Jamie said. "Honestly, if that's what she's gonna keep doing then I don't need her around," Piper said. Jamie opened the door for her and they headed inside. He locked up the gate and locked the door behind them. "I'll put this upstairs," Jamie said as he took her overnight bag upstairs to the master bedroom. Piper went into the kitchen and outside to the patio. Jamie came outside a little while later with wine for each of them and handed her a glass.

"What's wrong," Jamie asked. "Just blows my mind that she can't just be polite instead of being a psycho," Piper said. "You need to relax," Jamie said. "If she's the one that got him pushing my dang buttons, I swear I am gonna kick her backside to the moon," Piper said. "Babe, you're here. No more stress. She's gone," Jamie said as he slid his arm around her. "I know. I'm just floored that she would do that. It's not like he's her long-lost best friend or something. She slept with the guy," Piper said. He kissed her neck. "Eve was nice. That's all that mattered. Caroline being an idiot isn't messing with what we have, and it never will," Jamie said. "It's just embarrassing," Piper said. He kissed her and snuggled her to him. "I don't care what drama anyone else causes. I just want us happy. That's all," Jamie said. "I know. I love that you want that," Piper said. He kissed her. "And," Jamie teased. "And what else," Piper teased. "You still nervous about me coming with y'all," Jamie asked. "No. I just don't want us rushing into anything," Piper said. "I'm perfectly fine curled up in bed without doin anything," Jamie teased. "Oh really," Piper joked. He nodded. "Not saying that I wouldn't be tempted, but I can handle myself," Jamie joked. Piper shook her head and he leaned in and kissed her.

"You think so do you," Piper teased. "I know so," Jamie said. Piper took another sip of wine and he slid his hand in hers and walked Piper inside. "You alright," Jamie asked. Piper nodded and he sat down with her, snuggling her in close. Piper put her glass of wine down and Jamie wrapped his arms around her, sitting her in his lap. "So are you getting nervous," Jamie asked. Piper shook her head. "Not even. I know once the day comes I'll be beyond nervous, but it'll be alright. I know it will," Piper said. "Because I'm gonna be there," he asked. "About that. What did your work say about you wanting to be out every weekend," Piper asked. "They said it wasn't really an issue as long as I'm there Monday to Friday. They agreed that I'm done at 2 on Friday's so I can come out to meet you," Jamie said. "You sure," Piper asked. "Nobody is stopping me from spending every dang weekend with my girl," Jamie said. "If you can't and you have to be home," Piper said. He kissed her. "Then I come as soon as I can," Jamie said. "If you can't, it's not a problem," Piper replied. He shook his head. "I hate even thinking that I'm gonna be away from you. We can't go to the gym and do breakfast together," Jamie said. "You know that the bus isn't exactly a date situation," Piper said. He kissed her. "I just want to be with you," Jamie said. "I know," Piper said.

He put his wine down and turned her to face him. "What," Piper asked. "Come here," he said. She snuggled in closer. He leaned his head down and kissed her. It gave her goosebumps head to toe. The taste of her lips had him overheated in minutes. That kiss was like a drug that was beyond addictive. He slid his hands down her back and pulled her legs around him to straddle him. He kissed her again and got up, carrying her up the steps to the master bedroom, not letting go for even a second. The kiss didn't even break. When she felt her back against the bed, she noticed the sheets were different. He kissed her again and peeled his shirt off. "What are you up to," Piper asked. He kissed her. "Phone is staying downstairs. No interruptions," Jamie said knowing that it was the last chance before she left to have real alone time. "And just what were you planning there handsome," Piper asked. "Couple things," he said as he leaned in and kissed her.

He barely managed to let her up for air. He peeled her shirt off and wrapped his arms tight around her. "What," she teased noticing the look on his face. He went to undo her bra and kissed her before another word was said. He didn't want to let go for even a second. The bra slid to the floor and he kissed her again without even looking at the sexy golden glow of skin. "What," Piper asked, noticing him almost pause. "Just realized that you're almost bronzed. Totally sexy as all get out on you," Jamie said. "You sure this is what you want," Piper asked. "You that worried that I'll change my mind," he asked. Piper nodded, giving into the doubt that had been circling around her mind.

Chapter 8

"You're beautiful head to dang toe Piper. Don't you even see it," Jamie asked. Craziest thing, but it wasn't being nervous about getting ghosted after they slept together that worried her. She wasn't exactly a size 2. Every outfit that had been chosen for the tour, disguised what she hated about herself. She wasn't a six pack abs kind of woman. She never had been. She looked at Jamie and saw the chiseled abs and the muscles and asked herself over and over why he'd chosen her of all people. She was not exactly the most confident person, but she wasn't about to let it show. "I love that you see that," Piper replied doing her best to push the nerves out of her system. Once the jeans came off, he was going to see every single imperfection that she hated about herself. "You are sexy and beautiful just the way you are Piper. Why do you think I wanted to be in your life so dang badly," Jamie asked. "I'm not like other girls. I'm not the sexy tiny waist person," Piper said showing her vulnerability. "I want the whole dang package. I don't care about the outside stuff. I care about you. I want you," Jamie said as he leaned in to kiss her again. In the back of her mind, the doubt was festering like a pot about to boil over.

He devoured her lips, nibbling on one then switched to the other. Everything about her had Jamie hot, bothered and beyond the point of stopping. He didn't want to either. He wanted every inch of her wrapped around him. When they managed to come up for air, he peeled her jeans off, sliding them to the ground and kissed his way up her legs. "Jamie," Piper said. "Yes sexy woman of mine," he teased. "What are you up to," Piper asked. "Seducing my woman," he teased. He eased his way back up to her arms and she undid his jeans. "You alright," Jamie asked. Piper nodded. He leaned in and kissed her, kicking his jeans off and sliding his arms tight around her. "You sure," he asked as his hands slid to her backside. Piper nodded. "I'm sure," Piper replied. "Then why do you look scared," Jamie said. "I'm not. I just have a million things running through my head," Piper said. He kissed her. "I'm turning them off," Jamie teased. "Think so do you," Piper asked. He kissed her again, devouring her lips until he felt the goosebumps pop up again on her skin.

He slid the lacy nothings off of her and kicked his boxers to the floor. He leaned into her and it's like hormones took over from there. He made love to her and instead of hot and heavy, it was romance.

Her body curled around his and he lost himself in her. When he opened his eyes and looked into hers, they were almost a bright blue. Almost glowing. He kissed her again and his body gave into the heat. He had his arms so tight around her, he could feel the air go in and out of her lungs. He could feel her heart racing. He felt her fingernails almost dig into his shoulders. He was about to say the three words that every girl dreamt of but stopped himself. He knew that saying it before he really meant it wasn't right. He leaned into her, kissing her again and practically collapsed into her arms. Her legs slid around his hips and they entangled with his. "Piper," Jamie said as a finger lifted her face to meet his gaze. "Yes," Piper said. He kissed her. "You okay," he asked as he slid onto his side facing her. "I'm okay," Piper said. She had a smirk that was sexier than he could even explain. "I missed you today," he said. "I saw you this morning," Piper said. "Still missed you. I was thinking about you all dang day," Jamie said.

"And just what were you thinking about," Piper said. "Being alone without interruptions," Jamie said. "Oh really," Piper teased. "Just the reason why I plugged them in downstairs. No more interruptions and just us time. That's all I want," Jamie said. "You know that when I'm on the road it's gonna be harder to do that," Piper said. "That's why I wanted this tonight. Just you and me," Jamie said. "You're just intentionally being a sweetheart right now," Piper said. "This is how I feel. That's all," Jamie said. "Just promise me something," Piper said. "Which would be what sexy," Jamie asked as he pulled her closer. "Promise me that if you start feeling ignored or you're upset about something about this you tell me," Piper asked. "I know the industry Piper. I get that you're gonna be busy as all get out. Just remember that you need down time too. No phone downtime. I just wanna be there to spend it with you. To cheer you on from the side stage," Jamie said. Piper kissed him. "I love that, but I mean it. If something isn't right just tell me," Piper asked. He kissed her. "I'm not letting go. Not now," Jamie said. "And this is what made the difference," Piper teased. Jamie nodded. "The fact that you're worried about me walking out is what I wanted to hear. I get that you're working and you'll be insanely busy. I do. I've worked with artists that were recording on a dang tour bus," Jamie teased. "As long as you're sure," Piper replied. He smirked and leaned in for another kiss. Part of him wanted to just let go and scream those three words at the top of his lungs. The other part knew better. The silent side won out.

He curled up with her among the blankets. "You comfy," Jamie asked. Piper nodded. "How in the world did I get so dang lucky," Jamie asked. "Don't know. Might want to check for lucky charms," Piper teased. "I think I have one right here in my arms," Jamie teased. Piper shook her head and he snuggled her tight to him. "What am I gonna do with you," Piper asked. "I have a couple ideas," Jamie said as he yawned. "Did you set an alarm for the morning," Piper asked. Jamie nodded. "We'll be up in plenty of time," Jamie replied. Piper snuggled up to him and he leaned onto his back and Piper's head rested on his chest. Soon after, there was a quiet snore.

He was truly out cold. When she smirked and tried to get more comfortable, he held on like it was a knee jerk reaction.

Truthfully, Piper was happy that she'd finally found someone that accepted her the way she was. Only issue with it was, what would happen when the road got to be too much? She was determined to keep it out of her mind. She had to concentrate on the happy that she had at that moment. Just the fact that for one night, even if it was the only one, he accepted her the way she was. No telling her that she'd be prettier if she lost weight or she'd be more attractive if she got bigger breasts or a smaller nose or skinnier legs. He liked her the way she was, or at least he said he did.

The next morning, Piper woke up on her own side of the bed and Jamie gone from his side. She got up, cleaned up a bit, got dressed and ready to go and went downstairs to see Jamie's bag by the door. She walked into the kitchen and saw Jamie unplugging the phones and putting the cords into the case for his laptop. "What are you up to," Piper asked. "Made coffee and breakfast to go," Jamie said. "We have to go," Piper said. "You ready sexy," he asked. Piper nodded. He kissed her, handed her the orange juice, he locked up and turned his alarm on and they headed over to Piper's. When they got there, Harley was getting everything together. "What you up to," Piper asked. "Had to get a few things out of the fridge. The bus should be here any minute," Harley said.

Maybe 2 minutes later, the bus pulled up. They got their stuff loaded and Jamie took his bag and Piper's stuff to the stateroom. Everyone else started arriving and Piper grabbed a few last things from the house, locking it up and turning the alarm on. The officer at the gate let her know that they were gonna be there 24 hours a day until she got home. Piper nodded, thanked them and hopped on the bus. Jamie put the breakfast out for everyone and put the plates he'd made for Piper and himself aside. "Thank you for this," the band said. "Y'all are welcome. I had to use it up anyway. Since I'll be out with y'all for a bit, I figured that it would be appreciated," Jamie joked. "You can totally keep him around," Kurt joked. "I'll do my best y'all," Piper said. "So, how long do we have before we get there," Kyle asked. "13 hours," the driver said. "Damn," Jamie joked. "Which means sleep for a while and get settled. We can work on music around lunch," Piper suggested. "Good plan," the guys said. "I'm gonna sleep for a bit," Piper said. She headed to the stateroom with Jamie right behind her. She got settled, putting some of her stuff away. "You alright," Jamie asked. Piper nodded. "The nerves are kicking in now that it's all real," Piper said. "Jess meeting us," Jamie asked. Piper nodded. "She said she's gonna fly up tonight and meet us," Piper replied. She got everything where she wanted it and leaned onto the bed. "You sure you're okay," Jamie asked. Piper nodded. "I will be. I mean we have a ton of time to get used to it. We go from New York to Los Angeles for the first show. I have a few days where I can just relax a bit and do small stuff," Piper said.

"I got this week off. The whole week. I have to be back on the Monday for work I think, but I'm all yours," Jamie said. "Why did you get up so early," Piper asked. "I woke up at 4. Honestly, I had to pinch myself a couple times this morning. I thought I was still dreaming," Jamie joked. "So you aren't regretting last night," Piper asked. "Here's one thing I can't figure out. Why the heck would your manager be pushing you to go to the gym anyway," Jamie asked. "The stage show is demanding physically. She wants me to be able to do it without huffing and puffing. That's all," Piper said. "You sure that's all it is," he asked. "Meaning," Piper asked. "You're beautiful the way you are. You could be in shape for it just going for a walk every day or running. I just don't get why they'd want to change you," Jamie said. "Honestly, I wanted to get more fit anyway. Now I just have a reason to," Piper said. "You have to quit worrying that you're not skinny enough you know. I like the inside and the outside just the way it is," Jamie said. Piper smirked. "Well thank you," Piper replied. "You're not half-bad yourself either." "I mean it. So what if you don't fit in that stupid box they put women in. You make your own dang box that's 10 times better looking," Jamie teased. "A girl can get an over-inflated ego at the rate you're goin," Piper teased. "I mean it. You don't have to be a Carrie Underwood size to be on stage. You just be you. You are sexy as all get out to me," Jamie said. Piper kissed him. "I appreciate that," Piper said. "If that's the only reason why they're pushing you into having her as a trainer then tell them no," Jamie said. "Not gonna happen. I can see why they wanted me to do it. It does make me feel better and stronger," Piper said. "As long as it's because you want it," Jamie said.

Piper nodded and he snuggled her to him. They curled up together on the bed and within maybe 20 minutes, they were asleep. When Piper woke up maybe an hour later, Jamie was out cold with his arms tight around her. She slid out of his arms gently and went into the sitting area. "Hey," Harley said. "Hey yourself," Piper said as she grabbed herself a drink of water. "So, how are things goin," Harley asked quietly. "Good. Honestly, he's saying everything I could ever want him to say, but after the stupid stuff from my past I'm seriously finding it hard to believe that he's that good of a guy," Piper said. "He's trying. That's the difference. Like I said, he's a good egg. For once, you found a good one," Harley said. "One what," Keith asked. "Girl talk," Harley teased. "That Jamie guy is kinda cool. I mean, he brought breakfast," Keith joked. "And he brought bacon just the way I like it," Kurt said from his bunk. "Well since y'all like him so much," Piper joked.

"Seriously though," Harley said. "I agree with you. You know me though. See how things go and take it from there," Piper said. "Ever the doubter," Harley joked.

"Like you don't know why," Piper teased. They sat down, got the band into the sitting area and they closed the door to the bunks. They sat down and worked away on music. When Jamie woke up and heard Piper singing, he got a big ole grin ear to ear and just sat and listened. When they finished the part they were working on, he came in. "Now that is gonna make one heck of a song," Jamie said. "Well thank you," Harley teased. "So, where are we now," Jamie asked. "Just through North Carolina. We're stopping in a bit to refuel," the driver said. "And where would that be," Piper asked. "Yes we're by the water," the driver joked. "Perfect," Piper teased. They stopped for gas and were a quick walk away from the beach. They decided to stop and they all got out and went straight into the water.

Jamie grabbed Piper and dunked her into the water as they all splashed around while the bus was getting fueled up. Piper headed back to the beach and saw the driver. "Come on y'all. The bus is callin," Piper teased. They all headed back to the bus, hopped on and laughed as they headed back on the road. "And you thought bus life would be boring," Harley joked. They joked around and were laughing and working on music until they stopped for lunch. Piper got everything ordered and they sat down on the bus and relaxed. "This is quite literally the best burger I've ever had," Jamie said. "And it's not just because you were starved," Piper asked. "Nope. It's actually amazing," Jamie replied. Piper got a silly grin and the guys all agreed. Piper had her salad that she'd decided on and even it was amazing. The rest of the afternoon and into the early evening, they were working away on music and rehearsing what they had. They finally arrived a little after 6 and got checked into the hotel.

Piper and Jamie got to their room and the minute the door was closed, he picked her up, wrapped her legs around him and leaned her onto the massive bed. "What are you up to," Piper asked. "Nothin. Just glad we get a little alone time," Jamie teased. He kissed her, devouring her lips, and barely let her up for air. She looked in his eyes and he got a sexy little grin. "What," he asked. "What am I gonna do with you," Piper asked. He kissed her neck and his hands slid to her backside. "You get me all to yourself for an entire week. Whatever you wanna do," Jamie teased. Piper kissed him. Just as she did, there was a knock at the door. "Go figure," Jamie said. He got up and went to the door. "Hey Harley," Jamie said. "Hey yourself. We're heading down to grab dinner. Did y'all wanna come," Harley asked. "You mean you could hear my stomach from your room," Piper teased. "Girl, it's sonar. I hear your stomach growling from 2 floors away," Harley joked. Jamie smirked and they headed out with the rest of the band for dinner.

"And what time are we getting up tomorrow and don't you dare say 4," Kurt said. "We have to be there for sound check at 5:30 and we go on at 8. We have to go into hair and Harley and I have to go into makeup too. After that, we can chill at the hotel. We leave on Sunday morning," Piper said. "And where are y'all headed after that," Jamie asked. "LA then Seattle then whatever we have next on the tour dates," Piper joked. "The tour starts when," Jamie asked. "Thursday," Keith said. "Good. Then you have time to get some relaxation in before all of this," Jamie said. "Rehearsal and stuff then nights free maybe," Piper teased. "You'll be busy," Jamie teased. "So, since there's nobody else here to ask you, what are your intentions with our Piper," Keith asked. "Well, I think I'll keep her around for a long while. Kinda getting used to her," Jamie joked. "Oh really? And does that mean that you're thinking long-term," Kurt asked. "I don't even know, but honestly, yes," Jamie said. It hit Piper like a mack truck. "Really? News to me," Piper said. Jamie slid his hand in hers and held on. "And just what's that big future plan," Harley asked as she teased. "I don't know. I know I want to work my own hours," Jamie said. "And," Harley asked. "If you're asking if I'm planning to move out of Savannah, the answer is no," Jamie said. "Good," Harley teased. "Anything else y'all wanna ask," Jamie teased. "I have one question. What's with that guy Colt? The one that keeps causing trouble," Keith asked. "Not here," Piper said. "Then we're havin a party in your suite," Kurt joked. "Done," Piper said.

They finished dinner, paid for it and headed back to the hotel. Jamie got everyone a soda and they all sat down so Piper could update the band on what was going on. "And," Kurt asked. "Permanent restraining order. He left packages at the house that the police now have, he called and harassed until he got a response and even went as far as getting my friend's cell to contact me. It's a long-term restraining order. If he starts causing a fight then he's gonna end up in a jail cell," Piper said. "I don't get why though," Keith said. "He started a dang fight with Jamie. I wouldn't be surprised if he turned around and started another dang rumor. If he does, there's one hell of a kickback. Harley and I wrote a song to sort of musically kick his butt to the moon," Piper said. "What did he say to you," Keith asked. "He said that he was with Piper. I know he wasn't, but he was attempting to push buttons. He left that package and I wanted to kick his butt myself. I just want Piper safe. I know y'all can watch out for her if I'm back in Savannah at work," Jamie said. "That's what family is for," Kyle said. "Good," Jamie said. "I mean, you had me at crispy bacon this morning, but you're a good guy," Keith joked. "Well thanks," Jamie said.

They sat around and talked until almost 11 when Piper was starting to yawn. "I'm turnin in. We have to be up early y'all.

Go get some rest," Piper said. Everyone agreed and headed out. Jamie locked the door behind them and walked into the bedroom to see Piper washing her makeup off and changing into her pajamas. "You alright," Jamie asked. "I should've told them when it happened," Piper said. "Babe, it was hard for you period let alone tellin everyone. They didn't need to know what was in the box or anything else. Babe, you're alright. Nothing is gonna happen," Jamie said. "If Colt starts something I'm seriously gonna musically kick his backside to the dang moon," Piper said. "Then do it. Dedicate the song to him when you're back near home," Jamie said. "I was actually thinking about doing a show in Savannah. A one-off after the tour," Piper said. "Babe, just concentrate on one thing at a time," Jamie said. Piper kissed him. "Thank you," Piper said. He shook his head and slid his arms around her. "And what do you have to do for work," Piper asked. "Not a thing. Nothing," Jamie said. "So, you really got time completely off," Piper asked. Jamie nodded. "So, what do you wanna do," Piper said mid yawn. "You're goin to bed and I'm snuggling you to sleep," Jamie said. "Think so do you," Piper asked. He kissed her shoulder. Just get in bed," Jamie replied.

Piper grabbed her lotion and slid into the bed, opting to put her lotion on while she was on the bed. Besides the fact that it was one heck of a tease, he watched her like a hawk. When she was done, she slid under the covers and Jamie slid in with her, wrapping his arm around her and snuggled her to him. "What you want," Piper asked. "I'll give you a hint," he teased. He kissed her shoulder and snuggled her to him. "Piper," he said as she got goosebumps. "Yes," Piper replied. His hand slid to meet hers and their fingers entwined. "You sure you're okay with me staying," Jamie asked. Piper nodded. "Honestly, I'm kinda glad you are," Piper said. "Kinda," he asked. She turned to face him. "More than kinda," Piper said. He kissed her, devouring her lips and pulled her leg around his hip. "What," Piper asked. He kissed her again. "How in the world did I get this dang lucky," Jamie said. "Good question," Piper teased. He kissed her forehead and he snuggled her tight to him. "What," Piper asked. "Just thinking," Jamie said. Piper kissed him. "About what," Piper asked. "About you. About that question that your buddy asked," Jamie said. "Like what," Piper teased. "The one where Harley asked what my future plans were with you," Jamie replied. "Changing your answer," Piper asked. "Sorta," Jamie said. "And what's the new answer," Piper asked.

"I sorta think that we could work," Jamie said. "Sorta," Piper asked. "What do you think," Jamie asked. "I mean, it's not like we've known each other for years. It hasn't even been that long," Piper said. "But in a year," Jamie asked. "I don't know," Piper said. "Do you care about me," he asked. Piper nodded. "Of course," Piper said. "And if you got to that point where you said that L word," Jamie asked. "You're getting way too far ahead of yourself," Piper said. "But if it got that far," he asked. "I have no idea," Piper said. "If we got that far and we were in love, what would you do," Jamie asked. "We're not havin that conversation when it's been less than a month," Piper said. "Okay," Jamie said. "I know you're saying it because you don't want to fight about it, but if you want more then say it," Piper said. "I want more and I don't care how long it takes," Jamie replied. "Okay," Piper said. "What do you want," Jamie asked. "Other than sleep right now? I want someone who's my best friend and everything else. When and if that happens, then that next step happens. I would love to have kids and everything else, but not if he's not the right guy," Piper said. "And if it was me," Jamie asked. "Something specific that you're asking," Piper asked. "No," Jamie said. "I'd say we see how things go," Piper replied. She kissed him and he shook his head as his hand slid to her backside.

"I'm never gonna get a straight answer," Jamie joked. "For today, no," Piper said. "It's headin towards midnight," Jamie said. "Maybe tomorrow," Piper teased. "Piper," Jamie said. "If it's right then the sky's the limit," Piper said. "How many kids if you had a choice," Jamie asked. "Three," Piper said. "And big or little wedding," Jamie asked. "If I had to say it right now? Small. It'd end up huge though," Piper replied. "At least that's something," Jamie said. "Why are you talkin about all of that now, if you don't mind me asking," Piper asked. "Just seeing if we're thinking the same thing," Jamie replied. "You have a one-track mind about this stuff don't you," Piper asked. "Never did before we met," Jamie said. "We need sleep," Piper said. "Whatever else you wanna talk about, we do it tomorrow after the performance," Piper said. He nodded, kissed her neck and snuggled up to her. "Alright sexy," Jamie said. They relaxed and not long later, Piper was asleep in his arms. He kissed her neck and snuggled in tight to her.

The next morning, Piper did her workout, got showered and changed and packed and they all headed to do sound check. When they finished two run-throughs of the songs they were performing, Piper looked out and noticed the crowd starting to pack in. The nerves hit her. They headed off and they all went in to hair and makeup. Piper and Harley got changed and Jamie came in. "How you doing," Jamie asked. "Kinda hit me how crazy this is," Piper said. "You're all good. I promise you," Jamie said. "Do you see how many dang people are out there though," Piper asked. "You're fine. It just seems like more because it's daylight. That's all," Jamie said. Piper took a deep breath. "If I mess up," Piper said. "You're gonna be fine. I'm right beside you and they're behind you," Harley said. "Of course we are," Kurt said. "Like I said," Jamie said. Piper shook her head and tried to relax. "And I have breakfast organized since you said you didn't want to eat before the performance," Jamie said. "Thank you," Piper said. Jamie nodded and kissed her. "You got this," Jamie said. They finished doing hair and makeup and the stage tech said it was time. Jamie gave Piper a hug and headed to the outside stage.

They got to the side stage and Piper slid her earpieces in. When she got the cue, she headed onto the stage with the crowd going crazy. The song started and the crowd was singing along. It was one of those moments that only a big musician knows. She got everyone involved and the crowd was following everything. "One more," Piper asked at the end of the song. The crowd went crazy. "Y'all might remember this one. Somethin Good," Piper said. The crowd went nuts again and were singing along all over again. When they finished the song, the hosts came out to talk to her. "Wow. Pretty amazing right," the host asked. The crowd roared again. They asked a bunch of the usual questions then one she wasn't expecting at all. "So, a little bird told me that your new limited edition CD is out this week. I know that you are opening for our favorite Jason Wright. How many of y'all are going to that tour," the host asked as the crowd was almost screaming. "Well, all of you have wristbands. Look on the back of them. Five of y'all have a red heart on the back. Those five people come up this way," Piper said as 5 people came up on the stage, losing it completely. "Well aren't you guys lucky. They won pit tickets for the show in New York," the host said. They went nuts. The crowd even went nuts. "And for the rest of y'all who made it down here today, when you head out, each of you gets a free download of this next song on iTunes," Piper said. "And what's the name of this one," the host asked. "Found," Piper said. "Miss Piper, thank you so much for all of this today. One more song while we say goodbye for today," the host said as Piper gave her a quick hug. "This is Found," the host said. Piper got going with the song and everyone was singing along again. As soon as they were finished, Piper brought the winners out to get a few pictures and give out a few autographs. The rest of the band came out and got pictures together and signed an autograph or two and then they headed off.

Jamie slid his hand in Piper's and walked back into the studio to talk to the hosts and thank them. They finally headed off to the tour bus not long later and Piper and Jamie had their breakfast. "I have extra bacon and stuff for y'all just in case," Jamie said. "Keep this one around. I think I like him," Kurt joked. "Funny. I'm taken though," Jamie teased. "I bet," Harley teased. "And where we heading now," Keith asked. "Two radio interviews and then we get on the road to LA," Piper said. Jamie gave her a hug. "So, where we headed now," Jamie asked. "Radio station number one," Piper teased. Jamie smirked. They headed in not long later to the first station, then the second. When they finally finished, they hopped on the bus and Char messaged Piper. "We have two more but we can do them on the bus," Piper replied. "Done," Harley joked. Piper went to the stateroom with Jamie and called into the first one.

Question after question and there was no surprise at all. It wasn't until they asked whether a new love interest had inspired the music that she looked at Jamie. "Well, you could say that," Piper said. That was all she was gonna say and stuck to that. Even after the second one, she still wasn't about to divulge a darn thing. They finally finished just as they were stopping for lunch. "Not a single word," Jamie asked. Piper shook her head. "I'm not saying anything until we're at that level. When we're at an awards ceremony or something we can do all of that. I'm not gonna do it on a radio show or during a TV performance," Piper said. "You sure that's the only reason why," Jamie asked. "Quit thinkin it. It's not what you think," Piper said. "As long as you aren't trying to hide all of this," Jamie said. Piper shook her head. The bus stopped and everyone hopped off to get lunch. Harley knocked. "Do you want me to grab y'all lunch," Harley asked. Jamie looked. "Yes please," Piper said. "Just text me," Harley replied. Piper did just that.

"I'm not trying to hide anything. I just don't think that broadcasting it to everyone this soon is a good idea. It's not that I don't care and I don't want you around. I do want you here. I don't want you being stalked and getting questioned," Jamie said. "Then just say it," Jamie said. "No. I want my private life private for a while. Things are just getting crazy busy. When the tour starts, we can do something. I'm gonna have to say it anyway, but this way it's our choice," Piper said. "You sure," Jamie asked. Piper nodded. "Are you alright with it," Piper asked. Jamie nodded. "I get why you want to keep it quiet. I just don't wanna play the secret," Jamie said. Piper kissed him. "You aren't," Piper said. He looked at her. "And," he asked. "And you aren't gonna be. I just don't want it broadcasted on TV yet. I want us to have alone time," Piper said. He looked at her. "As long as you're sure," Jamie said. She nodded. "I'm sure," Piper said. He pulled her into his arms and kissed her. "You know that I'm not letting you change your mind," Jamie said. "Oh I know," Piper teased.

Harley went and got lunch and drinks for Jamie and Piper, putting them in the microwave and went and sat back outside with the guys. "What's up with Jamie and Piper," the guys asked. "They needed to talk alone," Harley said. "About what," Keith asked. "About relationship stuff," Piper said as she came out of the stateroom with Jamie. "We're heading off in 10 if you wanted to grab anything," the driver said. "Gimme 5," Piper said. She went in and grabbed a soda and a few snacks for the bus and came back on. Jamie was hanging out on the sofa with Kurt and Keith. Harley was heading back from her bunk. "And what's wrong," Piper asked. "Nothin," Kurt said. Piper shook her head. She grabbed her lunch, walked back to the stateroom and closed the door behind her. She had her lunch in peace and worked on lyrics. She just wanted one dang afternoon without the drama.

When the bus stopped to gas up, Jamie came down the hall and knocked at the door. Piper ignored it. It was like everyone on the bus was talking about her behind her back. Like she was that bullied girl in high school again. She finished working on the song she'd been picking away at and Harley came down the hall, knocked and came inside the stateroom. "You alright," Harley asked. "You wanna tell me what the quiet stuff was goin on," Piper asked. "He mentioned something to the guys and when you came in, they were just in the middle of talkin about it," Harley said. "And," Piper asked. "I overheard it," Harley said. "And what was the topic," Piper asked. "Can we just say that he'll tell you when he's ready," Harley asked. "Who's side are you on," Piper asked. "Piper, I'm on your side but you don't wanna hear it from me," Harley said. "Bad," Piper asked. "Girl, if it was bad he'd be under the bus," Harley said. Piper looked at her. "Piper, you're fine." "Still don't like it," Piper said. "You need to talk to him," Harley said. Piper shook her head. "We're stopping for dinner soon. Come on." "I'm fine," Piper said. "We're stopping at an actual restaurant. Are you good with pasta or something," Harley asked. "Just let me know where we stop," Piper replied. "Do you have a choice," Harley asked. "Steak or seafood," Piper said. "It's either that or we do barbecue," Harley said. "Just let me know," Piper said. Harley gave her a hug.

Harley closed the door and went down the hall to see Jamie on the extra bunk. "You alright," Harley asked. "She mad at me," Jamie asked. "She wants to know what you were talkin about," Harley said. "You didn't tell her right," Jamie asked. Harley shook her head. "I promised," Harley said. Jamie shook his head. "Something tells me that I'm not sleepin in there tonight," Jamie said. "Just go and talk to her instead of world war three," Harley said. She went and sat down on the sofa and the driver got her attention. "What's up," Harley asked. "There's a barbecue place that's just up here a little bit. I can get us up there but it's straight out barbecue," the driver said. "Sounds good to me. We have salad stuff if Piper wants it," Harley said. "Alright," the driver said. Harley went back to the bunks. "We're stopping at barbecue. Are y'all good with it," Harley asked. They all agreed. Jamie looked at Harley and she motioned towards talking to Piper. Jamie shook his head.

Harley texted Piper that they were stopping for barbecue. Piper thanked her and didn't come out of the stateroom. When they stopped a while later, the band hopped off to get dinner and Jamie got something for himself and Piper. He hopped back on the bus a little while later. He walked to the stateroom and knocked. "Babe, are you eating or what," Jamie asked. "I'm coming," Piper said. She opened the door and Jamie handed her a plate. "Thanks," Piper said. "Can we talk," Jamie asked. "Nope. Dinner then I'm getting some work in," Piper said. She headed outside with Jamie and sat down with everyone, having their dinner together. Jamie sat down beside her and the closer he got, the more annoyed Piper was. They all finished and Piper got leftovers for the next day of driving. She put them in the fridge and opened the wine, pouring a glass for herself. "Anyone else," Piper asked. Jamie nodded, got up and got a glass for himself and for Harley. "I'm turnin in. Night y'all," Piper said. "We should be stopping around midnight," the driver said. "You good in that extra bunk," Piper asked. "It's either that or we stop at the truck stop," the driver said. "Totally up to you. I'm even good with a hotel for now," Piper said. "Truck stop it is," the driver said. Piper headed back to the stateroom and Jamie stopped her.

"What would you like," Piper asked. "We're talking," Jamie said. "Pass," Piper said. She stepped over his leg and went into the stateroom. She was just about to close the door when Jamie came in. He closed the door behind him and Piper sat down. "What," she asked. "We're talkin. No more silent treatment. We're on a dang bus," Jamie said quietly. "And? You're the one that started whatever that was," Piper said. "You wanna know what we were talking about then just ask," Jamie said. "And," Piper asked. "We were talking about what the plan is future wise," Jamie said. "What, about your plan," Piper asked. "They wanted to know if I was thinkin about going ring shopping," Jamie said. "And," Piper asked. "I'm not about to lie," Jamie said. "You're getting way too dang far ahead of yourself," Piper said. "What do you want me to say," Jamie asked. "You need to stop Jamie. Stop pushing too far ahead. Just stop," Piper said. "You don't want me here now," Jamie asked. "Not if that's what you're putting in their heads," Piper said.

"Breathe," Jamie said. "What," Piper asked. "We were just talking hypothetical," Jamie said. "Just stop Jamie. If that's why you're here then you might as well go home," Piper said. "Woman, quit being so dang stubborn and let it freakin go," Jamie said. "You're seriously starting…" He kissed her, pulling her into his arms. "I'm telling you that I care about you and I wanna be with you. That's what I'm doing so quit with world war three," Jamie said. "Then don't even bring it up," Piper said. "Fine," Jamie said. "We done the fight?" Piper shook her head. "Stop causing one," Piper said. He shook his head and pulled her to him, devouring her lips. He leaned her onto the bed. "Quit. I get you're mad or upset or whatever. You can't keep flipping out and being mad. It's not like they don't see it," Jamie said. "I just don't want any stress about any of it," Piper said. "Then stop having a hissy fit and relax," Jamie said. "I'm tired and I need a decent night of sleep in a real bed," Piper said. Jamie kissed her. "Then put pajamas on and we go to bed," Jamie said. "Fine," Piper said. She got changed and went and washed her makeup off. "We're stopping at the truck stop in about an hour or two. Everyone good," the driver asked. "Thank you," Piper said. "Most welcome miss Piper," the driver said. She went back into the stateroom and Jamie had her phone in his hand.

"What's wrong," Piper asked. "Just putting your phone on the charger with mine," Jamie said. Piper kissed him. "Thank you," Piper said. He kissed her. "Now get in here and come get some sleep," Jamie said. Piper nodded, slid into the bed and flipped the light off. His arm pulled Piper to him and he snuggled her. "We alright," Jamie asked. Piper nodded and he turned her towards him. "What," Piper asked. He kissed her, devouring her lips. "No more fights. You get mad then we talk about it right then and there," Jamie said. Piper nodded. He leaned in and kissed her again and was about to make his move when Harley knocked at the door. "Yep," Piper said. "We're stopping in a bit. Do you need anything," Harley asked. "Nope. If you need something take one of the guys with you," Piper said. "I will girl. You two get some sleep," Harley joked. "Am I allowed to say that I'm glad there's a lock," he teased. Piper shook her head. "Bad," Piper teased. He kissed her and curled her practically into his arms. He slid her leg around him and devoured her lips. "What are you up to," Piper asked. "Taking advantage of the fact that it's 90% sound proof," Jamie teased as she got goosebumps. "Sleep," Piper said. He shook his head and she felt her pajamas slide up her torso. "Jamie," Piper said. He kissed her again and he slid her to her back and leaned into her arms.

His hands slid to the base of her back and she felt the weight of him against her. He kissed her and she slid her arms around him. "You alright," he asked. Piper nodded. He devoured her lips again and the kiss felt like it went on forever. When they were in the thralls of it, three words came out of his mouth that she wasn't expecting. "I want you," Jamie said as they kept going. Just as his body gave into her, he said them. The three words that Piper knew were coming. "I love you Piper," Jamie said as they kept going. When both of them collapsed and were catching their breath, he still hadn't moved from that spot. He leaned in for another kiss. "What did you just say," Piper asked. "What do you mean," Jamie asked. "Don't you even. Say it," Piper said as she was catching her breath. "The I love you thing," Jamie asked. "And where did that come from," Piper asked. He slid to his side and looked at her. "Was kinda thinkin about it today. I don't want to be without you," Jamie said. "And you waited until now," Piper asked. He kissed her. "I wasn't about to say it when we were in the middle of a fight," Jamie teased. Piper shook her head and kissed him. "We need sleep. We can talk about it in the morning," Piper said. "We're talking before or after working out," Jamie asked. "Before since we're on a bus," Piper teased. Jamie kissed her and they curled up together. Piper slid Jamie's t-shirt on and they curled up in bed as they both fell asleep.

Piper got up the next morning, seeing Jamie's arms still tight around her. "Where you goin," Jamie asked as he half-opened his eyes. "Food," Piper said. She knew they were back on the road. She could feel the bus moving. "Just stay," Jamie said. Piper shook her head. She slid her workout shorts on and came through the bunk area quietly and went and talked to the driver. "How many hours so we have left," Piper asked. "The other driver is coming so we can do straight through. The two of us are taking turns. We have about 30 hours left to drive," the driver said. "Alright," Piper said. "We're stopping for gas in about an hour," the driver said. "Much appreciated," Piper said. She went and brushed her hair and freshened up and sat down on the sofa. Jamie came out a few minutes later in joggers and a t-shirt. "What's up," Piper asked. "How we doin," Jamie asked. "They're driving straight through tonight. 30 hours left," Piper said. "So, we'll be there by tomorrow," Jamie said. Piper nodded. He handed her phone to her and sat down with her. Piper got up and closed the door to the bunks very quietly. "Hungry," Jamie asked. "I'll make something," Piper said. Piper made something and took some up to the driver. "Thank you Miss Piper," the driver said. "If anyone needs it, you do," Piper said. She came back, made something for herself and Jamie, including the bacon, and handed it to Jamie. She made coffee, pouring the three of them a cup and sat down with Jamie.

Chapter 9

"Well thank you beautiful," Jamie said. "You're most welcome," Piper said. "You feeling better," Jamie asked. "You mean since we slept a full 8 hours," Piper teased. "Do you," he asked. Piper nodded. "A little," Piper said. He kissed her. "Come and sit. We have all the time in the world," Jamie said. They had breakfast together and were just finishing her coffee when she heard movement in the bunk area. She smirked and put another pot of coffee on for Harley and the guys. When Harley came out, she barely said two words. "Coffee is on already for you. Juice is in the fridge. Bacon is in the microwave," Piper said. Piper nodded, got some food and her massive mug of coffee. She sat down on the chair, had her coffee in silence and didn't say a word until she'd had the last drop. "Thank you," Harley said. "You're most welcome," Piper said as Jamie's arms wrapped around Piper. "I guess you two made up," Harley joked. "Did our best," Jamie said. "How much longer are we on the bus," Harley asked. "Probably about 29 or so," Piper replied. "Those guys were up doin shots last night. I'm surprised if they even wake up," Harley teased.

"It's called road life," Jamie joked. "I'll pass," Harley joked. "Now that we're all workin on a full night of sleep, we can get going on actual music today. Gives us something to do," Piper said. Harley yawned and Piper shook her head. "Found out why the divorce was so dang quick," Harley said. "Girl, quit torturing yourself," Jamie said. "He got someone else pregnant," Harley said. "You alright," Piper asked. "Now he can make her miserable instead of me," Harley said. "You alright though," Jamie asked. Harley nodded. "I will be. Put it into some new music right," Harley asked. "Exactly," Piper said. "Once those guys wake up, I'm gonna wok on music. I just don't want to wake their butts up," Harley said. "So, what are we up to today," Jamie asked. "Lyrics, music, rehearsing and whatever else we have to do," Piper said. "So, you're alright if I go through emails and stuff," Jamie asked. Piper nodded. "Go for it," Piper said. She cleaned up and the guys came in one by one. "Coffee is in the pot and bacon is in the microwave," Piper said. "Thank you," the guys said as they sat down. "Most welcome. I'm going to get changed and chill. When y'all are awake let me know," Piper joked. She went back to the stateroom with Jamie and the minute the door was closed, he locked it and leaned her onto the bed.

"What are you up to," Piper asked. "Romancing my woman," Jamie said. "Oh really," Piper said. He leaned into her arms, devouring her lips. "Yep," he teased. "You realize that they're all awake," Piper said. He smirked. "And," he asked. "I have to get work done," Piper said. "And so do I, but we have time," Jamie said. Piper shook her head. He kissed her and slid his shirt off of her. "My favorite shirt," Jamie said. "Oh really," Piper said. He nodded. "Mine," he said. Piper shook her head. "I'm still getting ready to work," Piper said. He kissed her and peeled her shorts off. "I have to get work done," Piper said. He kissed her, locking the door, and slid his joggers off. "You are so totally getting ahead of yourself," Piper said. He leaned into her arms, devoured her lips and wrapped her legs around him until they were making love all over again. This time it was hotter, more intense and it was like they completely forgot where they were. They were quiet, but they were so much hotter. He devoured her lips until neither one of them had an ounce of energy left.

When they were done, they were curled up together under the blanket. "What are you up to," Piper asked. "Reminding you why you deserve to have someone that wants you around," Jamie said. "Oh really? Trying to make you irreplaceable," Piper joked. "Yep," Jamie said. "You're growin on me," Piper teased. He kissed her, devouring her lips again. "I don't wanna go home next week," Jamie said. "I know. I'm

164

gonna be goin back," Piper said. "Still gonna miss the heck out of you," Jamie said. "So, you meant that I love you thing," Piper asked. "I never would've said it if I didn't. Never," Jamie said. "As long as you're sure," Piper said. "Would you quit doubting everyone," Jamie said. "You can't blame me. I mean look at you and look at me. Not exactly the most likely pair," Piper replied. He kissed her. "You're beautiful the way you are and you know it," Jamie said. "Jamie," Piper said. He kissed her again and curled her into his arms. "Jamie," Piper said. "Don't even doubt it. You have me and I'm not going anywhere. You have to stop thinking that you aren't enough," Jamie said. "I just…" "Stop. If I didn't want every inch of you the way you are I wouldn't be here. I never would've even approached you. Size 2 or not, I want you. All of you," Jamie said. "And," Piper asked. "And no matter what, I'm not about to change my mind," Jamie said. "You quite finished," Piper teased. He kissed her. "Now I am," he teased.

Not long later, they got showered and dressed and Piper went and sat with the guys. She got going on some music while Jamie checked his emails for work. They kept going until they had one song completely finished and Jamie came in. "What's up," Keith said. "I have to be back on Saturday. Like Saturday coming," Jamie said. "We'll be back the Monday anyway," Keith said. "Alright," Jamie said. "Where's the show that Saturday," Harley asked. Piper grabbed the list. "Nashville I think," Piper said. "Good," Jamie said. "And why's that good," Piper teased. "Because I can drive up after I finish and come to the show," Jamie said. Piper shook her head. "And if we decided to go honky-tonkin in Nashville instead of comin home," Piper joked. "Then I'd throw you in the truck and drive you back," Jamie teased. "Good to know," Piper teased. Jamie kissed her and went to go through the rest of his emails. They stopped for gas and Piper hopped off to get some fresh air. "So, how much longer do we have," Keith asked the driver. "Another day on the road. We're picking up the other driver when we stop tonight," the driver said.

Keith and Kurt got lunch for everyone and Piper and Jamie just stretched out a bit. "You alright," Jamie asked. Piper nodded. "Just anxious to get there. I just wanted to get off the bus and away from the guys for a while," Piper said. "You sure you're alright," Jamie asked. Piper nodded. "I am. Believe it or not, I actually miss the gym," Piper teased. "Are you really that nervous about how you look," Jamie asked. "I'm gonna be on stage with a ton of people watching me. That's why. I don't wanna be the 300 pound musician," Piper said. "You're far from that," Jamie said. "I know, but believe it or not, I feel like I am sometimes," Piper said. "Those fans love you because of who you are not because of how you look," Jamie said. "I appreciate the compliment, but they are looking at my weight," Piper said. He kissed her. "Well, if you ask me, you're gorgeous inside and out," Jamie said. He kissed her and Piper shook her head. "You keep complimenting me like that I'm not gonna fit my ego onto that bus," Piper teased. He smirked. "Just remember what I said. That's all," Jamie said. "I appreciate that handsome," Piper said. "Y'all ready," the driver asked. Piper nodded.

They hopped onto the bus and finished out the rest of the drive for the day. When they got to the hotel, Piper and Jamie went to the gym while everyone else called their families and figured out dinner plans. As soon as they were done, they headed upstairs while Jamie called in their room service order. "We can go out," Piper said. Jamie shook his head. Piper took his phone and hung up. "We're goin out. We're stuck on a bus for 3 days, then we're goin out in public for diner," Piper said. "Alright," Jamie said. They got upstairs, they got showered and changed and got ready to head out for dinner. They reserved a table and went to head out. "Where y'all headed," Harley asked. "Dinner. I made the reservation for 3. You ready," Jamie asked. "5 minutes," Harley said. She got changed and came out to meet them by the elevator. Piper knew he had wanted it to be just the two of them, but also knew that not including Harley would mean hell on the bus.

They got to the restaurant and were seated in the quiet corner, away from prying eyes. Considering that they could walk to it, it was a pretty nice restaurant. They sat around and talked and had a quiet dinner before a fan caught sight of Piper in the corner of her eye. She looked over and saw Piper looking over. When the fan walked over towards them, Jamie almost laughed. "Totally called it," he joked. "Miss Piper, can you sign this for me," the fan asked. "Definitely," Piper said. She signed the autograph and the fan got a picture of Piper, Jamie and Harley with her. "Thank you," the fan said. "Most welcome. Don't forget to tag me in it," Piper said. The fan headed back to her table and Jamie almost laughed. "So much for that whole keeping your private life private," Jamie teased. "Was gonna happen sooner or later," Piper joked.

"I'm gonna ask you something and you can't laugh," Harley asked. "Yes I have single guy buddies and yes I'll bring them to a show so you can meet them," Jamie said. "Thank you," Harley replied. "And one of them works at the studio. He's a producer too," Jamie replied. "As long as he's a good guy," Piper said as Jamie's arm slid around Piper's shoulders. "Would ever even think of setting her up with a bad guy," Jamie said. "Picture," Harley asked. Jamie grabbed his phone and pulled up a picture of his buddy Carter. He showed Harley and her jaw dropped. "Damn," Harley said. "I'll call him tonight and tell him to call you," Jamie said as he texted Carter. "Damn. Well, alright then," Harley said. "Keeps your mind on good stuff," Piper said. When Harley heard the swoosh of the email sending, her heart was racing.

They paid for dinner and headed back to the hotel. When they got back, Jamie's phone buzzed with a text from Carter:

She's pretty dang sexy dude. Can't wait to meet her.

Jamie got a silly grin and showed Harley. "Meaning you're on for that date," Jamie said. "Dang. Way to go Jamie. You officially have a second job," Harley teased. "Well thank you but you haven't met him yet," Jamie teased. "I trust you," Harley said. "Alright then. Don't be surprised if your phone rings tonight," Jamie said. Harley nodded. Piper and Jamie headed into their room and Harley headed into hers as her cell rang. Needless to say, she spent the next 2 hours talking to Carter.

The door to the room closed and Piper went and got changed into pajamas. Jamie got changed and they curled up together on the bed. "You alright with her goin out with Carter," Jamie asked. "Who is he," Piper asked. "He's been single for a year or two. He wasn't gonna waist time on just anyone. He was there when we met," Jamie said. "Oh really," Piper joked. "He told me to go for it. I listened to his crazy butt and met this sexy woman I know," he joked. Piper kissed him and her phone buzzed. She looked and answered.

"Hey mom," Piper said. "And what are y'all up to," her mom asked. "Just chillin for a while before bed. Two days on a bus is getting to be too much," Piper said. "And the first show is Los Angeles right," her mom asked. "Yep. First show of many," Piper said. "Dad and I are coming down to the show in Nashville. You alright with that," her mom asked. "If you want to come, you just have to ask. I can get the tickets," Piper said. "We can get them," her mom said. "Just come down around 3. I'll get security to get you the passes. You can watch from the side stage," Piper said. Jamie shook his head. Meeting her folks was something he was in no way ready for. "You sure," her mom asked. "I can whenever you want to

come," Piper said. "Then we'll see you Saturday next week,"
her mom said. "Love you guys. I'll get dinner organized too,"
Piper said. "We love you back. See you then," her mom said.
They hung up and Piper took a look at the schedule again.
"This Saturday coming is New Orleans. The Saturday after is
Nashville," Piper said. "And I'll be there for it," Jamie said.
"Alright. You do know that means you'll be meeting them
right," Piper asked. "I may have to do a shot or two," Jamie
joked. "Whatever you want handsome," Piper replied. Within
an hour or so, Jamie was almost out cold and Piper was
starting to fall asleep. She pulled the blanket over them and
managed to flip off the light without waking Jamie up.

The next morning, Piper woke up and went to the gym to get
another workout in before they left. When she made it back
upstairs, Jamie had everything packed except her clothes for
the bus and her toiletries. "Well good mornin to you too,"
Jamie joked as she kissed him. "Shower and I'll be ready to
go," Piper said. "We're leavin at 8. Breakfast is on it's way
up," he teased. "Oh really," Piper said. "Yep. We're having
breakfast just us," Jamie said. Piper shook her head. "Of
course," Piper said. He kissed her again, pulling her into his
arms. He handed her a smoothie that he'd made and she
went to hop in the shower. A few minutes later, Piper felt
hands wrap around her. She turned to face him and Jamie
kissed her. "Breakfast," Piper joked. "On the table waitin on
you," he said as he kissed her. "I swear you have a one-track
mind," Piper said. He devoured her lips and picked her up,
leaning her against the wall of the shower. "What," Piper
asked. "Tempting as all get out right now," he said. Piper
kissed him. "We need to shower," Piper said. He kissed her
and that hot steamy shower sex just got 50 times hotter. The
mirror was fogged from the shower. When they finally
managed to come up for air, he leaned her under the spray of
the shower and washed the conditioner from her hair.

"Before we end up makin everyone late," Piper said as she slid to her feet.

"I know," Jamie said. He kissed her and she washed his hair for him. "I'll meet you in the TV room," Piper said. Jamie nodded and kissed her again. She slid out and got semi dressed. She brushed out her hair and put it into a ponytail and went and sat down. Jamie came out a few minutes later in nothing but a towel and sat down with her to have breakfast. "Dang. You totally went overboard," Piper teased noticing all the food. "Open that other one," Jamie said with a silly smirk. She opened it and saw strawberries cut into hearts and a key in the middle. "And what's all of this," Piper asked. "So, when you come back, you can be over at my place whenever you want," Jamie said. "You sure you want that," Piper asked. "Nobody else is gonna be there other than my sister on very rare occasion," Jamie said. "This is insane. You know that this is too much," Piper said. "Just think about it," Jamie asked. Piper nodded. "Alright," Piper said. He kissed her, they finished up the breakfast, including the strawberries, and Piper got dressed while Jamie got dressed and shaved.

Maybe 5 minutes later, Harley knocked with her suitcase in hand. "You ready to go or what," Harley asked. "And how was y'alls conversation last night," Piper joked. "Good. Nice guy," Harley said with a big ole grin ear to ear. "And," Piper asked. "He's comin out to the show in Nashville. We're goin out when we get back home for a few days after that," Harley said. "Like I said, a good guy," Jamie said as he came in dressed, shaved and ready to go. "You do know I'm gonna get you to spill the details on him," Harley said. "Oh, I know. It'll give me somethin to do," Jamie joked. "Y'all ready or what," Piper asked. Jamie kissed her. "Let's go," Jamie said. Just as the words passed his lips, Piper's phone buzzed. The bus was waiting on them downstairs. They headed downstairs, making sure the guys were coming. They got on the bus and were on the road. "Did everyone have breakfast," Piper asked. "That place is amazing," Kurt said. "I'm glad y'all liked it," Piper said.

They got settled and got down to work, playing around with new music ideas. Piper worked from the stateroom and Harley pulled Jamie aside, grilling him about Carter. "I need to know that he's really a good guy and I'm not getting myself into a bad situation," Harley said. "Honestly, he's protective of women that he cares about. That I do know," Jamie said. "But he's a good guy though right? Like he doesn't throw punches or anything," Harley said. "I wouldn't have ever set you two up if he was that kind of guy," Jamie said. "He knows that I'm on tour with Piper right," Harley asked. "Harley, trust me when I tell you that he's accepting. I'm in the studio as much as y'all would be on the road and so is he. He toured with an artist that wanted to work on his CD while he was on the road. He gets it. Also means that he'll want to come see you when you're on the road. I don't see that as bad when I want to be out here with Piper," Jamie replied. "As long as there's a spark," Harley said. "From what you're asking, I'm thinkin that you already found it," Jamie said. "Maybe. We'll see when I actually meet him," Harley said. "Just enjoy it. This is supposed to be the best part. The getting to know you part. Look how lucky I got," Jamie joked. "And you're only sayin that because I'm nearby," Piper replied. "Still true," Jamie teased.

Harley's phone buzzed and Jamie got up and went to sit with Piper. He grabbed his laptop and curled up on the bed with her. When his phone went off, Piper smirked and kept working on her music. He looked at his texts and then made a call. "Yep," Jamie said. "So, you're good. Saturday is covered. They're doing a pop up show. Monday definitely. I have weekends booked off and you finish at 3 on Fridays so you have time to get wherever you need to. You may have to

171

work the odd Sunday, but I can accommodate what you said you needed," the studio manager said. "Perfect. I appreciate it. Not this weekend but the following one I need off on the Thursday for the weekend," Jamie said. "No problem. I'll figure it out," the manager said. "See you when I get back," Jamie replied as he hung up. "And what was all of that," Piper asked. "We're good for this weekend and good for next weekend. All fixed. I can be out with y'all," Jamie said. "You still have work Jamie. I don't want you to put your life on hold to come on the road," Piper said. "It's not every weekend. I get it," Jamie said. "Seriously though," Piper said. "It's not gonna be every weekend. For the first couple weeks. It's not busy anyway," Jamie said. "You still have to be able to pay your bills," Piper teased. "Trust me. That's not a problem," Jamie replied. "You know you're gonna be spilling the secrets anyway so just say it now," Piper said.

"Babe, it's family stuff. It's not that big of a thing," Jamie said. "Talk," Piper said. "Let's leave it at enough to take care of me until I'm 150," Jamie said. "And," Piper asked. "I started a company that did really well and got bought out," Jamie said. "Now I have to drag it out of you," Piper teased. "Banking. That's all I'm saying," Jamie said. "So, you just do the music stuff for fun," Piper asked. Jamie nodded. "And that's only really part time. I have an office in New York that I go up to once in a while. I like working from home," Jamie said. "How many offices," Piper asked. "Three. Here, New York and Los Angeles," Jamie said. "Seriously," Piper asked. He nodded. "I go in to each one once or twice a month," Jamie said. "You were keeping it a secret why," Piper asked. He kissed her. "Because it doesn't matter," Jamie said. "You're killin me," Piper said. "It doesn't matter. Has nothing to do with you and me," Jamie said. "What am I gonna do with you," Piper asked.

Jamie slid her into his arms and kissed her. "Really make that much of a difference with us," he asked. "No, but knowing might've made me a little less apprehensive about you coming. I was worried that it was gonna interfere with work," Piper said. "Babe, I'll worry about my work. You just concentrate on the music," Jamie said. Piper kissed him. "I gather you're going into work when we're there," Piper asked. "When you're doin soundcheck. The rest of the time I'm right beside you," Jamie said. "Whatever you say," Piper joked. He kissed her. "I don't tell people because they start looking at me differently. That's all," Jamie said. "Your sister didn't exactly mention it either," Piper replied. "I asked her to keep it quiet. She loves to train people. She doesn't have to either, but she loves it. Like I love music," Jamie replied. Piper looked at him and he kissed her. "No more secrets," Piper said. "Want to hear the only other one," Jamie teased. "I swear if you're teasin intentionally," Piper joked. "We can be and go wherever the heck you want to. I just want you in my life," Jamie said. Piper kissed him. "Well, you can't get rid of me now," Piper joked. He kissed her and snuggled her to him. "Now it's your turn," Jamie said. "You know everything," Piper said. "You didn't just become a famous musician overnight," Jamie teased. "Not exactly famous, but it's getting there," Piper joked. "And," Jamie asked. "I was writing music when I first started. I have to perform to get a publishing contract," Piper said. "You sound amazing. Did you seriously even think about doubting yourself," Jamie asked. Piper nodded. "Always have," Piper replied.

He pulled her to him and they just sat and talked. When Harley knocked and heard them giggling, she had a big ole grin. "So, we're gonna be there in like 3 hours. The hotel has grocery delivery. Do y'all want anything," Harley asked. "Just fruit and milk," Piper said. "I'll get whatever you guys need. Does it have a kitchen," Jamie asked. "The suite y'all have does," Harley replied. "I'll handle it," Jamie replied. "Alright. We'll get a list. The other rooms only have regular fridges and stuff that is unless they upgrade it. Thanks Jamie," Harley said. "No problem," he replied. Piper looked at him. "You don't have to," Piper said. He nodded. "I have to go to the office anyway," Jamie said. She looked at him. "Seriously," Piper said. "And I'm getting some extra stuff," Jamie replied. "Just don't feel the need to overdo it alright," Piper asked. He kissed her. "I know sexy," Jamie teased.

They got organized and put all their stuff they'd need back into their bags. Just as they were about to bring their stuff into the sitting area to get ready for the hotel, he got a call and went and sat back in the stateroom. When the bus stopped, Piper wasn't about to interrupt his call. The bags went up to the suites and everyone was over the moon about the room upgrades. Jamie came out of the stateroom, slid her hand in his and they walked into the hotel and up to the suite. "Oh my goodness," Piper said. "I take it you like," Jamie asked. "Did you do this," Piper asked. Jamie nodded. "That way we all have the same pretty much. Everyone has their own kitchens," Jamie said. "This is too much," Piper said. "Points. I promise that's all it was," he said. "Jamie," Piper said. He kissed her. "It's taken care of," Jamie said. "Then I'm getting the groceries," Piper said. He shook his head. "Already ordered and they'll be here within maybe an hour," Jamie said. "You're doin too much," Piper said. He kissed her. "Stop worrying," Jamie said. Piper shook her head. "It's too much Jamie," she said. He picked her up and walked her into the bedroom and leaned her onto the bed. "You deserve this," he said. "You're not doing this at every hotel," Piper said. "Alright," he said. "Promise," Piper asked. He nodded and kissed her. "I promise," he replied.

They got settled and curled up together on the bed. Maybe 2 minutes later, just as they were getting comfortable, the groceries showed. Jamie put them away and came in with flowers for Piper. "What's all of this," Piper asked. "For you," he said as he put the vase with the flowers on the bedside table. "Thank you," Piper said as he leaned back into her arms and kissed her. "What am I gonna do with you," Piper asked. "Babe, don't worry about all of it. Just concentrate on work and stuff," Jamie said. "I'm not letting you spend all of this money when you don't have to," Piper said. "Babe, I promise you, it's alright," Jamie said. "No more after this alright," Piper said. He nodded and kissed her. His arms wrapped around her, sliding to her backside. Just as he was about to start undressing Piper and having his way with her, there was a knock at the door. "I am seriously considering a do not disturb sign," Jamie teased. Piper slid out of his arms and went to the door.

"Hey. We're heading down to rehearsal. Are you comin," Harley asked. "Two minutes," Piper said. Harley nodded with a little smirk. Harley went back down to her room and Piper walked back into the bedroom. "I know. I'll come with y'all then go into the office," Jamie said. Piper kissed him. "Just have to get changed." Piper slid into blue jeans and her sexy tee and Jamie slid into a suit. She almost caught herself drooling when she saw him. "What," Jamie asked. "Damn," Piper said. He walked over to her and kissed her. "And just think. All yours," he whispered as she got goosebumps.

The suit that was perfectly tailored to fit, the pants that showed off his sexy butt and the dress shirt just undone enough to be casual. He looked like he walked out of GQ magazine. "You ready beautiful," he asked. "Why do I feel underdressed," Piper joked. He kissed her and they headed out to the hall to meet everyone else to head to rehearsal. "What's with the suit," Keith asked. "Have to head into the office for a bit," Jamie said. "Office? I thought you worked at a recording studio," Keith said. "I do. That's sorta part-time," Jamie replied.

When they walked into the rehearsal space, Jason was waiting for them. "About time y'all got here," Jason said as he came over and gave Piper a hug. "We took the scenic route," Piper teased. "Jason, this is Jamie. Jamie, Jason," Piper said introducing them. "So, this is the infamous Jamie," Jason joked. "Nice to meet you," Jamie replied. "Dang. Alright. So, I came up with a couple ideas. At the end, we can do a duet. I picked one or two out and we can alternate at tour stops. Let me know which one you like," Jason said. He handed the two names to Piper and she shook her head. "Wow. I mean, they're both amazing. You sure you want those for the end," Piper asked. "Second or third from it. I always do that big one at the end," Jason said. "I guess we should run through them," Piper said. Jason nodded. Jamie sat down in the sofa to listen. They sat down on the edge of the stage and ran through them mic in hand. Jamie was in awe. "Both work," Jason said. "I totally agree," Jamie said. "Then you got yourself a deal," Piper teased. "Alright, I'm gonna get out of here so y'all can rehearse and stuff. Enjoy," Jason said as he gave Piper another quick hug goodbye. Piper grabbed her water and Jamie came over to her. "You goin to the office," Piper asked. Jamie nodded. "I'll be back at 6. I'll meet you guys at the hotel," Jamie said. Piper nodded. "Alright handsome," Piper said. He headed out and they got back to rehearsing.

"So, what does he mean office? That's kinda weird for someone who is just a producer. I mean what's with the suit," Harley asked. "He does the producing stuff for fun. I don't know everything else, but he's a good guy," Piper said. "I mean, they booked us in regular rooms and all of a sudden we're in half suites," Kurt said. "He said he got them upgraded," Piper said. "Girl, if he's the Georgia equivalent of Daddy Warbucks, I'm all in on you dating him," Keith joked. "Funny," Piper said.

"He makes you happy when you aren't being stubborn as all get out. He seems like a good guy," Kurt said. "Well thanks, but I didn't even know until today about the office stuff," Piper said. "That means you passed the test," Kyle joked. "Funny," Piper said. "He likes you. That I do know," Harley said. "Well, sorta more," Piper said. "He...he said that already," Harley asked. Piper nodded. "We sorta knew already. He told us he was thinking about future stuff," Kurt said. "We're supposed to be rehearsing. Can we just rehearse so we can go back to the hotel and chill," Piper said. "Fine, but if he starts going towards a big white wedding, you tell us," Keith said. "Just go get your guitar," Piper said.

They went back to rehearsing and did their staging. They had it down perfectly. They even rehearsed the new songs they'd written on the bus. When they were done, they even had those down just right. Piper looked at her phone and smirked. "What," Harley asked. "We have to get out of here before they kick us out," Piper teased. Keith smirked. "I wondered why my stomach was growling," Keith said. They got packed up and headed outside and headed back to the hotel. The guys stopped to go out for dinner and Harley opted to go to the hotel with Piper. "Carter is coming tonight. Is he working for Jamie or something," Harley asked. "I have no idea. I do know they're friends so I'd imagine maybe," Piper replied. "I'm goin to get changed then. If anything happens, I'll text you," Harley said. "Just be careful and don't do anything stupid," Piper teased. Harley nodded and they headed up the elevator. "I still can't believe that bomb he dropped on you," Harley said. "Wasn't exactly a bomb," Piper teased. Harley went into her suite and Piper went into hers.

She headed inside and looked into the master bath. She opted for the one thing she'd wanted while they were on the road. She slid out of her jeans and t-shirt and drew herself a hot bath. She slid in and closed her eyes for what felt like only

177

a moment. When she opened her eyes, Jamie was sliding in behind her. "Hey," Piper said as she leaned into his arms. "Hey yourself beautiful," Jamie said as his arms slid around her. "How was work," she asked. "Lots of paperwork. I have a meeting tomorrow that I can't miss. It's at 6. Should be done by 7:30. Means you sleep in," Jamie said. "Your sister is coming in," Piper said. "Then I'll find a way to wake you up so you're ready," he said. Piper shook her head. "Dirty mind," Piper joked. "That was the plan," Jamie joked. "And how was the rest of rehearsal?" "We even rehearsed the new ones we haven't recorded yet," Piper said. "So, you just have to go through the one with Jason and make sure everything else is all good," Jamie asked. Piper nodded. "I think we just have to go through the backdrops and stuff and then we're good. We start on Thursday," Piper said. "Meaning," he asked. "Two or three radio interviews tomorrow afternoon then Wednesday morning we perform on the morning show here. Then it's the last day before the madness. Jason and his wife just checked into the hotel. They're at the other end of the hall," Piper said.

His stomach grumbled and Piper got a silly grin. "Dinner," Piper asked. He nodded and kissed her. They slid out and he wrapped her up in a warm towel, wrapping one around his waist. "What did you want to do for dinner," Piper asked. "Already booked," he teased. He sent off a text. "What did you plan," Piper teased. "You'll see when it gets here," he joked. Piper went and slid into some silky lingerie, putting her hair up. "Damn," he said as he slid his jeans on. She put her lotion on and maybe 10 minutes later, dinner showed at the door for them complete with a white tablecloth and her wine perfectly chilled. "Jamie," Piper said. The waiter pulled out a chair for Piper and another for Jamie. They sat down together and the waiter headed out, leaving them to dinner. He slid the do not disturb onto the door. Jamie poured a glass of wine for Piper and another for himself and took the dome off the plates.

"Jamie," Piper said. "You said it was your favorite," he teased as she saw a bowl of she crab soup. "And that's just the appetizer," Jamie joked. Piper shook her head. They had their soup, then the steak and kale salad that she loved. "This was exactly what I wanted," Piper said. "Wait until you see dessert," he teased. "Jamie," Piper said. "We're sharing it," he joked. Piper shook her head and went to get up and clear the dishes. "What are you doin," Jamie asked. Piper kissed him. She cleared them, putting them into the kitchen and when she came back, the wine glasses were on the table with a plate of chocolate covered strawberries. "Jamie," Piper said. "Like I said, we're sharing it," he said. Piper kissed him and he pulled her into his lap. She straddled him and his arms wrapped tight around her, pulling her tight to him.

"I missed you," he said. "Oh really," Piper asked. He nodded and leaned in and kissed her. He devoured her lips until he was pawing at the silky lingerie. He slid it off and leaned her onto the sofa. She felt a soft blanket behind her and he devoured her lips. He kept going until he couldn't restrain himself. He undid the jeans and was about to kick them off when there was a knock at the door. Piper smirked. "Bed," she said. He nodded. Piper took the wine into the room and Jamie slid on a shirt and went and answered the door. "Long time no see," Piper heard from the bedroom. She went and grabbed a sundress she had and came into the TV room.

"You must be Piper," the man said. "Carter," Piper replied. The man nodded. "I was gonna go right over to see Harley, but I promised I'd stop in to see Jamie before I did," he said. "Nice to meet you," Piper said. "So, this is the lady you've been talking about," Carter said. "Now you get it," Jamie teased. "Definitely. She's beautiful," Carter said. "Well thank you," Piper replied. "Most welcome. I just wanted to let you know that the meeting was pushed to 7. They're not morning people like you," Carter joked. "I'll come over and get you before I go in then," Jamie said. "Sounds good. Y'all enjoy. I won't interrupt you anymore," Carter joked noticing that Jamie was obviously pawing at Piper. "Have fun tonight," Piper said. "I will. She sounds like an amazing lady," Carter said. "By the way, you make her cry anything but happy tears, I'm kickin your butt," Piper replied. Carter nodded. "I'll do my best," Carter joked. He headed out and Jamie locked the door, putting the night lock on and picked Piper up, walking back to the bedroom and devouring her lips all the way there.

He peeled her sundress off, throwing it on top of her suitcase and leaned her onto the bed. He threw the shirt on top of the suitcase and then leaned in to devour her lips again. "Jamie," Piper said. "Yes sexy," he said as he kicked his jeans to the floor. "I have to ask something and you can't get mad," Piper said. "Yes I work with him. He's the VP," Jamie said. "And I'd assume y'all are besties," Piper asked. He nodded as he kissed his way down her torso. "You sure he's a good guy," Piper asked. "Positive," he said. He kissed her hip and his phone buzzed. He worked his way up her torso and it went off again. "I'll…" He grabbed her hand and kissed her before she even suggested answering the phone. "I'm hating phones," he said when they came up for air. He slid her leg around his hip and leaned in, beyond hot and bothered. The sex was insane. Hot, nobody cares and nobody can hear us anyway sex that had every inch of her humming like a humming bird's wings. It's like every inch of her was on fire. They kept going until he all but collapsed into her arms. He wouldn't move. He didn't want to let go from that connection they had. Finally, still entangled, he rolled over, bringing her with him.

"What," Piper asked. "Is it bad that I want to turn the phone off when we're here," Jamie asked. "Nope. I almost feel the same way," Piper said. He snuggled her to him. "Now that you know all of the secrets, does it really even change anything," Jamie asked. Piper shook her head. "Not one bit. I still don't want you paying my way for stuff," Piper said. "One of the only dang women I've ever met that doesn't want the money," Jamie said. "It's nice to have, don't get me wrong. I just don't think it changes who you are," Piper said. "You're like the dang unicorn," Jamie said. "I'd like to think that," Piper teased. "To me you are," Jamie said. Piper kissed him. "And so are you," Piper said. He got up a little and handed her one of the glasses of wine. "Thank you handsome," Piper said. "Most welcome beautiful," Jamie said. "Tell me something? You could've had anyone you wanted," Piper said. "I wanted you. I want you. Nothing else to it," Jamie said. She kissed him and got up to get the strawberries. She came in and fed him one. "Damn," Jamie said. "Good," she asked. He nodded. They had strawberries and finished their glasses of wine and Jamie slid under the blankets. "Already," Piper joked. "Woman, get in here," he teased. She kissed him and slid under the blankets with him as he snuggled her to him. Needless to say, within maybe 5 minutes, Jamie was asleep. Piper grabbed her phone and noticed a text from Harley:

OMFG he's so much hotter in person. Did you figure out if he worked for Jamie?

Piper replied:

VP. Go have fun. I'm goin to bed. XX

Piper put the phone back on the charger beside Jamie's and saw another text come in:

I'll get it done. It'll be on your desk. See you there.

Piper ignored it, assuming it was probably just work then heard his phone buzz again:

I can come meet you in your suite

"Sleep," Jamie said. "Your phone woke me up," Piper replied. "Just my assistant," he said as he pulled her back to him. She closed her eyes and was out cold a few minutes later.

The next morning, Piper woke up and after freshening up, she left to go down to the gym. When she arrived, Jamie was cracking jokes with his sister. "Hey," Piper said as Jamie looked over. "Hey sexy," Jamie said. Piper kissed him and Jess was getting her workout organized. "You ready," Jess asked. Piper nodded. She did her workout and as soon as she was done, Jamie handed her a smoothie he'd had made at the bar. "Well thank you. So, when did you get in," Piper asked. "Last night around 11. I figured y'all needed sleep," Jess joked. "Well thanks for that. By the way, your bunk is nice and comfy," Jamie teased. "Of course," Jess joked. "Your room is alright right," Piper asked. "Beautiful. I even got a little yoga in. I really don't need that much room," Jess said. "It's only for a couple days anyway," Jamie said. "And what are you gonna be doin while Piper's workin," Jamie asked. "Either bugging you at the office or shopping. I have to do some meal plan stuff for my clients at home," Jess said. "And what exactly are you up to today," Jamie asked. "Nothing. Working on music, maybe shopping," Piper said. "Sounds like a fun day," Jamie joked. They all headed upstairs and Jamie put the order in for breakfast for himself and Piper and Jess just laughed. "What," Jamie teased. "Wrapped around her little finger," Jess joked. "Funny," Jamie said. They got upstairs and headed opposite directions to the rooms. "If you want to come shopping with me let me know Jess," Piper said. "Will do," Jess teased.

Chapter 10

They got into the suite and Jamie picked Piper up and walked her over to the bed. "What are you up to," Piper asked. He kissed her, devouring her lips. He leaned her onto it and leaned into her arms. "You have a meeting," Piper said. "Moved to 7:45," he said. "Jamie," Piper said. He kissed her again. "We have all the dang time in the world," Jamie said. "It's 6:30," Piper said. He kissed her again and peeled her shirt and sports bra off. Just as he was about to pull the shorts off, there was a knock at the door. He kissed her. "Stay right there," he said. He went and got the door, had the breakfast set up on the table and came back in to see Piper going into the bathroom filled with steam from the shower. "Damn," he said as he watched her disappear into the mist. He kicked his clothes off, locked the door to the suite and went into the shower right behind her. She rinsed out her shampoo and was just about to put the conditioner on when he came up behind her. "What happened to staying in bed," Jamie asked as his arms slid around her. "Wanted to shower and get ready," Piper teased. He turned her to face him and devoured her lips. He picked her up, leaning her against the wall of the shower and wrapping her legs around his hips. The sex was indescribable. So hot, it would've melted solid gold. So intense it made her forget completely where they were. He kept going until every ounce of energy was wiped out of her.

He finally slid her to her feet but refused to break the kiss. "Why do I get the feeling that you're up to something," Piper asked when they finally broke the kiss. He slid her under the hot water and she washed his hair for him. "Thank you," Jamie said. He rinsed the shampoo out and Piper kissed him, stepping out and wrapping herself in a warm towel. Her legs were still wobbly after the shower sex. She went and brushed out her hair then slid Jamie's t-shirt on. When he saw the shirt fall across her backside, he almost started drooling. "Dang," Jamie said. "Stop drooling. Come have breakfast," Piper said. He walked in wearing nothing but a towel. "Had to go taunting me didn't you," Jamie said. "I'm just having a chill day," Piper teased as she poured them each a mug of coffee. "And you're teasing. Plus you stole the shirt again," he joked. "And," Piper asked. "Don't make any plans for tonight. That's all I'm saying," Jamie said. "And why's that," Piper teased. "You'll see later," he joked. They had breakfast and their juice. "So, what are you gonna do today other than stealing my shirt," Jamie teased. "Go out shopping maybe. I have to do the radio interviews in maybe an hour. After that, nothin," Piper said. "Good. Then you'll need this," Jamie said as he got up and handed her an envelope. "Jamie," Piper said. "Just open it," he replied.

Piper opened the envelope and saw a credit card with her name on it. "And what's this," Piper asked. "So you can go shopping and have fun," Jamie said. "You realize I have my own right," Piper asked. "Just put it in your wallet," Jamie said. "I'm not using it," Piper said. He kissed her. "I know you won't. I still want you to go and have fun. Don't worry about anything else," Jamie said. "I'm not those other girls Jamie," Piper said. He kissed her. "I know. Just put it in your wallet," he said. Piper kissed him and nodded. "Alright," Piper said. They went and got dressed, finishing their coffee. Piper slid into the blue jeans and shirt that made Jamie drool. She was about to do her hair and makeup and Char called her.

"Hey," Piper said. "I'll be there around 1. That work," Char asked. "Sure. I'll see you when you get here," Piper replied. Jamie came over shirtless, in his dress pants and wearing the cologne that she loved. "And," Jamie asked as he kissed the back of her neck. "Have to do the radio stuff this afternoon with the band. Char is meeting me here at 1," Piper said. "Then you have time to shop a bit," he said as he kissed her shoulder. "You have meetings," Piper said. "Don't remind me," he teased. "It'll be fine," Piper said. "Just promise me that you'll call before the radio spot starts," he said. "I'll text," Piper teased. He nodded. "And tomorrow after the performance, you can show me the office," Piper said. "If that's what you want," he teased. Piper nodded. He leaned her chair back and kissed her.

"Now who's teasing," Piper said. He let her up and she finished doing her makeup then did her hair. When he came out with his suit jacket and shirt and tie on, she about drooled. She got up and walked over to him. "Hey handsome," Piper said. "Hey yourself," he said. "I'll call you," Piper said. He nodded. "Just promise me that you take security," Jamie said. Piper nodded. He leaned towards her and kissed her. "Let me know when you're on the way home," Piper said. He nodded. "I will," he said. "And if you're free for lunch," Piper said. "Then you can taunt me from across the table," he joked. Piper smirked and nodded. "Very true," she teased. "Tease," he joked. Piper kissed him, brushed her lipstick from his lips and walked him to the door. "I swear, if I come back and you're naked, you're so totally grounded," he teased. "Mental note. Taunt him when he's coming in from work," Piper said. "I'll be back as soon as I can. Promise," Jamie said. She walked him to the door and after another quick kiss, he headed out. Harley was just coming out of her room when he left and snuck into Piper's.

"Now you know you're spilling whatever it is," Harley said. "And good mornin to you too," Piper said. "What is goin on with you two? On the bus you were at each other's throats," Harley said. "We talked. I kept feeling like I was taking him away from his life," Piper said. "You mean now that you know he has money it's not that big of a deal," Harley asked. "Now that I know that I'm not tearing him away from things, it's a little easier. He's making his own schedule," Piper said. "It's about dang time," Harley said. "And how did the date go," Piper said. "First off, the man is hot. Really hot. When he took the dang jacket off, I was almost drooling. Plus, he's actually a really nice guy," Harley said. "That's good though right," Piper asked. "Too good. I mean, did you see him? He's too dang tempting," Harley said. "From what I heard, he's a good guy and he's an adult, not a kid in an adult body," Piper joked.

"That is true," Harley said. "And what did y'all end up doin last night," Piper asked. "Well, we kinda hung out and talked. We did dinner then headed back over and hung out in the suite," Harley said. "And he just left," Piper asked. "I walked him downstairs," Harley joked. "You are horrible. You said you weren't doing anything until you were ready and you were taking your time," Piper said. "Couldn't resist. One kiss and I was a dang puddle," Harley said. "Well, at least you know he's a good person. He wouldn't be around Jamie that close if he wasn't," Piper replied. "They're besties from what I heard," Harley said. "Good to know," Piper said. "Honestly, I really do like him. Like a lot. Like he slept on the dang sofa," Harley said. "Excuse me," Piper teased. "You heard me," Harley said. "The sofa? I mean, I know having restraint is one thing, but he really slept on the sofa," Piper asked. Harley nodded. "Dang," Piper replied. "I need something to wear tonight by the way. We need to hit a few shops," Harley said. "And what are y'all up to tonight," Piper asked. "Dinner and who knows what," Harley said. "Then let's go. We have to be back before Char gets here," Piper said. "She bringing the hair and makeup people," Harley asked. "Nope. We're on our own," Piper said.

They got Jess and they headed off to go shopping. Both Piper and Harley found a dress or two and a couple cute outfits and Jess got a few cute outfits. "And I heard someone had a date with Carter," Jess said. "He's a good guy," Harley said. "That he is. He always has been," Jess said. "Now I'm getting the details," Harley said. "I'm gonna wander around a little," Piper said. Just as she was about to step into the lingerie dressing room, her phone buzzed. She slid into something cute that she liked and looked at the phone:

Call me.

Piper picked up the phone and took a photo of her in the outfit and picked up the phone. "How's shoppin going," Jamie asked. "Not bad. Your sister's havin fun," Piper joked. "And where are you," Jamie asked. "Check your texts," Piper said as she sent the photo she'd taken. "You can't tease like that when I'm at work," Jamie said. "Should I get it," Piper asked. "On that card I gave you. Get a couple things," he teased. "I know that tone. What are you doin," Piper asked. "Locking the office door," he said.

Piper couldn't help but laugh. "Seriously," Piper asked. "You started it," Jamie teased. "And how's work really," Piper asked. "Long. 4 more meetings and then I'm all yours," Jamie said. "I don't even know when we're back," Piper said. "I may have one run a little late. If I'm not there when you get back then go do dinner with Harley," Jamie said. "I might. May just get something and bring it back," Piper said. "So, what else did you look at in that lingerie section," Jamie teased. Piper smirked. "Nothin yet," Piper said. "Piper," Jamie said. "Whatever I get, you'll see it later," Piper teased. "That a promise," he asked. Piper nodded. "Yep," Piper replied. "Alright. Go have fun and I'll see you tonight," Jamie said. "Okay handsome. You listening to the interview," Piper asked. "Of course. Even if I have to hide the earbuds," he joked. "See you tonight," Piper said as they hung up.

Piper finished in the lingerie section, complete with an extra bag. She headed off with Harley and Jess and they went off to the next shop then back to the hotel. "You ready for all of this today," Harley asked. "I'll have to be soon enough," Piper teased. "By the way, did you see that the photo from dinner went viral," Jess said. Jess handed her phone to Piper. It was all over the tv that she had a new man in her life. She also knew that meant that every interview was gonna include a million questions about her relationship with Jamie. She slid into what Char wanted her in and got started doing her hair. She touched up her makeup and freshened up. Maybe a half-hour later, Char showed. Harley was maybe 2 steps behind her. "Looking fantastic," Char said. "Thank you," Piper said. "Now, about this whole relationship thing that the press have their eyes on right now," Char said. "Gonna have to say it sooner or later," Piper said. "Just be prepared if they do ask. Did you mention it to Jamie," Char asked. Piper shook her head. "Guess I should," Piper said. "She can help me figure out what to wear," Harley said. Char went with Harley and Piper texted Jamie:

You still in a meeting?

Piper saw him replying:

Just going to head into another in 5. What's up?

Piper called him. "What's wrong," Jamie asked. "Remember that picture from the other night when we did dinner," Piper asked. "And," he asked. "Well, it's sorta gone viral. What do you want me to do about talking to the press about us," Piper asked. "Your choice. What did you want to do," Jamie asked. "Well, you're gonna have to listen and find out. I haven't exactly figured out how to say it," Piper said. "What do you want to say," Jamie asked. "No idea," Piper said. "You know how I feel. It's up to you beyond that," Jamie said. "Alright. Just wish me luck. I just don't want every interview turning into the Piper and Jamie show," Piper said. "You'll be fine. You always are," Jamie said. "Alright. Go to your meeting. I'll let you know how it goes," Piper said. "And I'm coming tomorrow morning. After that, we can do whatever you want," Jamie said. "Alright sexy. I'll see you tonight," Piper said. They hung up and Harley came back in. "You ready," Harley asked. Piper nodded. They left with the guys, knowing full well that she had to perform.

They arrived at interview number one and there were a bunch of fans waiting for autographs. Piper signed a few and headed inside, signing a few CD's while she waited. The guys went in and tuned their guitars and Piper looked at Harley who was tuning hers. "You got this," Harley said. Piper shook her head, took a gulp of her water and headed in. The earphones slid on and the interview started as soon as the song was over.

"We have to be the luckiest people in town because right this minute, we have the opening act for Jason Wright. We have Piper Adams in studio. Alright, well now we get to ask some of these fan questions that you've all been sending in," the DJ said. "Alright. Shoot," Piper said. "First question is Jay from Savannah. That's your hometown isn't it," the DJ asked. "One of my favorite places actually," Piper said. "Alright, so here's the question. After seeing your picture all over the internet, does this photo of you and a guy mean that you're together," the DJ asked. Piper took a look at it and saw Jamie's email on it. "Well, Jay in Savannah, yes he is. Pretty great guy too," Piper replied. "And tell us who the lucky guy is," the DJ asked. "He's a good guy. His name is Jamie," Piper said. "No last name," he asked. "Not unless he wants me to. Totally up to him," Piper joked. "Alright. I picked out a couple more then y'all get to hear why Piper's here. Question number two is from Mallory from New Orleans. She wants to know if you have a set list of your songs for the tour," the DJ said. "Well, we really don't. Every night we're switching the songs up. We're making it different every show for those big Jason fans that go to them all," Harley said. "About that set list. Is the new one on the list," the DJ asked. "Most definitely. One that

I know everyone will love," Piper said. "And what's this one," the DJ asked. "It's called Running from Sunset," Piper said. "You heard her y'all. This one live in studio – Running from Sunset," the DJ said as they started playing through the song.

When they finished, the lines were lighting up to ask Piper a question. "We are on the radio with the one and only Piper Adams. I have to ask, how does it feel opening for one of the biggest musicians of the year," the DJ asked. "Honestly, nerve racking. I am so dang nervous it's almost crazy. One thing I do know thought, is that none of us can wait for the show tonight. We're both over the moon," Piper said. "And is that special guy is going to be coming on tour with you," the DJ asked. "When he can," Piper replied. "And what does this special guy do," the DJ asked. "That's very private. We're leaving it at gainfully employed," Piper teased. "Okay. Two more questions and Piper is heading off. This one is a station question. Who has the tour that you'd love to be in next other than Jason," the DJ asked. "There's a bunch. Luke James, Mara Tyler, Big Town Love. Any of those. I've always been a big music fan," Piper said. "And the last question of the interview is from Emma in New York. She was the first winner of those tickets you gave away at the recording on the morning channel in New York. Firstly, she says thank you for giving her tickets to the show. Second, she wants to ask what inspired the Running from Sunset song," the DJ asked. "Every single girl has one of those moments where she doesn't want the night to end. That was based on one of those moments. When you meet a guy who is a gentleman and even lets you take things at your own pace, that's when you start wishing that time would slow down," Piper said. "And what's the next song that you brought for us," the DJ asked. "The one that everyone loved from the TV performance. This one is called Found," Piper said as the DJ pressed play on the song.

"That was absolutely amazing. Thank you so much for coming in to do all of this. I really appreciate this," the DJ said. "You're most welcome. Thank you for having me," Piper said. "We're doing one last goodbye and then you can head off," the DJ asked. "Definitely," Piper replied. They came back on the air. "Alright, so that's the newest two songs from Piper Adams. Who's ready for the giveaway time? The first 2 callers get an autographed copy of her brand new CD. For now, we hate to do it, but a quick goodbye to Piper Adams for coming down today. Thank you again Piper. It has been a blast," the DJ said. "And for all of y'all who are comin down to the show tomorrow night, see you there," Piper said. They put another one of Piper's songs on and after a quick photo with the DJ's she headed out with the band and off to the next interview.

She texted Jamie as soon as they got in the SUV to go to the next station. Her phone rang two seconds later. "Seriously planned that one didn't you," Piper asked. "Wanted to see what you'd say," Jamie joked. "You're grounded you know," Piper said. "I bet," Jamie joked. "What are you up to," Piper asked. "I swear I didn't do it there too," Jamie said. "You better not," Piper teased. "I'll let you know when I'm back. Another freaking fire to put out in the office," Jamie said. "Alright handsome. No more tricks," Piper teased. "And I love you back," Jamie joked. "See you tonight," Piper said as they hung up. They made their way to the next interview and headed straight into the studio. "And we have the one and the only Piper Adams in studio right now. Welcome Piper," the DJ said. "Well thank you," Piper replied. "Miss Piper is going to be rocking the Jason Wright show tomorrow night at the stadium. For all of you who don't have tickets, why don't you? For all of you that do, you have one heck of a show to look forward to. We'll get right into it. What do you have in store for the fans tomorrow night," the DJ asked. "Well, we have a ton of new music to share and of course Jason is going to blow everyone's minds. It'll be unmissable," Piper said.

She went through question after question, a live song or two and then came down to the fan questions. Piper almost laughed. "Alright, shoot," Piper said. "Single or dating," the DJ asked. "Dating," Piper said. "Not the answer we were expecting. Alright. Favorite Jason song?" "Deer in the Headlights," she said. "Unexpected. Favorite City," the DJ asked. "Well, I have a few. LA and Savannah Georgia," Piper said. "Favorite new song from your CD," the DJ asked. "Running from the Sunset and Found," Piper replied. "Double answer," the DJ asked. "My top 2. They're fan favorites too from what I heard," Piper replied. "And we have one of those two right now. This is Running from Sunset by Piper Adams." The DJ pressed play on the song and muted the microphones. "We're not allowed to ask about the guy are we," the DJ asked. Piper shook her head. "We're keeping things private. That's all," Piper replied. "Lucky guy," the DJ said. "He thinks so," Piper teased. "We have the rest of the tour dates. Can you sign a few CD's for giveaways," the DJ asked. "Definitely," Piper replied. "We have a couple more fan questions. After that, we're all good. We'll see you at the show tomorrow," the DJ asked. Piper nodded. They came back from the song and Piper smirked. "And that was Running from Sunset, the newest song by Piper Adams. Alright. As planned y'all, a few fan questions for the first 3 callers," the DJ said. The first one came through. "Alright. What's your question for the one and only Piper Adams," the DJ asked. "I am such a huge fan. Oh my goodness. Alright. My question is, are you doing meet and greets at the concert tonight," the caller asked. Piper looked over at Char and saw her nod. "Well, according to the super manager, the answer is yes. Just check out the website for info and I hope to see you tomorrow," Piper said. "If you can hold, you are gonna be on that list. Stay on the line," the DJ said as they went to the second caller and Char got the first line.

"Alright, caller number two. Shoot," the DJ said. "First off, I so want to be on that meet and greet list. So, here's the question. Who's the guy in the picture that I've seen a million times over," the caller asked as Piper recognized the voice. "That would be a great guy that I know. Let's leave it at that," Piper said. "Are y'all dating," the caller asked. "Yes," Piper said. "Alright thank you. Caller number three," the DJ said getting her out of divulging information on the air. "Oh my goodness. Alright. My question is, what would you do if you weren't in the music industry," the caller asked. "Dang. Had to do a hard question. Well, if I weren't in the music industry, I'd probably be writing books or being a tour guide in Savannah. Good question though," Piper said. "Alright y'all. And those are the three questions. Those three callers all have meet and greets for the show tonight. We have three passes left. They'll be up for winning at 5, 10 and 7am tomorrow morning. Piper, thank you so much for coming in. We will see you tomorrow night," the DJ said. "Can't wait. We'll see y'all tomorrow," Piper said. "And we have one more song for y'all. Piper, can you do the honors," the DJ asked. "Sure. This one is called Found off the new CD. By the way, for the three winners of the meet and greet, you're getting an autographed copy of the new CD too. Enjoy the song. Hope y'all love it," Piper said. The DJ turned the song on and got up to thank Piper for coming in. They got a quick photo for their social media and Piper headed out with Harley and the guys. Char got the information from the radio stations about the meet and greet winners and hopped in. They finally headed out and went back to the hotel.

"For someone that nervous, you were amazing," Char said. "It got easier as I went," Piper said. "You have two more with XM stations that we can do from the hotel. Other than that, everyone else can relax until tomorrow," Char said. They got back to the hotel and Char went up to Piper's suite with her. "I still don't get how y'all got upgraded to Jason's floor," Char said. "Blame it on Jamie," Piper teased. "So, since the meet and greet thing is now going to be huge, it's gonna start at 7. Before the show starts, y'all have to get ready to go and be set before 7. You go in at 7:15. That work," Char asked. Piper nodded. "Not an issue," Piper said. "Alright," Char said. They went into the suite and Char silenced the room phones and her cell and Piper went and did the XM radio call-in interviews. They all asked about the photo and Piper said it was a guy she was spending lots of time with. She left it at that. When she was done, she went through a few things with Char and then was finally alone.

She grabbed her cell, putting the ringer back on. There was no text from Jamie. She opted to wash the makeup off and relax. She slid into her t-shirt and leggings and tried to get work done on music for a while. Just as she got comfortable, there was a knock at the door. Piper got up and saw Harley. "Hey," Piper said. "Char finally leave," Harley asked. Piper nodded. "Just relaxing until he gets back," Piper said. "Carter is comin over. I need help figuring out what to wear," Harley said. "Girl, you bought 5 outfits today. You have a million options," Piper said. "Then help me do my hair and makeup," Harley said. Piper nodded. She did her hair, helped her with her makeup and helped her figure out what to wear. "You'll be fine," Piper said. "I still don't get how I ended up with a nice guy," Harley said. "You pushed me into one and I pushed you into one," Piper said. "We lucked out for once," Harley joked. Piper nodded.

Harley hung out with Piper until she got a text from Carter that he was on his way. Piper smirked. "Go. Have fun," Piper said. "What about you," Harley asked. "Hangin out and relaxing. Whenever he gets back, we'll do dinner," Piper said.

"If he flakes, you better call and let me know," Harley said. Piper nodded. "Girl, just go relax. Enjoy yourself," Piper said. Harley nodded. She gave Piper a hug and went to her room to put on perfume and freshen up. Piper went and slid into a hot bath, relaxed and when she stepped out, her phone buzzed. "Hey sexy," Jamie said. "And how are the meetings goin," Piper asked. "Long. One last one and I'm done for this trip," Jamie teased. "Good," Piper replied. "Did you eat," he asked. "Not yet. Harley is heading out with Carter so I have lots of alone time," Piper said. "I'll be back in an hour or so. Promise," Jamie said. "I'll get something sent over for dinner," Piper said. "Alright sexy. See you in a few," Jamie said. They hung up and Piper went and curled up on the sofa and went through dinner menus. She found something and got it ordered and just as Jamie was texting to say that he was on the way back, the food showed up.

Jamie walked in, saw the wine and glasses and got a grin ear to ear. Piper came in a few minutes later with dinner, plated and everything. "Well thank you," Jamie said. Piper kissed him and he slid his suit jacket and tie off. He sat down beside her and they had a quiet dinner just the two of them. That was exactly what they both wanted. "Where the heck did you find a place that had this," Jamie asked. "Just went through the menus. Kinda miss home," Piper said. He kissed her. "Me too to be honest. Don't worry. When I see you on the weekends I'll bring that soup you love with me," Jamie joked. "I know. Honestly, I don't know how Jason does it," Piper said. "He has his wife and the kids with him on the bus. He has a dang plane to fly him out too," Jamie teased. "I'll put that on the Santa list," Piper teased. He kissed her. "If you miss home, I'll find a way to get you back home," Jamie said. "Maybe it's just nerves," Piper said. They finished dinner and curled up on the sofa with their wine. "What am I gonna do with you," Jamie asked. "Which reminds me, Harley was actually getting butterflies waiting on Carter," Piper teased. "He likes her. Not that I'm surprised, but that's the first time I've seen him biting at the bit to finish work," Jamie joked. "Really," Piper asked. Jamie nodded. "Which reminds me. What time do you have to be there in the morning," Jamie asked with a mischievous grin. "6 I think? Meaning up at 5 and showered then going down to the studio to hair and makeup and soundcheck," Piper said. "Good. That means that we have time," Jamie said. "For what," Piper joked. "You to show me what you got in the lingerie store," he teased. Piper shook her head, kissed him and cleaned up the dishes. "Go. I'll clean them up," Jamie said.

Piper slid into the silky lingerie and came out to see him with a refill. "What you doin," Piper asked. "Getting us refills," Jamie said. He looked over and she was leaning against the door to the bedroom. "Damn," Jamie said. "You said you wanted to see," Piper said. He got up, put the wine on the bedside table and picked her up, carrying her to the bed. "I like," Jamie said. "I bet," Piper teased. His hand slid up the satin slightly covering her silky legs. "Damn," Jamie said. "You like," Piper asked. "And it's gonna look just as hot on the floor," Jamie whispered as it slid up her legs. She unbuttoned his shirt and slid it off of him. "How is it that one day of meetings and you're sexier than you were," Jamie said. "Distance makes the heart grow fonder," Piper teased. "Nope. That's not it," Jamie said. "Lingerie pictures," Piper joked. "Sexier when you teased. I think I over-missed you," Jamie teased as he kissed down her neck. "Think so do you," Piper asked. He nodded and undid his dress pants, sliding them to the floor. "This is pretty dang sexy," Jamie said. "You haven't seen all of it," Piper joked. "Oh damn," Jamie said. "What," Piper asked. "I swear, you keep teasing you may not be making it to that performance," Jamie said.

"Well, you could just look at the rest," Piper said. He slid it off of her, revealing the lace bra and panties. Before she even heard a reaction, his clothes hit the floor. He leaned into her, peeling every thread of clothing off of her. They were making love in minutes and just that visual of her in the lingerie had him way beyond hot and bothered. When they managed to finally come up for air, their legs were tangled. "I swear, you're way too damn tempting," Jamie said. "I guess that means you like it," Piper said. "More than you know. You're so damn sexy," Jamie said. "Well thank you," Piper said. "I was thinkin about you all day," Jamie said. "Oh really," Piper said taunting him. "What am I gonna do with you," Piper asked. "Move in with me," Jamie said. "You're insane. You know that right," Piper asked. He kissed her. "I wasn't joking," he whispered. "Jamie," Piper said. "I meant it. We can go wherever you need to. Do whatever you have to with the music career. I just want to know that I have you," Jamie said. "And if I'm in my own place," Piper asked. "We figure something out. We get a place together so it's ours," he replied. Piper shook her head. "Less than a month," Piper replied. "When you know you know right," Jamie asked. Piper looked at him. "We can talk when I'm back this week. Talk. Nothing else," Piper said. He kissed her. "Alright," he said.

That night, she was asleep in his arms. For once, she wasn't worried about her body or hiding or disguising what she didn't like about it. She had her confidence back for the first time in forever. Things were finally going the right way. Maybe it was just being away from home in a fancy hotel, but the worry about Colt was gone.

The next morning, Piper got up and did a quick workout with Jess then got showered and dressed and they all had breakfast together. "So, today is the first day of one heck of a ride y'all. It's not gonna be easy, but at least it'll be fun. I wouldn't want anyone else there with me but y'all," Piper

197

said. "We ready for all of this," Kurt asked. "We got this. Always will," Piper replied. They finished up and they headed down to the studio together and Jamie was right at Piper's side. They hopped into the car to get them to the TV studio and Piper was almost trembling she was no nervous. "You got this," Jamie whispered. She did a quick sound check with the band and they finished and headed into hair and makeup. "You got this. I promise," Jamie said. "Start of the longest day ever," Piper said. Jamie kissed her shoulder. "What do you need me to do," Jamie asked. "Make the nerves go away," Piper said. He kissed her and sat down beside her, holding her hand. "What are you nervous about," Jamie asked. "Had a bad feeling when I woke up. Like a bomb's about to drop," Piper said. "Maybe it's because the song is number one," Harley said trying to calm her down.

"I have no dang idea," Piper said. "What are you so worried about," Kurt asked. "I have a bad feeling. That's all," Piper said. "Then we'll fix it before we go on tonight," Kurt replied. They finished hair and makeup and said a quick prayer, then headed out to get going on their performance. All it was, was three songs. Three that blew everyone's mind. They finished and headed in for a quick interview then straight back to the hotel to get settled. "That was unbelievable," Jamie said. "Can you imagine how insane that show is gonna be tonight," Keith asked. "Quit makin me more nervous," Piper said. They got back to the hotel and headed to the suites to get packed up. Jamie and Piper went up to their suite and walked in to see sterling roses sitting on the table, complete with a note for Piper:

Don't ever doubt how amazing you are. Love you. Jamie

Piper looked at him. "And what's this," Piper asked. He kissed her. "It's true," he said. Piper shook her head. "Jamie," Piper said. He pulled her to him and kissed her again. "What am I gonna do with you," Piper asked. He kissed her again and walked her over to the bed. "What time are we checking out," Jamie asked. "Maybe an hour and a bit. Why? Don't you have work," Piper teased. He kissed her again, devouring her lips and was about to lean her onto the bed when there was a knock at the door. "Dang it," Jamie said. Piper smirked and walked over to the door. "Hey Jess," Piper said. "I mean dang," Jess said. "What," Piper asked. "You were amazing on that stage. It's like you've been doin this 25 years. Wow," Jess said. "Hey little sis," Jamie said as he came out of the master bedroom. "And what's the plan for the rest of the day," Jess asked. "Packing, soundcheck, rehearse a bit, interviews and then meet and greet and performance. After that we're headed off again," Piper said. "And where to this time," Jess asked. Piper grabbed the sheet she'd copied and gave one to Jess and one to Jamie. "So, west coast then across to Nashville for that concert next weekend. I mean, you're gonna be one busy lady," Jess said. "Thank you for coming with us," Piper said. "More than welcome. I even figured out bus workouts," Jess joked.

"That mean we're ready to go," Piper asked. "I just have to finish packing. After that, I'm ready to go," Jess said. "Alright. We're heading out in an hour. We're just gonna finish getting ready," Jamie said. "Alright. I'll see y'all in a couple," Jess said. As soon as the door was closed, Jamie locked it, picked Piper up and walked back into the master bedroom and leaned her back onto the bed. "Now where were we," Jamie asked. "I swear, you totally have a one-track mind today," Piper said. He kissed her, devouring her lips and started peeling her things off little by little. When their clothes were a puddle on the floor, he made love to her, never stopping or breaking the kiss. When they managed to come up for air, he pulled her to him as he leaned to his back. "What am I gonna do with you," Piper asked. "Stay with me and never let go," Jamie teased.

Piper kissed him. "We have to get up. The bus is gonna be coming," Piper said. "Party pooper," Jamie joked. She kissed him and went and washed the makeup off from the TV performance.

She got everything packed and double checked and Jamie got dressed and got the bags together. Piper came into the TV room and got her flowers. "You ready sexy," Jamie asked as he leaned over and kissed her. "I am handsome," Piper replied as she smirked. Just as they were about to head out, there was a knock at the door. "Yep," Piper said opening it. "You ready," Harley asked. Piper nodded. The doorman came up with a cart for the luggage and escorted them downstairs to the bus. Piper and Jamie hopped on, then Kurt, Keith and Kevin, then Char and Jess and last the driver. "Heading out in 5 if anyone's forgetting anything," the driver said. Not 2 minutes later, Harley's phone rang. "Yep," Harley said. "Hey," Carter replied. Harley went to her bunk and talked to Carter in the little privacy she had.

"Alright. What got her runnin off," Keith asked. "Hot guy that she likes," Piper joked. They got on the road and headed to the venue to see a huge amount of traffic. They got through it via a back route and paused to see a ton of fans running towards the bus. "Security is coming. Just stay put until they're here and the gate is up," the driver said. They went through the security gate and finally parked as the gate closed behind them and the wall of security was up. "Alright. We are parked and secured. Ready to go," the driver said. He hopped off and Piper looked at Jamie. Not 2 seconds later, Jason hopped on the bus.

"About time y'all got here. I thought I was gonna have to send out the search party," Jason joked as he came over and gave Piper a hug. "You remember Jamie right," Piper asked. "Nice seeing you again," Jason said. Jason said hi to everyone and when Harley came out, he gave her a hug.

"About time you woke up," Jason joked. "You done teasing," Harley asked. "Come on. We're just hanging for a bit before we get going on sound check. We're having barbecue tonight, so y'all better be hungry," Jason said. They all headed off and Piper snuck away to see what the stadium looked like. The minute she did, it's like her body was taken over by butterflies. Nerves was a complete understatement. "Oh my goodness," Piper said. "What," Jason said coming up behind her. "This place is freaking huge. I can't do this in front of all those people," Piper said. "Want the truth? You can maybe see the first ten rows. You won't be out here that long. When you finish, stand side stage and watch the lights. I promise you, those nerves will be gone after tonight," Jason said. "You sure I'm the right girl for this," Piper asked. "With those pipes? Heck yeah," Jason said. Piper shook her head. "This is absolutely insane," Piper said. "Wanna know a trick," Jason asked. "Sure," Piper said. He grabbed his favorite acoustic guitar. "Which song do you remember all the words to no matter what," Jason asked. "Dirt Road Memory," Piper said. He walked her to the edge of the stage and they sat down. Jamie saw from the side what he was doing and recorded.

"Close your eyes," Jason said. Piper did. He started playing the song and they sang through it together. It was so innocent and easy. The minute she opened her eyes, it was like the nerves had fizzed away. "I do it every dang show. Tomorrow we do one of yours," Jason said. Piper nodded and gave him a hug then just sat and looked out at all the seats that were about to be filled. Jason gave Jamie a guy hug on the way out and Jamie took Jason's place and sat down with her. "Well dang," Jamie said. "Beginning of an insane couple of months," Piper said. "Oh I know. Just ease yourself into it. You saw how crazy everyone was over seeing you. You got this," Jamie said. Piper kissed him and leaned her head onto his shoulder. "I still think I'm dreaming," she said. "And after tonight, you're living it," Jamie replied. She finally relaxed and they got up and headed backstage to hang with Jason, the band and his wife and kids.

By the time soundcheck was over, it was nearing entry time for the audience. Piper got warmed up, got hair and makeup done thanks to Jason's wife Kaylie, and got changed. Jamie had intentionally kept her phone in his pocket so nothing would distract them from day one of the tour. She went and did her meet and greet with the fans with every single one of them asking who the hot guy was. "Very amazing and one of a kind guy I met. Figured I'd keep him around," Piper teased. As soon as they finished with the last fan, Piper took a deep breath and had a quick drink with Jason. "You got this," Jason said. "Like he said," Jamie teased. Piper slid her monitors in and the band headed out. The crowd went insane. They started and Piper looked at Jamie. One quick kiss and she walked on stage.

Chapter 11

When the crowd went crazy, Piper got a big ole grin. The first song had the crowd singing along with her. "Y'all love that one," Piper asked. When she got nothing but cheers, she figured she'd start the second song. "And this one is called Found. I know y'all know it. Join in anytime," Piper teased. She sang through three more then opted to get everyone even more excited about Jason. By the time she stepped off stage, she was on a fan caused high. Jamie slid his hand in hers and they walked backstage. "Oh my goodness," Piper said. "No more nerves," Jamie asked. "Totally get why he does it. I mean wow," Piper said. "And," Jason asked as he came up behind her and handed her a drink. "I get it," Piper said. "You were amazing," Jason said. "Well thanks," Piper said with a big ole grin ear to ear. "So, we still on for that song," Jason asked. Piper nodded. "Second last one of the night. Deal," Jason asked. Piper nodded and he slid his ear monitors in and went to get ready to head on. Jamie walked Piper off to grab a drink. They sat down and were sitting and relaxing a bit when she heard the show start. Jason had the crowd going crazy.

"Now that is what I call the dream concert," Jamie said as his arms slid around Piper. "How the heck did I luck out," Piper asked. "You deserve that. You deserve to be here. It's about time you figured that out," Jamie said as he kissed her. "You know it's your fault right," Piper said. "And why's that," Jamie asked as she leaned into him. "Cause it is," Piper said. He kissed her neck. "I love you," he whispered. Piper got a silly grin and he held her that much tighter. The second last song came and Jamie looked at Piper. "Go get em," Jamie whispered. Piper kissed him, finished off her drink and headed back out to sing the duet with Jason. The minute she saw the lights and the crowd of people, it's like that performance high was back. They sang through the song and after a quick thanks hug from Jason, she headed off and went back to the bus with Jamie and the band. "Now that was freaking outstanding," Harley said. "Ya think," Piper asked. "If that's what this tour is gonna be like, heck yeah," Keith said. "And where are we heading next," Piper asked. "Vegas then we head to Arizona," Harley said. "This is insane," Piper said. "You were amazing," Keith said. "And y'all weren't bad yourselves. That was a whole new level of crazy," Piper said. "I mean, name one job in the world where you get to do that," Kurt asked. Just as the words passed his lips, Harley's phone buzzed. She answered and asked him to hold for a sec. "Where are we stopping next for a couple days," Harley asked. "Houston," the driver said. Harley went into the stateroom and talked to Carter alone.

Jamie got everyone a drink and they sat back and tried to relax. Not 20 minutes later, Jason hopped on. "Now that was absolutely amazing," Jason said. "Thank you for this," Piper said. "You deserve all the dang praise. They're not exactly accepting and they love you. You got this. No more nerves," Jason said. Piper nodded. Jamie handed him a drink to cheers. "Day one of 50," Jason teased. Piper nodded. They all had their drinks and cleaned up. "I'm hoppin on the bus. We'll see you at the next stop," Jason said. Piper nodded. He headed off and the second driver hopped on. "And we're off," the driver said. They headed off to the next stop. "I'm goin to call the wife," Keith said. "Ditto," Kurt said. "Me too," Kyle said. They headed to their bunk and Piper and Jamie were left on their own.

"You really were that good tonight," Jamie said. "Do you have my cell," Piper asked. Jamie slid it in her hand and within a matter of seconds, it buzzed. "What you up to," Jamie asked. "Come," Piper said. She made a video of the two of them. "Day one of the tour and honestly, I can't say thank you more. Jason is amazing and even better from my view. And then there's the one guy that calmed me down before this morning's performance. This guy right here is one of the greatest guys I know and I'm darn lucky to have him in my life," Piper said as he kissed her. "And for all of y'all wondering who this handsome guy here is, this right here is my boyfriend Jamie," Piper said. "Thank y'all again for all the support and see you at the next tour stop." She stopped the video and posted it to her social media. "You sure," Jamie asked. "Already done," Piper said. He kissed her. "Determined," Jamie asked. Piper nodded. "You said you wanted to shout it from the rooftops. This is the 2019 equivalent," Piper replied. He kissed her. "And what's next there superstar," Jamie asked. "Sleep," Piper said. He kissed her again, slid his hand in hers and walked her to the stateroom. "Two minutes," Piper said. She washed the makeup off and as she walked back, she heard Harley giggling on her phone. She walked back to the stateroom, closing the door and saw Jamie on his phone. "What's up," Piper asked. "Just catching up on news from home," Jamie said. "Anything interesting," Piper asked. Jamie shook his head.

She slid out of her stage clothes and got changed into sexy pajamas. "Had to go teasing again," Jamie said. Piper smirked and he slid his dress pants off, getting himself ready for bed. They curled up in the blankets and he leaned over and kissed her. "Sexiest girlfriend in the planet," Jamie said. Not 2 seconds later, there was a knock at the door. "Come on in Harley," Piper said as Jamie slid her to him and was spooning her. "So, I have a question. You alright if Carter comes when we're in Texas," Harley asked. "Girl, it's your room. Do whatever you want," Piper said. "You sure," Harley asked. "Just tell him to bring the papers from my desk," Jamie said. "Thanks," Harley said. "You know you don't have to ask," Piper said. Harley smirked. "Night y'all," Harley said.

Harley closed the door and Piper felt Jamie's breath on her neck, then the feel of his lips. "What you doin," Piper asked. He went for her shoulder and felt the bottom edge of the pajamas inching up her skin. "Jamie," Piper said. The backup driver knocked at the door. "What's up," Piper asked. He poked his head in. "Four hours and a bit just getting out of the traffic from the concert. Did you want to stay at a hotel or head over," the driver asked. "What's Jason doin," Piper asked. "Hotel tonight and going over in the morning," the driver said. "We'll go over and get a hotel closer to there," Piper said. "Alright," the driver said as he closed the door. "If you're asleep, I'll carry you in," Jamie said. Piper smirked. "And what else are you gonna be doin," Piper teased. He kissed her. "Come here and I'll tell you," Jamie teased. She turned to face him and he devoured her lips. "And what got you all hot and bothered," Piper asked. "I'll give you a hint," he teased. "What," Piper asked. "That video," he teased. Piper kissed him. "What am I gonna do with you," Piper teased. He kissed her again, devouring her lips until she was breathless in his arms.

He made love to her until they were both exhausted. She fell asleep in his arms and the only thing that woke her from that blissful sleep was a message from the driver letting her know they were in traffic. She slid her t-shirt on and saw a ton of replies to the video, and not one nasty negative reply until one popped up:

She's a bitch. Probably had to pay him.

Piper reported the comment and went to look up who's name was on that profile. When she saw Colt, she almost dropped her phone. She sent the info to Char, blocked Colt's profile and blocked him on the rest of her social media then felt an arm slide around her. "Get over here," Jamie teased. She slid back into the bed and tried to close her eyes. Maybe an hour later, she got a message from Char to call her in the morning. "You alright," Jamie asked. Piper nodded and he fell back asleep. She put it out of her mind and closed her eyes, determined to get some rest.

When the bus stopped, Piper was wide awake. She slid her joggers on with her runners, grabbed her overnight bag and got checked in. Jamie came in behind her and they headed to the room. The minute they were through the door, they curled back up on the bed and went back to sleep.

The next morning, Piper got up and did her workout with Jess while Jamie slept. "And why do you look like you're distracted," Jess asked. "Just something I heard last night," Piper replied. "You okay," Jess asked. "No idea. I kinda posted a video about Jamie and I and Colt made a nasty comment. I know he's starting something," Piper said. "Then ignore it and keep it out of your head," Jess said. "Tryin," Piper said. They finished the workout and headed back upstairs, ordering breakfast on the way up. When she got there, Jamie was going over emails. "Hey handsome," Piper said. "Hey yourself. Hey Jess," Jamie said. "Hey big bro," Jess said. "Why are you lookin so serious," Piper asked. "Didn't tell me what happened," Jamie said. "I'm goin to shower and stuff," Jess said excusing herself. "Meaning what," Piper asked as Jess headed off and Piper closed the door. "Colt started a problem last night," Jamie said. "And how would you know that super spy," Piper said. "He came after me on my Instagram," Jamie said. "I'll let Char know to come over," Piper said. She shot Char a text and sat down with Jamie. Just as she did, the room service showed. Piper got the door and they sat down to eat and relax.

"Why didn't you just tell me," Jamie asked. "Because you were asleep. Doesn't help anything if both of us are half-asleep," Piper said. "What are we gonna do," Jamie asked.

"He can kiss my butt. I've blocked him from all of my social media. He can't come after either of us," Piper said. "Alright," Jamie said as he followed her plan and blocked him from his social media as well. "You could've just told me," Jamie said. "And for right now, there's nothing else I can do. I'm not even in Savannah," Piper said. A minute or two later, there was a knock at the door. Jamie got up and answered and let Char in.

"Morning," Char said. "Good mornin," Piper replied. "Well, you are gonna be a little annoyed," Char said as she sat down and Piper handed her a cup of coffee. Jamie sat down beside Piper. "He's gone further than we noticed. He's attempted to trash you on the amazon site and the fan site. Whatever he's up to, he's determined to make the biggest problem possible. One email was flagged and was sent to the webmaster of the website. I don't want him causing even more problems," Char said. "Do I even want to know," Piper asked. "He said that he wanted to talk to you directly or he was going to make life very bad for you. An obvious threat. I notified the police," Char said. "As long as this doesn't mess up the tour for Jason," Piper said. "He's been notified from his publicist and said bitter exes is normal," Char said. "In other words, he's prepared," Piper teased. "Definitely. He's also said that if negative articles come out, he'll get them silenced completely. He doesn't want anyone messing with the tour any more than you do. Whatever it is, it may mean an extra interview or two," Char said. "Alright," Piper said. "And as for that video last night, very cute and I'm glad y'all did it on your own terms like you wanted," Char replied. "So, we're good," Piper asked. Char nodded.

Char headed out and Jamie slid Piper into his lap. "What," Piper asked. "So that gut instinct was right," he said. "I just hope he doesn't do anything else," Piper said. "You and me against the world right," he asked. Piper nodded and he kissed her, picking her up and walking into the bedroom.

"What are you up to," Piper asked. He kissed her again, devouring her lips and leaned her onto the bed, peeling her clothes off little by little. "Jamie," Piper said. "No interviews, no media stuff until later. We get us time," Jamie said. "Wasn't complaining," Piper teased. He shook his head with a big ole grin. "What," Piper asked. "I can just imagine how many emails I'm gonna have by Monday," Jamie joked. Piper kissed him and his jeans slid to the floor. He leaned into her and it was like they melded together. Like mixing two colors of paint just create a perfect new color. The faster it got, the hotter it was. Her legs were wrapped tight around him and almost locked. Letting go and coming up for air was totally against the rules at that point. When things kept going, she almost felt like he was proving that he was the one in control. Whatever it was, it was hot and she knew it.

When they finally crashed to the mattress, both of them were trying to catch their breaths. "You never answered me about that key," Jamie said as he curled his arm around her and snuggled her to him. "You seriously think that moving in is a good idea," Piper asked. "Harley can stay at your place. Just say yes," Jamie asked. "Still thinking about it," Piper said. He kissed her, devouring her lips. "Then just promise me that you'll stay a bit when you're home," Jamie replied. "How's this sound. When I get back from this little part, we can discuss it," Piper said. He kissed her. "Alright," he said. Piper kissed him and her phone buzzed. She shook her head. "You aren't moving," Jamie said. "Shower, get dressed," Piper replied. He shook his head. "You deserve relax time," Jamie said. "And just what did you have planned," Piper asked. "Me and you in this bed until you have to leave for interviews and stuff," Piper said. He kissed her and wrapped her leg around him as he felt his way up her silky legs. "Still don't know how you get your legs so dang soft," Jamie said. "Girl secret," Piper joked. "Just stay with me," he asked. "I thought more like go out for a walk, date day," Piper said. "Nobody else," he asked. Piper shook her head. "It's the first day you don't have to be at the office," Piper said. "Then I'll accept," he teased. Piper kissed him and he pulled her to him. "Promise me something," Jamie said. "What," Piper asked. "We still have date days no matter what," he asked. "Wouldn't have it any other way," Piper said. She slid out of his arms and went to go into the massive master bath. He got up and followed her into the shower as she turned the water on and the mirror started to fog up.

"What," Piper asked noticing the look on his face. He had that look like he was about to do something completely crazy. "Nothin," he teased as he slid her under the water of the rain head. He washed her hair and when she went to slide him under the water, he kissed her, devouring her lips. He picked her up, leaning her against the wall of the shower. When the kiss broke, he nibbled at her lip. "I want you so bad I can taste it," he said. "Oh really," Piper asked. He nodded. "What did I do that got you in my life," Jamie asked. "Took a chance. Just the right person at the right time," Piper said. He kissed her again and every inch of her wanted him just as much. There was just something about him. The fact that her imperfections were almost invisible to him was just one part of it. The shower sex caused every inch of the bathroom to be filled with mist from the hot water. When her feet slid to the ground, she leaned him under the hot water and washed his hair for him. When she went to wash his back, he had other plans. "Better idea," he whispered. He slid out of the shower, turning the water off and wrapped her up in a towel. She slid one around his waist and he carried her into the bedroom.

"Jamie," Piper said. He got the lotion from her bag and rubbed it into her back for her. She could feel his hot breath on her neck the entire time. "Much better," Jamie said as he slid the towel off and put lotion on her chest. "Now you're intentionally taunting," Piper said. "It's so this looks even better," Jamie said as he grabbed a box from the bedside table and slid a diamond solitaire necklace around her neck. "Jamie" Piper said. "Because I wanted to. You said everything needed sparkles right," he teased. Piper nodded then saw the necklace. It wasn't exactly subtle. The emerald-shaped diamond was just small enough to be subtle, but in no way hidden. "Jamie, this is too much," Piper said. "I saw it and I wanted you to have it," Jamie said. "Why," Piper asked. "You never ever fit into the box that everyone wanted you in. That's what I love about you. You don't care about the box," Jamie said. Piper kissed him. "Jamie," Piper said. "You don't have to ever fit in the box. All you have to do is be the woman I love," Jamie said. "Wow," Piper replied. "That video last night was what did it," Jamie said. "And if I hadn't," Piper asked. "Then I would've waited until you were ready," he replied. "Even if it means a ton of emails asking questions about it," Piper asked. "I love you either way," he teased. Piper kissed him and he wrapped his arms tight around her. "Just remember one thing," Jamie asked. "Which would be what handsome man of mine," Piper asked. "That I love you no matter what," Jamie said. "Meaning," Piper asked. "No matter what kind of crap he causes," Jamie said. Piper kissed him and he got up. "Let the date day commence," he joked.

They both got up and Piper slid on a sexy silky sundress. Jamie shook his head. "Had to keep teasing," Jamie said. "Oh I know. That was the plan handsome," Piper teased. "Are they radio interviews like call in or do you have to go to the studio," Jamie asked. "Call in probably. It's only 7:30," Piper teased. "And we have an appointment," Jamie said. "For what," Piper asked. "You'll see when we get there," he said. Piper did her hair and makeup, slid her shoes on and turned around to see him in jeans and a t-shirt. "Ready," he asked. Piper slid her phone in her purse, put her key card in and they headed out together. They stepped onto the elevator and he could smell the magnolia perfume she loved. "Had to put the dang perfume on that drives me crazy," he whispered as she got goosebumps. "That was the plan," Piper whispered.

They stepped off the elevator and got into the waiting car. "Where are we goin," Piper asked. "You'll see when we get there," Jamie teased. They drove and when they stopped at a lingerie store, she almost laughed. "Jamie," Piper said. "That's just part one," he teased. They hopped out and walked in with the doors locking behind them. "Whatever she wants," Jamie said. "Jamie," Piper said. "I'm sitting right here," he said as he sat down on the sofa with his Starbucks in hand. "Jamie," Piper said. "Go," he replied. She found a few things she liked, intentionally showing him one or two. "I mean really," Jamie said as she slid one leg out of the dressing room. "Come here then," Piper said. He got up and went in to look, seeing her in a lace, see-through piece of lingerie that had him drooling in a matter of minutes. "Damn," Jamie said. "Like," Piper asked. "Need a couple more," he teased. "Think so do you," Piper said. She slid it off and he kissed her. "Two I want you to try," Jamie said. Piper nodded. He slid out of the dressing room and the saleswoman brought them in. Both were white lace. One was satiny and the other had more lace than material.

When Piper looked at the tag, it said 'Bridal Collection'. "Jamie, why does this say bridal," Piper asked. "I don't care what it says. I think it would look great on you," Jamie said. She tried both on and they fit like a glove. As soon as she slid out of them, the saleswoman took them and put them into a bag for Piper. As soon as she stepped out, he slid his hand in hers and they left to wherever they were going next. "Jamie, just tell me what's going on," Piper asked. "I have a work event coming up and I want you with me. Figured we might as well look at a dress or two," Jamie said. "I know you're up to something. Just say whatever it is," Piper said. He kissed her and they pulled into the next store. They walked in and the saleswoman had a rack of dresses in Piper's size. She tried a few on and still hadn't found the right one. She grabbed another dress off the rack and slid it on. "Just show me," Jamie said. The saleswoman zipped it up for her and she looked in the mirror. "Damn," Piper said. "Understatement," Jamie said. It was pale pink satin with a short train but was just low enough in the back that it showed off all the work she'd been doing at the gym.

"Do you like," Piper asked. "Love. Show me another," Jamie said. "I need more than one," Piper asked. "Music awards coming up too," Jamie replied. Piper shook her head and went into the dressing room. When she walked in, there was a white satin dress waiting. "I'm not wearing a white dress," Piper said. "Just put the darn thing on," Jamie said. It was soft, flowy and fit perfectly to hide what she hated about herself. She stepped out and Jamie's jaw hit the floor. "Now that is a dress," Jamie said. "A little more bridal than red carpet," Piper said. "It does come in red, black and a pale blue," the saleswoman said. She looked at Jamie. "Red and the pale blue," Jamie said. The saleswoman nodded. "Jamie," Piper said. "Just get changed," Jamie said. "You're not telling me what you're up to," Piper asked. He shook his head with a cat that ate the canary grin. They headed out with 4 dresses in a suit bag. "You're planning something. Just tell me what it is," Piper said. "You'll see," he replied. Piper shook her head. "Fine," she said going along with his plan. They got to the next stop and he got her shoes. When they got back to the hotel, he rushed her past the lobby and up the elevator. "Jamie," Piper said. "You're the one that was teasing," Jamie said.

They got into the suite. The minute the door was closed, the dresses were laid across the chair and the lingerie bag was laid on top of it. "Jamie," Piper said. He walked over to her, picking her up. "What are you up to," Piper asked. He leaned her onto the bed and leaned into her arms, devouring her lips. "Jamie," Piper said when they came up for air. "What," he asked. "What's goin on," Piper asked. "I wanted us time where you felt like a million bucks. I wanted you to see yourself like I do," Jamie said. "You're just too much," Piper said. "I love you. Every inch of you whether you like it or not," he teased. "You are just full of surprises today," Piper said. Just as he was about to peel her sundress off, her phone buzzed. Jamie handed it to her. "Yep," Piper said. "Call in's are starting at 1:45. Are you back at the hotel," Char asked. "So you were in on it," Piper asked. "He wanted to do something special. Everything is a go for 1:45. I'll be there at 1:30," Char said. "Alright," Piper replied.

As soon as the phone hung up, Jamie slid that sundress off and kissed his way down her torso. "What are you up to," Piper asked. "Getting your mind off this morning," Jamie said. Piper kissed him. "Just being way too dang sweet," Piper teased. "If I told you what else I was planning, you'd kick my butt," he teased. "Jamie," Piper said. He kissed her again and slid her phone into his pocket. He slid his shirt off and he started sliding every inch of her clothing off. "By the way, we're getting massages," he teased. "Oh really," Piper asked. "They're coming up here at 11," he said. "Meaning another hour and a half before they're coming," Piper asked. He nodded with a smirk. "And just what do you have planned boyfriend of mine," she teased. He kissed her and his arms wrapped around her and slid to her backside.

"Jamie," Piper said. He devoured her lips and wrapped her legs around him. When they barely managed to come up for air, he made love to her until that last bit of energy was completely gone. They curled up among the blankets and a half hour later, Piper woke up. She slid out of his arms and got cleaned up a little. She was about to go into the TV room and let Jamie sleep when he woke up. "Where you goin," Jamie asked. "Checkin emails," Piper said. "Nope," he replied as he got her to come back to bed. "Why," Piper asked. "No work. I'm not even opening my laptop today. Not happening. You and me time," Jamie said. Piper kissed him. "Alright then," Piper said as he curled her into his arms and they curled up in bed just talking.

When the time came for the massages, they were side by side. They did a long relaxing massage and as soon as they were finished, he got up and helped Piper up. "Thank y'all," Piper said. "Most welcome," the masseuses said. They headed out and Piper and Jamie got changed and Piper fixed up her hair and makeup. "Your shoulders went down to normal," he joked. "Same to you," Piper said. He slid on a t-shirt and his blue jeans and when Piper looked over, she saw the concert tee. "Jamie," Piper said. "My girl's on it. Had to," Jamie said. Piper kissed him. "Ridiculous, but I love it," Piper said. He kissed her and just as they were about to sit, Char came. "I got it," Jamie said. He answered the door and saw Char. He shook his head hinting that it wasn't the time to mention whatever it was. They sat down and Char let her know who she was calling first. The first call went off without a hitch. The CD was promoted and the show was a hit. The second was just like the first. Not one problem. It wasn't until Piper heard her phone after they hung up that Jamie was intent on distracting her. "We have to head down anyway. We have sound check in an hour," Char said. "I can check my phone," Piper said. Jamie shook his head. "It's dead. I'll charge it for you," he said. He got the bags onto the bus with everyone else's and they headed off.

"Nice going on the interviews," Harley said. "Well thanks," Piper replied. Jess looked over at Jamie hinting that he needed to tell Piper whatever it was that he was hiding and he shook his head. "That's the third time I've seen that look. Just say whatever it is," Piper said. "It's nothing," Jamie replied. "Fine. Don't tell me," Piper said. They showed at the venue maybe a half hour later to see a ton of fans trying to run after the bus. "You know that will never ever get old. I used to do that when I was a teen," Harley joked. "You and every other fan in the planet," Kurt teased. They got parked and hopped out to see Jason playing corn hole with the band. "About time y'all showed," Jason joked. "Funny," Piper teased. He gave her a hug and went back to playing. "What time we doing sound check," Piper asked. "I'm starting in an hour and a bit. You're welcome to whenever you're ready," Jason said as she made her way up to the stage to do what Jason had said at the first show. She sat down on the edge of the stage. Somehow, this stadium seemed a heck of a lot bigger. "You alright," Jamie asked as he came over and sat with her.

"I'm good. Just getting the feel of all of this," Piper said. He kissed her. "You know it's gonna get easier," Jamie said. "I know. I just kinda like this idea," Piper teased. She got settled and calmed her nerves and the band came in to start sound check. Jamie moved over to the edge of the stage and listened to her. She finished, opting to put one of the newer songs in. They finally got things just right and Jason came out to play through the duet. "We're putting it in yours and that other one we did yesterday in mine. Does that work," Jason asked. "Sure," Piper said. They sang through it and after a quick hug, she headed off with the band and Jason started his sound check. They headed back over and played corn hole a while then went and relaxed a while on the bus. "Just tell me whatever it is," Piper said. "It's nothing," Jamie said. Even after they had dinner, nobody would say a word. Piper went into hair and makeup and Char was biting at the bit to tell her the news.

Piper did her meet and greet with the fans and when she stepped out, Jamie was hand in hand with her. "You alright," he asked. Piper nodded. "You spilling the beans," Piper asked. He shook his head. "It's up to Char," Jamie said. He kissed her and she shook her head. She touched up her makeup and freshened up a little and Jamie handed her a drink. "Thank you," Piper said. "You got this," Jamie said. "You better tell me after the show," Piper said. He nodded. They toasted and he gave her a huge hug. "You ready," the stage manager said. Piper nodded and the MC headed on to introduce Piper. They said a quick prayer backstage and as soon as the MC left the stage, the band headed on. When the crowd went crazy, Piper got butterflies. "You got this," Jamie said. Piper nodded, slid her monitors in and hit the stage with all the confidence in the world.

They finished the set and Jason came out to do the duet as a surprise. "Well, Miss Piper, I know you thought that I was comin out to do a duet, but we have a little news," Jason said. Piper looked at Jamie and shook her head. "So, there's sorta two pieces. One, your song Found just hit triple platinum," Jason said as they handed Harley the platinum plaque. "This is insane. It's all because of y'all," Piper said to the fans as they went crazy. "And there's one more piece of news," Jason said. Piper shook her head. "We just got news this morning that this lady right here has been nominated for her very first music award. The CMA award nominations came out and our friend Piper has been nominated for new female artist," Jason said. Piper burst into tears and so did Harley. Jason gave Piper a hug. "Well, you know, now we have to do that duet," Piper said. Jason nodded. "Done," Jason said. They did their duet and Jason gave Piper a quick hug and walked her off while Piper was still teary-eyed. "I can't believe this," Piper said. "I'm glad you liked that surprise," Jason said with a smirk. "Thank you," Piper said. "Like I said before, you deserve every second of it," Jason said. She handed off her microphone and walked over to Jamie. "And that's what the dresses were for," Piper teased. "Sorta," he joked. She shook her head and he wrapped his arms tight around her. "You are absolutely ridiculous," Piper said. "Always something up my sleeve love," Jamie said.

Jason finished his part of the show with another quick duet and they were off again. "I know you're up to something that you are determined that you're keeping a secret," Piper said. "Yep," Jamie said. Piper shook her head. "You're killin me," Piper said. "And a big congrats," Harley said. "If it weren't for y'all I wouldn't have even got close to that," Piper said. "I mean dang. Jason brought it out and everything," Harley said. "I was kinda totally stunned," Piper said. "You should be. This is totally insane," Kurt said. "All of it is," Piper said. "And what's next," Jamie asked. "The world," Harley teased. "The award and an entire shelf to follow," Keith said. "I love that," Piper said. "And what's the next stop," Harley asked. "From what it says on here, Phoenix then Dallas and Houston," Piper said. "So, we head to Dallas after the show tomorrow night," Harley asked. "Yep," Piper said.

Harley went to her bunk and talked to Carter and Jamie slid Piper into his lap as he wrapped his arms around her. "I'm so dang proud of you," Jamie said. "I can't believe you knew," Piper said. "That way there was no stress and no pressure. No worrying about the red carpet," Jamie said. "I guess it's a good thing that video came out," Piper teased. He kissed her. "What am I gonna do with you now superstar," Jamie teased. "Relax until we get to the next stop," Piper teased. "Better idea," he teased. The guys had gone off to call their wives and all they heard was the rain start drizzling outside. "Come with me," he whispered as he slid her from his lap. He walked her back to the stateroom and locked the door behind them, intentionally leaving her cell phone on the charger in the kitchen. Just as he was about to lean in for a kiss, the bus hit a bump, jostling them onto the bed. "Well that's one way of doing it," he teased. Piper shook her head and he leaned in and devoured her lips. "What," Piper asked. "About killed me having to hide that," Jamie teased. "I bet it did there handsome," Piper joked.

He started peeling her clothes off and he kissed his way down her body. Just as he was sliding the sexy lace lingerie off, there was a knock at the door. "Yep," Piper said as Jamie kicked his jeans off. "You're phone is ringing off the dang hook," Harley said. Jamie shook his head. He slid them back on and Piper slid under the blanket. Jamie opened the door as Harley smirked. "Thank you," Jamie said. "Most welcome," Harley said. He locked the door, kicked his jeans off and leaned into her as he slid her phone into the bedside table drawer. "Mine for the rest of the dang night. No phones allowed," Jamie joked. He kissed her again as his boxers slid to the floor. "You think so do you," Piper teased. He held her tight in his arms. "I know so," he replied. He kissed her again and just as he did, she could hear the phone going off. "Don't even think about it," Jamie said. He leaned into her and her legs, if by instinct, wrapped around him. He kissed every inch of her until she couldn't withstand the taunting anymore. With one intense move, he was covering her mouth with his and devouring her lips making that room feel like it was in the middle of a wall of flames. Her legs were almost trembling with every move. Piper opened her eyes and it was as if she was drowning in his eyes. That crystal green was so deep and so intense that she lost herself. They managed to come up for air a while later, covered in those little beads of sweat. He curled her into his arms and pulled the blanket up. "Like I said, mine," he replied. Piper kissed him. As the kiss broke, her phone went off again. "I have to," Piper said. He nodded and she grabbed her phone.

"Yep," Piper said. "I just wanted to call and congratulate you. It was on the news," Caroline said. "Well thank you," Piper said. "We have to come out and see you to celebrate," Caroline replied. "I'm in Arizona then Dallas and Houston and next week I'm in Nashville on the Saturday I think," Piper said. "Then we're going out. Definitely," Caroline said. "As long as you don't bring Colt, that's fine," Piper replied determined to be as far away from Colt as possible. Jamie nibbled at her neck, spooning her that much closer. "How was the show tonight," Caroline asked. "Good. I got the news about the nomination and a triple platinum plaque," Piper said. "I bet Jamie was happy," Caroline said sarcastically. "Meaning," Piper asked. "Nothing. Colt mentioned something and I didn't wanna bring it up," Caroline said. "I'm getting some rest. We can talk tomorrow," Piper said. "Alright. Lookin forward to next weekend," Caroline replied. "Alright," Piper said shaking her head. They hung up and Jamie kissed her shoulder. "Like I said, no phone is much better," Jamie said. "Especially since Colt's bad-mouthing you around Savannah," Piper replied. He kissed her again. "Don't worry about him. Just get some rest. He doesn't get to upset you," Jamie replied. Piper nodded and he linked their fingers.

When she woke up the next morning, he wasn't there. Truly, it was a first. She slid on her t-shirt and shorts and freshened up then came into the main sitting area. "Morning Beautiful," Jamie said. "Morning handsome. Where are we," Piper asked. "8 hours to go," the driver said. "Thank you," Piper replied. "Meaning writing time". Jamie kissed her. "Breakfast," he asked. "Did you eat," Piper asked. He nodded. "And I made something for Chuck," Jamie teased motioning towards the driver. "Well, I'm glad y'all had some fun this morning," Piper teased. "Kurt and Keith came out just from the bacon smell," the driver said. "I can just imagine," Piper said. "And I put an omelet in the microwave for you," Jamie said. Piper kissed him and went into the microwave to see the omelet plus heart-shaped bacon waiting. "This is just too cute," Piper said. "And there's juice in the fridge and coffee in the thermos thing," he teased. Piper got her breakfast and sat down with Jamie as he tried over and over to steal the bacon.

She cleaned up and sat down with him. "Jess is still out cold. She ended up hanging with the guys last night," Jamie teased. Piper kissed him. "And what do you have planned for this morning," Piper asked. "Going through emails and getting some paperwork finished," he teased. "Oh really. So, you brought homework," Piper teased. He kissed her. "Something like that," he said. Piper shook her head. "Alright then," she joked. She went and had a quick shower and got dressed before everyone else was up and sat down in the stateroom. Jamie came down the hall with his phone charger in hand, plugging it in for her and putting their phones on it. "What you doin back here," Jamie asked as he walked in and kissed her. "Working on lyric ideas. Playing around with a couple things," Piper said. "You know you didn't have to wake up so early," he said. "I slept 8 hours," Piper said. "More like 6 and a half. Time change," he teased. "I'm good. Bed was lonely anyway. What were you doin up," Piper asked. "Something just got stuck in my head and I couldn't sleep," he said. "Which was," Piper asked. He kissed her again and sat down with her. "I don't get why Caroline even wants to come out," Jamie said. "She doesn't like not being included," Piper said. "Still," Jamie said.

"What was bugging you about it," Piper asked. "I just get the feeling that she's helping Colt more than you think. I don't want to hate your friends or anything, but she's up to no good with that stuff. You know that right," he asked. "I'll handle her. We'll just make sure Colt is banned from all of the events," Piper said. He kissed her. "Did you want to invite Eve," he asked. "I would, but since my folks are coming, I'm thinking less is a better idea," Piper replied. "True. I just don't want him messing up a good thing. Getting you all upset before a show isn't exactly a great plan," Jamie said. "I know. I love that you know too," Piper teased. He snuggled her to him. "And what happens when you meet my folks?" "You getting them tickets or just backstage," he asked. "Jason can probably help getting a pit pass or two," Piper said. "As long as your okay with my folks coming," he said. "Oh really," Piper asked. He nodded. "Might as well meet on our terms," he joked. "And just where would we be going," Piper asked. "You're doing the show on the Saturday right," he asked. Piper nodded. "The next day we would be off," Piper said. "Fly in then. We can take them to the Ryman or something. We can all do lunch together," Jamie said. "That could work," Piper teased. He kissed her and her head leaned onto his shoulder. "We can figure it out closer to," Jamie said. Piper nodded. "Do you know where you're staying," Jamie asked. "I'd assume everyone would be heading back instead of staying. If not, we're probably at the Hilton downtown or something," Piper said. He kissed her again. "I'll ask Char when I see her tonight," Jamie said.

Within maybe a half hour, they were curled back up in bed and Piper was out cold in his arms. He watched her sleep, noticing that it was almost as if there weren't a care in the world. When his phone vibrated, he managed to get it without disturbing her blissful sleep. The message was from Char:

Need to talk to Piper asap. That Colt guy has officially gone to the press with his lies. She needs to know. No interviews for her until we discuss. Ask her to contact me please.

Jamie shook his head. Piper had no idea of the bomb that was about to drop. He had no idea what would happen, but it would be more than she could handle. He just thanked his lucky stars that he was there a few more days to get her through. That blissful sleep was gonna be harder when she found out.

Chapter 12

Piper got up a little while later to see Jamie going through emails. "What are you up to," Piper asked. "Just checking over a few things. I checked with Char. She has you booked at the Union Station Hotel. I got a suite for each of our folks. More than enough room," Jamie said. "All that while I was asleep," Piper asked. He nodded. "Anything else happen?" "Not a whole lot," he replied. She kissed him and he pulled her into his lap. "Yes," Piper asked. He put his phone on the counter and pulled her legs around him. "Say you'll move in," Jamie asked. "I live two doors down. I'm not moving," Piper teased. He leaned her onto her back and leaned into her arms. "Negotiate," he asked. Piper nodded. "I'm not changing my mind," Piper teased. He kissed her, devouring her lips. "Don't move," he said. He got up and closed the door. Just as he went to come over to the bed, her phone went off. He silenced it and saw Char's name. Now wasn't the time.

"What was that," Piper asked. "It can wait," he said. Piper shook her head. "Until," Piper asked. "Until we finish negotiating," he joked. He kissed her and leaned into her arms. "And you think it's gonna be that easy," Piper teased. "I think that if it takes another 6 hours then I'm good with it," he joked. Piper shook her head. "Still not doing it," Piper said. "If we find a house that's in that same area that we both like," he asked. "There isn't one unless you build it," Piper said. "Then we build it. We get a house just the way we want plus 5 or 6 extra bedrooms so we will never have to move," he teased. "And what are you filling those with," Piper asked. "Closets," he joked. Piper shook her head. "Seriously," she asked. "It's not like there isn't land. The house between us isn't exactly fitting in with the area anyway. We can buy it and turn it into a massive lot and a house done just like we want it. It works," Jamie said. "If," Piper said. "They're moving anyway. They're putting the house up in a few days," Jamie replied. "We can talk about it. That's all," Piper replied.

Not 15 minutes later, her phone rang with her mom's ringtone. "You letting me get it," Piper asked. "Alright, but it's not my fault if you get too distracted," he joked. Piper grabbed her cell. "Hi mom," Piper said. "Hey there," her dad said. "What's up," Piper asked. "We're flying in and we land in Nashville at 10am. Is that alright," her dad asked. "Shouldn't be a problem. We're staying at the Union Station Hotel. That one I used to drool over. Jamie booked the rooms," Piper said. "Then we'll meet you there," her dad asked. "Definitely," Piper said. "Alright. Tell him we said hi," her dad said. "I will. By the way, I have a little good news," Piper said as he kissed her stomach and inched her shirt up her torso. "And what's the good news," her dad asked as he nibbled through her bra. "I got nominated for a CMA. It's huge," Piper said. "That's amazing," he said. "If I get it, I'm gonna have to make an award wall," Piper teased. "I'm proud of you. You worked so hard," her dad said as he got up to her neck. "I'm kinda proud too. I'll tell y'all all about it in Nashville," Piper said. "Alright. Go get some work done. We love you," her dad said. "Love you too," Piper replied. They hung up just as he was starting to peel her shorts off. "You are relentless," Piper said. "Just another reason why you love me," he teased.

"Oh really," Piper asked. He nodded. Before he managed to make another move, there was a knock at the door. Piper slid her shirt back down. "Yep," Piper said. "You comin to get work done or what lady," Harley joked. "Three steps ahead of y'all. Was working on lyrics," Piper replied. "Let's go," Harley teased. Jamie kissed Piper. "You know this isn't over," Jamie said. "If you can get the neighbor to go along with it then we'll take it from there. Deal," Piper asked. He nodded. "We still aren't done," he joked. Piper kissed him. "When do you have to go back," Piper asked. "Monday night," Jamie said. "Since my folks and yours are coming, I have to go into the studio and help one of the artists finish up. If we're done sooner than later, I can come meet you in Houston or wherever." "I guess," Piper joked. He shook his head. "Determined," he teased. "You realize that the studio thing is just fun. You work hard enough at the big office," Piper said. "Once this artist is done, I'm all yours," he said. "Good answer," Piper teased. She got up and went to work on music with Harley and Jamie called Char.

"Have you talked to her," Char asked. "Not yet. I don't want to do it when everyone else is around," Jamie said. "I have to tell her Jamie. She has to put out a statement," Char said. "I know what she'd say," Jamie replied. "If she signs off on it, I'll agree to it," Char said. "I'll talk to her when we get there," Jamie said. "See you in Phoenix," Char said as she hung up. Kurt closed the door to the bunks and came back to the stateroom. "Just spill it," Kurt said. "I have to talk to Piper before anyone else," Jamie said. "That Colt guy up to no good," he asked. "That's one way of putting it," Jamie replied. "Honestly, don't tell her before she goes on. Do it when y'all are alone. Just give me the sign and I'll get the guys to scatter," Kurt said. "Appreciate it," Jamie said. Kurt went to get some music work done with Piper and Harley and Jamie sent a message to the real estate agent friend of his about that house.

They worked away at the song Piper had been playing around with and got music. She hadn't even finished writing lyrics, but by the time they arrived in Phoenix, the song was done and recorded even if that was only on her phone. "I'm in love with that song. Damn," Piper said. Jamie came out and leaned against the door frame. "And what's it called," Jamie asked. "Lost and Found," Piper replied. "Damn," Jamie said. "It was stuck in my head for days," Piper said. "And we're here," the

driver said as the security gate closed behind them. Jamie
motioned towards Kurt. "Anyone hungry," Piper teased.
"Understatement," Harley said. Kurt shot Jamie a look like he
apologized. They went and got lunch and sat outside and
relaxed a bit. Piper did her sound check with Jason and came
back to get her outfit picked out. Jamie walked onto the bus
behind her, trying to talk to her. "What you wearin," Jamie
asked. "Thinking the black leather and the silver top," Piper
said. She slid into the outfit and Char hopped on the bus.
Jamie shook his head and Char gave him a look. "And," Piper
asked. "Perfect," he said. He slid his black shirt on with his
black jeans and Piper went into the arena to go to hair and
makeup.

Jamie shook his head. "I can't," he said. Char walked over to
Harley and asked the hair and makeup team to step out for a
minute. "What's wrong," Piper asked. "We're having a little
issue. Something came up," Char said. "Just say whatever it
is," Piper said knowing that the one thing she was worried
about was ready to drop a bomb. "So, after that situation
that we dealt with last night, there was another issue. He's
gone to the press with a complete lie. We all know it is," Char
said. "And what did he say," Piper asked. "Doesn't matter,"
Char said. "Yeah it does," Piper said. "He said that you were
sleeping with him and only with Jamie for looks. Like I said,
it's a line of BS," Char said. "And," Piper asked. "He's trying to
tear y'all down," Char said. "There is no way in hell I am
letting a guy like that ruin everything. Not happening. No
how, no way. No guy is tearing down what I've spent years
building up. I'm nominated for a dang award and the press
aren't gonna stop asking now. The man takes his damn
clothes off for a living," Piper said as the weight of the
problem seemed to feel heavier and heavier. "Piper, we can't
make him leave you alone. We tried a cease and desist. He
hasn't backed off. It's like someone's paying him to come

after you. Whoever you ticked off isn't about to back off that easily," Char said. "Then find out who," Piper replied.

Char headed off and Piper tried calming herself down. "He's not gonna mess this up. Jason knows that he's up to something. He's not gonna let him mess things up," he said. "This is not gonna mess this up tonight. After how well things went last night, I'm not letting it go there," Piper replied. He kissed her. They came in and finished hair and makeup and they headed off to the meet and greet. "Just ignore his stupid crap," Jamie said. Piper nodded, kissed him, brushed her lipstick from his lips and walked in.

Piper finally finished the meet and greet and went outside to get a little air. Jamie was right behind her. "Piper," he said. "Did you know," Piper asked. "I didn't want to tell you until we had a little time. I didn't want to mess yesterday up either," Jamie replied. "I appreciate that. Honestly, I need to keep my mind on the show. I can't do this Colt crap tonight," Piper said. "I know it's the last thing you wanna deal with. He's gonna keep going. Char managed to buy you 24 hours before people are gonna be asking questions," Jamie said. She looked at Harley. "I have an idea," Piper said. "Uh oh," Jamie said. "I know how to deal with it, but I need another day," Piper said. "I don't even wanna know," Jamie joked. Piper kissed him. He walked her inside and they went over to the band. "I need your help tonight. I need to do a song and I need everyone doing it together," Piper said. "Done," Kurt said. "Alright. This one is not gonna be an easy night," Piper said. "Whatever it is, leave it here," Keith said. Piper nodded. They said a quick prayer and warmed up to go on. The band went on and after a quick kiss to Jamie, Piper headed on that stage to a stadium of roaring fans. It was exactly what she needed. She had a room full of people cheering her on.

The show was amazing. Even the duet was great. As soon as they were done, Jason's bus and Piper's headed off to Texas. "So, what's this plan," Keith asked. "Y'all are gonna hear about it anyway and I know Harley's gonna want to kick butt. Colt went to the press," Piper said. "About what? You didn't do anything," Harley said. "He said that I was sleeping with him and only with Jamie for the money," Piper said. "Oh lord. Seriously? He needs a life," Harley said. "We're gonna do something I swore I didn't want to do. I know that the fans would love it plus everyone loves a good revenge song," Piper said. "Girl, I knew that's what you were thinkin," Harley said. Piper looked at Jamie. "Totally up to you. Sounds like a plan to me as long as it's not directed at me," Jamie said. "Deal," Piper said. Jamie kissed her and she got going on some lyrics. The guys fidgeted with the music half from what Piper was humming. By midnight, they had a big dent in the song. Jamie just watched. He was in awe of her. By 1:30, they had a big enough dent in the song to get some rest. Piper washed her makeup off and brushed out the hairspray and went into the stateroom.

When she walked in, Jamie was curled up on the bed. "Saved you room. Get in here," Jamie said as Piper closed the door and locked it. She slid the phones onto the charger and slid into the bed with him. "Babe," Jamie said. "Yes handsome," Piper said. "I know that it was the last thing you wanted to hear, but you took it like a trooper," Jamie said. "I had to. If they'd seen how upset I really was, they'd be telling me to kick his backside," Piper said. "Babe, he's pushing a button. Instead of stooping to his level, you're doing things your way. You're showing him that he can't hurt you. That you're better than him. That's all that matters," Jamie said. She snuggled to him. "What," he asked noticing the gears in her mind turning. "Just figured out the perfect song name," Piper said. "Which is," he asked. "You can't break me," Piper said. "Sorta like that Kelsea Ballerini song Miss me more," Jamie asked. Piper nodded. "Exactly like it. Hits just where it needs to," Piper said. "That mean you're goin back to workin on it," Jamie asked. "Sleep first," Piper said. "Good answer," he said as he kissed her. "I know why you didn't tell me," Piper said. "It was such a good day. I didn't want him messing it up," Jamie said. "I know. I'm glad you didn't. It'll be fine," Piper said. "Like we said, he can't break me down. He doesn't get to do that to anyone," Piper said. "All that matters is you right now," Jamie said. "What am I supposed to do about him though," Piper asked. "My security team is handling it. He was served a cease and desist," Jamie said. "Still gonna look bad in the press," Piper said. Jamie kissed her. "Like you said, worry about you," Jamie said.

Piper kissed him and he snuggled her tight to him. "What," Piper asked. He kissed her, devouring her lips and slid her leg around him. "And what do you want," Piper teased. "My woman," he said. "Oh really," Piper asked. "Kinda like you too". "Just like," he asked. "Workin on it," Piper said. "Just workin on it? Really," he said as he peeled his shirt off. "Workin on it," Piper teased. "You are so in for it," Jamie said as he peeled her t-shirt off, revealing the silky skin underneath. "Much better," Jamie said. "And why's that," Piper asked. He kissed her, leaning into her arms. "Because even if you aren't gonna say it, I know you do," Jamie said. "You're still on that," Piper teased. He kissed her. "I know you do," he said. "Maybe," Piper replied. He kissed her again and that kiss just made the entire room feel like the a/c was broken. "Piper," he said when they came up for air. "Yes sexy," Piper said. "I love you," he said. "And you think it's that easy," Piper teased. "Piper," he said. "When you know you'll know," Piper replied. He kissed her and snuggled into her arms. He made love to her until he had spent every ounce of energy. When he collapsed into her arms, he slid to the side and Piper turned to face him. "What," he asked. "What am I gonna do when you have to go home," Piper asked.

"Miss the heck outta me," Jamie answered. Piper kissed him. "You think so," she joked. "You will. You'll miss me something fierce," he said. "Probably," Piper said. He kissed her. "Probably my butt," he joked. "Definitely," Piper said. "That's more like it," he said. Piper kissed him. "Never ever give up," she said. "What on earth would make you think I ever will," Jamie asked. Piper kissed him and curled up into his arms. She actually fell asleep on his shoulder. "Love you," he said. "Like you too," Piper said. He shook his head and within maybe 2 minutes, he was out cold.

Piper woke up the next morning and Jamie was still out cold. Whatever it was that had him upset the day before, he had obviously got past it. Piper slid out of his arms and put her workout clothes on, going into the sitting area to work on the song. By the time Keith was awake, she had the rest of the lyrics. She handed them to him and after a quick read, his jaw dropped. "I mean dang lady," Keith said. "One way of telling him where to go," Piper said. "This is crazy awesome. Okay. I'm gonna pick at the song until I can get the music just right. We can go over it when everyone's up," Keith said. Piper nodded. "You really like," Piper asked. "The best way to say screw you without directing it towards him," Keith said. "That was sorta the plan," Piper said. "Well, you did it. How you doing with all of it," Keith asked. "Just annoys me that he thinks it'll make a difference. He's not exactly a decent person," Piper said. "If he starts another problem or tries to show up, just tell me if Jamie's not here alright," Keith asked. "I will. I appreciate it," Piper said. "Appreciate what," Jamie asked as he yawned and pulled his shirt on. "Being my bodyguard when you head home," Piper said.

"Well at least I know I have backup," Jamie joked. Piper kissed him. "What time do you think we're coming in," Piper asked. "Probably around 1. Y'all can get checked into the hotel and get settled," the driver said. "Awesome. Thank you," Piper said. "Most welcome Miss Piper," the driver said. Piper made breakfast for everyone and brought some to the driver with a fresh coffee. "Girl, this omelet is amazing," Keith said. "Well thank you," Piper said putting some aside for everyone else in the microwave. "You know I am not just dating her for her cooking, but it's a pretty good perk," Jamie joked. Piper kissed him, topping off the coffee and sat down with him.

"So, we don't have a show until when," Keith asked. "Thursday I think. We're doing Houston then Dallas and San Antonio then start working our way towards Nashville," Piper said. "Last weekend," Jamie said. "Don't remind me," Piper said. The rest of the band got up and so did Jess. "Breakfast is in the microwave," Piper said. "And how goes the work on the song," Kurt asked. "Got the lyrics done and Keith got a head start on the music," Piper said. "Meaning we may be performing it tonight," Kurt asked. "Tomorrow," Piper said. "Then we're rehearsing once it's done," Keith asked. Piper nodded. "I need a lady opinion on it," Piper teased. "You got me and Jess," Harley said. "Perfect," Piper said.

They all hung out and worked away on the song until Jamie slid his hand in Piper's and walked her to the stateroom. "What's up," Piper asked as he closed the door. "Char texted," Jamie said. Piper looked at it and called her on speakerphone. "What's up," Piper asked. "Four interviews. I booked them for tomorrow," Char said. "I think we have a solution and it'll be tomorrow night," Piper said. "What," Char asked inquisitively. "Well, we're workin on a new song. It's a woman power song. It'll cover the BS," Piper said. "Alright. Just let me know if y'all are 100% doing it," Char said. "We are. The song will be done today," Piper said. "I can get y'all into a recording studio tomorrow morning if you can handle it," Char said. "Alright," Piper said. "And since I know I'm on speakerphone, Jamie can you take care of it," Char asked. "Definitely," Jamie said. "Alright then. The interviews will be just before the show and we can get them to come down to the show to see the song," Char said. "Perfect," Piper said. "And by the way, I have a revised tour list. He added dates. Y'all have November to end of January off. It's because the weather situation gets hairy after November," Char said. "Alright," Piper said.

They got to the hotel finally, got checked into the suites and managed to finish the song with everyone happy. They were all 100% behind it. Piper was just worried that Colt would get worse. "We got this. You don't need to keep worrying," Keith said. "Jamie," Piper said. "Babe, this one is gonna be huge. When we finish recording, it's gonna be on every dang cell phone in the world. You're good," Jamie said. "Can we go in today before I change my mind," Piper asked. Jamie went and made a call and got a message back that they were welcome to come in. "Let's go," Jamie said.

Truly it was the first time she'd seen him doing the one thing he loved to do. He was beyond good at it. He was amazing. By the time dinner hit, they had a good first run at it. By the time it got to 10pm, the song was done. They all sat down in the main room and Jamie pressed play on the recording. They listened through the lyrics and the music. It was perfect. It was the exact way Piper wanted it. It would hit the exact notes she wanted. It was exactly what she wanted to say and do. He wasn't ever breaking her now. Colt was either going to get ten times worse, or he was gonna back off and never go near her again. She hoped it meant he'd back off.

Piper let Char know the recording was complete and after 10 minutes of the song in hand, Char had a press release drawn up. She sent it to Piper for confirmation and Piper rewrote the entire thing, sending it back to Char. Within 10 minutes, Char called. "What's up," Piper asked. "You mean since I'm listening to it on repeat," Char joked. "What'd the label say," Piper asked. "They're releasing it. We're putting something on the website and we need you to do a post. You good with that," Char asked. "Nobody's gonna see it," Piper said. "You have almost a million followers. Just go on," Char said. "Send me the link and I'll post it. We got this," Piper said. "The interviews start at 10. I'll meet y'all at the hotel," Char said.

Piper got everyone together. She made a decision about the right thing to say and ran with it. "I know that y'all have heard about some really messed up rumors that started recently. So you hear it from me, they're a load of bull. Before you meet the right one, there are always bad eggs. The guy who started those rumors was one really bad egg. Now for the good stuff. There's a new song to download online tonight that'll be on the next CD. It's called You Can't Break Me. The link is in the post. Go get it. When someone tries to take anyone down, this is how we handle it. Hope y'all love it and see you at the next tour stop," Piper said. She went into Instagram and posted it complete with the link to the new song. It went to her Twitter, Instagram, Facebook and everything else. "What do you think," Piper asked. "If this doesn't get him to screw off, I don't know what will," Jamie said. "You were amazing," Piper said. "Pretty great yourself," Jamie said as Piper slid into his lap. "Seriously though, that was pretty great. We haven't recorded like this in forever," Keith said. "And it was a million times better than last time," Kurt said. "Meaning we found our new producer," Piper joked. Jamie smirked. "Deal," Jamie said. Piper kissed him. "Now can we go back and get sleep so I can go hang with Carter," Harley said. "Alright," Piper said.

They all headed off and went back to the hotel. The minute they were through the door to their suite, Jamie kissed Piper.

"And what's that for," Piper asked as he locked the door behind them. "Because I love you. I get that the stupid crap with him just made things hard, but that song was absolutely amazing. He doesn't get to break you or even think about trying," Jamie said. "That's what I said. That's why we wrote it," Piper said. "Babe, I had no idea that's how good it was gonna turn out. That was amazing," Jamie said. "Something tells me that song is gonna be a regular every night," Piper teased. Jamie kissed her. "I'm proud of you," he said. Piper kissed him. "I'm proud of you too. You haven't even threatened to whoop his butt," Piper teased. He kissed her. "That's because I'm not back in Savannah yet," he teased. Piper slid her shirt off and went for the shower. Jamie grabbed them each a glass of wine and put it on the bedside table. He followed the trail of clothes, putting them into the laundry bag and walked into the bathroom. He slid into the shower behind her and saw her trying to take a deep breath. All of that strength was just a façade. He wrapped his arms around her and she turned to kiss him. "You alright," Jamie asked as he washed her hair for her. "I don't get why he feels the need to do this stupid stuff," Piper said.

"You want the truth," Jamie asked. "What," Piper asked. "He wants you. That's it. You. He knows he can't get you. You're an amazing woman and he's just pissed that you wouldn't accept him," Jamie said. "I don't even know if that's enough," Piper said. "You made a statement. One hell of one," Jamie said. Piper kissed him and they stepped out of the shower. He wrapped a towel around her, wrapped one around himself and carried her to the bed, leaning her onto it. "Now you get to relax. Three days of no stress," Jamie said. "Except I have interviews thanks to idiot," Piper said. He kissed her. "For tonight then, he doesn't exist," Jamie replied. He leaned in and kissed her again, curling up into her arms. "You are just so dang cute," Piper teased. He kissed her. "Love you too," he teased. He curled up on the bed with her and one hot kiss led to making out. That led to the hottest sex they'd ever had. Something about that song had him hot and bothered. She'd fought back with the one thing he couldn't ignore. He also knew that the song was gonna be number one in a heartbeat. It was one of the best songs he'd heard in a long time. He knew that it was all from her heart. That's what made it so important. The fact that standing up to Colt got him hot under the collar, had him even more turned on. They kept going and going. She was on top, then he was, then he kissed her with an intense kiss and they kept going until her toes were curled so tight they cramped. Finally, he collapsed into other arms and with one last kiss, he lost all control.

"I love you," Jamie said when he finally managed to catch his breath. Piper kissed him. "Still nothin," he joked. "You'll know," Piper said. He kissed her and she leaned against his shoulder and he curled his arm around her and pulled her to him. "You alright," he asked. "My legs are still shaking," Piper joked. He kissed her. "I don't ever wanna let go," Jamie said. "Good. I don't want you to either," Piper replied. He looked at her. "Piper," Jamie said. "I don't. I know that you…" He kissed her before she said another word. That was better than hearing those three words. That feeling that she had was so much more than saying I love you. "Piper," he said. "Mm," Piper replied. "I got some good news," Jamie said. "Which is," Piper asked as she pulled up the blankets and snuggled into him. "That house between ours. They accepted the offer on the house," Jamie said. "What," Piper asked. "Meaning we build what we want and we don't have to move," Jamie said. "That house is bigger than mine," Piper said. "Then we tear one of ours down or both and build what we want," Jamie said. "Who's are we getting rid of," Piper asked. "Up to you. Whoever's house we take down, we stay in the other together," Jamie said. "That's insane," Piper said. "Have 4 architects working on it. Sorta decided on one thing we definitely need," Jamie said. "Which is," Piper asked. "Recording studio so you can record instead of doing it on your phone," Jamie said.

Piper smirked and shook her head. "I love the idea," Piper said as she yawned. He kissed her forehead and snuggled her to him. "Just determined to get me to move in aren't you". "I just want you to be happy and have what you want instead of settling," Jamie said. "Jamie, a huge house is a great dream, but I don't need something huge. If I'm touring, I'm never gonna get to enjoy it," Piper said. He kissed her. "You will. Whatever happens in the future, you will. We just make it our way. Huge tub to relax, huge master with a balcony so we can sit on the porch and have coffee. We can even put a glider loveseat so we can just relax out there," he said. Piper looked at him. "Thought of everything," Piper teased. "And a room or three in case little feet come in our lives," he said. "Planning everything out," Piper teased. "As long as we're together, I don't care what else happens. I only need you," Jamie said. He kissed her and Piper snuggled in tighter. "All I need is a big tub, somewhere to write and us," Piper said. "Nice throwing that in," he teased. "We need to get some rest," Piper said. "Just wake me up before you go do the workout. I'll go with you alright," Jamie asked. Piper nodded, kissed him and they curled up and were asleep not long later.

The next morning, Piper woke up and went to get ready for the gym when Jamie woke up. "Two minutes," Jamie said. Piper nodded. He got dressed and they headed down to meet Jess at the gym before the insanity began with the press. Jamie couldn't help the smile he had ear to ear. "What is with the perma-grin today big bro," Jess asked. "Nothin. We were just talking last night. Realized how amazing my woman is,"

Jamie said. "You're making me nauseous," Jess said. They did the workout as Jamie saw the difference after just a couple weeks. She even held her head higher. That thought that Char and Piper's label had tried to change her was gone. They wanted her to be able to walk head high onto those stages without worrying. The fact that it made her even sexier to him was just an added bonus. Every time she stepped on that stage, she was stronger, more powerful and so full of confidence it was overflowing to everyone else.

They finished up and Jess pulled Jamie aside as Piper finished stretching out. "Dude, you were in dreamland. What's goin on," Jess asked. "I love her. Every dang day it just gets bigger. She went from not letting anyone get close because she was afraid of being judged to hitting that stage with her head held high," Jamie said. "You are totally whipped," Jess said. "Dang right I am," Jamie said. He came back into the gym area, helped Piper finish stretching out and they headed up to the suite. "How are you feeling," Jess asked. "Good. Tired but good," Piper said. "You may need to amp up what you're eating," Jess said. "Spinach and cheese omelets, turkey bacon and yogurt. That's what you told me to have," Jamie teased. "Well if both of y'all are doin it," Jess teased. "I'm good. I miss not being able to work out on the bus. That's my only issue," Piper said. "We'll figure something out," Jess said. "What are you up to today little sis," Jamie asked. "Meeting up with Harrison. He flew in to hang out a bit," Jess said. "Her man," Jamie teased. "You know you can invite him to the show if you want," Piper said. "I appreciate that. I'll ask him," Jess said. They stepped off the elevator and Jess went her way while Piper and Jamie went down to the suite.

Jamie called breakfast in and just as they were about to sit down and relax, Harley knocked at the door. "Come on in Harley," Jamie said as he opened the door. "Did you see the news this morning," Piper asked. "Just got back from the gym.

What's up," Piper asked. She handed her phone to Piper. In big letters across the screen was the one thing Piper totally wasn't expecting:

Country Songstress hits number one on the iTunes and Billboard Charts with a midnight release. Piper Adams hits back with a new song – You Can't Break Me.

"You're kidding right," Piper asked. "It's in 5 magazines and on MSN. Trust me, it's real," Harley said. "There's no way," Piper said. "Girl, we did it. We really really did it," Harley said. Piper wrapped her arms around Jamie. "Looks like that plan went just perfectly," Jamie said. Piper hugged Harley and when the breakfast showed, Piper was more than tempted to turn the juice into mimosas. "This is insane," Piper said. "We are celebrating today girl. Whatever you wanna do," Harley said. "Go get changed then. I have to do interviews and all of y'all are comin," Piper said. "Done. I'll message the guys and let them know," Harley said as she headed back to her room. Piper looked at Jamie with a grin ear to ear. "What," he asked. "All your fault," Piper said. "You wrote it," he replied. Piper kissed him. Just as she was about to start crying tears of joy, there was a knock at the door.

Piper answered and the room service waiter came in and set the table up for breakfast and put the food at the table. "Thank you," Piper said. The waiter left and they sat down and had a quick breakfast. "This is so dang good," Piper said. "Could be because you're hungry," he teased. Piper kissed him. "You know that you're comin today right," Piper asked. He nodded. "If that's what you want sexy," Jamie said. Piper kissed him again. They finished breakfast and went and hopped in the shower, then went and got dressed. Piper slid on the one outfit she loved that had been packed for interviews. She put the extensions in, did her makeup and just as she was about to get up, Jamie smirked. "What," she asked. "You're missing something," Jamie teased. "Which would be what," Piper asked. He kissed her. "Now you're good," he joked. Piper shook her head and slid her shoes on. Jamie put on her favorite cologne and just as they were about to head out, Char called.

"Yep," Piper said. "You ready to go? The interviews start in a half hour," Char said. "If I'm goin, we're all going. We wrote the song together," Piper said. "Already notified. We'll meet y'all downstairs. We have to get goin asap," Char said. "On the way down," Piper said. They headed downstairs and Piper and Jamie hopped into the car to go to the first stop. They arrived and Piper and Jamie stepped out hand in hand. They walked in and Piper and Jamie sat down and the band was right behind her. She knew what bringing Jamie would mean, and she didn't care. She didn't even let go of his hand.

"Miss Piper Adams just stepped into the studio y'all. You've been requesting that song all morning and now we finally get to ask the question everyone wants to know the answer to. Firstly, a big welcome to y'all and your guest," the DJ said. "Well thank you. We are so happy to be here," Piper said. "I have to cut to the chase. What is the story behind the song we've been listening to on repeat since midnight," the DJ asked. "Well, a rumor was spread by someone I used to know and instead of hitting back and turning things into a Twitter war, I opted for higher ground. That song was about how I feel now. I'm lucky to have all of these amazing people in my life and since they're pretty much family, nobody is getting close to messing that up for any of us," Piper replied. "And this must be the man that everyone is talking about. Jamie, you are one lucky man," the DJ said. "That I am," Jamie replied. "One question Piper, is that song added to the set list for the next shows," the DJ asked. "Well, that's totally up to the fans. If you want it on the set list, it will be," Piper said. "We may need a few more copies at this rate. We've played it by request at least 10 times since midnight. Everyone is loving that song. Also, a huge congrats for the CMA nom. That's huge for a new artist," the DJ said. "Honestly, I thought that I was dreaming that moment. I'm just happy that this awesome group of people were right there at my side for it. I don't know where I'd be without them," Piper said as Kurt and Keith rubbed her shoulder as a thank you. "I can just imagine. So, was the song a group collab or did you do it on your own," the DJ asked. "All of our stuff is usually a group collab. Sometimes I can pull a couple off about 80 percent, but finishing the whole thing as a team has always been the way we work," Piper said. "Very rare," the DJ said. "And that's what makes us family as well," Piper said. "Well y'all, for the first two callers you can ask miss Piper any question you want," the DJ said.

Jamie almost laughed. "Alright. I need to know the joke," the DJ teased. "One of the last interviews I did, Jamie called in to tease," Piper joked. "That's totally not happening today," the DJ teased. "Alright. Caller number one." "I love the new song Miss Piper. My question is, what did you mean by the song," the caller asked. "The inspiration you mean. Well, I've seen how amazing Kelsea Ballerini did with Miss me more. I wanted a song that had that same power. That same empowerment. I wanted the listeners to know that they didn't have to take it when people aren't good to them or nice to them. Standing up for yourself is the best thing you can do in any situation. This song was just a way to fight back. When you have a bad breakup, you need a song to pull you out of that funk. This is that song for me and I hope that all of y'all feel the same way," Piper said. "Amazing," the DJ said. "We all thought it was something missing. Kelsea started it," Piper joked. "Alright, caller number two," the DJ said. "Miss Harley, what's the one dream you're still holding onto that you hope happens," the caller asked. She looked at Harley and Jamie. "That is a super amazing question. The one dream is that every woman or guy that I know has the one thing that makes them happy. Whether it be a boyfriend or a girlfriend, I want everyone to be happy. I don't want anyone to feel defeated. I don't want anyone feeling like they are less than. I want everyone to know that they have someone even if that someone is just a song. This song could even help people that are bullied to get their confidence back," Piper said.

"We were discussing that on the show the other day. There are so many people bullied out there. You've had struggles in your past. What's your advice," the DJ asked. "I learned one very big lesson and it took most of my life to learn it. I didn't have the greatest friends in my younger years. I got teased for my weight, for my glasses, for my braces and even for acne. I got teased because people thought I wasn't slim enough to perform. Women get that standard all the time. I got told by someone that looks aren't why I'm on that tour. They're not why I have the people around me that I do now. There's nothing to hide. I'm me. I'm imperfect, have an I hate my clothes day and have those down moments just like everyone else. Stop judging yourself by how others see you. Love you the way you are. Don't settle for someone who doesn't want you the way you are. There are good ones out there," Piper said as she looked at Jamie.

They finished up the questions and Piper introduced the new song. After a quick thank you to the DJ and a couple photos for promo, They headed out. "Girl, you didn't have to do all that," Keith said. "Yeah I did. It's because all of y'all that the song is out there," Piper said. "Where we goin next," Harley asked. "Three more stations and we're back at the hotel," Char said. "We don't need to be there right," Kurt asked. "Wifey flying in," Piper asked. Kurt nodded. "Y'all can go if you want. Jamie's comin," Piper replied. "Good," Jamie teased. Harley hugged Piper at the next stop and Jamie and

Piper went into the next interview while the car took everyone back to the hotel. "You sure," Jamie asked. "They're gonna ask and I'd rather you were there," Piper said. He kissed her.

The next stop was the same and then the one after that just got better. By the time they made it back to the hotel, Piper was eager to just get out and enjoy herself. "What are we doin today," Piper asked. "We're goin out so I can show my sexy woman off," Jamie said. "And where are we going," Piper asked. "You'll see when we get there," he teased. They got back to the hotel, Piper got changed and they headed out. "Jamie," Piper said. "You'll see when we get there," he teased. They arrived an hour or so later and all Piper saw was sand. "Galveston," Piper said. He slid her sandals off, slid his runners and socks off and rolled his pants up. "Walk on the beach," he said. Piper kissed him and they walked together hand in hand. When she heard camera clicks, she tuned them right out. They finished their walk and went back to the car. "Lunch," Jamie asked. Piper nodded. "Date day," Piper said.

They hopped back in the car and Piper thought they were going back to the hotel. Instead, they ended up at a mall. "Jamie," Piper said. "There's a store in here that I wanted you to see," he said as he started to get butterflies. They stopped at a little shop outside of the main mall and Piper saw furniture. "And what's this," Piper asked. "You'll see when we get in there," Jamie said. They hopped out of the car and went inside. "Jamie. About time," the shop keeper said. "Henry, this is Piper. Babe, my buddy Henry," Jamie said. "Nice to meet you," Piper replied as he shook her hand. "How is it going," Jamie asked. "Almost finished. Just have to pick out the stain like I said," Henry replied. "For what," Piper asked. Henry walked them back to the workshop he had and unveiled it; a headboard that was so intricately carved that it looked like a piece of artwork. "The posts like you said you

243

wanted plus that design that we were talking about," Henry said. She saw the magnolias, what looked like a live oak with Spanish moss and hearts as the leaves of the flowers. "This is beautiful," Piper said. "It's her choice," Jamie said. "For what," Piper asked. "Come choose a color," Henry said. She looked through them and chose one that was clear to show off the details of the carving. "I had a feeling that's what you would want," Henry said. "It's too beautiful for it to be covered up," Piper said. Just as she looked harder, she saw what looked like two rings entwined in the center. "What's that," Piper asked. "Never seen a double knot in the wood. I honestly didn't want to touch it," Henry said as he winked at Jamie.

"You two are up to something. Just say whatever it is," Piper said. "Future idea," Jamie said. Piper shook her head. "And you needed my input why," Piper asked. "First piece for the new house. He's working on one other one but he's not showing us until we need it," Jamie teased. "Meaning what," Piper asked. "Not gonna jinx it Miss Piper," Henry said. "Alright then. It really is absolutely beautiful," Piper said. "Did you want to show her the other pieces you were asking about," Henry asked. Jamie nodded. Henry showed her the sofa, the oversized chair, the live edge tables and the dining table with live edge on all four edges. "These are amazing," Piper said. "They'll be delivered for next week," Henry said. "Much appreciated my friend," Jamie said. "Nice meeting you and thank you," Piper said. They headed out and hopped into the car. "What are you up to," Piper asked. "I'm glad you asked," Jamie replied.

Chapter 13

"Jamie," Piper said. He kissed her. "Figured if we were moving in together we should have some furniture that's ours instead of yours or mine," Jamie said. "You know I didn't say yes right," Piper asked. "And I got the house plans from three different architects and they're in 3d on my iPad. We pick one and go from there," he said. "Jamie," Piper replied. "Pick one," he replied. He showed them to her and her jaw almost hit the floor. "Jamie," Piper said. "What do you think," he asked. "This looks like a dang hotel or a palace," Piper said. "Now look at the other two," Jamie said. Both of them were the dare to dream places. She shook her head. "It's too much Jamie. Way too much. It's like you're building a castle," Piper said. "Look at the third one," he said. She looked and it was a lot more toned down. It had everything they wanted and wasn't so massive. It had 6 bedrooms, but it didn't feel like it. "Now that's more realistic," Piper said. "You didn't see the master," he replied. He showed her and her jaw hit the ground. "That's like a dang fantasy room," Piper said. "So we both have tons of room and a huge balcony to relax on," he replied. "Jamie," Piper said. "You like," he asked. Piper nodded. "It's beautiful," Piper said as she saw the glassed in sun porch. The oversized pool and hot tub was breathtaking. "This would take months," Piper said. "And we have time. You can move in to my place or the other way around. Whatever you want to do, we can do it," Jamie said.

"Jamie, I don't even know what to say," Piper said. "Say that we can do this," Jamie said. "You're talkin something crazy," Piper said. "Piper," he said. "You sure that's what you want? I'm gonna be..." He kissed her. "I've never been so dang sure in my life," Jamie said. Piper shook her head. "Since your place has all the security and everything, we can go over there, but Harley is staying with me," Piper said. "We'll figure it out. The guest house at my place is almost 2500 square feet. That way she has her own space," Jamie said. "I can't believe I'm even saying this," Piper said. "I love you," he said. "You're still nuts," Piper teased. He kissed her again and she slid into his arms. "Best day in a long dang time," Jamie said. Piper nodded. "I still can't believe this," Piper said. "And," he asked. "And what," Piper asked. "I swear if you don't just say it, I am seriously…" "Say what," Piper said. He shook his head. "Jamie." They headed back to the hotel and just as they were about to stop to turn into the hotel, she looked at him. "What," he asked. "We can finish the conversation upstairs," Piper said.

Jamie was pissed. Actually, pissed was an understatement. They headed in and went up to the suite. "Just say whatever the hell it is," Jamie said. She got him a glass of wine and handed it to him. "What," he asked. "Do you think I wanted that moment when there's a cab driver there," Piper asked. "Meaning what," he asked. "Forget it," Piper said. She went in and slid her dressy shoes off and went over to see Harley.

"You alright," Harley asked when Piper opened the door. "Not even a little," Piper said. "What's wrong," Harley asked. "He's not the right one," Piper said. "And you're saying that now why," Harley asked. "He practically demanded that I said I love him. Who the heck does that," Piper said. "You alright," Harley asked. Piper shook her head. "Do you want me to talk to him," he asked. "Not worth the time," Piper said. "Girl, just tell him how you feel. You know you love him," Harley said. "He bought the house between mine and his and he's building a house for us. His freaking guest house is huge. He offered it to you. He just makes plans without even asking me or waiting for a damn decision," Piper said. "You need to breathe. You're hallucinating," Harley said. "Not even a little. He had someone carve a headboard for our bed and started talking about cribs. This is freaking insane," Harley said. "You were talkin about it too when y'all first met," Harley said.

"Two bottles of wine in but not like that," Piper said. "What do you want me to do," Harley asked. "I can't do this," Piper said. "You're losin your marbles. You love him and you dang well know you do. Stop flipping out. You're just losing it because he's jumping ahead instead of waiting for you to catch up," Harley said. Piper shook her head. "I need to go. Anywhere," Piper said. "You need to quit outrunning what you want and just be with him," Harley said.

Piper shook her head. Harley walked her out to the balcony and told her to take a couple deep breaths. Not 2 minutes later, Jamie knocked at the door. Piper shook her head. "Hey," Harley said. "She in here," Jamie asked. "She's outside. Just let her breathe for a minute," Harley said. "Piper," Jamie said. Piper shook her head. "She'll come over in a couple," Harley said. He shook his head. "Piper, come here," Jamie said. "Hell no," Piper said. "Piper," he said. "I'll bring her over," Harley said. "Fine," Jamie said as he walked off and went down to his sister's room to talk to her.

"What's goin on," Jess asked as Jamie walked in. "I tried and she still won't say it. I just handed her everything she wanted and she walked away. She actually left the dang suite," Jamie said. "I told you not to push. Jamie, give the woman a break. She got harassed by her dang ex and had to bare her damn soul today. Breathe. Let her do things when she's ready and quit tryin to talk her into it," Jess said. "She won't even talk to me," Jamie said. "Then stop being a jackass," Jess said. "Nice," Jamie said. "Money doesn't buy Piper. Don't you get that," Jess asked. "Meaning what," he asked. "Meaning she's not there for what you can give her money wise. She's there because she cares even if the words don't come the way you want them to," Jess said. "In other words I just messed up the one thing I want more than all the money in the world," Jamie said. "Maybe," Jess said. He looked at Jess and shook his head. She saw the frustration and the desperation. She'd never seen it in him before. It was like Piper brought out every vulnerability he had. "I have to get her back," Jamie said. "Don't push. Promise me," Jess said. He nodded. He gave Jess a hug and she swore that she felt a tear on her shoulder. "Jamie," Jess said. "Yep," he replied brushing a tear away. "Dang. She broke my brother," Jess said. He kissed her cheek and went to walk down the hall when he saw Piper going into the suite. He heard the door close and it's like a lump locked itself into his throat.

He walked down the hall and went into the suite to hear the water running in the bathroom and the lock click on the door. He poured himself another glass of wine and poured a second, putting it on the bedside table. He sat on the edge of the bed, almost trying to stare a hole through the bathroom door. "Piper," Jamie said. She didn't answer. The longer she ignored him, the more desperate he started to feel. He had never ever been around anyone that could cause that reaction from him, but Piper could without even trying. He was way past loving her. He needed her like a drug addict needed a hit. She was his drug of choice. Her voice, the taste of her lips, the feel of her skin on his. All of it was his only craving. He could live without food and water. Piper was something he couldn't live without.

When he took the last sip of wine from his glass, he heard the water draining from the tub. He watched the door, taking a labored breath. Piper unlocked the door and Jamie looked up. She walked past him and put her jeans and a t-shirt on, put her hair in a ponytail and walked into the TV room. "We need to talk," Jamie said. "Nothing to talk about," Piper said. He walked into the TV room and she went to walk into the bedroom and he grabbed her hand, linking their fingers and pulling her back to him. "Let go," Piper said. "I can't," he said. "You want your way so damn bad that you're willing to start world war three. That's what you want? To get your way on command? That's not me Jamie. Never has been and never will be," Piper said as she pulled her hand away and went and sat down on the chair by the sliding door to the balcony.

She slid the door open, letting the breeze waft in. "Talk to me," Jamie asked. "About what," Piper asked. "I shouldn't have pushed," Jamie said. "Demanded," Piper replied intentionally correcting him. "Every time we talk about the future I jump in with both feet," Jamie said. "And I'm in the shallow end alone," Piper replied. "Tell me what you want," Jamie asked. "Nothing. I don't care about the house or the furniture or anything. I don't care if I'm in a freakin 900 square foot box. We don't want the same things Jamie. You made that obvious," Piper replied. "All I want is you. That's it. Just you. Nothing else. I don't care about the house. I just can't do this without you. I don't want to," Jamie said. She shook her head and almost laughed. "What," he asked. "Nothing," Piper replied. In her mind, she played through what she really wanted to say, knowing that it would kill him. She wanted to tell him that if he hadn't started a dang fight, she was going to say those three words he craved. She couldn't do it. Hitting him with that would hurt him so much more than he deserved. She bit her tongue instead. "Tell me that we can fix this," Jamie asked. She just shook her head. "Maybe we just need time," Piper replied. "Meaning," he asked. "You have to go work in the studio. Maybe we just need time apart for a little while," Piper replied.

"Piper, please. I don't care about going back. You're more important right now," he said. "Then maybe I just get..." "No," he said. "Get my own room," Piper replied. He shook his head. "Please," he asked. "I can't Jamie. Not if you're gonna keep pushing me into saying and doing stuff I don't want to do. I just need to be alone for a while," Piper said. "Piper," he said. "Why are we even doing this? You don't want me Jamie. You want your way. It's more important,"

Piper said. "Don't do this," he said. "You want to be the one who controls all of it. I'm not that submissive Jamie. I never have been and I never ever will be," Piper replied. "I want you. I want us. I can't do this without you," Jamie said. "You don't want me Jamie. You want someone who's gonna do what you want when you want," Piper said. He shook his head. "Do you want to know what I want? I want you and me together whether you ever say I love you or not. I don't care where we are. I don't care if we're on that bus the rest of our lives. I want you with me. I need you in my life," he said. "I don't...I can't," Piper said. She brushed tears away and he shook his head. "Do you want me," Jamie asked. "I do, but I know..." He kissed her. He picked her up from the chair and sat her on the bed beside him. "I'm not losing you," he said. "You don't want someone who isn't gonna do what you want," Piper said. "Yeah I do. I love you. I'm not losing you over this. All of this other crap can wait. You're more important than all of it," Jamie said. "And," Piper asked. "I'm not about to lose you," Jamie said. Piper shook her head. She got up and walked into the TV room.

He shook his head and walked in to hand her the glass of wine and saw her brushing tears away again. "Baby," Jamie said. Piper shook her head. He handed her the glass of wine. "I don't want it," Piper said. "It's your wine," he said. Piper took the glass. "Thanks," Piper said. "Am I allowed to sit," he asked. "Whatever," Piper said. "I love you. You know that right," Jamie asked. "Doesn't change anything," Piper said. "What do I have to say," Jamie asked. "Nothing," Piper said. "Tell me what to say to fix this," Jamie asked. Piper drank the entire glass and put it on the table. "Please," Jamie said. Piper shook her head and got up. He pulled her into his lap. "Enough," Piper said. She went to get up and he pulled her back to his lap. "Jamie," Piper said. "Don't walk away," Jamie said. "Let go," Piper said. He kissed her, devouring her lips and his hands held her face. "I love you. You know that right," Jamie asked. Piper nodded. "I'm not gonna stop." She slid out of his lap and went into the bedroom.

"Tell me what to do," Jamie said. "Just leave me alone," Piper said. "I can't do that. You know that," Jamie said. Piper shook her head. She texted Harley that she needed a lifeline. The reply back:

You love him. Just say the dang words. I'm not letting you break off with the one guy that I know dang well that you want. Go and talk to him before I lock y'all in a closet.

Piper went outside and sat on the balcony alone. She leaned back on the chair and he picked her up out of the chair and carried her back inside. He laid her on the bed and sat down beside her. "I can't leave," he said. "Jamie, what part of you don't want me don't you get," Piper asked. He kissed her. "The part where I am not leaving your side," Jamie said. "Why? Just answer that. Why are you so dang determined to rush through all of this," Piper asked. "You want the truth," he asked. Piper nodded. "I am so damn petrified of losing you altogether that I'm trying to hold on with both dang hands. That's why," Jamie said. "I'm not goin anywhere Jamie. I'm sitting right here trying to tell you that you have to quit trying to jump ahead of everything. You want me to move in, then you tell me that you're building a house so we have more than enough room. One minute you're fine with me waiting to say that I care and the next you're practically demanding I say it. You can't just push until you get your way," Piper said. He kissed her. "The stuff with Colt threw me alright? Who knows what he's gonna do next," Jamie said. "I said that and you told me I was nuts," Piper teased. He shook his head. "I just want to bury him. I don't want him doing anything or trying to come after you. It's not fair to you. Please just let me protect you from him," Jamie said. "I'm fighting my own fight with him Jamie. He's gonna keep going if it's you fighting. I want it over. I get that you're worried, but you're letting him ruin this relationship. You want more. I know you do. I just don't know if I'm even ready yet," Piper asked. "I'm fine with it. I just don't want to lose you," Jamie said. "As long as you don't push, I'm not gonna leave. You go too far too fast, I'm not gonna be trying to catch up," Piper replied. He looked at her, linking their hands. "Don't leave me," Jamie said.

That was all he was worried about. Living without her when he had to be back at work was bad enough, but never seeing her again was never gonna be an option for him. He had the craziest things running through his head. The fact that he already had a ring for her was the biggest. He knew the minute they met. That feeling got even stronger the minute he first kissed her. Even more the first time they slept together. Letting go was not in any way an option. He gave her a hug and didn't want to let go. "I love you Piper. More than you even know, I do," Jamie said. "I care about you too, but you have to slow the heck down," Piper said. He kissed her and slid onto the bed, lying down beside her. He curled her into his arms and thanked his lucky stars that she was still there.

They got up a while later and opted to go and have dinner, just the two of them. They got to the restaurant and they escorted them to a quiet table in the back so everyone wouldn't be staring. "You sure you're alright," Jamie asked. Piper nodded. "I will be," Piper said. They ordered and within no less than 5 minutes, a few people were staring. "Is it bad that I just wanna turn all of the fan stuff off for a night," Piper asked. "You had a bad day. That's all it was," Jamie said. "Still," Piper replied. He poured them another glass of wine and one of the on-lookers made their way over to their table. "Miss Piper, can we get your autograph," they said. "Sure," Piper said as he smirked. She signed the autographs and they got their dinner. Piper was determined to finish as fast as possible so they could get their privacy back. As soon as they were done, they paid and headed out.

When they got back to the hotel, Piper saw Jason heading in. "And how was dinner," Piper asked. "Good. How was date night," Jason teased. "Definitely interesting. Was a good dinner though," Jamie said. "So, what's the plan for tomorrow," Jason's wife asked. "Nothin at all. Rehearsing the new song," Piper said. "By the way, way to go on that one. My daughters have been cranking it since it came out," Jason said. "That was totally a team effort, but thank you," Piper said. "I think we all kinda needed that song," Jason said. "I think even kids needed it," Piper said. They headed into the elevator and headed upstairs. "You tellin me that you managed to get that song written and recorded in 2 days," Jason asked. "Helps having Jamie around," Piper said. "I may call on you for some help sometime," Jason said. "Not a problem. Just let me know," Jamie said.

Piper and Jamie went into the suite and Piper slid out of the dressy shoes. "You okay," Jamie asked. "I know that you say that you're fine with taking our time on all of the house stuff, but are you really," Piper asked. "As long as I know that I still have you, I'm fine with whatever you want. We can wait on the house stuff. It's gonna be a long while to get the blueprints approved and stuff anyway. We just start whenever we're ready or however we want to do it," Jamie said. "You sure," Piper asked. "Doesn't mean I don't want it and that I don't love you. It means that we do it when we decide to," Jamie said. "We," Piper asked. He nodded and leaned in to kiss her. "I am not letting you go for anything in the entire world," Jamie said. He kissed her and her phone buzzed. Piper grabbed it. "What's up," Piper asked seeing Char's name on the call display. "So, there's a little news. Firstly, the song is goin real well and almost has a million downloads already," Char said. "Seriously," Piper asked. "Yep," Char replied. "Okay. What's the rest of the news," Piper asked. "You're performing at the awards. They want the new song," Char replied. "Really," Piper asked. "You're the star you wanted to be," Char said. "This is crazy," Piper said. "That one song made one heck of a big difference. It's number one on every chart. It even beat Jason's song," Char said. "Meaning I should do a video right," Piper asked. "Meaning you're getting a couple days off next week. We're doing it Monday," Char said. "Where," Piper asked. "You have a couple options. Savannah at Forsyth or Wormsloe or we can do it in the Outer Banks," Char said. "I'll run it by Jamie and I'll let you know," Piper said. "We put requests out for all of them. I'm hoping it's in Savannah so you can be home a while," Char said. "Sounds perfect," Piper said.

They hung up and Jamie looked at her. "Home," he said. Piper nodded. "Let's just hope that Colt doesn't try to ruin it," Piper replied. "Don't worry about him. Worse comes to worse, I get him thrown in the jail for a couple days," Jamie joked. "Not funny," Piper said. "We can handle it either way," Jamie said. "So, we have to do the video and then you meet my folks," Piper said. "And you meet mine," Jamie replied. "What do you think," Piper asked. "You can use the house if you want to for anything," Jamie said intentionally staying off the topic of the real reason he wanted to meet them. "Alright. I'll let her know," Piper replied. He kissed her and slid his hand in hers and walked her into the bedroom. "What," Piper asked. "We're watchin a movie tonight. Last night before the shows start again," Jamie said. "Alright," Piper said. She slid on her t-shirt and Jamie kissed her. "Where are you goin," Jamie asked. "Nowhere," Piper replied. He shook his head. "You realize that's my shirt right," Jamie asked. "Nope," Piper said. "You are seriously gonna go stealing my shirt," Jamie asked. Piper nodded. "My shirt," Piper replied. He shook his head.

"Just come over and sit. The movie is starting in like 15 minutes," Jamie said. Piper got each of them a glass of wine and they curled up in the bed. Jamie flipped the TV on and the movie was just coming on. "And what movie are we watching," Piper asked. "We can either watch Gone with the Wind or we watch The Lucky one," Jamie said. "If I say Lucky One," Piper asked. "Then we're gonna need more wine," he teased. Piper shook her head. "Just turn the movie on," Piper said. "Question. About this whole meet the folks thing. You sure you still want that," Jamie asked. "My folks are coming either way," Piper said. "And," he asked. "And nothin," Piper replied. "So, if I went and talked to your dad for a little while you wouldn't be mad right," Jamie asked. "As long as it's not for any ring reasons," Piper said. He kissed her. "I'm not about to have that fight with you again. I just want to pick his brain about some stuff," Jamie said. "Like I said, as long as it doesn't have anything to do with you and me," Piper replied. In the back of his mind, he knew exactly what he wanted to ask. The fact that Piper would lose her marbles altogether if she knew didn't matter. It was the true gentleman thing to do and he wasn't losing that opportunity while he had it. They curled up and watched the movie, as he watched her nod off towards the end.

He smirked and slid her under the covers with him as he turned the TV off and turned the light out. The sheer fact that she was asleep in his arms made him almost breathe a sigh of relief. He wasn't letting go of her for anything. He kissed her forehead and she snuggled in a little more. He heard his phone buzz and grabbed his phone. One look at the screen and he answered albeit quietly. "Yep," Jamie said. "That ring you were lookin at is ready for pickup. Did you want me to pick it up and send it to the Savannah office," his assistant asked. "Sure," Jamie said. "Alright. It should be here by noon tomorrow. You're back tomorrow right," his assistant asked.

"Monday," Jamie replied. "Alright. We'll see you Monday then. The pilot will meet you in New Orleans which is the last show this week that she has. See you Monday," his assistant said. "Alright," Jamie said. "And Mr. Hastings, congratulations," his assistant said. Jamie put the phone back on the charger beside Piper's and closed his eyes. He was dang lucky she'd slept through that call. He kissed her forehead again and was out cold a few minutes later.

Piper went to get up in the morning and Jamie's arm was tight around her. She tried to slip away from him and he held on tighter. "Where you goin," Jamie asked. "To hang with your sister. Sleep," Piper said. "Nope. I'm goin with you," Jamie said. "You'd have to kinda get up," Piper said. He kissed her and rolled over, kissing her again. "Jamie," Piper said. "What," he asked brushing the hair out of her face. "I'm getting up," Piper said. "Fine. Party pooper," he teased. She kissed him again and slid out of the bed. She put her workout stuff on and Jamie got up and slid on his joggers and a tank. "You really coming with us," Piper asked. He nodded. "I'm not letting y'all go off alone," Jamie teased. They came downstairs and saw Jess warming up in the gym. They did the workout as Jamie just watched in awe. "Why are you starin," Piper asked. "Can't help it," Jamie said. They finished the workouts and headed upstairs to grab breakfast.

"What time do you have to go down to the stadium," Jamie asked. "Probably 3. Honestly, I'm just glad that I don't have to do all the press stuff first," Piper said. "The press is gonna be there. They're coming just for that song," Jamie said. "You know it's like the first song right," Piper said. "Then they're gone when you're finished it. Babe, that song is even more amazing every time I hear it," he said. Piper kissed him. They had a quick breakfast and Piper's phone went off. "Yep," Piper said. "We need you at the arena at 1. Three interviews came up and one of them is an XM station. It's huge. They 're interviewing Jason as well," Char said. "Alright. We'll be there," Piper replied. "See you at 1," Char said as they hung up. "So much for a day to relax. You alright to do this tonight," Jamie asked. "I don't exactly have a choice," Piper teased. "What if you did something like a private performance of it where they could ask whatever questions they want to ask," Jamie asked. "We can message Char and ask her," Piper said. "Might make it easier, but you know they still want to see how the fans react," Jamie said. Piper kissed him. "We have 5 1/2 hours to relax just us. No work talk," Piper teased. He kissed her. He picked her up, walked into the bathroom and proceeded to peel every inch of her clothes off. He turned the shower on and slid his workout gear off. They stepped into the steamy hot shower and he slid her under the hot water.

One kiss. Just one. One that lasted until both of them were soaked, but that kiss didn't break. He leaned her up against the wall of the shower, devouring her lips. The morning sex was somehow hotter than any moment they'd had. When they came up for air, it was only for him to nibble and kiss her neck or shoulder. When her body was shaking in his arms, he slid her to her feet. "I want you so dang bad I can taste it," Jamie whispered. "Good," Piper said. He shook his head and kissed her. She washed his hair for him, then washed hers. As they stepped out, his phone was ringing again. He kissed Piper and went and grabbed his cell.

Piper dried her hair and slid her jean shorts and tank on. "What? Tell me you're joking," Jamie said. Piper shook her head, put lotion on and checked her emails. When she saw one from her security at the house, she about lost it:

We managed to keep the house safe, but there was an issue at the gate. A gentleman was turned away and tried to find another way into the house. We doubled up security and managed to stop him before he made it up the back steps.

Jamie looked at Piper. "You alright," Jamie asked. "What happened," Piper asked. "You tell me," Jamie said. "Someone tried getting into my house," Piper said. "Colt," Jamie said. "Meaning," Piper asked. "He tried to get into my place too," Jamie said. "Like I said, that whole idea about movin in together and building the new house means him trying to bust through the gate every time," Piper said. "Were you thinking about it," Jamie asked as he took a gulp of his water. "Just saying all the more reason to hold off until he's stopped causing drama," Piper said. Jamie shook his head. "Babe, you can't outrun his stupidness. He's always gonna be an idiot," Jamie said. "And how do you think things are gonna be fixed," Piper asked. "We're fine. I'm saying that putting him in a hole would be amazing," Jamie teased. "I just don't get how all of the crap he'd done didn't get him put in a jail cell permanently," Piper said. "If he does anything else he might be," Jamie said. "I think I'm just had it with him," Piper said. He kissed her. "We'll figure it out. You know how I feel and I know that you aren't ready yet," Jamie said. "You can handle that," Piper asked. "As long as I have you, I don't care about the rest of it. If you decide you're ready whenever you are then we're full steam ahead. I kinda think that I came up with a blueprint idea that blends a little of each with the look I know you want. The plans were approved anyway, so we can do things in your time," Jamie said. He wasn't about to start that fight all over again.

"Jamie," Piper said. "Yes sexy," he said. "Thank you for not pushing," Piper said. "I just want you happy," Jamie said. She kissed him and he sent off the private performance idea to Char. She sprayed her perfume on and Jamie shook his head. "Had to didn't you," Jamie asked. Piper nodded. "Your favorite and my lucky perfume," Piper said. He sat down on the edge of the bed and slid his jeans on. "So, what do you want to do," Jamie asked. "About him? Honestly, we're heading home for Monday. When I get there, I'll deal with him," Piper replied. He kissed her. "Did I ever tell you that you're brilliant," he asked. Piper kissed him. "Suck up," Piper teased. "And what are we doin this morning anyway," Jamie asked. "What do you have planned," Piper asked. "We're goin out and getting away from the city for a while. We're relaxing instead of being all stressed," Jamie said. "Whatever you wanna do. It's up to you today," Piper said. "Then we're definitely getting out of here, but I think you'll need jeans," Jamie said. She slid into her beat up blue jeans that he loved and got their things, heading out. "Where are we headed," Piper asked. "To the one thing I know you haven't done in forever probably and something that means just you and me," Jamie said.

They got to the ranch that he'd decided on and walked around to meet the horses. "This is what we're doin," Piper asked. He nodded. "We can go on separate horses or we can go on one together. Totally up to you," Jamie said. "Then I say we go on separate," Piper said. "Because we're gonna race," he asked. "Maybe," Piper joked. They got down to the horses that they were taking out and got them saddled and headed off. The open field was away from stress and drama and away from the prying eyes of the press. He knew exactly what he wanted and he knew that's what she needed. They got to the live oak at the back of the property and they hopped off and walked the horses to where they could get some water.

"What's up," Piper asked. "You didn't tell me that you are practically an expert," Jamie said. "Just been a bit. Used to be my way to unwind," Piper said. "Well, just between you and me, you were amazing," Jamie said. "Well thank you handsome," Piper said. "You sure you're alright," he asked. Piper kissed him. "I will be. There's nothing either of us can do while we're away," Piper said. "Will you let me add security to your place," he asked. Piper nodded. It was the first time she'd just let it happen. In the back of his mind, he wondered if he'd finally got her to trust him. They hung out and just relaxed by the tree. "And what else would you like to do this mornin since we have another couple hours," Piper asked. "We are hanging out just us alone," Jamie said. "What did you want to do," Piper asked. "Had a couple plans. I'd love to go and look around and go shopping, but I also don't want to have us have to deal with the fans and stuff," Jamie said. Piper kissed him. "I appreciate that," Piper said. "I love you. You having that smile is all I need," Jamie said. Piper shook her head. "What am I gonna do with you," Piper asked. "I have a couple ideas," he joked. "We're gonna have to go back to the hotel and stuff," Piper replied. "We could," he joked. Not 2 minutes later, her phone buzzed. They sat down under the tree and Piper put the call on speaker.

"Hey Char," Piper said. "I think that idea may work. Sort of cuts down on the time that we are doing interviews. Are you alright with them hanging to do a few shots during the show," Char asked. "Most definitely. I just thought it'd be easier to have everyone in one room," Piper said. "It is a good plan. Just be prepared for more questions than you are expecting," Char said. "We kinda figured it would mean that we could somewhat control the questions," Jamie said. "It's a good point," Char said. "We'll try to keep them off the conversation about Colt. We're keeping him out of the subjects. Jamie will probably be one of the people they ask about," Char said. "Not a problem," Jamie said. "Alright. I'll see you there at 1ish. You have to do two sound checks now if that's alright," Char said. "See you then," Piper replied.

They hung up and Jamie snuggled her close to him. "You ready to head back," Jamie asked. Piper almost laughed. "Definitely," Piper said. They hopped onto a horse together and the other followed them back to the stables. Once the horses had their treats, Piper and Jamie left hand in hand. "We still have a little while. What else did you wanna do," Jamie asked. "Your day," Piper said. "Then we're going to relax while we can at the hotel," Jamie said. "Sure," Piper said. They got back and went up to the suite. When they walked in, flowers were on the counter. "Jamie," Piper said. He shook his head. He grabbed the card and saw another note from Colt:

When you want a real man, let me know.

Jamie threw the flowers in the trash and turned to see Piper. "Tell me that he didn't do this," Piper said. "He's tailing you wherever you are," Jamie said. "Then we have to do something. At least we're goin home Sunday after the show," Piper said. "What are you gonna do about him," Jamie asked. "Talk to the cops and get it solved permanently," Piper said. "I just don't want you getting hurt. I don't want him doing something stupid and coming after you," Jamie said. Piper kissed him. "Nobody is getting to either of us," Piper said. He kissed her. "Alright," Jamie said. They sat down on the sofa and curled up together until they had to leave. They just sat and talked until Harley came knocking to head down to the bus. They got their bags together, loaded them up and hopped onto the bus, checking out of the suite.

When they got to the stadium, they headed in and Piper got warmed up. She did sound check on the big stage and the little one and when she came back to the sitting area, Jamie handed her a drink. "You sounded amazing," Jamie said. Piper kissed him. "I'm not ready for all of this. I am gonna dread that performance," Piper said. "Babe, you'll be fine. I promise you," Jamie said. "And when they ask a million questions about Colt," Piper asked. "Team work," Jamie replied. Piper nodded.

They relaxed and Piper warmed up and ran through the song with the band. "Y'all ready for this," Piper asked. "We got ya," Keith said. Piper got changed and touched her makeup up and went in to do the performance for the press. They were thee and waiting and the room was full. "Now what," Piper asked before she stepped in. "Now you go and kick butt," Jamie said. "You're comin right," Piper asked. "I'll be right behind you," Jamie said. Piper kissed him and they all went inside to a room full of people. "Hey y'all. Thank you for coming. I guess we can start off with a few questions," Piper said as everyone got settled. She got a bunch of the regular questions about tours and being on the road and the new CD and without fail, the questions started about Colt. "Well, for those asking, since I know you all want to know, the new song was my response to the gentleman that started those rumors. All of them are false. He was turned down flat for even one date and did all of that for revenge for me leaving him in the wind," Piper said. "So, the rumors that he started are all fabricated," one of the reporters asked. "Everything from his mouth is a fabricated lie that he made up," Piper replied. "This is the song that I wrote when that rumor started as my response. I'd love to hear what you think." They played through the song and Jamie had a huge grin ear to ear. He was so dang proud he was worried he'd explode.

By the end of the performance, she had every reporter happy. They were all happy and loved the song – her goal was successful. Piper and the band went and they had a quick dinner together. "You sure you're ready for all of this," Harley asked. "It's gonna be alright. We got this," Piper said. "You're in way too dang good of a mood," Harley teased. "Blame that on Jamie," Piper said. "I guess y'all made up," Harley said to herself. "Something like that," Piper said. Jamie looked at Harley, wondering what was going on with her and Carter. "How's Carter," Jamie asked intentionally poking the bear.

"Good. He's coming tonight," Harley said. "That mean y'all are sharing a bunk," Keith asked. "That means we're meeting y'all in Houston before we go to San Antonio," Harley said. Jamie smirked. "That means you have a bunk to yourself," Piper teased. Jamie shook his head. "You're killin me," Jamie said. He looked down and read an email that he'd just received and his attitude completely changed. "Does this mean that there's no fighting on the bus," Kurt asked. "Yep," Piper replied. "That include us," Jamie asked. Piper nodded. "Alright then" Jamie replied. His arm slid around her waist, pulling her to him. "So, what now," the guys asked. "Now, we have a little bit to chill before I have to do the meet and greet. I have to go for 7," Piper said. "I have to go call the wife. I'll meet y'all at the bus," Kurt said. Piper nodded. Keith went to make a call, Kyle even. Harley went off and called Carter leaving Piper and Jamie alone. "What," Piper asked.

Jamie slid his hand in hers and walked her into the extra dressing room in the venue, closing the door and locking it behind them. "What," Piper asked. He kissed her, leaning her against the wall. "What are you up to," Piper asked. He kissed her. When she felt his phone buzz in his pocket, he shook his head and ignored it, pulling at her t-shirt. "Jamie," Piper said. He kissed her again. "Not happening," Piper said. "And why's that," he asked as he leaned down and was nibbling at her neck. "Because I have to go to hair and makeup and get changed," Piper said. He kissed her. "Then it won't matter if I mess your lipstick," Jamie said. Her phone buzzed two minutes later. "No," Jamie said. He kissed her. That kiss had her toes curling in her shoes. "Jamie," Piper said when they came up for air. "Fine," he said. She looked and it was Harley looking for her.

He kissed her again and his hands slid to her backside as he kissed down her shoulder and up her neck, nibbling at her ear. "I have…" He kissed her again, silencing her. "It's 5:30.

We have time," he said as he picked her up, wrapping her legs around him and pinning her to the wall. "Jamie," Piper said as she felt his phone go off again. "Not happening," he replied. Piper kissed him and he slid her to her feet. "What," Piper asked. "We're going straight to the hotel in San Antonio," Jamie said. "Why," Piper asked. "Because that way we don't have to change hotels again and we have more time alone," Jamie said. "If that's what you want," Piper said. "We have plans," he replied. "And what exactly do you have planned," Piper asked. She could feel the hot breath on her neck as he nibbled and kissed. "We are gonna be busy," he replied. Piper shook her head and he kissed her. Not 2 minutes later, her phone buzzed with a message from the hair and makeup team asking where she was. "Five minutes," Jamie said. She kissed him and grabbed her phone. "Reply to text," Piper said to Siri. She said she'd be there in 5 and he devoured her lips. She pressed send and Jamie kissed her, taking her breath away. "I love you, he said as he nibbled at her ear again. Her phone buzzed again that they had to get going on her hair and makeup. "Now you know why I wanted to leave early," Jamie said. She kissed him and they headed out of the room and went into the dressing room where the hair and makeup team were waiting.

Chapter 14

Jamie sat down in the chair beside Piper. "What," Piper asked. "Nothing," Jamie said. "Then stop staring at me like I'm a dang meal," Piper replied. "And what are you wearing tonight," Jamie asked. The stylist came over, bringing a top that Jamie was sure was way too dang sexy for the stage. "Excuse me," Jamie said. "It's fine," Piper said. "You're not wearing that," Jamie said. Piper looked at him. "Alright then, you're in the red," the stylist said. Piper looked at him and shook her head. He semi-approved. She shot him a look and he shook his head. They needed to talk. Something was brewing and it was driving him nuts. "What," Piper asked. Jamie looked at his phone and showed her the email he'd received that had him in a bad mood since dinner:

Mr. Hastings

It's come to my attention that the woman you are seeing is a liability. The situation has been brought to my attention that the woman you are with is not only engaged, but is with a gentleman who wants their relationship in the public eye. As you are a very private man, I'd suggest that you remove yourself from the situation before your private life becomes public. The gentleman she is with has attempted a second break in at the house. We are unsure what to make of this, but verified that the two of you have no relationship. Please contact me to discuss. – Jacob Harker

"And who's that," Piper asked. "My PR guy for the company," Jamie said. "He's started again," Piper asked. "I don't want you at your place alone. Are you alright with that," Jamie asked. Piper shook her head. "I'll handle him when we're back. Nobody is messing with the good mood after that performance for the press," Piper said. He kissed her hand as he held on that much tighter. "He busted into the house," Jamie said. "Then obviously your house needs more security,"

Piper teased. He shook his head. She had no idea who she was dealing with. "I came up with a solution to that problem," Jamie said. "Which one," Piper asked. He shook his head. She knew exactly what he was talking about and wasn't about to bring it up. It had already been such a good day. She wasn't letting him mess with it.

When they finished with the hair and makeup, she was even more breathtaking. She went and slid into the red outfit with the black leather leggings. She'd planned on saving it for when they got back to Georgia. She slid her heels on and he couldn't move. "What," Piper asked. His jaw dropped. He couldn't move. It was like he was in slow-motion. He gulped and the stylist smirked. "I guess he likes it," she said. Piper nodded. "Jamie," Piper said. He looked at her and the only thing running through his mind was how long they had until they were in the hotel room alone. Piper stepped out of the room and he went behind her, sliding his hand in hers. "What is with you," Piper asked as she sprayed his favorite perfume on. "Tease," he joked. They walked into the meet and greet and the fans who were lined up were losing it.

Once it was finished, he walked with her. She freshened up her makeup and went for the bathroom. "Where are you goin," Jamie asked. Piper shook her head. She freshened up and went back out to the hall. She slid her ear monitors in and the stage manager handed her microphone to her. Harley and the rest of the band came up behind her. "Lookin good there superstar," Keith said. "Well thank you," Piper said. Harley came around the corner and hung up from her call with Carter. She gave Jamie a dirty look. Obviously, she'd heard about the email.

They said a quick prayer and Jason came up behind her. "Good choice," Jason teased as she noticed he had on his Falcons t-shirt. "We still doin the duet," Piper asked. Jason nodded. "During my set," Jason said. "Works for me," Piper said. He gave everyone a shot and they did it quickly. The band headed on and Piper warmed up. "Piper," Jamie said. She nodded, slid her ear monitors in and went on stage, ignoring what that email said.

Jamie sat and watched and was in awe again. How she managed to compartmentalize, he'd never quite understand. He saw her whisper something to the band. He knew that meant a change in the set list. "How many of y'all have ever had to deal with someone that didn't take no for an answer," Piper asked as the crowd replied back with hooting and hollering. "And how many of y'all ever wanted to tell an ex where to go," she said to another roar. "This one is your payback. Your revenge song. Y'all might know it as You Can't Break Me," Piper said as they all went nuts for the song. She had a way about her and he couldn't get it off his mind. Knowing that he got to take her home meant that he was gonna win. She played through it then took a drink and looked right at him. "Alright y'all. Since I know you loved that one, we thought we'd surprise you with one that was our first big song from the CD. Y'all have it right," Piper teased hyping the crowd up. They went crazy. "This one is called Mine," Piper said. Jamie hadn't heard it in rehearsal. He knew it was on the CD, but he never thought she'd be performing it. When the crowd started to sing along, he paid closer attention.

It was the last song of the set. She signed a quick autograph or two at the front of the stage and headed off. She walked towards Jamie and went right past him, sliding her ear monitors out. "Piper," Jamie said. She kept walking. That email had her pissed as all get out. She played a good game on the stage, but the minute the lights weren't on her, she was livid. She walked into grab another drink, making herself a double jack and coke. He grabbed it out of her hand. One

267

look and she took it back walking out to get some air. She drank it in what seemed like one gulp. She was more than pissed. Getting on a bus and moving her house to the other side of town was the only idea on her mind. "Piper," Jamie said as he came up behind her. "Leave me be," Piper said. He tried to slide his hand in hers and she brushed him off. She walked back towards the stage and grabbed a ginger ale. "Hey girl," Jason's wife Kaylie said. "Hey," Piper replied. "You alright? You look like you're about to shoot fireballs," Kaylie said. "Something like that," Piper said as Jamie realized he was completely and utterly screwed.

Kaylie did her best to calm Piper down. "You heading home next weekend," she asked. "Monday actually. I'm doing a video for the song. Should be good," Piper said. "You know you're welcome to come up to Nashville. Y'all can come hang at the house," she said. "Might be an idea," Piper said. They sat around and talked, and Keith came over to talk to Jamie. The entire time, his eyes were on Piper. A little while later, the stage manager let Piper know that she had to be on at 10. Piper nodded. She looked at her watch and saw that she had a half hour to go. She walked up towards the stage and Jamie grabbed her hand, pulling her to him.

"What," Piper asked. "Come with me," Jamie said. Piper shook her head. "No," she replied. The makeup artist came over and touched her makeup up, fluffed up her hair and handed her the black jacket she had to go with the outfit. "Thank you," Piper said. The makeup artist smirked and Piper slid the jacket on. "Are we talking about this," Jamie asked. "Right now, no. I can't change the fact that your stupid lawyer believes that psycho. That's up to you to change. If that's how he's reacting, we're done," Piper said. "Piper," he said. "You follow what the lawyers suggest. Enjoy," Piper said. "What are you saying? What happened to today," Jamie asked. "Maybe you should tell your stupid lawyer that," Piper replied. She walked off and headed to the stage, knowing that she'd be heading on any minute.

She finished the performance with Jason, headed off, gave his wife a hug and went to the dressing room. She grabbed her stuff and headed onto the bus. When she stepped on, the guys were already chilling and playing video games. "I thought you were heading to the hotel with Jamie," Keith asked. "Going to wash the makeup off and put normal clothes on," Piper said. Jamie came out of the stateroom with her bag and his, grabbing her hand. "What," Piper asked. "Off," he replied. She stepped off the bus. "What," Piper asked. "We're goin," Jamie said. She grabbed her bag and went to walk back on the bus. "Have fun," Piper said. She put her bag in the stateroom and went to wash the makeup off. She slid the extensions out and when she emerged from the bathroom, the bus was empty except for Jamie. "No," Piper said. "We're going to talk," Jamie said. "I'm goin to bed alone," Piper said. "Off," Jamie said. She shook her head. "You wanna go then go. I'm stayin on the bus," Piper replied.

He was about to snap, but he knew he couldn't. He grabbed her hand, pulled her to him and went to kiss her and she backed off. "Piper, don't," Jamie said. "I didn't do a dang thing," Piper said. "Babe, please," Jamie asked. Piper shook her head. "I'm going to bed. Alone," Piper replied. He grabbed her hand, walked her off the bus and opened the door to the waiting car. The driver put the bags in the trunk and they headed off before the concert let out at all. "Jamie, do you even listen to me," Piper said. "I'm not having this conversation until we're alone," Jamie said. "Meaning," she said. He pulled up the reply he'd sent to his lawyer and handed her the phone:

Mr Harker.

While I appreciate the concern, you don't know what the hell you're talking about. No she's not engaged to him. No she has never had a relationship with him. He's a psychopath that won't back off. As for telling me what to do with my private life, please obsess over your own and leave mine alone. We're happy together. If I need anything from you, I'll let you know. If you can't accept that I'm running my own life, I will accept your resignation. – Jamie

"Obviously your staff have an issue," Piper said. "Piper I can't control everyone else. My security staff like you. The staff at the house like you. Everyone is on board except for the PR team. You never met them. They don't know what I do. They're at the office in Savannah," Jamie said. "Enjoy," Piper said. "Piper," he said. "No. If they wanna be that one sided and they aren't gonna bother getting all the info then just leave me alone. Do what they freakin want," Piper said. She slid as far away from him as she could. They pulled into the helipad and Piper shook her head. "What," Piper asked. He hopped out and got her door as the driver loaded the bags into the helicopter. "What in the heck," Piper asked. He opened the door and helped her into the seat then hopped onto the seat beside her. "What are you doin," Piper asked. "Taking the faster route," Jamie said. He told her to put the earphones on and she wouldn't. He slid them on her ears. "Stop causing such a dang issue," Jamie said. Piper shook her head. "Whatever," Piper said. They landed a little while later and he helped her off. They headed down to the suite that he'd already booked and checked into.

They walked in to see candles, wine chilling and flowers. Piper shook her head. Like that was gonna fix anything that had happened. He put the bags in the master bedroom and when he came back in, Piper was on the balcony. He looked at the wine and poured two glasses. He walked out and handed one to her. Piper shook her head. "Where are you goin," Jamie asked. She walked inside and went into the bedroom. She slid out of the heels. "We need to talk about this," Jamie said. "Why? You lost your marbles when you got that email at dinner and went ballistic. Obviously, his opinion matters," Piper said. "Not like you think it does," Jamie said. She put her bag on the bed and slid her slip on shoes on. "Piper," he said. "I'm not playing this game Jamie. One minute we're fine, the next you're letting your stupid PR people tell you what to do with your private life. I'm not what you want and obviously, I'm not what anyone else on your staff wants," Piper said. She zipped her bag up and carried it to the door. "What are you doing," he asked. "What I should've done a long-ass time ago," Piper said. She went to grab her phone to get a second room key and he slid the phone out of her hand. "Stay," Jamie said. "Then you're sleeping on the sofa," Piper said.

The idea of it irritated him. She knew just how to press that dang button. The one button that would push him into going too far and completely scaring her away. He moved towards her and she shook her head. "Leave me alone," Piper said. He shook his head and slid his hand in hers. "And while we're at it, what the hell did you think you were doin trying to tell me what to wear on stage?" "You mean because you'd practically be hanging out of it," Jamie asked. "Right. You forget I tried it all on. I'm good," Piper said. Just that comment had her convinced that she was wearing the sexiest of the outfits the next show if only to completely defy him. "Why can't you just talk to me," Jamie asked. "I'm done. If that's how things are going down with your stupid idiot PR people then I'm done," Piper said. "Piper," he said. "Just leave me alone," Piper said. She went into the bedroom, noticing the bag back on the bed. She grabbed her joggers and a t-shirt and went into the bathroom. She locked the door behind her, showered and washed the hairspray from her hair and rinsed that feeling of anger off of her.

She slid out, dried off and slid into her joggers and t-shirt. When she stepped out, he was standing right there waiting. "What," Piper asked. "You talking to me or not," Jamie asked. "Answer would be…" He kissed her, enveloping her lips with his. He picked her up and wrapped her legs around him. He walked over to the bed and leaned her onto it. "What are you doing," Piper asked. "Ending this fight," Jamie said. Piper shook her head. "Let go," Piper said. "No," he said. "Jamie," Piper said. "You're gonna listen to me if I have to make you listen," Jamie said. "Meaning what," Piper asked. "I don't care what anyone else in the dang planet says about you and me. I want you. Nobody's changing that. End of discussion," Jamie said. "You're full of it," Piper said. "You're driving me insane," Jamie said. "I'm done playing stupid games. Let go of me," Piper said. "You don't get it do you," Jamie asked. She pushed him off of her and he almost slid to the floor. "Damn you," Jamie said. Piper shook her head and walked into the TV room. "You're seriously doing this right now," Jamie asked. "Leave me alone," Piper said. He walked into the TV room and he saw the anger building.

"Tell me what you want from me," Jamie asked. "Just go home," Piper said. "No," he replied. "At some point you have to just accept that things aren't gonna…" Jamie leaned over and kissed her. "Aren't gonna what," he asked. "You telling the people that don't believe in this to screw off isn't gonna change anything. It's like 12 dang strikes against me," Piper said. "When we get back, we are going in to deal with him. I said we. You and me. I'm not walking away from this because he's a dick," Jamie said. "Did you ever think he might be right," Piper asked. "He's so far from the truth he wouldn't know it if it hit him with a transport truck," Jamie replied.

"Whatever," Piper said. "Then we enjoy the rest of the weekend and I prove it to you when we're back," Jamie said. "How," Piper asked. "Because I made a decision," Jamie said. "And what's that," she asked. "I'm going ahead with the house," he said. "Good luck with that," Piper said. "I can come stay at your place once it gets to that point," Jamie said. Piper shook her head. "I said no," Piper said. "I'm doing it for myself," Jamie said. She shook her head and in the back of her mind, she was glad she wouldn't have to deal with it because she'd be on tour. "Maybe it'll work out for you," Piper said. "You alright with me being at your place with you," Jamie asked. "I'll be on the road," Piper replied. She was making excuses.

"We're not having another fight about it," Jamie said. "And you should probably do your best to keep your house in one piece as long as you can," Piper said. She wanted to kick his butt. Assuming he would be welcome at her house had her seeing red. She wasn't over that horrid email no matter what he said. "I was supposed to work out with Jess," Piper said. "I let her know where we were. She'll be here at 5:30," Jamie said. Piper shook her head. She walked into the bedroom and charged her phone. She slid under the blankets and turned off the light. "Seriously," Jamie said. He blew the candles out and locked the door, coming into the bedroom. He put his shirt and jeans on the chair and slid into the bed. "What are you doin," Piper asked. "Quit," Jamie said. His arm slid around her and he pulled her to him. His arms wrapped around her. "What," Piper asked. "I don't want to go to bed mad," Jamie said. "Then don't," Piper replied. He kissed her shoulder. "Just don't." "Why," he said. "Jamie," Piper said. He snuggled in tight, refusing to let go. If that's all he was getting, he wasn't letting go.

The next morning, he woke up to an empty bed. Even the pillow and blanket were gone. He walked into the TV room and she was having breakfast at the table alone. "How was the workout," he asked. "Fine," Piper said. She was still mad. Honestly, it made her even hotter. He went to kiss her and she brushed him off. He shook his head and saw she'd ordered something for him. When he looked, it was bacon and an omelet. He poured himself a cup of coffee and ate, staring intently at her. "What," Piper asked. "You know we're talking," Jamie said. Piper didn't even look up from her phone. "What's goin on?" "Nothin," Piper said. He slid it out of her hand and looked and saw an article written about her from the Dallas newspaper. It was a good review and not even a word about Colt's issues that he'd caused. "What's wrong with it," Jamie asked. Piper shook her head. She took her phone back and went to check the Savannah news. She didn't see any Colt issues for once. She checked the rumor mill aka texted Caroline.

What's up?

Caroline replied.

Just heard that the concert went great. How are you?

She knew that meant nothing was going around the rumor mill. Two seconds later, her phone buzzed. "Hey," Piper said. "What's shakin," Caroline asked. "Just thought I'd see how things were," Piper replied. "As in did Colt start more drama," Caroline asked. "Yep," Piper said. "He's kinda been quiet. I don't know if that's because he tried more crap with trying to get your place or what," Caroline said. "Just keep me posted," Piper said. "I will girl. Talk to you later," Caroline said as she finished getting ready for work.

"What," Jamie asked noticing her glaring at him. "Nothing," Piper said. He knew that somehow they'd work it out, but Piper being that pissed was making him hot. "We're talking. We have 6 freaking hours to hash this crap out," Jamie said.

"Better idea. Go home," Piper said. "Still," Jamie asked. "Never changed," Piper said. He walked towards her and she backed up until he had her backed into a corner of the bedroom. "What," Piper asked. He had her in his grasp. He was the one in control. One way or another, he was getting her to talk to him and end this stupid fight. "I want you in my life. Doesn't matter what anyone else says no matter who they are," Jamie said. "Whatever," Piper said. He lifted her chin so their eyes met. "Whether you believe me or not, I love you. I'm not changing a dang thing. I'm not letting anyone mess this up," Jamie said. "You say that now," Piper replied. "It's not changing. I refuse to turn that off Piper. I want you. I love you and I am not walking out on this because of someone else," Jamie said. Piper shrugged. "Can I move," Piper asked. He shook his head. "I want you. When are you gonna get it through your head that no matter what anyone else says or does I'm not leaving your side," Jamie asked. "When I know that it's true and you aren't gonna do what you did after reading that email," Piper said. She knew. The minute he dragged her into that empty room, she knew.

"I want you to talk to me. If you're mad, say it. Deal," he asked. "You're the one that kept it to yourself," Piper said. "When nobody else was around was my only prerequisite. Nobody needed to hear it," Jamie said. "What did you say to Harley," Piper asked. "Carter mentioned that he didn't think that you and I were a good idea. She was worried about you. She wanted to make sure that I didn't hurt you," Jamie said. In the back of her mind, the words if you only knew were screamed. "Guess she's gonna know then," Piper said. "Piper, we were perfectly fine yesterday morning. I love you. We went and spent that day together and all that busted it up was a stupid email," Jamie said. "One that you took to heart," Piper said. She tried brushing him away and he linked their fingers and pinned her to the wall. "Jamie," Piper said. "I'm not losing you over some stupid email," Jamie said. "Doesn't change anything Jamie. You read it and took it to heart," Piper said. He shook his head and he kissed her, devouring her lips. He peeled her shirt off and then that stupid sports bra. Nothing she could say would stop him.

He kissed her and picked her up. "Put.." He devoured her lips and leaned her onto the bed, holding her hands above her head with one hand and getting her shorts off with the other. "Jamie," Piper said. He kissed her again and kicked his boxers off. "Jamie, stop," Piper said. "What," he asked as he leaned on top of her feeling her heart racing with his. "This isn't gonna fix this," Piper said. "Only thing that is, is in Savannah," he replied. "Then tell him to come and we straighten it out once and for all on my turf," Piper said. He kissed her. "Alright," Jamie said. The sheer fact that he had her at his mercy was making him even more turned on. She was doing her best to distract him. He leaned into her and devoured her lips. Waiting one more second wasn't an option. The sex was hot, insane, intense and passionate, but like they were working out their aggressions. They kept going until her body was throbbing in his arms. When they finally gave into the heat, he rolled over, leaning onto his side. "I don't want to fight about this anymore," Jamie said. "Doesn't change anything Jamie. You don't get how much that hurts. I was already insecure enough before all of this and then that happens," Piper said. She went to get up. "Where are you going," Jamie asked. She shook her head, got up and walked into the bathroom, sliding into the shower alone.

She was just rinsing the conditioner out when Jamie's arms slid around her. "I'm sorry," Jamie said. She broke his grasp and rinsed out the conditioner. She felt lips on her chest. "What are…" Jamie kissed her and the kisses trailed up her chest to her neck and then her shoulder. "What are you doin," Piper asked. "Making the most of the morning," Jamie asked. She brushed him off and stepped out of the shower, wrapping herself in a towel. She grabbed her phone and sat down on the bed seeing a text from Harley to call her asap.

"What's up," Piper asked. "Where did y'all vanish to," Harley asked. "We're staying down in San Antonio. Jamie decided we needed to talk alone," Piper said. "I can't believe him," Harley said. "Why," Piper asked. "Carter told me what his PR guy said. He didn't even have the balls to defend you," Harley said. "Babe, stop. Leave them alone," Piper heard Carter say. "He did after he told me about the email," Piper replied. "I don't want you getting hurt. There are other…" "Just ignore her. He probably lit into the dang PR team. If you sat down with them, they'd see you're a good person," Carter said. "Doesn't mean I'm not still pissed," Piper said. Jamie opened the door and was looking her up and down like she was covered in pink and green spots. "He loves you. We all know that. Just take what that idiot says with a grain of salt. He also thought that living anywhere but LA was stupid," Carter said. "I appreciate that," Piper said. "Just talk to him. He's not gonna steer you wrong," Carter said. "Thanks," Piper replied. "He around," Carter asked. Piper handed the phone to Jamie and he grabbed her hand, pulling her to him before she could walk off.

"Yep," Jamie said. "You know he's causing shit right? He's not looking at things clearly," Carter said. "I know. I've been trying to explain that to her but she's not exactly listening. Honestly, letting him go is the next option," Jamie said. "You need to get through to him," Carter said. "Working on it," Jamie said. "Just go make up so I don't have to hear about it," Carter joked. "Will do. Thank you," Jamie said. They hung up and Piper broke free from his grasp. She slid her jean shorts and t-shirt on and went into the TV room. He shook his head, walked in with nothing but a towel on and grabbed her hand, walking her into the bedroom. "What," Piper asked. He kissed

her. "We're finishing this today," Jamie said. "Meaning what,"
Piper asked. He called Mr. Harker. "Jack," Piper said. "Sir," the
PR guy said. "Did you receive the email," Jamie asked. "I
thought maybe we should be discussing it before you brush
off the suggestion," Jack said. "Then you can come down to
the show so we can discuss it," Jamie said. "Sir," Jack said.
"Just go to the airport. The plane will be waiting," Jamie
replied. "Yes sir," Jack said as he hung up and Jamie ended
the speakerphone call.

"Hope y'all have a nice chat," Piper said. "We," Jamie replied.
"I have rehearsal to do," Piper said. "I didn't say it was
optional," Jamie said. "And I don't take orders," Piper replied.
He looked at her and shook his head, pulling her tight to him
as the towel fell from around his hips. "Come here," he said.
"Jamie, enough," Piper said. "Do you want me," Jamie asked.
"Has nothing to do with it," Piper said. "Yes or no," he asked.
"With you ordering me around and telling me what to do,
no," Piper replied. "He's not in control of who I date or who I
don't," Jamie said. "Whatever," Piper said as she tried to walk
away. He pulled her to him and devoured her lips. "What,"
Piper asked as they came up for air. "I'm not walking away
and I'm not gonna just stand here and watch you leave,"
Jamie said. "Just give me space," Piper said. He kissed her.
"Shirt," Jamie said. "What," Piper asked. He motioned
towards the t-shirt. "No," Piper said. "You don't need it," he
replied. "And why is that," Piper asked. He went into the
closet and handed her a suit bag. "You're seriously doing it
again? You're telling me what..." He kissed her. "We're going
out," Jamie said. He kissed her and slid his boxers on. He
looked over and saw her open the suit bag and he put his
jeans on. He was getting turned on all over again watching
her bend over to open the suit bag. He turned his gaze and
freshened up in the bathroom intentionally skipping his
morning shave.

He walked over to her as she slid the dress from the bag. "Jamie," Piper said. "Try it on," he said. "We're not going anywhere," Piper said. "Yeah we are, and if he's coming down here then you have to look the part," Jamie said. Piper looked at him. She shook her head and walked out of the bedroom. She sat down, sliding her earbuds in. Damn it. Why the heck did she have to fight him on every single thing. He walked into the TV room and looked at her without even a shirt. "Please," Jamie asked. "You want me to look the damn part. Seriously? You're actually saying that," Piper asked fighting him on every detail. "I want you to wear it. I got it for you. I know you'll look beautiful in it. Please," he asked. "Why," Piper asked. "Please just put it on," Jamie asked. "Where am I going that I need something that dressy," Piper asked. She was driving him crazy. "It's a sundress. It's not a straight jacket," Jamie said. It was a floral slip dress that she was convinced was beyond overdressed and would look horrible. She hated shopping anyway, but that dress was just going to drive her over the edge. "Fine, but if I don't like it, it's going back in the bag," Piper said. Jamie nodded. She had no idea that he'd got it made to fit her.

Piper slid into it and it hugged her just a little. She looked in the mirror and shook her head. "I'm doing a sound check and performing. Way overdressed," Piper said as she went to slide it off. Jack would back off when he saw her in that dress. He'd leave her alone. He'd stop trying to destroy the only happiness that he'd ever found. "I don't even have shoes," Piper said. Jamie handed her the shoes from the suit bag. "Jamie, this isn't me," Piper said. "We're going out for lunch anyway," Jamie said. "I have to be at the venue at 2 for sound check," Piper said. "We have time. They have your stuff for the stage and we can bring your shorts and stuff with us," Jamie said. Piper grabbed her beat up jeans and t-shirt and her hoodie and put them in a bag. "We'll fly in," Jamie replied. Piper shook her head. "Whatever," Piper said. He kissed her, put on his cologne and they put their things into the closet. They headed off, with the extra bag of clothes in hand and went up to the helipad. "Where are we going," Piper asked. "Dallas," he replied.

She almost rolled her eyes at the thought. Being put on the hot seat because of his idiot PR team wasn't her idea of a fun afternoon. When they landed, Piper stepped out and Jamie walked her into the other hotel. "What in the...." "We're doing this on your turf. You have Harley and Carter on your side with me," Jamie replied. "You mean the completely pointless meeting," Piper said. He kissed her cheek. Jack's flight should be landing any minute. The helicopter ride to the venue would maybe be 10 minutes. "Nice dress," Harley said coming in. "Thanks I think," Piper said as she gave Harley a hug. Carter shook Jamie's hand. "You alright," Carter asked. Piper nodded. "Thanks," Piper said as he gave her a hug and motioned towards Jamie that it was the perfect dress. They each got a sweet tea and Jack came in. "Sir," Jack said realizing he was the target in the firing squad.

"You wanted to talk about the email that you sent," Jamie said. "I understand it was not taken the way I had wanted it to," Jack said. "Well, I still think that you are going to have to accept that you're gonna end up having your past all over the papers." "I'm the one that complained that she hadn't said a word about the two of us together," Jamie said. "I just know that you don't want your past in the spotlight and if the two of you are a couple, it will be everywhere. If someone lashes out at the other, you can end up having things ruined. My job is to protect you," Jack said. "As for that crack you made about Piper and I not being good," Jamie asked. He looked at Piper in that dress and shook his head. "I just was unsure about the entire thing. It's nothing against Miss Piper," Jack said trying to backpedal or avoid insulting her. "In future, you say one negative thing about Piper, I will personally have you removed from the company," Jamie said. "Yes sir," Jack said. Piper got up and Jamie grabbed her hand. She broke his grasp and walked out of the room. She grabbed the bag and went and slid her jeans and t-shirt on. She rolled her jeans up and slid her feet into the water at the pool.

That room was stifling. That man lying through his teeth had her blood boiling. Piper shook that feeling off trying to concentrate on the tour and if she wanted to change the set list up. Her phone buzzed in her pocket. She saw Jamie's name on the display and ignored the call. "You're actually ignoring my calls now," Jamie asked. "Go away," Piper said. He walked over to her and slid his socks and shoes off. He rolled his jeans up and sat down with her. "You alright," Jamie asked. Piper moved away from him. "You are driving me nuts," Piper said. "I love you. I'm trying to fix this so nobody is against you and you walk out," Jamie asked. "Damn right," Piper said. She grabbed her shoes and socks and walked off, phone and purse in hand. She walked into the hotel and saw Harley. "You alright," Carter asked. Piper nodded. "Jamie's by the pool," Piper said. Carter kissed Harley and walked out to the pool, while Piper and Harley went up to the suite.

"What happened," Harley asked. "I can't do this Harley. I can't just sit there and not want to kick that stupid idiot's butt," Piper replied. "You can't just walk off. The guy is tryin," Harley said. "So, now you're on his side," Piper asked. "Girl, I'm not doin anything. I don't want you all upset because of his stupid staff," Harley said. "I want him but I don't want his stupid crap," Piper said. "Do you love him," Harley asked. "Doesn't matter," Piper replied. Harley shook her head. "Yeah it does. Yes or no," Harley asked. "Not like this," Piper said. "What do you want me to do," Harley asked. "I don't know," Piper said. "Here's my one question. If you had a choice between walkin away or staying and being with him good or bad," Harley asked. "I don't know," Piper replied. Her phone went off and she ignored it. She was not in the mood. "He loves you. We all know it. We can all see it," Harley said. Piper shook her head. "I'm not playing with him anymore," Piper said. "Meaning," Harley asked. "Meaning if one of his idiot staff doesn't like me, they either get fired or I leave and get on with my dang life alone," Piper said.

"Really," Jamie said as Piper jumped. "Yes really," she said. Jamie looked at her. "What?" "Excuse us," Jamie said. He slid his hand in Piper's, pulled her to him and walked her to the hall and down to the ladies bathroom, locking the door behind them. He checked to make sure nobody else was there and she went to walk out. "Where do you think you're goin? You can't just say that and walk off," Jamie said. "I am," Piper replied. "Tell me you didn't mean that," Jamie asked. "I meant it. If they want to start a dang problem and try to break what we have then there's the decision. They go or I do," Piper said. "He admitted that he made a mistake," Jamie said. "Knee jerk reaction is the real reaction," Piper said. He shook his head. "Piper, you have to negotiate. You have to make him see what I do," Jamie said. "I'm not playing Jamie. If that's how he feels then he can go screw himself. You wanna take his side then I'm sure I can find something else to do," Piper said. He grabbed her hand, pulling her into his arms and leaned her against the wall.

"What," Piper asked. He kissed her and devoured her lips. "Let go," Piper said. "No," he replied. "Jamie, enough. I'm not playing this stupid game with you," Piper said. "He's the head of PR for the company. I hired him a long time ago. He's old school. That's all," Jamie said. "Jamie, the man hates me and wants me gone. I'm not playing. Bad enough I had to deal with my high school friends bullying me. I'm not about to let someone that works for you do it too," Piper said. "Piper, please," Jamie said. She got out of his arms, unlocked the door and walked out. She walked out the front and hopped in the SUV to go over to the venue. If nothing else, hanging with Jason would get her mind off all of it.

She got down to the arena and Jason was watching the game. Piper got on the bus, changed into shorts and a t-shirt and went and hung out with Jason, his wife and the kids. "You alright," Jason asked noticing that she was beyond mad. Piper shook her head. "There's something to be said for an easier life without the drama," Piper said. "What happened," Jason asked. "He's driving me insane. Someone at his company doesn't like me around him and told him to dump me," Piper said. "Dang," Kaylie said. Piper nodded. "Now I'm just annoyed," Piper said. "You know that you can always come hang with us if you want to," Jason said. "I appreciate that," Piper said.

Maybe 20 minutes later, Jason's phone went off. "Yep," Jason said. "There's a Jamie Hastings at the gate," the security man said. "Yep. He's fine," Jason said. Jamie came walking in and went straight over to where Jason was sitting. By then, the bus was there and Kurt, Keith and the rest of the band had come over to watch the game. Jamie walked over to Piper. "Hey buddy," Jason said. "Hi. Who's winning," Jamie asked trying to not make a scene. "Dawgs as always," Jason said. "Excuse us for a minute," Jamie said as he grabbed Piper's hand and walked her to the empty bus and straight back to the stateroom.

"What," Piper asked. "You walked out," he said. "Yeah I did. I'm not having this fight again with you. If that idiot is determined to make you walk away then walk. I don't need the extra stress," Piper said. He shook his head and Piper just about lost it. "What," Piper asked. "You aren't the one that's leaving. I'm not gonna let some paper pusher mess with my life," Jamie said. "He already did," Piper said. "Piper, just stop.

You have to trust me at some point," Jamie said. "If he'd said that I was bad for your image what would you have said," Piper asked. "That he needs to mind his own dang business. That he doesn't control what I do or don't do," Jamie said. "You seem to have reacted just the dang way he wanted," Piper said. "I love you. Stop trying to make this harder than it is. He was put in his place. End of discussion," Jamie said. "You're so dang full of it that it's floating," Piper said. Jamie shook his head. Two seconds later, his phone was buzzing in his pocket. "What," Jamie said. "Mr. Harker on the line for you," his assistant said. He put the call on speaker.

"What did you want," Jamie asked. "Sir, I'm still unsure even after today," Mr. Harker said. "If you even think about disrespecting her you're gonna be looking for a new job," Jamie said. "Sir, I'm just concerned after we got more information on that Colt person," Mr. Harker said. "Which would be what? Which lie is he concocting today," Jamie asked. "He said that Miss Piper is his fiancée. Sir, I get that it's not true, but the public perception is going to be an issue," Mr. Harker said. "If you can't handle that then you shouldn't be in that position in my company," Jamie said. He wouldn't let Piper leave the room and wasn't letting her hands go. "I'm trying to come up with a response to it that won't cause more of an issue," Mr. Harker said. "Can you hold for a moment," Jamie asked. "Yes sir," Mr. Harker said as Jamie put him on hold. "And," Jamie asked. "Let go of my arm," Piper said. "No. What's your solution since he's not giving you one you want," Jamie asked. "Instagram," Piper replied. "And then," Jamie asked. She shook her head. "Press release about us will shut his stupid butt up." "When I decide that it's worth doing," Piper said. He gave her a look and she took the call off mute.

"We're opting to go the press release and social media response. If you don't agree," Jamie said. "Sir, I'm just not sure that's the smartest idea. The perception is still going to be negative," Mr. Harker said. "You don't get to make that call. You either do what I ask or find some boxes to pack your office," Jamie said as he hung up. "Like I said," Piper said as she went to walk out. He pulled her to him and kissed her. "You're not walking out of this room until you talk to me," Jamie said. "I'm done talking. You're going home anyway," Piper said. "And you're coming with me," Jamie replied. "No I'm not," Piper said. "You have a video to shoot," he said. "And I need 24 damn hours without this stupid crap going on," Piper said. Her phone buzzed two minutes later.

Chapter 15

"Char," Piper said. "We're gonna have to do a press conference and social media push. Colt's started again," Char said. "I heard," Piper replied. "What would you think of having Jamie in the new video," Char asked. "No. Not happening," Piper said. "You alright with the social media push? Y'all can do a video like you did last time. You may have to do an interview or two as well," Char replied. "I need 24 hours," Piper replied. "You have it. I'll meet you at the show tomorrow and we can go over the next step. You alright," Char asked. "The fact that I want to thoroughly rip his face off," Piper said. "Gotcha," Char said. "Is there nothing legally," Piper asked. "We served him with a slander and cease and desist. We talked to the police and told them that he's violating the orders. They said they'd take care of it, but it hasn't exactly stopped him," Char said. "Gag order," Piper asked. "The lawyers are drawing it up. I know that you don't want to deal with this, but you're gonna have to," Char said. "Alright," Piper said. "Just relax this afternoon and try to calm down. We can work on it tomorrow. Today, just watch the game," Char said. "Thanks," Piper replied.

"And," Jamie asked. "I need air," Piper said. "Sit and just tell me," Jamie said. Piper shook her head, pushed past him and walked out the door, out of the bus and walked over towards the stage, sitting on the edge of it trying to clear her head. Jamie looked at her from the edge of the stage as the lights were being set up. He couldn't do a dang thing to fix this for her. It's like the dang world was against them and he was powerless. "Piper," Jamie said. "Just leave me alone," Piper said. "I'm not leaving your side. We have to fix this together," Jamie said. "Nothing's getting fixed until I go home and handle it myself with a dang tire iron," Piper said. "Baby," he said. "Jamie please," Piper said. He saw Jason's wife looking over and flagged her over. Jamie traded places with her and sat to fake watching the game so Piper could talk to her.

"You look like you're about to lose it," Jason's wife Kaylie said. "Just a long day," Piper said. "I heard about the stupid rumor stuff," she said. "I mean, how the heck do I even handle that," Piper asked. "Jason and I went through it. We just ignored them and eventually they just went away. When we show that we're not effected by them, they just go away because they're not getting any attention," Kaylie said. "The more I ignore this the worse it gets," Piper said. "Tell me what happened," Kaylie asked. Piper told her and she was stunned. "That is just so dang wrong. I think I came up with a way better idea though. Jase and I can do a video with y'all and it gets twice as far," Kaylie said. "I don't want y'all dragged into this," Piper said. "You had a rough enough day Piper. Let someone help," Kaylie asked. Piper gave her a hug. "Just makes it worse that Jamie's stupid PR guy pretty much said for him to dump me," Piper said. "He wouldn't," Kaylie said. "I don't even know that for sure," Piper said. "Girl, he tells everyone how much he loves you all the dang time. He's not gonna go," Kaylie said. "He's better off going. He doesn't need this," Piper said. Kaylie gave her a big ole hug as Piper's eyes welled up. "Don't you dare let anyone see you cry over this. You're an amazing woman Piper. One I'm dang glad that Jase gets to be on tour with. Don't ever cry over someone being an idiot," Kaylie said. Piper hugged her back and it's like there was a release of the flood gates. The built-up anger was fading even if it was only in trickles.

Kaylie walked Piper to the bus, did her hair and makeup and they did a quick video. Kaylie talked about how Piper was the greatest and she was so glad she was on the tour. The second part was about bullying and even the big country stars have to handle stuff like that. "No matter who you are, or what you do, everyone has to deal with bullies. The one thing we both want y'all to know is that you always have support. You just have to ask. Right Piper," Kaylie asked. "Definitely. That's why You Can't Break Me is an anti-bullying anthem. You get bullied, blare it. We're all in the same boat y'all," Piper said. "Now for all of y'all that are bullied, don't forget to tell your folks. Tell a teacher. Tell the police. Nobody deserves to be bullied no matter what," Kaylie said as she finished the video and posted it to Instagram. That was the first step and somehow, it relieved a little bit of the pressure and stress. Kaylie grabbed Piper's phone and copied the videos to her phone and posted them to her Instagram, twitter and Facebook. "Step one," Kaylie said. Piper gave her a hug. "I appreciate this," Piper said. "Girl, we're stickin together. That's why I'm here," Kaylie said. They stepped off the bus and walked over towards Jamie and Jason.

"And what were y'all up to," Jason asked as Kaylie grabbed his cell and posted the video on his Instagram. "If that doesn't make a difference, I don't know what will," Kaylie said. Piper gave her another hug. "I really do appreciate this," Piper replied. "And what did y'all do," Jason asked. Kaylie showed him and he smirked. "I approve," Jason teased. Piper looked at her phone a couple minutes later and there were hundreds of comments and loves. Piper looked and there was only one negative comment:

Nice try. See you at home – Colt.

Piper deleted, blocked and reported the comment. He was banned from the profile. Step two was complete. She banned him from every social media account she had. He couldn't get to her anymore. She took her life back. Jamie looked at Piper and she wouldn't even make eye contact. Piper went and found her outfit in the dressing room. She made sure it was just right and went to walk out when Jamie closed the door. "What," Piper asked. He looked at her and locked it. "You're telling me what the heck is goin on," Jamie said. "I'm not playing anymore Jamie. As far as I'm concerned, that stupid PR guy is just as bad as Colt. I'm dealing with this my way. I don't care if you're not part of it either," Piper said. He walked over to her, pulled her to him and devoured her lips. "I love you. Whatever you're doing, I'm cheering you on. Just tell me," Jamie said. "Kaylie came up with an idea off the cuff and we ran with it. So far it looks like it's working," Piper said. "And," he asked. "You're not gonna be involved. It shuts that stupid guy up," Piper said. Jamie looked at her as she could see him starting to get annoyed. "What?" "When are you gonna understand that I don't care what anyone else says," Jamie asked. "When I actually see that it doesn't," Piper said. She went to walk towards the door and he pulled her back to him. "What," Piper asked.

Jamie kissed her, devouring her lips and he picked her up, sitting her on the counter. "Jamie," Piper said. He kissed her neck, her shoulder and then slid the strap of her tank from her shoulder. "What are you up to," Piper asked. He peeled her shirt off and went for her bra. "Jamie," Piper said. She felt the back of her bra come undone. "Jamie, quit," Piper said. "I'm not letting go," Jamie said. His shirt came off, and threw it to the counter on top of hers. "We aren't doing this here," Piper said. He kissed her, devouring her lips, silencing her complaints. He undid her jean shorts and slid them off. "Jamie," Piper said. He went for the button of his jeans and she stopped him. He smirked. "What," Piper asked. "Not gonna be that easy," he teased. "Jamie, I have to…" He silenced her with another kiss and brushed her hand away, undoing his jeans. She fidgeted, trying to fight off the kiss. "What's wrong," he asked. "I'm not doing this in here," Piper said. Before she knew it, the barely nothing lace panties were on the counter and they were having sex on that counter. When her toes were about to curl and her legs were trembling, he kept going. He wanted every inch of her curled around him. It got harder, more powerful and when he finally stopped, she felt like her legs had turned to jelly. He didn't move. "What," Piper asked. "I'm not leaving no matter what anyone else says. You know that right," Jamie asked. "I just can't handle that stupid crap Jamie. I get bullied enough from Colt," Piper said. "Nobody is laying a hand on you ever again," Jamie said.

She finally slid to her feet, even though her legs barely held her. She got re-dressed and Jamie kissed her. "What time is sound check," he asked. Piper looked at her Fitbit. "Half hour at the earliest," Piper said. "Sound check then we can sit down and figure out a game plan long-term. I wanna see what you two did," Jamie said. "We just did a video that's anti-bullying and stuff," Piper said. "Do you need me to do anything," he asked. Piper shook her head. He kissed her. "I don't want to fight with you about it anymore," Jamie said. "Either do I, but I'm not the one that caused this," Piper said. He kissed her and pulled his jeans up and slid his shirt on. "I'm going alright," Piper asked. "Before we do, what are you wearing tonight," he asked. "You're not gonna like it," Piper said. He shook his head. "Whatever you want," Jamie replied.

He'd backed down, even if it was only to prevent yet another fight. He kissed her. He slid his hand in hers, unlocked the door and they walked out together. Piper shook her head and they went outside. "Hey Piper," Kaylie said. "What's up," Piper asked as Jamie's arm slid around her waist, pulling her to him. "2900 loves and it got re-posted by 50 other celebs. You're officially trending," Kaylie said. "And," Piper asked. "And it's only growing. You got the upper hand back," Kaylie joked. "Thank you," Piper said giving her a hug. "Girl, if that's all it takes, that's the easy stuff," Kaylie replied. They headed back over to the rest of the gang and Piper saw the stage manager coming towards them. "Sound check when you're ready Miss Piper," the stage manager said.

Piper went with the band and did sound check. "Better mood," Harley asked as they stepped on the stage. Piper nodded. By the time they were done, Jamie was sitting in the front row, watching her. They headed off and Jamie followed. Jason went on and got going on his sound check and Piper went and got on the bus, opting to have a power nap. Jamie closed the stateroom door and slid onto the bed beside her, wrapping his arm around her waist and almost spooning her. The fact that she didn't fight him made him think that the fight they had was over. When she woke up, Jamie was out cold. She went and had a quick shower and slid her simple sundress on. She slid into her flip-flops and grabbed her cell and keys and walked off to grab something to eat.

"I was wondering where y'all took off to," Harley said as Carter sat down beside her. "Needed a nap. Jamie was working," Piper said. "Starved," Harley asked teasingly. Piper nodded and grabbed herself a plate of the seafood pasta and salad. She grabbed her bottle of water and went and sat down. Harley felt a tug at her leg a minute later along with little hands. "Kevie," Kaylie said. Piper smirked. She picked him up and he snuggled Piper. "You hiding from mama," Piper asked. He giggled. "Well, if that's where you want to be," Kaylie joked. "Ma," the little boy said reaching for Kaylie. "Just a little heartbreaker," Piper joked. He still had one arm coiled around Piper. "Well then, I guess mama's just gonna have to sit over here," Kaylie said. "He's just so darn cute," Piper said. "Someday you'll have one of your own girl," Kaylie joked. Kevie walked over to Kaylie. "Ma," he said. "You doin better," Kaylie whispered. Piper nodded.

They finished up dinner and Piper got Jamie a plate, bringing it back to the bus for him. "Thank you," Jamie said as he came out of the shower in nothing but a towel. "Most welcome," Piper teased. She kissed him and headed into hair and makeup to get ready to go on. She slid into the outfit and put a robe over it. Within maybe an hour and a half, her hair and makeup was done and so was Harley's. "Lookin good," Harley said. "Thank you," Piper said showing off the robe. "You sure you're alright," Harley asked. "Better now," Piper said. "Good," Harley said. Piper slid her heels on, spraying her perfume. "Ready," the security guy said. Piper nodded. She walked down the hall and the fans were screaming. She finished a little while later, freshened up and headed over towards the stage when she felt an arm wrap around her waist. "Hey," Piper said. "Hey yourself. How was the meet and greet," Jamie asked. "Not bad. A pile of people saying they loved that post," Piper replied. "Good. Just wanted to make sure I saw you before you went on," Jamie said. She shook her head. "And why's that," Piper asked. "Don't make me have to show you again," Jamie whispered. She got a silly grin and Jason headed on stage with lucky shots before she went on. "You got this girl. I'm so dang proud of you," Jason said. "Thank you," Piper said. They said a quick prayer, did the shot and the band headed on. Jamie kissed the nape of her neck. She smirked. She slid her ear monitors in, got her microphone and headed on to a arena full of cheering fans.

By the time she was done on stage, her adrenalin hit the roof. Jason gave her a high five. "Great show there," Jason said. "Thank you. I meant to ask you which song you wanted to do tonight," Piper asked. "Came up with a good plan. We're doin an older one. We're doing Dusty Road. You alright with it," Jason asked. Piper nodded. "Definitely," Piper said. She stepped down to the ground and went and grabbed a drink, opting for ginger ale. "What are you doing," Jamie asked as he came up behind her. The little hairs on her neck almost stood at attention. "Getting a drink. What are you doin,"

Piper asked. "We're leaving when that last song is done to go back to the hotel," Jamie said. "I kinda wanted to hang out with everyone," Piper said. "Tomorrow," Jamie replied. She nodded and walked back over towards the stage to watch Jason wow the crowd. "We're heading to San Antonio as soon as the show is done. Did you want to meet up and work out tomorrow," Kaylie asked. "Sure," Piper replied.

As soon as her duet with Jason was done, she headed backstage. Jamie grabbed her hand. The bus headed off with Harley and the guys and Piper and Jamie went off to head to the helipad back to their hotel. "You feeling any better," Jamie asked. "No," Piper said. "Babe, we can't control other people. We can only control ourselves," Jamie said. "Doesn't mean that I don't want to kick that idiot's butt," Piper said. "I can't do anything about him. Please just stop," Jamie said. "Maybe you should go home," Piper replied. He leaned his head back in the helicopter, determined not to have another fight with her. When they got back to their hotel, Piper went in and had a long hot shower alone, washed the makeup off and washed that anger off of her. When she stepped out, he saw a makeup free sexy woman. His woman.

Piper slid her t-shirt on and grabbed a bottle of water. "Piper," Jamie said as he sat on the bed shirtless in just his boxers. "No," Piper replied. He shook his head. In the back of his mind, he was saying please just let this crap be over. He walked into the TV room and saw Piper getting comfortable on the sofa. "Quit. Get in here and get some sleep," Jamie said. "No. I'm fine here," Piper said. He looked at her, shook his head and gave her a warning. "Either you get in there or I'm carrying you," Jamie said. "Just leave..." He picked her up, flipped her over his shoulder and walked into the bedroom, lying her onto the bed. "Why can't you just leave me alone," Piper asked. "Because you need sleep and the stupid sofa isn't enough," Jamie said. "I'm fine," Piper replied. He shook his head. "Just close your dang eyes and go to sleep. We start over with a new dang day tomorrow," Jamie said. He flipped the light off, wrapped an arm around her and pulled her tight to him as they both tried to sleep.

The next morning, Piper woke up and got dressed. She slid out the door before Jamie even noticed she was gone. She worked out with Jess and Kaylie and when she came back to the suite, Jamie was waiting with breakfast. "Good timing," Jamie said as he poured the milk in his coffee. Piper grabbed something and went into the bedroom. She had her breakfast while she went through emails. Jamie shook his head and brought the food into the bedroom and sat down with her. "Can't just sit alone," Piper asked. "Did you eat," he asked. She shook her head. "Yes," Piper said. He looked at her. "Piper," he said. "I had the dang omelet. Leave me be," Piper said. He took the rest of the food back to the TV room and shook his head. He grabbed his laptop and went to check emails. There was no way possible that it would be worse than the previous day.

When he got into his email, there was more than a few emails that he knew would put Piper in a mood. "What," Piper asked. "Nothing," Jamie said. "Whatever," Piper said. She finished going through her emails then checked the Instagram account. The post was one of the best she'd ever had. It made a difference. Colt wasn't able to see anything that she'd posted and never would again. A few minutes later, Char messaged her:

Are you awake?

Piper smirked and called her. "Yep," Piper said. "That video went viral. The TV stations have played it more than once since y'all did it. You doing alright," Char asked. "Sort of," Piper replied. "The interviews are pretty much cancelled for today after that hit the airwaves yesterday. I have you on a

flight to Savannah right after the show tonight. Are you alright with that," Char asked. "One sec," Piper said. "Leaving after the show to go back. You alright flying," Piper asked. "Already organized. We're leaving as soon as we can get there," Jamie said. "Already handled. We'll see you in Savannah," Piper said. "We're shooting at Wormsloe, Forsyth and at the house. We found one near you," Char said. "Jamie already offered his place plus it has more security," Piper said. "Alright. We'll figure it out. See you tomorrow," Char said. They hung up and Jamie looked at her. "What," Piper asked. "I love you. You know that right," he asked. "Whatever you saw in those emails just say it," Piper said. "Do you want this," Jamie asked. "Meaning what," she asked. "Do you want us. You and me. Disregard the stupid crap with my ex PR guy. Do you want you and me," Jamie asked. "I don't want everyone against it. I don't want to worry that you're gonna do what they want," Piper said. "Yes or no," he asked. She looked at him. "I don't even know anymore," Piper said. "Do you love me," he asked. "Jamie," Piper said. He looked at her like the next words she said would make or break him. He gulped. "I care. I just...I'm scared," Piper replied finally.

"Why the hell are you scared," Jamie asked. "Because every time I get close and things are good, something takes a shot at it. Especially when it's your business stuff," Piper said. "He's gone Piper. Nobody is pushing you out of my life. Nobody. Do you love me," he asked again hoping for a straight answer. "Jamie," Piper said. "Please just give me a straight answer," Jamie said. "I do, but I..." He got up, walked over and kissed her. "Come with me," Jamie said. "I have..." He pulled her to her feet before she could even protest. He turned the hot shower on then proceeded to pin her against the wall and peel every inch of her clothes off, kicking his joggers to the side. He picked her up, wrapped her legs around him and carried her into the shower. "What are you

doin," Piper asked as he slid her under the spray of the shower.

"We're goin out," Jamie said. He kissed her and slid her to her feet, washing her hair. "Jamie, I can handle it," she said. He devoured her lips, rinsed her hair off and picked her up, wrapping her legs around his waist and leaned her against the wall of the shower. "What," Piper asked. He had her arms pinned. "Jamie," Piper said. Before she said another word, they were having sex. Her entire body was wrapped around him. She was almost pulsating. He barely managed to let her up even for air. That kiss was so hot, so hard, so intense that he lost himself in it. Like he was falling down a bottomless tunnel. The sex got faster, hotter. When they finally came up for air, he kissed her neck, almost nibbling at it. The sex got even harder. Even more intense meant that she was almost trembling in his arms. When they finally stopped, he almost collapsed to the floor. She slid to her feet and he shook his head. "What," Piper asked. "Where are you goin," he asked. She kissed him and went to step out. He pulled her back to him and had her leaned face first against the wall and kept going. "Jamie," Piper said as it got even harder. When he finally drained himself of every ounce of energy, he pulled her to him from behind and kissed her neck. "Finish your shower," Piper said. He nodded. Piper shook her head and stepped out, wrapping herself in a towel.

She went into the bedroom and sat down on the edge of the bed, trying to regain her footing. She was still shaking. Just as she had finally managed to stand up, there was a knock at the door. "Jamie," Piper said. "Can you," he asked with a smile she could almost hear in his voice. She slid her robe on and went to the door. "A package arrived for Mr. Hastings," the room service attendant said. "Thank you," Piper replied. They handed Piper the package and she closed the door, walking into the bedroom and putting it on the counter. Jamie came

up behind her. "What was it," he asked. "It's on the counter," Piper said. She hadn't even looked. A baby blue tiffany's box with a silver bow and she didn't even look. In the back of his mind, he knew that box would be burning a hole in his pocket. He didn't want to wait.

He put it in the outside pocket of his suit bag and got dressed. Piper blew her hair dry and when she turned it off, Jamie was in nothing but his blue jeans. "Come here a sec," Jamie said. He slid his hand in hers and they sat down in the TV room. "What," Piper asked. "That PR guy who was causing trouble is gone. You know that right," Jamie asked. "Whatever you say," Piper said. "Everyone else in my staff at the house and anywhere else is supportive. You know that right?" Piper nodded. He looked at her. "Are you alright with us being together or do you want to leave," Jamie asked. "Get to the point," Piper said. "I don't wanna fight with you about this stuff anymore alright? No more worrying about stupid emails saying BS," Jamie said. "What are you getting at," Piper asked. "That I want us to be alright. I don't wanna fight anymore," Jamie said. "I just don't want to end up fighting because someone in your stupid staff doesn't approve. I'm not a socialite. I'm not a debutante. I'm just imperfect, not skinny, not in any way a size two me. I guess according to them you're slumming it with me," Piper said. "If anyone even looks at you that way, I'll fire them on the damn spot," Jamie said. "Jamie," Piper replied. "Nobody is ever disrespecting you or I'll whoop some serious butt," Jamie replied.

Piper shook her head. "What's all of this about," Piper asked. "Promise me something," Jamie said. "Which would be," Piper asked. "Promise me that there's no more walking away or walking out," Jamie asked. "I won't if you give me space when I ask," Piper said. He kissed her and snuggled her to him. He kissed her. "You gonna tell me what's wrong?" Piper asked. "I just want to make sure we're alright," Jamie said. "Whatever you're up to, just spill," Piper replied. He kissed her. "And if you start getting pissed at something, you have to tell me," Jamie said. She nodded. "Why do I have the feeling like there are gears turning?" "When we're back in Savannah, things are fine. It's when I'm stuck on the road instead of being home," Piper said. He kissed her and gave her a hug. "Travelling isn't exactly easy. Just let me help you if you start getting overwhelmed," Jamie said. Piper nodded. He kissed her and went into the bedroom staring at that bag that was delivered. Piper shook her head, ignoring the bag altogether. Jamie sent off an email and text just as she was coming into the room. "What," Piper asked. "Nothin. Just making sure that things are a go for after the show," he said.

When he got a "Yes Sir," reply back, Piper shook her head. "I know you're up to something," Piper said as she finished packing up her bag and got dressed. "You think so do you," Jamie asked as his phone pinged with an email. He took a look, replied back and finished getting everything into his bag to head out after the show. "And what's with the texts and emails," Piper asked. "Work," Jamie said. Piper looked at him. "It's Sunday," she said. "Office still runs even if I'm not there," Jamie said. Piper shook her head, finished doing the double check to make sure they weren't forgetting anything and opted to go out for a while. "You gonna tell me what was in the bag," Piper asked. "Something for my mom for her birthday next week," Jamie said as he lied through his teeth.

Jamie's phone went off a minute or two later. "Yep," Jamie said. "So we're moving it up to tonight," Jamie's mom asked. "If you can," he replied. "Why don't we just come next weekend," his mom said. "If you can't, it's fine," Jamie said. "We'll meet you there. You said 3 right," his mom asked. "Yes," Jamie said. "Alright. Tonight it is," his mom said. They hung up and Piper looked at him. "Just spill it," Piper said.

"Nothing. I have to get something from the office and they're sending it over," Jamie said. "We're gonna be in Savannah tomorrow," Piper said. "I know, but it's at my office in LA," Jamie said continuing to lie. What he had planned was gonna blow Piper's mind. It was a solution to the entire Colt problem. He had everything he needed. All that they had left to do was go to the last arena for the week.

"What time do we have to be over there," Jamie asked. "Two I think. We have time to just relax," Piper said. "And what would you like to do for the rest of the morning," Jamie asked. "Up to you," Piper said. He kissed her and they headed out. "Where are we goin," Piper asked. "Out for a bit," Jamie said. He checked his watch. Just in enough time to get a few things at the outlet mall before the insanity started. When they finally left, not only did Piper get new lingerie that he drooled over, but had a dress or two that she wasn't expecting. "I still don't know why I need that dress," Piper said. "Because I said so," he said. He smirked, they went and grabbed their things and checked out of the hotel and they went over to meet up with the rest of the gang at the bus. Piper put her things and Jamie's in the stateroom and they headed to the venue.

When they arrived, Jason was hanging out with his team. Piper, Jamie, Harley and everyone else hopped off and they all hung out together. At around 1:30, Jamie went to go to the washroom, or at least that's where he said he was. He walked out to security and met his folks and Piper's. "Nice timing y'all," Jamie said as he gave them a hug. "So, what's the big news," his dad asked. "Remember that conversation we had when Piper and I had just started dating," Jamie asked. Piper's dad nodded. "I need to ask you guys for your blessing," Jamie said. "What," his mom asked. "I'm waiting until we're back in Savannah I think, but I need to do this the right way," Jamie said. "As long as you make her happy," her dad said. Jamie gave him a hug and he heard Piper on the stage doing sound check. "Perfect timing," Jamie said. He walked everyone in and introduced them to everyone. Quietly, they snuck in while she was doing sound check and everyone grabbed a seat. She was even better than usual. That confidence was back. She did the new song and two of the alternates just in case then looked over and saw Jamie sitting with her folks and his. Harley started laughing. "Good thing we're done," Piper said as they finished the sound check.

"What in the world," Piper said as she came around and went over to her folks. "Surprise," her mom teased. Piper looked at Jamie. "I knew you were up to something," Piper said as she kissed him. "Babe, this is my mom and dad. Mom and dad, my girl Piper," Jamie said. They both gave her a hug. "You were pretty amazing," Jamie's mom said. "Well thank you. How on earth did you pull this off without…" "This morning when you were asking what I was doing," Jamie said. Piper shook her head. "I'm so glad y'all are here," Piper said as she gave her mom and dad another hug. She had absolutely no idea what he was up to, but at that point, she had the people there that she needed. They went back over to the bus and sat around outside to just talk and hang out. Her band came and hung out and when Jason finished sound check, they all went and had dinner together. "Are y'all staying for the show tonight," Piper asked. Jamie nodded. "All arranged thanks to Kaylie," Jamie said. "Girl," Piper said. "Had to. Have fun tonight y'all," Kaylie said with a little grin while she fed the kids.

Piper gave everyone a hug and kiss and went in to freshen up, get changed and get into hair and makeup. They handed her the silver sparkle outfit and she slid it on. Felt better than it did the first time she'd tried it on. She sat down and they started on her hair, then her makeup. By the time she was done, she looked like a movie star. "Think you're missing something," Jamie said. "Which would be what," Piper asked. He slid a bracelet on her wrist. It had the sparkle she needed. "Well, this is kinda pretty," Piper teased. He kissed her neck. "Thought you'd need it," he joked. That's not what was in that bag. He hoped beyond hope that she'd forget that bag was even in existence. "You ready for the meet and greet," Jamie asked. "Depends. What else are you surprising me with tonight," Piper asked. He kissed her and she brushed her lipstick off his lips. "Nothin else planned. I just wanted to make tonight special. You deserved it after all that crap the past couple days," Jamie said. Piper gave him a hug and he walked hand in hand with her to the meet and greet. "Come," Piper said. He gave her a hug and went with her.

As soon as they were finished, Piper went back and freshened up and touched her makeup up. "So, where are their seats," Piper asked. "I think relatively close to the front," Jamie said. Piper smirked. "You sure that you aren't up to somethin else," Piper teased. "Absolutely nothing," Jamie said. He kissed her forehead and she slid her ear monitors in. "You ready," he asked. Piper nodded. She slid them out, did a little prayer with the band and they had a quick shot before they headed on. Every one of them had a silly grin ear to ear. Whatever they were up to, Piper had absolutely no idea. They started the performance and by the third song, they opted for one that Piper had written when she met Jamie – Him. "There's this guy that I met. Y'all probably remember seeing pictures on Instagram," Piper said. The crowd cheered. Jamie stepped out onto the stage and walked over to her. "Y'all, you know this face don't you," Piper joked. Jamie walked over and kissed her. "This is one I wrote when we first met. This one is called Him," Piper said. Jamie waved and headed back side stage while his folks and Piper's watched from the VIP booth. Jamie sat there proud as all get out and watched.

She'd got so much better at it since that first show. She'd finally found a comfort level and showed it all off. He just watched and it just got him turned on. As soon as she was finished, she headed off stage and he kissed her. "Pretty amazing there sexy girlfriend of mine," Jamie said. "Well thank you handsome," Piper said. "Our folks are comin back here. You alright with it," he asked. Piper kissed him. "Thank you for that surprise," Piper said. "Even if you didn't say it, you needed them," Jamie replied. Their parents came backstage and came straight over to Piper and gave her a huge hug. The I'm proud of you's and congrats moments were what she needed. Little did she know that was only the beginning.

When the show was finished, they hung out with their folks for a little bit then went to head back to the airport. Their folks went back home and they headed back on the plane with everyone. "Finally," Harley said. "Didn't really think there was any point in y'all takin the bus when we were flying back," Jamie said. "Well thank you," Harley said as she curled up with Carter. Jamie had a Cheshire grin ear to ear and Harley looked over at him. She motioned towards Piper and he subtly shook his head. "What," Piper asked. "Nothin," Jamie said. They got back a couple of hours later and Jamie got the bags into the car. They hopped into the SUV and went back to the house while Harley went to Carter's.

"And just what else did you have planned," Piper asked as she fell asleep on Jamie's shoulder. "A couple things," he teased. He looked over and smirked. "What," Piper asked. "Nothin," he said. He wrapped his arm around her and she leaned her head on his shoulder. "I know you're up to something. Just say it," Piper said. "I wasn't. I just know that you needed them," Jamie said. "Where are we goin," Piper asked. "My place," he said. They pulled in, hopped out and went inside. Jamie carried her upstairs and leaned her onto the bed.

"Have to..." He kissed her. He slid her out of her jeans and t-shirt and she went and washed the makeup off. When she came back to bed, she slid under the soft satiny sheets with him and curled up in his arms. "Love you," he said. "I love you too," Piper said as she closed her eyes and fell asleep.

The next morning, they got up and went to the gym to workout with Jess side by side. For once, Colt wasn't there to distract or harass them and Jamie didn't have to threaten to kick his butt. They'd found a solution. That simple block button was all they needed. They headed back to the house and he made breakfast. "And what's all of this," Piper asked. "Since we have to go do that video thing today," Jamie said. "What time," Piper asked. "We start at 12," Jamie replied. "We," Piper asked. He nodded. "You are ridiculous," Piper said. He kissed her and they ate then cleaned up. "You alright with being over here," he asked. "I still have to go home," Piper said. He kissed her. "Right now, we're going upstairs," Jamie said. "Was already there. I have to go get clothes," Piper said. He picked her up, threw her over his shoulder and walked upstairs. "Jamie," Piper said. He put her down when they got to the master bedroom. "All of my stuff is at my place," Piper said. "Would you just look," Jamie said pointing out the closet. She looked over and saw dresses, shirts, skirts, jeans. "What's this," Piper asked. "So you don't have to keep running home," Jamie said. "We said we weren't rushing things," Piper replied. "We aren't. It's so you don't have to run home all the time. You'll have clothes here," he said. "Hinting that we're going that direction," Piper asked. "We do it in whatever time you need. I just want us to be able to have fun without taking off," Jamie said. Piper shook her head.

"Babe," Jamie said. She shook her head and went downstairs. She grabbed her suitcase that she'd brought home and left, heading back over to her place. She headed inside, locked up behind her and walked up to the master, bringing her bag with her. Her phone went off and she ignored it. She got unpacked, threw clothes into the laundry and got her clothes together for the weekend. When her phone went off again, she looked and ignored the call. Talking to Jamie was something she didn't want. She had a quick shower, freshened up and went downstairs to grab a coffee. She poured herself a mug and got a message from Char that she was sending hair and makeup to the house. Piper moisturized her legs and slid her robe on. Within maybe 20 minutes, there was a buzz at the gate. "Miss Piper, there is a miss Jane and miss Cara at the gate. They said they're here for hair and makeup," the security guy said. "Just let them in. I'll meet them at the door. Thank you," Piper said. She walked down the steps and the glam squad came in with Harley two steps behind them. "About time you made it back there giggles," Piper teased. "Slept in," Harley replied.

The hair and makeup for both of them looked amazing. "Did we figure out where we're going first," Piper asked. "I think Wormsloe since it's always insane busy, they want to get it out of the way so the tourists can come in," Harley said. Two minutes later, Piper got the itinerary for locations. They were finishing the day off in a concert venue that she'd played at when they started. "I guess we're finishing all of this today," Piper said. "And we're doing one for that other song. The Him video," Harley said. "When," Piper asked. "Tomorrow. They figured we can get it all in while we're on break," Piper said. She saw the second email. The other video was mostly going to be at Tybee and at the house. Piper shook her head knowing that she meant Jamie's.

"Why do you look like y'all got in another dang fight," Harley said. "It's fine," Piper said. "What happened," Harley asked. "He bought me a whole new dang wardrobe and has it in the closet at his place," Piper said. "And? That's a good thing," Harley said. "Whatever," Piper replied. Harley shook her head. The car showed a minute or two later and they hopped in with the hair and makeup people. They got down to Wormsloe and got changed into wardrobe. She did her best to brush off the annoyance that she'd had when Jamie had practically moved her into the house. Had he really just disregarded what she wanted completely? Was he really that self-centered? "Ready," Char asked. Piper nodded. They did that part of the video and it felt like they'd been there for days. When that was done, they headed to the next stop. By 2pm, that section was done. Around 7, they were heading over to the live performance part of the video. Piper got changed, they re-did her hair and makeup, and everyone else's, and they got warmed up. "Piper," Char said. "Yep," she said. "Jamie is coming for this shot. Just an idea, but we thought ending with you running into his arms," Char said. "Maybe a better idea not to," Piper said. "Won't be an issue," Jamie said. "Alright. We ready," Char asked. "Give Piper and Jamie a minute," Harley said pushing Piper into talking to Jamie.

Everyone headed out, leaving Jamie and Piper alone in a quiet room. "What," Piper asked. "I was trying to do something nice," Jamie said. "I'm sure someone else will be damn happy that you're buying them. That's not me," Piper said. She went to walk out and he stopped her, blocking her from opening the door and pinned her to it. "I was trying to make it easier so you didn't have to vanish in the morning. So you'd be comfortable. Why can't you just say thank you," Jamie asked. Piper shook her head. "Can you move please? I have work to do," Piper said. "Not until you just talk to me. I'm not trying to cause a dang problem," Jamie said. "Then stop trying to buy me. Stop trying to throw money around to impress me. It doesn't work Jamie. I don't impress that easy. I said I wasn't ready yet. Period. Not do something and I'll adapt," Piper said. "You realize how ridiculous you sound," Jamie asked.

"Do you realize how ridiculous this is that I have to repeat myself over and over? I said no to moving in together. Period. I am walking out of this room and finishing this video shoot then I'm going home to my house. End of discussion," Piper said.

Chapter 16

By the time they finished the stage performance part of the video, Piper was more than ready to go home – alone. They did the last scene where she walked over to Jamie and did her best to ignore all of the drama he'd caused. They finished the scene and Piper went to back up and get changed and Jamie pulled her back to him, devouring her lips. She finally pushed him and walked off. She got changed into street clothes and took the extensions out. The minute she was about to walk out of the dressing room, Jamie stopped her again.

"What," Piper asked. "We're not gonna have this stupid fight again. I did it so that we can relax and just be instead of the back and forth crap. When you're at your place, you have stuff there. When you're at my place, you have clothes to change in the morning," Jamie said. "Move," Piper said. "Don't do this," Jamie said. She looked at him. "Please just move," Piper asked. "I can't. Not if I'm about to lose the only dang thing in the world that I can't live without," Jamie said. "You push until I snap. That's what you do," Piper said. "You have no idea what's going on do you," Jamie asked. "Meaning what," Piper asked. He shook his head, pulled her to him and kissed her. "I love you. I'm not letting you leave," Jamie said. "I need to just go home Jamie. I need my own dang space. I didn't want us to move in yet, because I'm not ready and instead you just push me into it like you didn't hear a dang thing I said," Piper said. "I heard you. I swear I heard you. I just thought it'd be convenient to have stuff at my place too. That's all it was," Jamie said. "I can't do this," Piper said. He kissed her again and picked her up, sitting her on the edge of the counter.

"I love you. I can't just walk out and pretend that this is over," Jamie said. "Jamie, stop pushing. Please. Just stop trying to take things twenty steps ahead when we don't have to," Piper said. "I want to take a step forward. Something," Jamie said. "Then ask me. I don't wanna move in right now. I'm in the middle of a dang tour. Moving at all isn't an option," Piper said. He kissed her. "Tell me what you want. Do you want us," he asked. "Jamie," Piper said. "Do you want us to be together," he asked. "Of course," Piper said. "Instead of leaving stuff at my house, are you alright with me getting stuff so you have stuff there," he said. "Since you already did it," Piper asked. "Just answer the dang question. I just did it so it was convenient. That's it," Jamie said. "I'm not moving in," Piper said. "Come and stay while you're home," he asked. "You're not listening," Piper said. He kissed her. "I am. You have 3 days before you're gone again. Just come. Please," Jamie said. Piper shook her head. "Why do I even bother," Piper said. She went to hop off the counter and he stopped her. "Jamie," she said.

"I need you to hear me Piper. You want me to hear you and I do. Just hear me out. I hate waking up without you. I hate worrying that Colt is gonna do something and harm you. I want you with me. I get that you don't wanna move in tomorrow. I just want you with me as much as we can be. Please," he asked. "Why? Why did you even call my folks and yours to bring them to the show," Piper asked. "Because I wanted to meet them before next weekend. I knew that you needed them after what's been going on," Jamie said. "I get that you want this to progress a certain way, but you just aren't hearing me," Piper said. He kissed her. "I am. I just miss you somethin crazy if you're not there. I don't wanna wake up without you," Jamie said. "What do you want from me," Piper asked. He devoured her lips. "I want you. I want every inch of you. No more stupid fighting. Just come and be with me. Stay with me. I want us to at least try," Jamie said. "I have my own place," Piper said. "I get that. I do, but can't we just try," Jamie asked. "Why," Piper asked. He looked in her eyes. "I want you. I want you with me in the morning instead of having to run down the street. I want to fall asleep with you in my arms. What's wrong with that," Jamie asked. Piper shook her head. "I just want space to myself Jamie. I want to be able to have my friends over whenever. Do you even understand," Piper asked. He devoured her lips, pulling her legs around him. "I understand. It's not like you couldn't have that and us both under the same roof," Jamie said. She shook her head. "What am I gonna do with you," Piper asked. "What," he asked. "Only hearing yourself talk," Piper said. He shook her head. "Do you remember what you said last night," he asked. "Meaning," Piper asked. "You said the one thing you said you were never going to," Jamie said.

"Jamie," Piper said. "I want us to have a dang future instead of you putting the breaks on when you get scared," Jamie said. "Meaning what," Piper asked. "Meaning you and me against the dang world," he said. Piper shook her head. "I just didn't like being blindsided," Piper said. He kissed her, devouring her lips again and pulled her tight to him. "I love you. I get that I went overboard. I'm sorry it blind sided you. I just want you in my life. I want you with me," Jamie said. "Determined," Piper said. "Convinced that we're meant to be together," Jamie said. "Next thing you know, you're gonna go and tear that house down and build the three houses into one," Piper said. "I might," Jamie said. "You're not funny," Piper said. "We have time. You're on tour for a while anyway. We just wait until it's almost done to connect mine," he teased. "Jamie, you're completely insane. You realize that right," Piper asked. "In love with you," he said. They managed to calm things down until he had her convinced to stay at his house that night. It was perfect timing for what he had planned. He kissed her and slid her off the counter. "I'm goin home," Piper said. "Later," he teased.

They got out to the SUV and saw Harley and Carter talking by
the other SUV. "Y'all heading out," Carter asked. Jamie
nodded. "See y'all tomorrow," Jamie replied. Harley smirked.
Something was goin on and Piper was intentionally being
kept out of the loop. "You gonna tell me what's going on,"
Piper asked. "Nope," he said. "Jamie," Piper said. "What
makes you think anything's goin on," Jamie asked. "Because I
know that look. You're up to somethin," Piper said. He kissed
her and wrapped his arm around her. She shook her head and
when they pulled back in to his place, they headed inside to
see flowers, candles and a dinner table set up for two. "And
what's all of this," Piper asked. "Just come and sit," Jamie said
as his driver put her bag and purse upstairs in the master
bedroom.

Jamie pulled the chair out and she sat down, noticing her
favorite wine. "Jamie, I know you're up to somethin," Piper
said. "I wanted us to have a relaxing dinner. We never get a
chance to do this," Jamie said. "I still say you're up to
somethin," Piper said. Jamie shook his head and sat down
with her. He poured each of them a glass of wine and the
appetizer came out. "What is this," Piper asked. "Romaine
hearts, artichoke hearts and veggies," the waiter said. Even
the cucumber was in the shape of a heart. Piper shook her
head. They had a quiet meal, finishing their appetizer. When
the waiter took the plates, Jamie kissed her. "What," Piper
asked. "Was just thinkin," he teased. "About what," Piper
asked. "Do you want to stay tonight with me," he asked. "At
least you asked this time," she joked. "Is that a yes," he
asked. "Or we can just go to my place," Piper said. He shook
his head with a little grin. The next part of the meal came out
– lobster and steak with two shrimp in the shape of a heart.
"Jamie," Piper said. "Date night dinner," he teased. Piper
shook her head. They finished dinner and just as she was
about to pour another glass, the waiter came out with

dessert. "And what's this," Piper asked. "Dessert," he teased. She looked at him. "I know you're seriously up to somethin," Piper said. The waiter put the dessert in front of Piper. "Where's yours," Piper asked. He got a silly little grin. "We're sharing," he teased. The waiter took the cover off of it and she saw chocolate covered strawberries and chocolate whipped cream. "You think I'm sharing do you," Piper asked. Jamie nodded and leaned over to kiss her. "You sure nothin else is going on," Piper asked. "I don't wanna fight anymore. I hate fighting with you," Jamie said. "We have to start listening to each other," Piper said. He kissed her. "Deal," he replied. He got up and pulled her chair out.

He slid his hand in hers and walked her over to the sofa. "Come sit," Jamie said. "I know you're totally up to something. Drop the bomb," Piper said. He kissed her. "No bombs. I get I screwed up. I know it was a little much to go get you all new clothes and stuff," Jamie said. "I get helping me out if it's an event or something, but you can't really expect that I'm just gonna drop my place and run here," Piper said. He kissed her. "Do you wanna know what was in my head," he asked. "Might be nice," Piper said. "I have been in love with you since the day we met. I couldn't get you off my dang mind," Jamie said. "Oh really," Piper teased. "Still can't. The other night when we got in that stupid fight, I couldn't even think straight. It's like I'd lost my left arm. I don't wanna be without you. Even when you're on the road, I still wanna be there. It sounds ridiculous, but I really want to," Jamie said. "Why," Piper asked. "I can't think when you aren't around. I try to go to work and all I think about is you and I before I went to work, what I want to do to you after," he teased. "You're ridiculous," Piper said. "I wasn't joking. I don't wanna ever have to know that feeling again," Jamie said. "What are you saying," Piper asked. "I wanna be with you. Here, your place, the bus, a random hotel. I don't care where," Jamie said. "Jamie, all I am trying to say is that I don't want us to rush. I know that the whole moving in thing isn't a big thing for you, but it is for me," Piper said. "Well, what if we had a compromise," Jamie asked.

"What would that be," Piper asked. "When you're home on a break, you stay here. When you're away, we stay wherever you want," Jamie teased. "So, you're saying basically, that you want me to move in here so I can be here when I'm home," Piper said. "I'd like you to. I know it's taking the next step and if it's too much, I get it," Jamie said. "I just don't want Harley there alone," Piper said. "I don't think that's gonna be an issue. She's getting a lot closer with Carter," Jamie said. "And you're suggesting that they'll be at the house," Piper asked. He nodded. "Or they'll be at his place in Charleston," Jamie said. "That house was my dream house Jamie. I got it renovated so it was exactly the way I wanted," Piper said. "It's up to you. I really want you to stay with me," Jamie said. "You know that means bringing my stuff over here," Piper said. "That means it can all be done in a day or so," Jamie replied. He kissed her hoping beyond hope that it meant she was staying. He reached into his pocket and slid the keyring in her hand. "What's this," Piper asked. "A key for the house. There's a key on there for the garage too," Jamie said. "Why would I need a key for that," Piper asked. "That way you can use whichever car you want to," Jamie replied. "What," Piper asked. "Three sports cars and the SUV's," Jamie said.

"Jamie," Piper said. "And there's room for your truck. Like I said, we can figure it out," Jamie said. "All of this is a little much," Piper said. "I just want to be with you," Jamie said. "Can we just take it one step at a time? The moving in stuff then the other stuff," Piper asked. He nodded. He wasn't about to tell her that he'd already added her to his car insurance. "As long as we're together," Jamie said. He kissed her. "Fine. I'll move in," Piper said. "Good," Jamie said. "And what else did you want," Piper asked as she sipped her wine. Jamie kissed her, grabbed the dessert and walked upstairs, putting the strawberries on the dresser by the bed. "Jamie," Piper said. "I even got that body wash you love," Jamie said. He kissed her shoulder and his arms slid around her waist. "Jamie," Piper said. "What," he said as he kissed his way up her neck. "What are you doin," she asked as he slid his shirt off. "Nothin," he said as he peeled her shirt off.

"Jamie," Piper said. "Mm," he said as he kissed her side. "What are you doin," Piper asked. "Seducing my woman," he replied. She went to turn to face him as her breaths started to speed up. "Don't move," he said. He slid her heels off and undid her jeans. "Jamie," Piper said. "Step out of them." "No," Piper replied. He turned her to face him. "What's wrong," he asked. "What are you up to," Piper asked. He kissed her, undoing her jeans. He pushed them to the floor and picked her up, wrapping her legs around him. He leaned her onto the bed and kicked his jeans off along with his boxers. "Jamie," Piper said. He devoured her lips, overpowering hers and nibbling as he did it. The kiss deepened and she felt his hand slide her lace panties off. He pulled her bra to the side and kissed her from her lips, all the way down her torso. Just as he got to her hip, her phone went off. "Don't even think about it," Jamie said. "I have to. It's Char," Piper replied. He kissed her again and pinned her arms down. "My night," Jamie said as he kissed her again. "It's about the shoot tomorrow," Piper said. "She's waiting," he replied.

She was almost trembling in his arms. She knew if she tried to get up to leave, he would only get worse. Instead, she gave in. When he looked in her eyes, it's like he was free falling through the blue. It's when he couldn't restrain himself and started making love that he felt like he was out of body. They kept going and going. It's like it wasn't enough. Even when he thought he couldn't, he kept going. When he finally collapsed in her arms, her legs were shaking and so were his. "Your plan all night," Piper teased as she steadied her breathing. "Was thinkin about it all damn day," he teased. "I bet," she teased. He kissed her again. "I was thinking," he said as he managed to catch his breath. "What," Piper asked. He kissed her. "What if we just hung out the rest of the week? Stay over here," Jamie asked. "One day at a time," Piper said. He kissed her. "We can do this if it's what you want," Jamie said. "Can we talk about it in the morning," Piper asked. He kissed her. "Alright, but don't think that you're gonna sneak out on me," he teased. "Meaning what," Piper asked. "Meaning there's a full gym at my place. My sister can come over here," Jamie said. "You should probably ask her," Piper said. He kissed her. He grabbed his phone from the counter, texted her and within a minute or two, she'd replied back with a smiley face emoji. "She'll be here," Jamie said. "Can you get my phone," Piper asked. He kissed her, got up and grabbed her phone, handing it to her.

She looked and saw a text from Colt:

Welcome home. Is it my turn?

Piper dropped it and Jamie grabbed her phone. He slid his jeans on, suggested that she got dressed and went to talk to security. "What's wrong," his head of security asked. He showed him the message. "Hotel," his head of security asked. "Piper's house cleared," Jamie asked. "She has more security there plus the police," his head of security said. He nodded and went to talk to security while Jamie went upstairs. "I'm right aren't I? Being at my place is safer," Piper asked. "For right now, no. We're either staying in Charleston or we're going to a hotel," Jamie said. "You realize this is nuts right," Piper asked. He kissed her. "Please," Jamie said. "I have to do the video in the morning," Piper said. "Follow me," Jamie said. They left, got in the SUV and went to the helipad. "Where are we going," Piper asked. "Charleston. I have a condo there," Jamie said. They headed off and when they made it to Charleston, they hopped off the helicopter and went straight to his condo. "We have to message your sister," Piper said.

Jamie handed Piper his phone and they got to the building. "Sir," his other security man said. "Just for tonight," Jamie said. The security guy nodded and Piper headed inside with Jamie. The lights came up and the view was amazing. "This is where you live? Seriously," Piper asked. "Sort of a business condo," Jamie said. "Pretty amazing," Piper replied. His phone buzzed a minute later. He looked at his phone. There was a camera in his bedroom. A tiny pinhole camera, but it was still bad. Piper was going to lose it. He replied back:

Just make sure it's gone and check the rest of the house. I want him in a jail cell by the end of the night.

"And who was that," Piper asked as she came into the bedroom in his t-shirt. "They found out how he knew we were there," Jamie said. "And," Piper asked. "It's being fixed," Jamie said. "So, all in all we were better off being at my place," Piper said. "We're staying here and flying back tomorrow so you can meet Char," Jamie said. He handed Piper her phone and she messaged Char that she was in Charleston for the night. When her phone pinged, Piper looked. "Well, we don't have to be there until 10am," Piper said. "Then we can go back early and watch the sunrise," Jamie replied. "And what happens when he doesn't stop," Piper asked. He kissed her. "Then I'll handle it once and for all. He's not starting another war," Jamie said. She looked at him. "What am I gonna do with you," Piper asked. "Meaning," Jamie asked. "Meaning I am perfectly capable of handling him," Piper said. "By all means go ahead," Jamie said. "I'm goin home," Piper said. "Just stay tonight. It's late," he said. Piper looked at him.

"I'm going back to my house in the morning," Piper said. He nodded and came over to her. The closer he got, the more she tried to back up. When her back hit the cold wall of the master bedroom, he smirked and leaned up against her. "What is up with you," Piper asked. "Nothin," he said. He kissed her and had her almost pinned. "Jamie," Piper said. "I'm not the one who bumped into the wall," Jamie said. He kissed her and one hand slid to her side. "What are you up to," Piper asked as her knees were almost shaking. His arm slid around her to her backside. "Come here," he said. "I'm going to sleep," Piper said. He shook his head. "Jamie, don't start," Piper teased. He gave her that look. "Not happening," Piper said as she heard his phone go off. "Aren't you getting that," Piper asked. He shook his head. "Sorta busy," Jamie said. "I'm going to sleep. I have a ton of stuff to do tomorrow," Piper said. He pulled her to him and walked her to the bed. Two seconds later, her phone went off. Piper grabbed it.

"Piper," Char said. "What's up," Piper replied. "Have a little change of plans. We're doing the shoot early instead like sunrise," Char said. "Where's the first location," Piper asked. "Wormsloe. It's what you said you wanted right," Char asked. "What time," Piper asked. We're going for 4 if that's alright," Char said. Piper looked at the clock. "Can we not do sunset," Piper asked. "That could work instead," Char said. "We're up in Charleston. Security issue at Jamie's," Piper said. "Not a problem," Char said. "We'll be back before 6. I'm doing a quick workout then I'm all yours," Piper said. "Alright. We'll see you at 9," Char replied. "Thanks," Piper said. They hung up and Jamie kissed her. "What in the world has got into you," Piper asked. "Call it addicted," he teased.

He slid her phone to the charger and kissed her. "Jamie," Piper said. He smirked. "Yes sexy," he teased. "You're up to something," Piper said. "Trying my best to get that shirt off," he teased. "You're acting insane," Piper said. He kissed her. Just as he was about to slide the shirt off of her, his phone went off. He shook his head, grabbed it and propped himself up. "Yes," Jamie said. "The cameras have been cleared and destroyed. The police have him in custody," his security man said. "Good," Jamie replied. "What," Piper asked when he put the phone on the charging pad beside hers. "We can go whenever we're ready. He's in police custody," Jamie said. "For now. I've heard that before," Piper said. "For tonight, we can sleep easy. He's not coming near either of us," Jamie replied.

"And," Piper asked. "And what," he replied. "You gonna tell me what all of this is about," Piper asked. "Meaning what," he asked. "Candles, rose petals and dinner with flowers everywhere," Piper said. "Not allowed to make things romantic now," he asked. "Not if you're up to something that you're keeping a dang secret," Piper said. "You'll find out soon enough," he teased. "Meaning what," Piper asked. He kissed her and peeled the shirt over her head. He pulled the covers up and curled her into his arms. "Jamie," Piper said. "I screwed up. I was making it up to you," Jamie said. "Then it's gonna take more than that," Piper teased. He shook his head and pulled her to him. "Such as," he asked. "Just remember that I do things my way," Piper said. "You alright with the house stuff," he asked. "When I know if Harley is gonna need somewhere to stay," Piper replied. "Carter will have that handled if I know him at all," Jamie said. "We're gonna be on tour Jamie. I don't even have time to go visit my folks let alone work on a house," Piper said. "I can get your things moved over here. Like I said, it won't take long," he said. "I don't have time to move Jamie. I don't even have time to go to the dang gym in the morning," Piper said. "Do you want to," Jamie asked. Piper nodded. "Then it will be done. We can change whatever you want to. We can put a recording studio in the new section of the house. We can put in a bigger gym," Jamie said.

"Do I get to add what I want," Piper asked. "Depends. Does it include a bigger bedroom," he teased. "For me," Piper said. "Tease," he joked. "I want to have my own space for when I need it," Piper said. "How about a sun porch with porch swings or gliders," Jamie said. She looked at him. "Stop reading my mind," Piper said. "Big porch," Jamie asked. Piper nodded. "Double wrap around porch on both floors," he asked. "With the option of shatter proof glass," Piper said. "I can figure something out," Jamie said. "Meaning," Piper asked. "More like bullet proof," he replied. "And," Piper asked. "We should be alright," Jamie said. "Meaning what," Piper asked. "They're taking that other house down tomorrow. In a couple months it'll be connected to my house and then we have free reign," Jamie said. "And my place," Piper asked. "We can have that added so there's a space no matter what for Harley," Jamie said. "So, it's gonna be one huge massive 15000 square foot property," Piper teased. "Works for me. Private entrances, huge master bathroom, master suite and even a reading room if you want it," Jamie said. "Falcons room," Piper asked. "Definitely. Comfy chairs for watching the games when we don't want to be at the stadium," Jamie said. "What," Piper asked. "I have season tickets. Always have," he said. "See, if you'd told me that I wouldn't have caused a problem," Piper joked. "That easily impressed? All I had to do was mention tickets," he joked. Piper kissed him. "Something like that," she said.

They managed to get some rest finally and headed back to Savannah. After a quick workout, they ate, showered and he went into the studio while Piper went off to the video shoot.

By the end of the day, she was beyond exhausted. They did the final shot of walking off into the sunset and it was a wrap. Two in one week was a little much. "And where did you disappear to," Harley asked. "When," Piper asked. "You weren't at the house last night obviously. Looked like you hadn't been there in weeks," Harley said. "Well, we sorta came to a decision," Piper said. "Meaning what," Harley asked. "Before I start that, how's Carter," Piper asked. "Amazing," she replied. "So y'all are workin out," Piper asked. Harley nodded. "He's amazing," Harley said. "And," Piper asked. "He asked me to move in, but I'm not doing it. I'm staying at the house. I don't want you there alone," Harley said.

"Well, about that," Piper said. "You're really doin it," Harley asked. "We talked. A lot. I didn't want you not having anywhere to go if things didn't work with Carter," Piper said. "I know that I'll always have a place to stay. I just want to make sure that I wasn't holding you back. He's a good guy Piper. He really is," Harley said. "Just don't let him talk you into something stupid," Piper said. "Like you," Harley joked. "Exactly," Piper said. She shook her head. "How the heck it took you this long to realize that he's head over heels I will never quite understand," Harley said. "That's not it. He's used to being in charge. So am I," Piper said. "So the two control freaks can't lose control," Harley joked. "Okay Miss Fifty Shades addict," Piper teased. "Just because we're reenacting a couple scenes from Grey," Harley joked. "I don't even wanna know," Piper said. "Let's leave it at you don't need to worry. If I need you, I know where you are. You're allowed to be happy," Harley said. Piper gave her a hug. "This mean that you're giving the guy a chance finally," Kurt asked. "All y'all are on his side," Piper teased. "Definitely," Keith said.

Piper shook her head. She washed the makeup off and slid into her jeans and t-shirt. "We going to celebrate and get dinner or something," Keith asked. "Call the wives y'all," Piper said calling the Olde Pink House. "Miss Piper," the hostess said. "Is the private dining room available for a quick dinner," Piper asked. "For you, definitely," the hostess replied. "We'll see you in a half hour or so," Piper said. "We'll make sure the soup is on," the hostess joked. Piper shook her head. "Half hour. We'll meet you at the restaurant," Piper said. She texted Jamie that they were going to the restaurant and got no reply. She put on a little lipstick and they hopped into the SUV that had originally picked them up. She looked at the driver, ensuring it was the same original driver. "What," Harley asked. Piper shook her head. They got to the restaurant and she headed in with Harley. Just as the guys were arriving, Piper's phone dinged:

Still at the studio. Dinner is on me. Left something at the house for you. Hope it all went well.

Piper replied back:

Hey handsome. Did you want me to bring you home some soup? I can bring it to the studio.

As soon as she saw the read notification, her phone buzzed:

Tempting. Very tempting. I'd never get anything done. I'll meet you in bed. And yes I would love a couple bowls. Love you

Piper smirked. "I guess he's not coming," Harley asked as Carter walked in. "Hi Carter," Piper said. "Hello," Carter said. He kissed Piper's cheek and kissed Harley. The guys came in a little while later with their wives and a bottle of Piper's favorite wine came to the table. "We didn't order that," Piper said. "Was a gift from Mr. Hastings," the waitress said. "Thank you," Piper said. Everyone else ordered whatever they wanted and the waitress looked at Piper. "We're putting a few bowls aside for you. What else would you like," the waitress asked. "Soup and the chicken Caesar," Piper said. "Very good," the waitress said. "I wanted to thank y'all for the past day or two. I know it's a lot in a short period of time, but we have two videos under our belts. Its huge," Piper said. "And when you win that CMA," Keith joked. "It's all because of you," Piper said. "Girl, if you hadn't written the dang songs," Kurt said. "Y'all helped," Piper teased. Kurt smirked. They hung out, had a long relaxing dinner and just as they were bringing the 6 bowls of soup to Piper, her phone buzzed:

Dinner is paid for. Changed my mind. Bring soup. And wine. And you in lingerie. And nothing else. ;-)

Piper shook her head. "Did we need the bill," Keith asked. "Already taken care of," Piper said. "Thank you," everyone said. "Now go home and enjoy. 24 more hours at home before we leave," Piper said. They all headed out and Piper got another bottle of wine. "Thank you," Piper said. The hostess smirked and Piper walked outside to see Jamie's security. "Miss Piper," the security guy said. "He wants..." "He let us know. We're heading over now," his security guy said. They arrived 20 minutes later. "Miss Piper," the security guy said as he opened the door. He walked her into the studio and up to where Jamie was. She went in and Jamie's hands were running through his head. He was beyond frustrated. It was taking longer than he thought and he was getting annoyed.

"Anything that soup can fix," Piper said quietly in his ear as he got goosebumps. "You wearing lingerie," he teased. "Under my jeans and t-shirt," Piper joked. He turned to kiss her and pulled her into his lap. She put the soup on the counter and he turned to face the studio. "Take ten," Jamie said. The artist he was working with nodded and came in. "This must be

Piper," the man said. "Babe, my cousin Andrew. Andrew, my girl Piper," Jamie said. "Andrew Hart," Piper said. He nodded. "I've heard all about you," Andrew said. "I bet," Piper teased. "I'm just gonna eat. Feel free to go grab dinner," Jamie said. "Or just another cup of Starbucks. Back in 10," Andrew said as he headed off with his band mates.

"Hey," Piper said. "Hey yourself sexy," he said. "Stuck," Piper asked. He nodded and kissed her neck. "Have your soup," she said. "And you even brought the wine," he teased. "They packed it," Piper said. "Then we have extra for tomorrow so you can have a day to relax," Jamie said. "Or I can add more crab and lobster," Piper said. "Tease," he joked. "You sir, have work to do. I just wanted to make sure you ate," Piper said. "Stay until I am done tonight," Jamie asked. "Why," Piper asked. He gave her that look. He was worried that something else would happen and he wouldn't be there. "Jamie," Piper said. "He only has the studio for another hour and a half. We can go home after that," Jamie said. Piper kissed him. "I'm going to go and get some sleep while I wait for you in bed," Piper said. "No," he said. Piper kissed him again. "I'll take the soup and put it in the fridge at home. Whenever you're done, I'll be in bed," Piper said. He shook his head. "Colt is in jail. He's not getting out. The officer said he'd keep me apprised of what's going on," Piper said. "I still don't want you at the house alone," Jamie said. His security guy came in. "Sir," he said. "Is Colt still in custody," Jamie asked. "Yes." "If Piper goes back to the house with you, sweep the house before she goes in and keep her safe," Jamie said. He nodded and left the room. He kissed her again. "An hour and a half max," Jamie said. Piper nodded. "Alright handsome," Piper said. She headed out and he went back to work. "Andrew, let's get this done. I have plans tomorrow," Jamie said.

Piper got to the house, put the soup and the wine into the fridge and walked upstairs. She put the phone on the wireless charging pad and slid out of her clothes, opting for a shower before bed. She stepped out, wrapped herself in a towel and went and slid one of Jamie's t-shirts on. She dried her hair with the towel and put lotion on her skin. She slid into the bed and her phone went off. "Yep," Piper said. "Where are you," Jamie said. "In bed," Piper said. "Oh really," Jamie said. "Yes," Piper said. "And what are you wearing," he teased. "You'll see when you get here," Piper said. "Thank you by the way," he said. "For what," Piper replied. "I was frustrated from hunger," he teased. "Kinda figured that. Are y'all finished," Piper asked. "Almost. Have a little left to do, but it'll be done in the morning," Jamie said. "See you when you get home," Piper said. "Love you," he said. "Back at ya," Piper teased. "Someday," he teased. They hung up and Piper turned the light off and curled up on the bed.

A half hour later, the other side of the bed was empty. She closed her eyes. When she woke up another hour later, there was nobody else in the bed. She got up, slid his robe on and saw a light on in his office. She walked over and leaned against the door jam. "What you doin," Piper asked. "Had to check something," Jamie said. "And I thought you wanted to come to bed," Piper teased. "The police officer called me," Jamie said. "And," Piper asked as she yawned. "In the morning," Jamie said as he didn't want to upset her before bed. "Say it," Piper said. "In the morning," Jamie replied. "Now," Piper said. "You need sleep. I don't want you getting upset," Jamie said. "He's out isn't he," Piper asked. "On bail," Jamie replied. "And who posted it," Piper asked. "No idea. The officer is getting the info," Jamie said. "Come to bed," Piper said. "In a minute," Jamie said.

Piper walked back upstairs, put the robe across the chair and slid under the blankets, falling back asleep. Not long later, Jamie came upstairs and saw her asleep in his bed. The first time she hadn't started a fight about staying. The first time

she'd just let him have his way without repercussions. He slid
out of his shirt, jeans, socks and shoes. He washed up before
bed and slid into the bed beside her. When his arm slid
around her, she all but refused to move. He slid closer to her
and nuzzled her neck. "About time," Piper said. He kissed her
shoulder. "Sleep," Piper said. He smirked. He nuzzled her ear
and as he was about to move his hand to inch that shirt up,
she linked their fingers and stopped him. "Good night sexy,"
Jamie said.

The next morning, Piper woke up to an empty bed. She
looked and it was almost as if he had never been in bed. She
got up, slid her workout gear on and went downstairs. "Do
you know where Jamie is," Piper asked his security. "He went
into the studio. He said he wanted to make sure the music
was done so you had the day together," his security guy said.
"Nobody went with him," Piper asked. "He has two other
security people with him. He asked that I stayed here to keep
an eye on you," the security guy said. Two minutes later,
there was a knock at the door. Piper went to answer. "Jess,"
Piper asked. "Hey. Jamie said you were doing the workouts
here now," Jess teased. "Eliminates the cat calling I assume,"
Piper joked. They went up to the gym and did the workout.
"Damn. You look amazing," Jess said. "Even though I didn't
even really get to work out on the bus," Piper said. "We can
do them anywhere. It's just a matter of bringing what we
need," Jess said. She finished her workout and they went
downstairs and had breakfast. "Where is my brother
anyway," Jess asked. "At the studio. Something about
finishing what he started last night," Piper said.

Piper texted Jamie:

Good morning handsome. You coming home or avoiding me?
Was I talking in my sleep?

When she got no reply, Piper shook her head. "I'll stay until he's back," Jess said. "I appreciate it," Piper said. "So, when did you decide to move in," Jess asked. "Jamie did his best to talk me into it," Piper teased. "As long as you're happy. Just remember that. He hates the word no, but being honest with what you want is important. Nobody gets to bully you into it," Jess said. "Oh I know that. Honestly, I was just worried that Harley would have nowhere to go if it didn't work with Carter, but I guess it is," Piper teased. "Carter is a good guy. He always has been. Nobody was really good enough for Carter, but I guess Jamie thinks they're good together. Just take care of you alright? Don't let him start talking you into crazy stuff," Jess said. "What crazy stuff are we talking about," Jamie teased as he leaned over and kissed Piper. "Anything that involves whisking her away from working out or the tour for her work," Jess teased as she gave him a hug. "How was the workout," Jamie asked. "Good. She's looking great," Jess said. "Always has," Jamie teased. Piper shook her head. "Y'all can quit talking about me like I'm a piece of meat," Piper said. Jamie smirked. She walked upstairs to go and have a shower.

"Did you get it," Jess asked. Jamie nodded. "And the earrings to match," he said. "I can't believe you," Jess said. "Just don't make it freaking obvious alright," Jamie asked. Jess nodded and gave him a hug. "I'm heading home. Take care of your girl," Jess said. Jamie nodded. He peeled his shirt off and walked upstairs. He kicked his jeans off, laying them on the edge of the bed and walked into the master bathroom, slipping in behind Piper in the shower. "Hey," Jamie said. "Really nice," Piper said. "What," he asked. She rinsed the conditioner out and washed her body from head to toe. She bumped up against him and his hand slid to her side as his nails grazed her hip. She rinsed off and stepped out of the shower, wrapping herself in a warm towel.

He shook his head watching her leave the bathroom. She went into the bedroom, slid her t-shirt and blue jeans on and went and sat outside, opting for sunshine and the warm summer breeze. She sat down to write, or at least attempt to when Jamie came out in nothing but a towel. "Piper," Jamie said. "What," she said. "Come inside for a minute," he asked. "I'm good," Piper said. He slid his hand in hers and pulled her to him. "Jamie, I'm fine," Piper said. "Come," he asked.

Chapter 17

She came in and walked over to the bed. "What would you like," Piper asked. "You have to go tomorrow. Are you alright if we hang together today," he asked. "You mean since you didn't bother to even stay in bed last night," Piper asked. He shook his head. "I had stuff spinning around my head. I couldn't sleep," Jamie said. "You realize that you actually need sleep right," Piper asked. "He got out. I was practically jumping every time I heard a noise. I didn't wanna wake you up. I slept on the chair," Jamie said. Piper shook her head. "Whatever," Piper said. "The first dang time I just stay and you won't sleep in the bed with me. What's the point of me even being here," Piper asked. He went to grab her hand to pull her to him and she pulled away. She grabbed her pen and notebook and walked off. She went downstairs and put her phone in her purse. "Miss Piper, do you have a list of what you wanted us to bring over to the house," his security guy asked. "I'll go with you," Piper said. "I appreciate that, but if you can just…" "I'm going," Piper said. She grabbed her purse and walked over with his security.

They walked over to the house and headed inside. Piper walked up to the master bedroom and saw her clothes. "What did you want us to take," the security guy said. "Can I just have a few minutes," Piper asked. He nodded and stepped out. She looked over all of the clothes. Some were lucky outfits, some were perfectly beat up blue jeans. She picked out her favorite shoes, purses, dresses and then she felt someone looking at her. She turned around and saw Jamie. "What are you doing," Jamie asked. "Just picking out what I need," Piper said. "We're taking it all over to the house. You don't have to pick and choose," he said. Piper shook her head. "Why do you want me there if you're not even gonna sleep with me," Piper asked. "I was having nightmares about him. I didn't want to wake you up with my tossing and turning," Jamie said. She shrugged. "Then I might as well sleep here," Piper said. He kissed her neck. "Stop." "I love you," he said. "Funny way of showing it," Piper said. He shook his head. He had 48 hours before everything in his world was gonna change. 48 hours left to get her to look at him that way again.

"Come back to the house. They can take everything to the house and you can go through it there," Jamie said. "What's the freaking rush," Piper said as she put a couple pairs of jeans aside. "You're leaving in the morning," Jamie said. "Have fun at work," Piper said. She went back to going through her things. Jamie motioned towards the security team and asked them to take it to the house. He handed her a bag to put her clothes in from her drawers. "What are you..." "Like I said, go through it at the house," Jamie said. Piper shook her head. He emptied the drawers and one of the other security guys took the bag. "Harley still has stuff here," Piper said. "Bathroom," he said. She took out the few items still in her bathroom and closed the door. "What," Piper asked. He kissed her and sat her up on the counter, closing the door.

"Jamie, enough," Piper said. She went to slide off and he stopped her. "You're stuff is in good hands. Is there anything else that you have to have at the house," Jamie asked. "My pillows," Piper said. "And," he asked. "My wine," Piper teased. "Not an issue. Anything else," Jamie asked. "My pictures. My guitar. My notebooks. I would like my sofa and chairs," Piper said. "It will be brought over. Come over to the house," Jamie said. "You're not even sleeping with me. I might as well be here," Piper said. He kissed her. "After not being able to sleep last night, I will from now on," Jamie said. Piper shook her head. "And I call..." He kissed her. "We're going. Now," Jamie said. He grabbed her hand, opened the bathroom door and walked her downstairs. "Guitar, sofa and

chairs, notebooks and books from her library. All the clothes.
Bring Harley's as well. We'll put them in the guest room,"
Jamie said. "TV's," his security guy asked. Piper nodded. "As
you wish," Jamie said. The other security people walked them
back to Jamie's.

"Seriously," Piper said. "He tried to get into your house last
night. Indulge me," Jamie said. "What," Piper asked. "That's
why we're staying at my place tonight," Jamie said. "How am
I getting to the venue tomorrow," Piper asked. "Flying
everyone out to meet the bus," he replied. "New Orleans,
Memphis and Nash," Piper said. "Won't be that bad. Three
days and you're back," Jamie said. "Or I just stay on the bus
and go to the next stop while you work," Piper said. "You
trying to get rid of me again," he asked. Piper nodded. They
walked into the house and Piper went outside. "Stubborn
pain in the...Piper, come inside," Jamie asked.

Piper ignored him. He walked outside. "Tell me what you
want me to do," Jamie asked. "You left," Piper said. He shook
his head. "I figured if I couldn't sleep, I might as well finish the
work on the CD so I had time alone with you," Jamie said.
"Waking up alone wasn't part of the deal," Piper said. He
kissed her. "Come inside," he asked. She walked in and saw
her sofa going upstairs. "Where are you taking that," Piper
asked. "Upstairs. Sitting room. Your sofa and chairs and your
TV," Jamie said. "What," Piper asked. "Upstairs sitting room,"
he said. He walked her upstairs and it was set up like a hotel
suite. The sofa and chairs were cleaned and set up with the
TV. "This way if we have anyone over, they have somewhere
to sit or you have somewhere to sit that makes you feel like
home," Jamie said. She went into the bedroom and saw her
clothes organized by color on the other side of the closet
from Jamie's things. Jewelry was even put into a case. Her
lingerie was even organized in the drawer. She noticed a few
extra things among what she'd left at the house. "And what's

the extra lace stuff," Piper asked. "Couple extra things you might like. I added in a few dresses too," Jamie said. "You know how I feel about dresses," Piper said. He kissed her. "They were made for you," he said. She saw heels mixed with her cowboy boots. Her socks were even organized by color. "And your toiletry stuff is in the master bathroom," Jamie said. "That easy," Piper asked. Jamie kissed her. "Now, come with me," Jamie said.

They walked back into the bedroom and he sat her down in the chair he'd slept in more than once. "I need you to promise me something," Jamie asked. "Such as," Piper asked. "If we are doing this, I need to know that you aren't gonna walk away. That you aren't gonna just get up one morning and leave me," Jamie said. He had a look in his eyes that showed his desperation. That his happiness at that moment depended on her answer. "Just remember that I won't just up and vanish unless I need time to cool off. That's why I said to set that other bedroom up. I'll have space to just cool off if I'm upset," Piper said. "Promise me," Jamie asked. "I can't promise it'll never happen, but I can promise that I'll come back when I cool down. Even if I just go for a walk on the beach," Piper said. He looked at her. "I can't lose you," Jamie said. Piper kissed him. "I can't promise we're never gonna fight. I can promise that we'll figure it out," Piper said. "I love you. You know that right," he asked. Piper nodded. He kissed her. "What's all of this about," Piper asked. "Nightmares over and over again that you leave and never come back," Jamie said. "That's why you can't sleep," Piper asked. He nodded.

"Just remember that I'm right there. If I'm on tour, you're there. I'm not gonna just disappear," Piper said. He kissed her again. "What is all of this about?" "Do you want kids," he asked. "When and if it ever happens," Piper said. "Big or small wedding if you had a choice," Jamie asked. "Why are we having this conversation again," Piper asked. "Answer," Jamie asked. "Probably small," Piper said.

"Nanny or no nanny," Jamie asked. "Totally not having this conversation. Why are we even talking about this," Piper asked. "No nanny," he asked. "It'd help but I don't want someone else raising my kid," Piper said. "Good," he said. "Jamie, why are you talking crazy," Piper asked. He kissed her. "Because we never talked about it," Jamie said. "You're talking about marriage issues. We're not married. We just freakin moved in together today. A little much," Piper said. "We needed to talk about it," Jamie said. She shook her head. "Can I go and get some work done on my writing," Piper asked like a little kid asking the teacher to go to the washroom. "We are going out just us tonight," Jamie said. Piper nodded. "If that's what you want," Piper said. "We get a night to just relax," he said. Piper nodded. "Just let me know what to wear," Piper teased. He kissed her and they went downstairs, just as they were bringing in her TV and a few other things from the house.

Piper messaged Harley that her things were in the guest room at Jamie's. Two minutes later, her phone went off. "At Jamie's? Did I read that right," Harley asked. "For now, that's the plan," Piper said. "You're seriously going along with the massive house thing," Harley asked. "You have a place here if you need it. The house is yours until we figure out what to do with it," Piper said. "Alright, but I was gonna kinda tell you that Carter asked me to move in," Harley said. "I swear this is all planned out," Piper teased. "I'll come get my stuff on our next break," Harley said. "Alright girl. You know we're gonna be talkin about all of this," Piper teased. "I know. By the way, thank Jamie for introducing us," Harley teased. "You can thank him this weekend. He's comin," Piper said. "Alright girl. Go enjoy the last day of freedom," Harley joked.

Jamie walked downstairs, laptop in hand and sat down with Piper. "Need an opinion," Jamie said. "Alright," Piper said. He put the laptop down and pressed play. "Objective opinion," he said. They watched the video of what had to be a dream house. Wrap around porches, live oaks with Spanish moss and porch swings were outside. The inside came up on the screen. The pristine floors, the dream kitchen, the massive tv room, library, game room then a butler pantry and room for the security staff that was more like their own house. The staircase to the second level was dreamy. The 10 bedrooms, the elaborate bathrooms, the gym, the media room and the football room were all absolutely amazing. Last on the video was a nursery and children's room. "It's beautiful, but it's a little big," Piper said. She saw the massive 6 car garage then the huge pool. "Jamie, I get wanting elaborate, but it's too much for just you and me and the security staff. It's way too much," Piper said. "What's missing," Jamie asked. "Recording studio. It's still too much," Piper said. "Then we do it together," Jamie said. Piper nodded. He made a call and within 20 minutes, the architect was at the house to go over ideas.

They sat down to discuss it and the planning began. The bedrooms, the bathrooms, the nursery, the master suite, the master bath. They were done within the first half hour. "Office with lots of room, tv room, huge footprint for the kitchen, the office for the security staff. All of that was next. "What else did you need," the architect asked. "Piper needs a studio," Jamie said. "Alright," the architect said. "It just seems cold to me. Like it's flaunting things. Something more southern looking but still with all the security we need. We don't need a massive pool. I'm happy with a hot tub, a small pool and a garden with a fire pit. I know it's not exactly extravagant, but that's what I want," Piper said. Jamie's arm slid around her. "I'll have the updated video for you by

Sunday if that's alright. It'll be beautiful. Softer and less cold feeling works," the architect said. "Alright," Piper said. He headed out and Piper tried to get some writing in. Jamie walked over and kissed her. "More southern," he asked. "We're in Georgia. Southern works," Piper teased.

He worked away on emails for a little while and she got a little bit written. "What did you want to do today," Jamie asked. "Go out somewhere away from all of this insanity for a while," Piper said. He kissed her, put his laptop in his office and took her hand. "Where are we goin," Piper asked. "Park. We can walk around Forsyth, go and walk on Broughton, get ice cream," he said. She kissed him and shook her head. "Throw your run gear on then," Jamie said. "And where else are we goin," Piper asked. "We can do the walking path at Wormsloe," Jamie replied. Piper smirked and kissed him. She went and put her shorts, tank and runners on. He came up behind her as she put her hair into a ponytail. "What," Piper asked. He kissed her neck. "I kinda like," he joked. She shook her head and he slid into his run gear. They headed to Wormsloe and went off on the walk. "You know, I had no idea they had that set up for a wedding," Jamie said as they walked past the altar that was all trees. "Cute," Piper said. He smirked. "You're up to something. Just spill it," Piper said. He kissed her. They kept going. They saw everything and there was a nagging feeling. "Jamie," Piper said. "Yes beautiful," Jamie said. "What is all this marriage talk about," Piper asked. "Just stuff I wanted to know. We've been together a while and we never even talked about it," Jamie said as they made it back to that altar.

"Jamie," Piper said. It was an ask me anything moment. "Yep," he asked. "You never answered any of those questions you asked me," Piper said. "We see things the same way. I want something small for a wedding, I hate the idea of nannies and I'd have as many kids as we can if we can. I don't wanna have them with anyone else," Jamie said. "We just moved in together. Don't you think this is a little much," Piper asked. "At least we had the conversation," Jamie said. Piper shook her head. "Just promise me that you aren't jumping even further ahead," Piper asked. He kissed her.

They got back to the hotel, freshened up and got changed for dinner. "Where are we goin," Piper asked. "You'll see when we get there," he teased. He kissed her and his security guy Jackson came up to the master bedroom. "Sir," he said. "Yep," Jamie said. "The reservation has been made as per your request. They'll be expecting you in about an hour and a bit," he said. "Thank you. Piper, you met Jackson right," Jamie asked. "Nice to meet you," Piper said. "He's your security," Jamie said. "Since when do I need security," Piper asked. "When you're out or whatever, you need security," Jamie said. "Whatever," Piper said. Jackson went back downstairs. "Jamie," Piper said. "When I'm not there, you need security. You can do whatever you want to. I just need to know that you're safe," Jamie said. "Alright," Piper replied. Fighting with him was pointless.

That night, they left for wherever he'd planned to go and when they pulled into the Mansion on Forsyth, she couldn't help but laugh. "And what are we doing here," Piper asked. "Dinner. Private dining room just us," he said. She knew he was up to something. They sat down and had a long romantic dinner, headed off for a walk through the park to see the fountain all lit up and then headed back to the house. "What time are you leaving in the morning," Jamie asked. "I think 8 or something. We're meeting at the airport," Piper said. "The pilot will meet you there. I'll come down later tomorrow. I have a meeting with the studio tomorrow," Jamie said. Piper nodded. "Alright," she said.

The next 2 days of performances were amazing. When they finally got to Nashville, Piper's folks and Jamie's were there waiting. "Y'all are just so cute. Good timing," Piper said as she gave them each a hug. "How was the flight," Piper asked. "Good," her mom said. Piper hugged them again and Jamie came up behind her. "All checked into the hotel," Jamie said as he gave everyone their room keys. "Lookin forward to tonight," her dad said. "I'm just glad y'all could come out for this. At least you know your way around a little," Piper joked. They sat around and chatted and the stage manager came over to Piper. "Miss Piper, sound check is in 10 minutes," the stage manager said. "I'm gonna head over. Y'all are welcome to come hang and watch," Piper said.

By the time she was done sound check, she knew something else was going on. Jason was staying away and giving her room. Even didn't come over. By the time everyone had finished sound check, it was time to eat before getting ready. Jamie's folks, hers and the band were all together. They even went as far as making crab linguine alfredo. She shrugged it off, but there was a nagging feeling. When she excused herself to go to hair and makeup, Jason's wife came in to get her ready. "I know something is goin on. Just say it," Piper said. "Just wanted to do it myself. My mom is looking after the kiddos this weekend," Kaylie said. When Piper looked in the mirror at the end, she looked amazing. "Wow," Piper said. "And what are you wearing," Kaylie asked. Piper picked out the red and Kaylie smirked and handed her the silver. "Seriously," Piper asked. "It matches the glitter on your eyes," Kaylie said. She knew it was a distraction.

She did Harley's hair and makeup while Piper went in to do her meet and greet. When that was done, Piper touched up her lipstick and put perfume on. "Look amazing," Kaylie said. "Kinda need jewelry," Piper said. Kaylie put a bracelet on her, put the sexy earrings in and sent Piper on her way. She got up to the stage and Harley came up behind her. "You ready," Harley asked. Piper nodded. Harley gave her a hug and they did a quick shot, said a quick prayer and the band headed on. The crowd was going nuts. "Hey y'all," Piper said. "I think you might remember this one. This is You Can't Break Me," Piper said as she started singing the song everyone loved.

She saw her folks singing along. "A special shout out to two pretty amazing couples. Give them a big hand y'all. My folks," Piper said. The crowd roared. She saw her mom getting teary-eyed. "This one is one I know she loves. Dedicated to my folks and this handsome guy I know," Piper said. "This one is called Him," Piper replied. The crowd was singing along with it. At the end of the song, there was another spotlight that came up. Piper turned around and saw Jamie walking towards her. "Y'all remember this handsome guy don't you," Piper teased. He gave her a huge hug. She started getting butterflies. Jason was standing side stage with Kaylie. It's like everyone was watching. He pulled out a microphone. "Y'all know what an amazing woman Piper is right," Jamie asked as the crowd roared. She shook her head. "I may have inspired that song, but she inspired me in so many ways. I'm lucky to have her in my life and I hope that I'll be able to spend forever with her," Jamie said as he got down on his knee with the ring in hand. "Jamie," Piper said without the microphone. "Make me the happiest guy ever and marry me," he asked. "You're absolutely ridiculous," she said quietly. "I love you. Marry me," he asked. "Couldn't just do this at Forsyth," Piper teased. "Go big or go home," he teased. She nodded. "Y'all she said yes," Harley said. He opened the box and her jaw almost hit the stage. "Jamie," Piper said. He slid the ring on her finger and kissed her. She shook her head. He kissed her forehead. "We're celebrating after," Jamie said. Piper nodded, he kissed her again and headed off stage. Jason shook his hand and gave him a guy hug, Kaylie gave him a hug.

"Well, back to what we were up to," Piper said brushing a tear or two away. They sang Forever Mine, Found and then sang Heartbeat and headed off. The minute she was off the stage, Kaylie and Jason gave her a huge hug and her folks ran right to her. "So that's why," Piper said as her mom hugged her. "Like I said, you needed the silver," Kaylie joked. "What am I gonna do with you," Piper asked as Jamie wrapped his arm around her. "Marry me," he whispered. Jason came over and gave her a huge hug. "Congrats superstar," Jason said. "All of y'all had this planned," Piper said. "If it helps, we didn't know either," Harley teased as she opened the champagne and poured glasses for everyone. She looked at the ring – cushion cut and an emerald shaped ring with diamonds along the edges. It was breathtaking. "Did you design this," Piper asked. Jamie nodded. She shook her head and he pulled her to him. "So, about that nursery," Jamie teased. "You're absolutely ridiculous," Piper said. "Now that you have everyone in that room stunned," Piper said.

"Congrats," Char said as she came up behind them. "Thank you," Piper said giving her a hug. "Can I talk to you a second," Char asked. Piper stepped away. "What's up," Piper asked. "Problem came up. I didn't want to mention it to you after that beautiful proposal, but it's kind of a big issue," Char said. "Which is," Piper asked. "Colt just released another tidbit of gossip and the papers are running wild," Char said. "Which was," Piper asked. "He said that you were pregnant with his child," Char said. So much for that relaxing night.

To Be Continued…..

73916673R00205

Made in the USA
Columbia, SC
08 September 2019